# *welcome to*
# moonlight harbor

# SHEILA ROBERTS

## *welcome to* moonlight harbor

mira

mira

ISBN-13: 978-0-7783-6805-2

Recycling programs
for this product may
not exist in your area.

Welcome to Moonlight Harbor

Copyright © 2018 by Roberts Ink LLC

To the Dreamscape Beach Babes

Dear Reader,

I'm excited to be launching a new series against one of my favorite settings—the beach! Our family has some modest digs down at the ocean and it's our favorite place to get away. We love our little town and the friends we've made there. I never get tired of walking the sandy shore and watching the waves roll in.

And the beach is the perfect place to go when, like my main character, Jenna Jones, you need to hit Restart in your life. Her story is all about reshaping your life and who you are, dreaming new dreams. I hope you'll enjoy your stay at the Driftwood Inn and fall in love with the town of Moonlight Harbor and its residents as much as I have. Come back, stay often. And remember, life is good at the beach!

*Sheila*

# Chapter One

*To Do:*
*Clean office*
*See dentist at noon*
*Drop Sabrina off at Mom's*
*Meet everyone at Casa Roja at six*
*Or just tell them I've got bubonic plague and cancel*

The four women seated at a corner booth in the Mexican restaurant were getting increasingly noisier with each round of drinks. Cinco de Mayo had come and gone, but these ladies still had something to celebrate, as they were all dressed in body-con dresses or slinky tops over skinny jeans, in killer shoes and wearing boas. There were four of them, all pretty, all still in their thirties—except the guest of honor, who was wearing a black dress, a sombrero and a frown. She was turning forty.

It was going to take a while for her to get as jovial as the others (like about a million years), considering what she'd just gotten for her birthday. A divorce.

"Here's to being free of rotten scum-sucking, cheating husbands," toasted Celeste, sister of the guest of honor. She was thirty-five, single and always in a party mood.

The birthday girl, Jenna Jones, formerly Jenna Petit,

took another sip of her mojito. She could get completely sloshed if she wanted. She wasn't driving and she didn't have to worry about setting a good example for her daughter, Sabrina, who was spending the night with Grandma. Later, if they could still work their cell phones, the gang would be calling Uber and getting driven home and poured into their houses or, in the case of sister Celeste, apartments, so there was no need to worry about driving drunk. But Jenna wasn't a big drinker, even when she was in a party mood, and tonight she was as far from that as a woman could get.

What was there to party about when you were getting divorced and turning (ick!) forty? Still, that mojito was going down pretty easily. And she was inhaling the chips and salsa. At the rate she was going she'd be getting five extra pounds for her birthday as well as a divorce.

"Just think, you can make a whole new start," said her best friend Brittany. Brittany was happily married with three kids. What did she know about new starts? Still, she was trying to put a positive spin on things.

"And who knows? Maybe the second time around you'll meet a business tycoon," said Jenna's other bestie Vanita.

"Or someone who works at Amazon and owns a ton of stock," put in Celeste.

"I'd take the stock in a heartbeat," Jenna said, "but I'm so over men." She'd given up on love. Maybe, judging from the chewed fingernails and grown-out highlights in her hair, she'd given up on herself, too. She felt shipwrecked. What was the point of building a rescue fire? The next ship to come along would probably also flounder.

"No, you're over *man*," Brittany corrected. "You can't give up on the whole species because of one loser. You

don't want to go through the rest of your life celibate."
She shuddered, as if celibacy was akin to leprosy.

"Anyway, there're some good ones out there somewhere," said Vanita, who, at thirty-six, was still single
and looking. "They're just hiding," she added with a guf-
faw, and took another drink of her margarita.

"That's for sure," agreed Celeste, who was also looking now that This-is-it Relationship Number Three had
ended. With her green eyes, platinum hair, pouty lips
and perfect body, it probably wouldn't take her long to
find a replacement. "Men. Can't live with 'em, can't…"
Her brows furrowed. "Live with 'em."

Jenna hadn't been able to live with hers, that was for
sure. Not once she learned Mr. Sensitive Artist had another muse on the side—a redhead who painted murals
and was equally sensitive. And had big boobs. That had
nothing to do with why they were together, Damien had
insisted. They were *soul mates.*

Funny, he'd said the same thing to Jenna once. It
looked like some souls could have as many mates as
they wanted.

Damien Petit: handsome, charming…rat. When they
first got together Jenna had thought he was brilliant.
They'd met at a club in the U District. He'd been the
darling of the University of Washington Art Department. He'd looked like a work of art himself, with brooding eyes and the perfectly chiseled features of a marble
statue. She'd been going to school to become a massage
therapist. She, who had never gotten beyond painting
tiles and decorating cakes, had been in awe. A real artist. His medium was unrecyclable detritus. Junk.

Too bad she hadn't seen the symbolism in that back

when they first got together. All she'd seen was his creativity.

She was seeing that in full bloom now. Damien had certainly found a creative way to support himself and his new woman—with spousal support from Jenna.

Seriously? She'd barely be able to support herself and Sabrina once the dust settled.

Nonetheless, the court had deemed that she had been the main support of the family and poor, struggling artist Damien needed transitional help while he readied himself to get out there in the big, bad world and earn money on his own. Her reward for being the responsible one in the marriage was to support the irresponsible one. So now, he was living in the basement of his parents' house, cozy as a cockroach with the new woman, and Jenna was footing the bill for their art supplies. Was this fair? Was this right? Was this any way to start off her fortieth year?

Her sister nudged her. "Hey. Smile. We're having fun here."

Jenna forced her lips up. "Fun."

"You can't keep brooding about the junk jerk."

"I'm not," Jenna lied.

"Yeah, you are. I can see it in your eyes."

"I know it's not fair you have to pay him money," put in Brittany, "but that's how things work today. You know, women's rights and all. If men can pay us spousal support we can pay them, too."

"Since when does women's rights give your ex the right to skip off like a fifteen-year-old with his new bimbo and you pay for the fun?" Jenna demanded.

It was sick and wrong. She'd carried him for years, working as a massage therapist while he dabbled away, selling a piece of art here and there. They'd lived on her salary supplemented by an annual check at Christmas from his folks, who wanted to encourage him to pursue his dream of artistic success, and grocery care packages from her mom, who worked as a checker at the local Safeway. And her grandparents, God bless them, had always given her a nice, fat check for her birthday. Shocking how quickly those fat checks always shrank. Damien drank up money like a thirsty plant, investing it in his art…and certain substances to help him with his creative process.

Maybe everyone shouldn't have helped them so much. Maybe they should have let Damien become a starving artist, literally. Then he might have grown up and gotten a job.

They'd had more than one discussion about that. "And when," he'd demanded, "am I supposed to do my art?"

"Evenings? Weekends?"

He'd looked heavenward and shaken his head. "As if you can just turn on creativity like a faucet."

One of Jenna's clients was an aspiring writer with a family who worked thirty hours a week. She managed to turn on the faucet every Saturday morning.

There was obviously something wrong with Damien's pipes. "I need time to think, time for things to come together."

Something had come together all right. With Aurora Benedict, whose mother had obviously watched one too many Disney movies.

Jenna probably should have packed it in long before Aurora came slinking along, admitted what she'd known after only a couple of years into the marriage: that it had been a mistake. But after she'd gotten pregnant she'd wanted desperately to make things work, so she'd kept her head down and kept plowing forward through rough waters.

Now she and Damien were through and it still didn't look like clear sailing ahead.

"Game time," Celeste announced. "We are going to see who can wish the worst fate on the scum-sucking cheater. I have a prize for the winner." She dug in her capacious Michael Kors purse and pulled out a Seattle Chocolates chocolate bar and everyone, including the birthday girl, let out an *ooh*.

"Okay, I'll go first," Brittany said. "May he fall in a Dumpster looking for junk and not be able to climb out."

"I'll drink to that," Jenna said, and did.

"Oh, that's lame," scoffed Vanita.

"So, you think you can do better?" Brittany challenged.

"Absolutely," she said, flipping her long, black hair. "May he wind up in the Museum of Bad Art."

"There is such a thing?" Jenna asked.

"Oh, yeah." Vanita grinned.

"Ha!" Celeste crowed. "That would serve him right."

Jenna shook her head. "That will never happen. To be fair, he is good."

"Good at being a cheating scum-sucker," Celeste reminded her, and took a drink.

Vanita tried again. "Okay, then, how about this one? May a thousand camels spit on his work."

"Or a thousand first-graders," added Celeste, who taught first grade.

"How about this one? May the ghost of van Gogh haunt him and cut off his ear," Brittany offered.

Vanita made a face and set down the chip she was about to bite into. "Ew."

"Ew is right," Jenna agreed. "But I'm feeling bloodthirsty tonight so I'll drink to that. I think that one's your winner," she said to her sister.

Celeste shook her head. "Oh, no. I can do better than that."

"Go for it," urged Brittany.

Celeste's smile turned wicked. "May his 'paintbrush' shrivel and fall off."

"And to think you teach children," Jenna said, rolling her eyes.

Nonetheless, the double entendre had them all laughing uproariously.

"Okay, I win the chocolate," Celeste said.

"You haven't given Jenna a chance," pointed out Brittany.

"Go ahead, try and beat that," Celeste said, waving the chocolate bar in front of Jenna.

"I can't. It's yours."

Their waiter, a cute twentysomething Latino, came over. "Are you ladies ready for another drink?"

"We'd better eat," Jenna said. Her mojito was going to her head.

Celeste overrode her. "We've got plenty of night left. Bring us more drinks," she told the waiter. "And more chips." She held up the empty bowl.

"Anything you ladies want," he said, and smiled at Jenna.

Celeste nudged her as he walked away. "Did you hear that? Anything you want."

"Not in the market," Jenna said firmly, shaking her head and making the sombrero wobble. Tonight she hated men.

But, she decided, she did like mojitos, and her second one went down just fine.

So did the third. *Olé.*

\* \* \*

Saturday morning, she woke up with gremlins sand-blasting her brain and her mouth tasting like she'd feasted on cat litter instead of enchiladas. She rolled out of bed and staggered to the bathroom where she tried to silence the gremlins with aspirin and a huge glass of water. Then she made the mistake of looking in the mirror.

Ugh. Who was that woman with the ratty, long, blond-gone hair? Her bloodshot eyes were more red than blue and the circles under them made her look a decade older than what she'd just turned. Well, she *felt* a decade older than what she'd just turned.

A shower would help. Maybe.

Or maybe not. She still didn't look so hot, even after she'd blown out her hair and put on some makeup. But, oh, well. At least the gremlins had taken a lunch break.

She got in her ten-year-old Toyota (thank God they made those cars to run forever—this one would have to) and drove to her mother's house to pick up her daughter.

She found her mother stretched out on the couch with a romance novel. Unlike Jenna, Melody Jones, Mel to her friends, looked rested, refreshed and ready for a new day. In her early sixties, she was still an attractive woman, slender with a youthful face and the gray hairs well hidden under a sandy brown that was only slightly lighter than her original color.

"Hello, birthday girl," Mel greeted her. "Did you have fun last night?"

As the night wore on Jenna had been distracted from her misery. That probably counted as fun, so she said, "Yes."

"Looks like you could use some coffee," Mel said, and led her into the kitchen.

"How's my baby?" Jenna asked.

"She's good. She just got in the shower. We stayed up late last night."

Jenna settled at the kitchen table. "What did she think of your taste in movies?"

"She was impressed, naturally. Every girl should have to watch *Pretty in Pink* and *Jane Eyre*."

"And?" Jenna prompted.

"Okay, so I showed her *Grease*. It's a classic."

"About hoods and hoes."

"I don't know how you can say that about an iconic movie," Mom said. "Anyway, I explained a few things to her, so it came with a moral."

"What? You, too, can look like Olivia Newton-John?"

Mel shrugged. "Something like that. Now, tell me. What all did you girls do?"

"Not much. We just went out for dinner."

"Dinner is nice," Mel said, and set a cup of coffee in front of Jenna. She pulled a bottle of Jenna's favorite caramel-flavored creamer from the fridge and set it on the table, watching while Jenna poured in a generous slosh. "I know this is going to be the beginning of a wonderful new year for you."

"I have no way to go but up."

"That's right. And you know…"

"Every storm brings a rainbow," Jenna finished with her.

"I firmly believe that."

"And you should know." She'd had her share of storms. "I don't know how you did it," Jenna said. "Surviving losing Dad when we were so young, raising us single-handedly."

"Hardly single-handedly. I had Gram and Gramps and

Grandma and Grandpa Jones, as well. Yes, we each have to fight our own fight, but God always puts someone in our corner to help us."

"I'm glad you're in my corner," Jenna said. "You're my hero."

Jenna had been almost five and Celeste a baby when their father had been killed in a car accident. It had been sudden, no chance for her mom to say goodbye. There was little that Jenna remembered about her father beyond sitting on his shoulders when they milled with the crowd at the Puyallup Fair or stood watching the Seafair parade in downtown Seattle, that and the scrape of his five-o'clock shadow when he kissed her good-night.

What stuck in her mind most was her mom, holding her on her lap, sitting at this very kitchen table and saying to Gram, "He was my everything."

That read well in books, but maybe in real life it wasn't good to make a man your everything. Even the good ones left you.

At least her dad hadn't left voluntarily. Her mom had chosen a good man. So had Gram, whose husband was also gone now. Both women had picked wisely and knew what good looked like.

Too bad Jenna hadn't listened to them when they tried to warn her about Damien. "Honey, there's no hurry," her mom had said.

Yes, there was. She'd wanted to be with him *now*.

"Are you sure he's what you really want?" Gram had asked. "He seems a little…"

"What?" Jenna had prompted.

"Egotistical," Gram had ventured.

"He's confident," Jenna had replied. "There's a difference."

"Yes, there is," Gram had said. "Are you sure you know what it is?" she'd added, making Jenna scowl.

"I'm just not sure he's the right man for you," Mel had worried.

"Of course he is," Jenna had insisted, because at twenty-three she knew it all. And Damien had been so glamorous, so exciting. Look how well their names went together—Damien and Jenna, Jenna and Damien. Oh, yes, perfect.

And so it was for a time…until she began to see the flaws. Gram had been right: he was egotistical. Narcissistic. Irresponsible. Those flaws she could live with. Those she did live with. But then came the one flaw she couldn't accept. Unfaithful.

Not that he'd asked her to accept it. Not that he'd asked her to keep him. Or even to forgive him. "I can't help how I feel," he'd said.

That was it. Harsh reality came in like a strong wind and blew away the last of the fantasy.

But here was Melody Jones, living proof that a woman could survive the loss of her love, could climb out of the rubble after all her dreams collapsed and rebuild her life. She'd worked hard at a job that kept her on her feet all day and had still managed to make PTA meetings. She'd hosted tea parties when her girls were little and sleepovers when they became teenagers. And, in between all that, she'd managed to make time for herself, starting a book club with some of the neighbors. That book club still met every month. And her mom still found time for sleepovers, now with her granddaughter.

Surely, if she could overcome the loss of her man, Jenna could overcome the loss of what she'd thought her man was.

Mel smiled at her and slid a card-size envelope across the table. "Happy birthday."

"You already gave me my birthday present," Jenna said. Her mother had given her a motivational book about new beginnings by Muriel Sterling with a fifty-dollar bill tucked inside. Jenna would read the book (once she was ready to face the fact that she did, indeed, have to make a new beginning) and she planned to hoard the fifty like a miser. You could buy a lot of lentils and beans with fifty bucks.

"This isn't from me. It's from your aunt Edie."

"Aunt Edie?"

She hadn't seen her great-aunt in years, but she had fond memories of those childhood summer visits with her at Moonlight Harbor—beachcombing for agates, baking cookies with Aunt Edie while her parrot, Jolly Roger, squawked all the silly things Uncle Ralph had taught him, listening to the waves crash as she lay in the old antique bed in the guest room at night with her sister. She remembered digging clams with Uncle Ralph, sitting next to her mother in front of a roaring beach fire, using her arm to shield her face from the heat of the flame as she roasted a hot dog. Those visits had been as golden as the sunsets.

But after getting together with Damien, life had filled with drama and responsibilities, and after one quick visit, the beach town on the Washington coast had faded into a memory. Maybe she'd say to heck with the lentils and beans, spend that birthday money Mom had given her and go see Aunt Edie.

She pulled the card out of the envelope. All pastel flowers and birds, the outside read *For a Lovely Niece*. The inside had a sappy poem telling her she was special and wishing her joy in everything she did, and was signed, *Love, Aunt Edie.* No Uncle Ralph. He'd been gone for several years.

Aunt Edie had stuffed a letter inside the card. The writing was small but firm.

Dear Jenna,
I know you've gone through some very hard times, but I also know that like all the women in our family, you are strong and you'll come through just fine.

Your grandmother told me you could use a new start and I would like to give it to you. I want you to come to Moonlight Harbor and help me revamp and run the Driftwood Inn. Like me, it's getting old and it needs some help. I plan to bequeath it to you on my death. The will is already drawn up, signed and witnessed, so I hope you won't refuse my offer.

Of course, I know your cousin Winston would love to get his grubby mitts on it, but he won't. The boy is useless. And besides, you know I've always had a soft spot for you in my heart. You're a good girl who's always been kind enough to send Christmas cards and homemade fudge for my birthday. Uncle Ralph loved you like a daughter. So do I, and since we never had children of our own you're the closest thing I have to one. I know your mother and grandmother won't mind sharing.

Please say you'll come.
Love, Aunt Edie

Jenna hardly knew what to say. "She wants to leave me the motel." She had to be misreading.

She checked again. No, there it was, in Aunt Edie's tight little scrawl.

Her mom smiled. "I think this could be your rainbow."

Not just the rainbow, the pot of gold, as well!

# Chapter Two

*To Do:*
*Give notice to landlord*
*Put furniture on craigslist*
*Contact school re: taking Sabrina out early*
*Start packing up office and call clients*
*Tell skunkball ex we're moving (like he'll even care)*

What an unexpected and amazing gift. Jenna and her daughter would have a home. On the beach! No more rent. No, better than that, they would own something that could produce income for them, a good income, certainly more than she made now. She handed over the letter for her mother to read.

"I knew she was going to do this. It's just what you need," Mom said when she'd finished. "And the best news is you won't get it right away. By the time you inherit, hopefully your three-year spousal support sentence will be up and a certain someone won't have any claim to it."

"Unless Aunt Edie dies," Jenna said, reality splashing cold water on her euphoria. Then Damien would be right there with his hand out, demanding half of everything she'd inherit. "I mean, obviously I wouldn't want her to, anyway," she added, realizing how she'd sounded.

She loved Aunt Edie and hoped the sweet, old woman lived to be a hundred. There weren't enough Aunt Edies in the world.

Mom handed back the letter. "I wouldn't worry about that. All the women in our line are long-lived. She's eighty-two but she's in good health. No, this is a blessing, no doubt about it."

"I still can't believe it," Jenna said. It all seemed too good to be true.

"Can't believe what?"

Jenna looked up to see her daughter had entered the room. Sabrina was wearing a pink T-shirt and denim shorts, which showed off long, coltish legs. She'd gotten Jenna's blue eyes and round face and her nose, which, if Jenna did say so herself, wasn't a bad nose at all, and she had a pretty, full mouth under it—a mouth which was turned down a lot lately. Her reddish blond shoulder-length hair was freshly washed and blown-out, and she'd covered the few scattered zits on her face with concealer. She was a cute fourteen-year-old. Down the road, she'd be a beautiful woman.

If she lived that long. There were times when Jenna wanted to throttle her. Teenage girls could be stinkers (Jenna knew—she'd been one), but teenage girls whose parents were splitting could be minimonsters.

Who could blame them, though? When the grown-ups in their lives screwed up and the toxic spill splashed on them, they were bound to react. Jenna tried to be patient with the pouting, the tantrums and the accusations, but sometimes it was hard, especially when her daughter pointed out that if she'd been nicer to Daddy he'd have never left.

In those moments, Jenna bit her tongue until it bled.

She'd have liked nothing better than to inform her daughter that she had been nice to Daddy until he started being nice to another woman. If Sabrina wanted to make someone the villain she should cast her father in the role.

But Jenna also knew that father-daughter relationships were important. In spite of all the love her mother had lavished on her, she'd yearned for her own daddy so many times growing up. What Sabrina had with her father wasn't stellar—she was hardly a top priority for him, coming in somewhere after his art, his new woman and basically all things Damien—but it was better than nothing, and Jenna wanted to try and keep it intact. Sabrina had often volunteered to be his helper when he went in search of his *unrecyclable detritus* (junk), and they shared a fondness for horror movies, something Jenna had never really approved of him letting her watch. But at least it was something they did together. Okay, he did it and let Sabrina join him. Still, it put them side by side on the couch on a Friday night.

There'd been no horror movie marathons allowed since he moved out—another thing her daughter held against her. But Jenna had remained firm. Their life had been enough of a horror movie the past year as it was, and she preferred to fill her daughter's mind with more beautiful and positive images than terrified teens and spurting blood.

When Jenna wasn't worrying about money she was worrying about Sabrina. She'd gone from being a straight-A student to getting Cs and Ds. She was barely speaking to Jenna these days and she had discovered the definition of *surly*. So far, the changes had been limited to an overall bad attitude and nothing more dramatic or dangerous. But Jenna knew that teenage angst could easily spiral into something much darker and more serious, so she walked around holding her breath, her shoulders tight, fearful that things could take a turn for the worse at any moment. She and Sabrina had tried going to a counselor but Sabrina had refused to open up. Sometimes Jenna wished she could clone herself because she sure needed a massage therapist.

Other moms who'd been through this assured her that her listing ship would right itself eventually. Meanwhile, though, she was captaining it alone. There'd been no custody battle and very few visits with Daddy. The blame for this was also laid on Jenna's doorstep, and again Jenna had kept her mouth shut.

"You've got the house," Damien had pointed out. "I'm in no position to take her."

Of course not. There was only room for two in the basement love nest. Damien couldn't be bothered obviously, and Aurora the muse probably didn't want the competition.

So both mother and daughter had been rejected, by a man who didn't deserve either of them. But now all that misery was about to get shoved into the past. Now they had a bright future looming, a new start.

"I have some amazing news," Jenna said to her daughter. "We get to live at a beach motel in Moonlight Harbor." Her voice was quivering with excitement. Heck, her whole body was quivering.

Eagerness transformed Sabrina from sulky to adorable. "For the whole summer? Wow! Can Marigold come visit?"

"Of course she can. But…we're not going just for the summer."

The eagerness paused. "What do you mean?"

"We get to move there. My great-aunt, your great-great-aunt—"

"Live there?" Sabrina interrupted.

"Yes. Your great-great-aunt—"

"Live there?" Sabrina stared at Jenna as if she'd announced they were going to prison.

"Now you sound like Aunt Edie's parrot," Jenna teased, trying to cushion what was shaping up to be a bumpy ride. "She has this parrot named Jolly Roger…"

Sabrina's brows dipped right along with the edges of her mouth. "I don't want to move."

"Oh, darling, it's so much fun down at the beach," put in Mel, trying to help. "You'll love it."

"No, I won't," Sabrina corrected her, her voice tinged with panic. "All my friends are here."

"You'll make new friends," Jenna said. Like that was assuring to a fourteen-year-old?

*Blink. Blink, blink.* Oh, no, there it was, the nervous tic that had plagued her during her messy marriage, returning with a vengeance. She thought she'd gotten rid of it when Damien left.

Sabrina's hands fisted. "I don't want to make new friends! I don't want to leave Marigold."

Asking Sabrina to leave behind the girl who had been her bff since they were in the fourth grade was the equivalent of asking her to cut off her arm, especially in light of the fact that her father had stepped out of the picture. How could Jenna have forgotten so quickly the passion of those young years, the desperate need to keep your friends and your footing on an ever-shifting social ladder? Best friends were a young girl's emotional anchor. Crap. Crap, crap, crap, crap, crap.

"I won't go!" Sabrina cried. "I'll stay with Daddy."

Jenna's right eye twitched. "Baby, you can't stay with Daddy. He can't take you right now. We've already talked about that."

"But you said we'd always be close by, that I could see him whenever I want."

Big-mouth her. "You'll still be able to see him."

"No, I won't. Not if we move away."

"It's not that far." Well, not compared to someplace like Texas.

"I won't go. You can't make me!"

Sabrina turned and fled and Jenna's excitement crumbled faster than a sand castle under assault from an incoming tide. She heaved a sigh. "I guess I'll call Aunt Edie."

"Don't you dare," her mother said. "This is an opportunity for you to make a better life for yourself and your daughter."

"Some new life if she ends up hating me even more than she already does."

"She doesn't hate you."

"No, she adores me. Anyone can see that."

"She's angry that her father's gone. You make a good scapegoat."

Jenna frowned. "He's the one who screwed up and I'm the one being punished."

"That's about the size of it," Mom said.

"I should stay here. Maybe once Jenna's done with school…"

"The opportunity might not be there. Aunt Edie needs help now. And, frankly, so do you. Not having to pay rent would make all the difference."

"I'm not doing that bad," Jenna protested.

"You're not exactly making a fortune. And once

Damien starts taking a bite out of your paycheck you'll have even less."

"We could move in with you," Jenna suggested hopefully. Her mom didn't live that far away. Sabrina wouldn't even have to change schools.

"Of course you could," Mel agreed. "And you know I'd be glad to have you. But how long do you think your daughter would put up with sharing that second bedroom with you?" She shook her head. "I'm afraid none of us can be any help in this. You have one set of grandparents in an over-fifty community in Olympia and a grandmother in a one-bedroom condo in Bremerton. Sabrina wouldn't be allowed in one place and she wouldn't be happy in the other any more than she would be here. And the truth is, she's not going to be happy anywhere for a while. You know that."

"But at least she'd be with her best friend if I stayed. At least I wouldn't have to change schools on her."

Mel cocked an eyebrow. "And she's doing so well where she is."

Jenna's head suddenly hurt.

"Honey, you have to think beyond these next few months," her mother said as Jenna tried to rub away the ache at her temples.

"I don't know. It's a big step."

"Most first steps are. And yes, you can stay where you are and play it safe. You can keep limping along with the clients you have. I can slip you money once in a while, and so can your grandparents. But it will never be enough to keep you very high above the poverty level. Once we die—"

"Don't even say that," Jenna interrupted. Her mother and the grandparents had been her safety net over the last year, as well as her rooting section, coaches and therapists (and therapy with Mom had been free). She couldn't imagine life without any of them. She especially couldn't imagine life without her mother, who was both her role model and her best friend.

"We're not planning on it anytime soon," Mel said. "Once I'm gone you'll have my life insurance money. And you girls are in the grandparents' wills. Although the recession dipped into Gram and Gramps's retirement pretty heavily—but still."

"Can we not talk about this?" Sheesh.

"My point is that, while down the road you'll inherit a small nest egg, it doesn't help you now. You have to live. Go to the beach and you can live comfortably. You can build a future."

Jenna tried to imagine herself getting her daughter on board with this plan now that she'd seen Sabrina's reaction. She couldn't. The motel had looked like such a godsend, but really…

"I know what you're thinking," Mom said, making Jenna's brow furrow and her lips turn as far down at the corners as her daughter's had only a moment ago. "Stop it right now. You can't keep doing what you've been doing and expect to do well, not with how your life's changed."

Deep down she knew her mother was right. And deep down she did want to make a new start and do something special with the rest of her life. But…

"You're like a snail that's outgrown its shell. You have to move on, expand your life. Adapt or die, darling."

"And is that what I'm supposed to tell Sabrina?" Jenna retorted irritably.

"No. You simply tell her this is how it has to be. Children are resilient. She'll adjust."

"I don't know." Only a moment ago this had looked like a great opportunity. What if it turned out to be a great mistake?

"You're not moving to the edge of the earth," Mel said. "Her friend can come visit. She can come here and stay with me and see her father. Tell her it will be fine."

"Like you told me when I kept asking where Daddy was?"

"Exactly. And it did turn out all right, didn't it? You had a happy childhood."

She had. After her father died the relatives had circled around their bereft little family, making sure both Jenna and Celeste got plenty of love and attention. The grandpas stepped up to the plate, taking the girls to father-daughter dances and coming to their music recitals and volleyball games along with the grandmas. Uncle Ralph had made visits to the beach an adventure, teaching the girls how to bait a crab trap and how to work a clam gun. When they'd gotten older he'd also scared away boys he deemed unworthy of his great-nieces, which had turned out to be most of the boys they ever met. That had perturbed them both, but they'd loved him, anyway. And Aunt Edie, she'd always been there, smiling and ready to help the girls make wind chimes out of bits of driftwood and seashells or to bake cookies together. On rainy June evenings they'd all played hearts and crazy eights or, Jenna's favorite, Monopoly.

She'd always won at Monopoly. Now she had a chance to win in real life. But she didn't want to win at the expense of her relationship with her daughter. Resilient or not, kids still paid the price for their parents' mistakes.

But surely living at the beach wouldn't be a bad price to pay. Maybe Sabrina would love to dig for clams and make wind chimes. Maybe she'd be as in awe of the spectacle of waves racing to throw themselves on the sandy beach as Jenna had once been.

If Jenna could just get her down there.

"This could be good for Sabrina, too, you know," her mom said, as if reading her mind. "Her father really isn't a very positive influence."

"He's still her father."

"Let him be her father from a distance. It's what he wants, anyway."

"Yes, it is."

Sad, but true. Damien and his slimy lawyer had done a great job of pulling the wool over the judge's eyes. He'd come away with a very loose arrangement, visitation rights but no responsibility. He'd be the same father he'd been when they were together, barely involved.

"Someday, she'll figure out who the real bad guy is," said Mel.

Jenna sighed. "Part of me wants that, wants to be exonerated. But part of me… Jeez, Mom, he's her dad. I hate the idea of her ever realizing what a pathetic one he is."

"She will, and it will be hard. But she'll survive. She's strong, like her mama," Mel added with a smile. Then she sobered. "Meanwhile, remember who's the child here and who's the adult. It's up to you to move you girls to a better future even though your daughter isn't able to see it. You have to do what's right even if it's not what's popular."

How many times had her mother told her that when she was young? She smiled. "How did you get to be so wise?"

"Lots of stupid mistakes," Mel replied, although Jenna couldn't remember her mother ever doing anything stupid. "Trust me when I tell you that you need to take advantage of this. Don't let the fear of the unknown keep you tethered in a place where you can't prosper. And you know I'm not simply talking about money."

Jenna nodded. Mom was right. She'd fallen into quicksand and now someone was offering to pull her out. She'd be crazy not to take that helping hand. And she wanted this. She wanted to feel alive again instead of like one of the walking dead. And the move would be good for Sabrina, too. Fresh air, healthy outdoor activities, a summer of fun to distract her from the dark clouds her parents had blown over her life.

How was she going to convince Sabrina of that?

She took a deep breath and followed her daughter to the guest bedroom, praying all the way that somehow the right words would drop into her mind.

She found Sabrina on the bed, listening to her iPod, tears streaking down her face. Clothes lay scattered around the floor. The book she'd been reading leaned against a corner, its pages fanned out, obviously hurled there in a fit of anger. Sabrina pretended not to see her mother, but the vicious kick at a pair of jeans gave her away.

*Oh, boy.* Both eyes went into action. *Blink, blink, twitch, twitch.*

Jenna forced her eyelids to stay in place and sat down next to her daughter on the bed. Sabrina shifted so her face was turned to the wall.

Jenna laid a hand on her arm. Sabrina yanked it away.

"Sabrina."

Sabrina took out her earbuds and glared at Jenna. "It's not fair," she spat.

That much was definitely true. None of what had happened was fair. She sighed. "I know."

"You're ruining my life," Sabrina wailed.

No. Damien was ruining her life. He'd ruined both their lives. But that wasn't something she'd say out loud. "I'm trying to get us out of the ruins, Sabrina. I'm sorry Daddy and I couldn't stay together." *I'm sorry your dad's a shit.* "But this is how things have turned out, and I don't want us to keep sitting around being miserable. I want to do something that's good for our future." This was way too philosophical. Jenna tried a new tack. "I want to be able to afford nice clothes for you. I want to be able to pay for all those school activities you're going to want to do when you start high school. I want to be able to save for your college education. I want to try and make things better for us." Sabrina was sitting with her lips pressed together, a river of tears flowing down her cheeks. "Can you understand that at all?" Jenna asked.

Sabrina bit her lip and nodded. "But I don't want to move," she said in a small voice.

"I don't want to move you," Jenna said. "But I think, in the long run, this will be good for us. Can you try and keep an open mind?"

Sabrina burst into sobs.

"I'll take that as a yes," Jenna said, and hugged her.

At last Sabrina's sobs began to subside. She wiped at her nose. "What if I hate it there?"

"What if you give it a chance?" Jenna countered. "It really is a great town," she hurried on. "They have this cute ice cream parlor where you can get about a million flavors of ice cream. And there's miniature golf and go-carts. Lots of friendly people. Your aunt Celeste and I used to meet so many cute boys at the beach," she added, sure that would clinch the deal. Her daughter was frowning, but at least she'd stopped crying.

"Can Marigold come?"

"She can visit as soon as we get settled. How's that?"

The frown shrank slightly and Sabrina said a reluctant okay. Then added, "But what if I hate it?"

Back to that again. "You won't," Jenna assured her. *Dear God, pleeease let me be right about that.*

# Chapter Three

*To Do:*
*Finish packing up kitchen and craft stuff*
*Call Aunt Edie with ETA*
*Rent trailer*
*Buy chocolate for grumpy daughter*

The first Saturday in June found Jenna Jones and her daughter on their way to Moonlight Harbor, towing behind their car a tiny rented trailer filled with their most valued possessions—scrapbooks, crafting supplies, clothes, Sabrina's bike and Jenna's massage table and oils and other business necessities, just in case she needed to supplement their income from the motel. Or in case she got the itch to do massage, which was highly likely, since she loved what she did. Most of the furniture had been sold, and that had given her some extra cash. Her linens and the Wedgwood china Gram had given her had been stored in Mom's basement, along with Sabrina's bedroom set, after Jenna realized that would have been the final straw for her daughter.

Big clue: "My bed? You're selling my bed?"

"Aunt Edie will have a bed for you," Jenna had assured her.

"But it won't be my bed," she'd argued. "And what if we don't like it there? We won't have beds when we come home."

"Honey, this is going to be our home." At that, Sabrina had looked thunderous and Jenna's nervous tic had reappeared. "Okay, we won't sell your bed." No bed selling.

Taking Sabrina out of school early turned out to be the one thing Jenna had done right in her daughter's eyes. Sabrina's grades weren't getting any better. Her teachers were all mean and she hated school. Jenna hoped she'd be in a better frame of mind come fall.

Daddy didn't bother to come see his daughter off. Instead, he'd texted her. Have fun at the beach. Keep an eye out for detritus for me. As always, all about him.

"She doesn't want to go, you know," he'd told Jenna when he'd dropped Sabrina off the week before, after a father-daughter run to Dairy Queen that Sabrina had instigated.

"She'll like it once she's there," Jenna had insisted. If she kept saying it often enough surely it would become true. "And it will help the budget if we have a place to live rent-free while I help my aunt run the motel." She'd conveniently neglected to inform him that she was going to inherit said motel. She may have been stupid when she'd married him, but she wasn't going to be stupid now that she was divorced from him.

"Well, at least that way you'll have enough money to pay me what you owe me."

Yep, all about him. "You mean I'll have enough to pay you what you're leeching off me," she'd said, which had sent him roaring off in his truck while Jenna was left steaming.

Now, though, as they entered Harbor County, home of

beachside towns, fishing ports and relaxation, the frustration and fury got left behind like unclaimed baggage. So what if the sky was gray and drizzly? The future was sunny. They crested the rise outside of Aberdeen and, in between the giant firs, caught sight of the Pacific Ocean in the distance.

"There it is," Jenna said, sounding like an Oklahoma land-rush pioneer pointing out the Promised Land.

Sabrina was plugged into her iPod and ignored her. So far her enthusiasm for their new adventure had been underwhelming. But wait till she saw the town.

Jenna could hardly wait. Other than one quick visit after her high school graduation and a honeymoon weekend with Damien, she'd been MIA since her sophomore year in high school. Her first real job, working at the local McDonald's, had kept her away. Then came the friend with the house on Hood Canal where there were boys galore, followed by a couple of boyfriends. Then, of course, along came Damien, who didn't fall in love with Moonlight Harbor like she'd hoped. After they married, it seemed as if every time she planned to visit her aunt something came up that prevented her from going. Damien demanded a lot of attention.

Actually, more than a lot. Looking back on her life it seemed she'd married a psychic vampire. As their marriage progressed he grew bigger and she grew smaller, an insignificant planet orbiting him. Scrapbooking and various craft projects fell by the wayside. How could scrapbooking and refurbishing old furniture compare to Art? And, by the way, had she finished those posters for his exhibition?

She'd been crushed when he'd found another woman. Now she couldn't help but wonder if Aurora had actually done her a favor and set her free, allowing her to come back to a place that had given her a happy childhood. Maybe it would give her a happy adulthood, too.

They drove through Aberdeen and then Quinault, a small town that had given up on logging and was working its way back to prosperity. "We're almost there," Jenna said to Sabrina after another few miles. "Beachcombing, whale watching, cute boys."

That last item on the list made Sabrina smile, proof that she'd been able to hear her mother all along. She pulled out an earbud. "Can we get ice cream?"

"Of course we can. You can't go to Moonlight Harbor and not get ice cream at the ice cream parlor."

At last they reached their destination. There was the same white-rock gateway to the town that Jenna remembered, one of the first things to go up when the town was new.

Hmm. She didn't remember the molehills rising like tiny mountains from the grass on both sides of the gateway. But there were flowers in the flower beds. Someone cared. And maybe they didn't want to hurt the moles. She knew the many deer who roamed the town were a protected species, so why not the moles?

They turned in and started down the main road through town, Harbor Boulevard, named for the harbor that sat at the south end of town. Once a bustling harbor with a ferry service to Westhaven, a busy fishing town across the bay, it had gotten silted in over the years and was no longer viable for commercial use, although the pier was still there.

The town's lifeblood was now tourism, and shops and restaurants abounded, with a couple of small, dated motels sandwiched in between. Many of the businesses were housed in buildings that had gone up in the sixties. But some new buildings had also sprung up, including an eye-catching group of cabana-style shops all painted in beachy colors of turquoise and mint green, yellow and an orange that made Jenna think of Creamsicles, offering everything from women's clothing to kites. And there was a new addition, an art gallery. If Damien had known about that maybe they'd have made more trips to the beach. The seafood restaurant shaped like a lighthouse was still in business. Jenna had always loved the whimsy of that place.

In spite of the drizzle, people were out shopping. Many of them were seniors (hardly surprising considering the fact that there was a large retirement community there), but Jenna saw a few young families and some couples, as well. Where were the cute boys?

As if reading her mind, Sabrina asked, "Where are the kids my age?"

"They're here." Somewhere.

Jenna stole a look at her daughter. She was assessing the town and so far she didn't look impressed.

Farther ahead, on the left, sat Good Times Ice Cream Parlor, one of Jenna's favorite haunts when she was her daughter's age. Right next to it was the Go-Go Carts go-cart track and the Paradise Fun-Plex, which consisted of a miniature golf course and an arcade. This should improve Sabrina's mood.

Indeed it did. Her daughter was actually smiling.

"You ready for ice cream?" Jenna asked.

Sabrina nodded and they pulled in. The parlor itself was housed in one-half of the square building, painted pink with white trim. An arcade took up the other half.

And next to that was the go-cart track and the miniature golf course. Good times indeed.

A giant cement strawberry ice cream cone sat out in front of the ice cream parlor, perfect for photo ops, although with the drizzle no one was bothering. Inside several people sat in booths or at little white wrought-iron tables and enjoyed double-scoop cones, sundaes and milkshakes. A retired couple frowned at a woman with a crying toddler who was trying to pay for ice cream for two little boys who were chasing each other back and forth. A middle-aged couple shared what looked like a hot-fudge sundae. A couple of teenage girls and a boy with scraggly hair, wearing a Seahawks sweatshirt over baggy jeans, stood at the counter, selecting ice cream while the pimply-faced boy behind the counter waited for them to decide.

He caught sight of Sabrina and his eyes widened in appreciation. She gave him a discouraging frown. His customers turned to see what he was staring at and the other boy smiled at Sabrina. She smiled back, but the two girls gave her the stare of death, which of course brought back her frown.

Meanwhile, the woman with the squalling child and rambunctious boys had finished paying and left, leaving the woman behind the counter free to wait on Jenna and Sabrina.

She was in her sixties with a smile as wide as her girth. Her hair was almost all gray now but Jenna would know that round, smiling face anywhere. Nora Singleton had been dishing out ice cream since Jenna was a kid.

"Hello, ladies, what will you have?" she asked.

"I'll have a big order of sunshine," Jenna said, quoting what she used to tell Nora whenever it was rain⸍

Nora squinted at her. "Jenna?"

Jenna nodded. "I'm back."

"Well, welcome back. We haven't seen you around here in ages."

"It's been too long," Jenna agreed.

"Your aunt said you'd be coming to help her. I'm so glad. The poor thing's been struggling ever since Ralph died." She shook her head. "Hardly any of her family even made it down for the funeral."

Jenna had been one of the ones who hadn't made it. But life had gotten in the way. When Uncle Ralph died, she'd been too busy coping with a miscarriage to want to go anywhere. Instead, she'd sent flowers. It was the best she could do at the time. Anyway, she was here now, and that was what counted.

"It's good you're here," Nora said. She turned her hundred-watt smile on Sabrina. "And who is this?"

"This is my daughter, Sabrina," Jenna said, and Sabrina murmured a polite, "Nice to meet you." She may have been unhappy about getting uprooted but it wasn't stopping her from showing good manners, and Jenna was proud of her.

"You are just as cute as your mom was at your age. You'll have all the boys after you," Nora predicted, making Sabrina blush. "What kind of ice cream would you like?"

Sabrina looked down the rows of tubs. "Bubble Gum?"

"One of our most popular. How about we top it with a scoop of Deer Poop?"

's eyes shot open. "Excuse me?"

late with chocolate-covered raisins," Jenna

miled and nodded. "Okay."

"And how about you, Jenna? No, wait, let me guess. One scoop of Sand Pebble for you."

"Sand Pebble?" Sabrina scanned the tubs.

"Butter Brickle with peanuts."

"What's Butter Brickle?" Sabrina asked.

Nora rolled her eyes. "What have you been feeding this poor child?"

"Obviously, not enough ice cream," Jenna said.

"Obviously," Nora agreed. "And how about a second scoop?"

Neither Jenna's budget nor her waistline needed a second scoop. "I think one will do."

"I hope you're not passing up a second scoop because you're dieting. You obviously don't need to."

"If I eat too much of your ice cream, I will," Jenna said.

"I can't think of a better way to get fat," Nora said with a grin, and got busy scooping out their treats.

"It looks like you've expanded," Jenna said, motioning to the neighboring fun-plex.

"Yes, we have. My boys, Beau and Beck, run all that. In fact, adding the arcade and the bumper cars was Beck's idea. Needless to say, it was a good one."

"So your boys are still here?" Jenna asked.

"Oh, yes. You can't take fishermen away from the beach. My daughter moved away but she comes down to visit. Okay, Bubble Gum and Deer Poop," she said, giving Sabrina two giant scoops in a waffle cone. "That's our welcome to town serving," she said with a wink.

She refused to take Jenna's money once she'd handed over the cones. "Consider it a welcome home gift."

Back in the car, Jenna offered her cone to Sabrina to sample. "Good, isn't it?"

Sabrina nodded. "I like Bubble Gum better."

"I did, too, until I discovered Sand Pebble and Wild Huckleberry," Jenna said, and started the car.

They continued down Harbor Boulevard past more shops and restaurants, many looking a little tired and in need of paint, and a place to rent bikes and mopeds. "Can we do that?" asked Sabrina.

"When you're old enough to drive," Jenna said, making her frown.

Off-shoot streets with names like Beach Way and Razor Clam led to the other main drag, Sand Dune Drive, which ran parallel to the boulevard. The streets also took people either to the beach in one direction, past more shops, or away from the water to the neighborhoods where the natives lived. On Sand Dune Drive visitors could find a grocery store and pharmacy, as well as the library and the police and fire departments and city hall, and the Seaview Medical Building, which wasn't much bigger than a house, to name a few. Jenna pointed to a restaurant in a faded red building. Red-checked curtains at the restaurant windows gave it a homey, welcoming look. "The Pizza Palace has the best pizza in the world. We'll have to go there."

Sabrina nodded eagerly. Pizza was her all-time favorite food.

Next to that sat a low building that housed Sunken Treasures Consignments and a new shop called Cindy's Candies, which was sure to be a hit with Sabrina. Across the way sat the Drunken Sailor, the town's popular pub, and here was something new, Cannabis Central. Well, there was a good pairing. It was hardly surprising that the town would now have a pot shop. Ever since Washington legalized marijuana, pot stores had been popping up all over like acne on a teenager's face.

More tourist treats awaited them past the roundabout. "What's that?" Sabrina asked, staring at the building with an entrance shaped like a giant gaping shark's mouth. A young family stood posing inside the mouth while the dad snapped their picture.

"That's Something Fishy. It's a souvenir shop. They sell everything from saltwater taffy and postcards to preserved baby sharks in a tube."

Sabrina made a face. "Ewww."

"Yes, ewww to that, but they have a lot of fun things in there. Tomorrow I'll take you in and you can check it out. In fact, we'll do a tour of the town. How's that sound?"

Sabrina nodded. "Good."

Good? That was good. Jenna smiled.

More motels began to appear—a Quality Inn, a Best Western with a restaurant sandwiched between, and a beautiful old Victorian B and B with a long front porch, complete with wicker chairs for lounging. It was painted white with blue trim. One word summed it up: charming.

Sabrina's eyes lit up at the sight of it. "Is that our motel?"

"No. That's the Oyster Inn. It's gorgeous inside. I remember eating in their restaurant for Gram's birthday one year when we were all down visiting. I was ten and it was the first time I'd been in such a fancy place. Linens on the tables, fine crystal, my first ever crab cocktail. From what I hear the restaurant's still as nice. We'll have to go there and order you a crab cocktail."

"Does our motel have a restaurant?" Sabrina asked.

"No, but there's one next to it. And the motel has a pool."

Sabrina smiled and took off a big bite of her ice cream. Ice cream, pizza and a pool. Jenna had scored some major points.

The two cars in front of them began to slow down. "Why's everybody stopping?" Sabrina asked.

"Look," Jenna said, pointing.

Farther ahead a deer and her fawn strolled across the road. A woman in the car ahead of them leaned out and snapped a picture with her phone.

"Wow," Sabrina breathed, impressed.

Mama and baby made it to the other side and traffic—all three cars—began to move again.

"Pretty cool, huh?" Jenna said, and Sabrina nodded.

Good. Another favorable impression made.

Until they got to the end of Motel Row and finally came to the Driftwood Inn. Charming it was not. What had happened to it? If not for the sign hanging askew and blowing in the wind Jenna would have thought she was at the wrong address. The roof covering the long string of twenty rooms was missing shingles and one of the rooms had a board where there should have been a window. Once the place had been the color of a cloudless sky. Now it was faded and the paint was peeling, and a blackish mold was forming colonies on the walls of the motel. As for the promised pool, she didn't dare look. The chain-link fence around it was bent and sad. A couple of ancient lounge chairs sat on the cement deck. One was tipped over. If there was water in that pool it was probably contaminated. A lone car, a gas hog from another era, brave enough to traverse the potholes in the parking lot, was camped at an end unit.

Sabrina looked around them in horror. "This place is a dump."

It was. And the small, two-story gabled house next to it, Aunt Edie's home, wasn't in much better shape. Its paint, also once a cheery blue, was as faded and chipped as the motel's. The long porch and its railing needed painting and a couple of the steps were leaning at a slant like something in a carnival fun house. The trees and bushes had been taken over by some kind of hanging moss. The lace curtains at the windows and the big pot of flowers on the porch made a vain attempt to dress up the place.

Sabrina had followed Jenna's gaze. "That's where we're gonna live?"

Jenna's right eye twitched. "Don't worry. We'll fix it up." *Blink, blink.*

Too young for a vote of confidence, Sabrina said, "I want to go home."

"Hey, now. Where's your sense of adventure?"

Sabrina looked at her as if she were insane. "You're kidding, right?"

"At least it's got a restaurant next door."

All right, not really a restaurant. The Seafood Shack, situated on the other side of the parking lot, was barely big enough to support the giant wooden razor clam perched on its roof. But it was a novelty. People liked novelties, and having a place to eat right next to your motel was a bonus. Guests could just walk over and grab something.

Not that there was anyone walking across the parking lot or anyone inside the Seafood Shack grabbing. Well, lunch hour was past, so that was hardly surprising.

The gentle rain was becoming less gentle, pouring

down in an angry patter. "Come on," Jenna said. "Let's go see Aunt Edie. And don't say anything rude about the motel," she added as they walked up the front steps. "Okay?"

"I wasn't going to," Sabrina said irritably. "You taught me better than that."

The doorbell didn't appear to work, so Jenna knocked on the door. She heard the chattering of a bird, and then muffled footsteps. "I'm coming," called a thready little-old-lady voice.

"When?" Sabrina muttered.

It felt like forever standing on the porch with the rain soaking their sweaters and hair. "You don't move so fast when you get to be Aunt Edie's age," said Jenna.

She'd barely finished speaking when the door opened. There stood her great-aunt. She was wearing jeans and tennis shoes and a sweatshirt with a seahorse on it that had Moonlight Harbor scrawled across it. Her hair was the same tightly permed cherry red it had always been, and she was still wearing her usual coral lipstick on lips that had grown thin with age. Silver earrings shaped like sand dollars hung from her ears and a collection of rings decorated her hands. To top off the ensemble, a pair of red reading glasses hung from a chain around her neck.

"Jenna!" She held her arms wide and Jenna bent to step into her embrace. Aunt Edie had always been petite, but it seemed she'd shrunk since Jenna last saw her. She still smelled like White Shoulders, her favorite perfume.

Aunt Edie turned her loose and smiled at Sabrina. "And this must be your lovely daughter. Sabrina, I'm so happy to meet you at last." She held out her arms, giving Sabrina no polite option but to also accept a hug, which, well-mannered child that she was, she did. "I can't tell you how much it means to have you both coming here to live with me."

"We're not staying for sure," Sabrina said as she pulled back, and cast a look at her mother that begged her not to make any wild promises.

Aunt Edie's brows pinched together. "You're not?"

"Don't worry, Aunt Edie, we're here to stay," Jenna said, and shot Sabrina a warning look. The way her eye was twitching, she hoped Sabrina didn't think she was winking at her.

The look she received in return spoke volumes about parental betrayal, even though Jenna had not made any promises about returning to Seattle. That option was all in her daughter's mind.

"Well, come on in. I made oatmeal cookies just this morning, and I've got pink lemonade."

Her aunt's oatmeal cookies had been a childhood favorite. "Thanks," Jenna said.

"It's not a very nice day," Aunt Edie observed as she led the way into the living room, "which is a shame, because it's so pretty here when the sun's shining. June's a little iffy weather-wise," she told Sabrina, "but in July it's heaven."

Sabrina was polite enough to nod but she didn't look all that thrilled to see heaven in July.

The living room was almost as badly in need of paint as the outside of the house, but it was cozy, with its furniture arranged for conversation, the old woodstove in the corner ready to take off the chill on a winter's day. Jenna remembered the braided throw rug on the hardwood floor, and there was the same old brown sofa sleeper bed that cousin Winston had often occupied when there was an overload of girls in the house. One of Aunt

Edie's hand-crocheted afghans was draped over the back of it. She still had the little stuffed chair upholstered with a sand-dollar-print fabric that Jenna had always favored. And there sat Aunt Edie's antique rocking chair and Uncle Ralph's old recliner. Seeing the recliner empty put a lump in Jenna's throat. As they entered the room a parrot with plumage in varying shades of green perched inside a giant cage in the corner fluttered his wings and greeted them. "No solicitors!"

"Now, Roger, behave yourself," Aunt Edie scolded.

"Roger, behave yourself," echoed the bird, who'd obviously heard that a few times.

Sabrina walked over to the cage to get a better look and Jenna followed her. The parrot was walking back and forth on his perch now, excited over having an audience.

"Are you a pretty bird?" Jenna asked him.

"Roger's a pretty bird," he said. "Give me whiskey," he added.

That had always made Jenna giggle. In her present mood, Sabrina wasn't about to even smile. "Weird," she said.

"Uncle Ralph was a bad influence," said Aunt Edie. "You girls sit down and make yourselves at home and I'll fetch the cookies. Would you like milk or lemonade, dear?" she asked Sabrina.

"Milk, please."

At last her daughter was managing to remain polite. Jenna smiled at her encouragingly. Sabrina didn't smile back.

"And, Jenna?"

"Cookies and milk sounds great."

"All right, then." Aunt Edie nodded and started for the kitchen.

"Do you want some help?" Jenna asked.

"No, no. I can manage," she said, and disappeared.

"Isn't she sweet?" Jenna said to her daughter.

Sabrina's polite mask fell away. "Why did you tell her we're staying? We're not for sure staying."

"Sweetie, we don't have a house anymore. Remember?"

"You said we didn't have to stay if I didn't like it," Sabrina said, eyes flashing. "You lied to me."

"No, I didn't. I said give it a chance."

"Well, I have."

"No, you haven't. We just got here."

"I don't want to be here," Sabrina said, her voice rising.

Aunt Edie picked that moment to return with a tray bearing a plate of cookies and two glasses of milk. Her steps faltered and for a moment Jenna thought she was going to drop everything.

She rushed over to her aunt and took the tray. "Here, let me help you with that."

"Oh, thank you, dear," Aunt Edie said, looking flustered. If only she didn't still have such good hearing.

Sabrina clenched her jaw and plopped onto the sand-dollar chair and Jenna joined Aunt Edie on the couch. Two against one. The atmosphere felt charged as if there was about to be a squall of epic proportions right there in the living room.

Aunt Edie cleared her throat and picked up the plate, offering it to Sabrina. Sabrina shook her head. "No, thanks."

"We just had ice cream," Jenna said.

"Oh."

"But I'd still love a cookie," Jenna hurried to say. "Your oatmeal cookies are the best."

That brought out a smile. "You always did like them."

Jenna helped herself to one and took a bite. Aunt Edie hadn't lost her touch. "It's as good as I remember."

"And you're just as sweet as I remember."

Not for the first time, Jenna found herself wishing she'd made the time to come down and see Aunt Edie. If only she'd come to visit when Sabrina was younger maybe her girl would have fallen in love with the place, too. Maybe then she'd have been happy to be there.

"I'm sorry I didn't get here for Uncle Ralph's funeral," Jenna said.

"You wrote a lovely note, and you sent those beautiful flowers. Anyway, I know you've been busy, dealing with…" She cleared her throat. "Things."

Like crummy husbands. Jenna nodded and took another bite of cookie and Jolly Roger informed them all that he was a pretty bird. "Give me whiskey. Pretty bird, pretty bird. Roger's a pretty bird. Ralph? Ralph, where are you?"

Roger was certainly contributing more to the conversation than Sabrina. Jenna sighed inwardly. This house felt like a haven to her, but Sabrina was looking at it like it was prison.

Jenna and her aunt visited a few more minutes, while Sabrina sat in her chair and brooded.

"Maybe you'd like to see your rooms," Aunt Edie suggested.

"Good idea," Jenna said. "Want to see your room?" she asked her daughter, keeping her voice gentle and coaxing.

Sabrina bit her lip and nodded. She was close to tears. Now, so was Jenna.

"I have you in the blue room and I thought Sabrina might enjoy being in the doll room," Aunt Edie said, and started to get up.

"Don't bother to get up," Jenna told her. "We can find our way."

Aunt Edie nodded and subsided back against the couch cushions.

Jenna led the way upstairs, bracing herself for what would come once they were out of earshot.

Sabrina didn't wait until they were in her room. She started in as soon as they reached the landing. "I don't see why we have to be here."

"We have to be here because right now we *need* to be here. Sweetie, Aunt Edie is letting us stay rent-free. That's going to really help with the budget and right now I need help with the budget. I'm doing what I think is best for us." Honestly, how many more times would they have to have this conversation?

"Daddy's paying child support. We can live on that."

Child support? With what? "Who told you that?"

Sabrina blinked. "He is, isn't he?"

Of course he wasn't. He was still just a child in a big body. Jenna wanted to scream, *No, he's not paying anything. I'm supporting him and his new girlfriend while he pretends to train for life in the real world. I'm carrying the load and he's sitting around making statues out of old shoes.* This was what happened when you didn't listen to your mother and your grandmother. This was what happened when you fell stupidly, besottedly, in love with an illusion masquerading as a man. Now she had to foot the bill while he supposedly trained for a new job.

She reined in her temper. Hard. "No, he's not." The words came out like chipped rock.

"But he said—" Sabrina stopped midsentence, seeing the expression on Jenna's face.

"What did he say?"

"He said he gave up a lot for us."

Oh, yes, he'd have been famous by then if it hadn't been for the burden of caring for a wife and child. Damien Petit, thwarted genius.

"He did," Jenna said. "And he loves you." Not as much as he loved himself. There was no one he loved as much as he loved himself.

No, wait. Maybe that wasn't fair. He loved art. He lived it and breathed it. Damien hadn't been cut out for a normal life. Maybe this mess was as much Jenna's fault for not seeing that as it was Damien's for being who he was.

"You know your dad's a great artist," she said. "But he's not famous yet. And he's struggling." How cliché, but it was the best she could do. "Right now, we're all struggling. But things are going to get better."

She opened the door to the room that would be her daughter's. Sabrina looked in and took a step back. "It's creepy."

Maybe it was a little if you weren't into dolls. They were everywhere, crowded into a curio cabinet, lolling on the bed, having a tea party in the window seat. Even the antique dresser hadn't escaped. A clown doll was making himself at home there. The room housed every imaginable type of doll—baby dolls, porcelain costumed ones, Barbies, even a three-foot-high little girl from the fifties that had fascinated Jenna when she was young. That one was standing in the corner, ready to play.

"Am I supposed to be able to sleep in here?" Sabrina asked, eyeing the collection as if they were all about to come to life. That was what happened when you watched too many horror movies.

"I'll take this room. You can have the blue room," Jenna said, and led her to the next room.

It was well named and sweet with its blue walls and the blue bedspread with a seashell pattern stitched into it covering an antique iron double bed that had been painted cream. White sheer curtains at the window framed a mesmerizing view of the Pacific Ocean, its giant swells frothing their way to the beach.

Sabrina walked to the window and looked out silently. No comment on the room or the view.

Jenna came and stood behind her and put her hands on her shoulders.

Sabrina covered her face. "If you'd been nicer to Daddy he'd have stayed and we wouldn't be here."

There it was again, the familiar chorus. "Sabrina, sometimes things don't work out between people and it has nothing to do with anyone being nice."

"Go away!" Sabrina cried, and began to sob.

Jenna sighed and obliged.

Back in the living room Jolly Roger greeted her. "Give me whiskey, give me whiskey."

*I could use one, too.* Did Aunt Edie know how to make mojitos?

*This will work,* Jenna told herself sternly. Aunt Edie needed her help. Sabrina needed her to be wise and carve out a secure future for her.

And, darn it all, she was going to do both.

# Chapter Four

*To Do:*
*Unpack*
*Return trailer*
*Go to bed early and recover*

Aunt Edie looked at Jenna with concern when she came back into the living room. "Your daughter's not happy with our arrangement."

There was an understatement. "Right now my daughter's not happy about anything," Jenna said, and fell onto the couch.

Aunt Edie twisted the large agate ring on her middle finger. "I'd hoped this would help you. I thought we'd all be so happy..." Her words fell away and she gave the ring another twist.

Jenna reached out to hold her aunt's hand. "We will be." She wasn't sure who she was trying to convince, Aunt Edie or herself. "It's just going to take her a little time to adjust."

Aunt Edie nodded and made a brave attempt at a smile.

"The divorce has been hard on her. Even though her dad's never been much of a father, he's all she's got. Moving away, well, that just makes it easier for him to ignore her and for her to blame me."

"It's never easy to admit when your father's no better than seagull droppings."

Good old Aunt Edie, she always did have a way with words. "Everyone tried to warn me. I was just so…"

"In love," Aunt Edie finished. "Of course you were. And I remember when you brought him to visit. He was a handsome young man with all that straight, dark hair and that Roman nose, that perfect physique. He was a beautiful work of art."

"Only on the outside," Jenna said, and helped herself to another cookie.

"We all make mistakes, dear."

"You didn't. Uncle Ralph was great."

Aunt Edie took a cookie and inspected it. "Well, your Uncle Ralph wasn't the first."

Jenna stared at her in astonishment. "He wasn't?"

"No. My first love was a banker."

"A banker," Jenna repeated, trying to process this new information. It was hard to think of her free-spirited aunt married to a staid businessman. "Nobody ever told me."

Aunt Edie nodded. "Oh, yes, he was quite the catch. He looked so handsome in a suit. And he could dance beautifully. He beat me, you know."

This time Jenna's mouth dropped and she set aside her cookie. "Seriously?"

"Back when I was young you didn't talk about those things in polite society. Not in my circle, anyway. That sort of thing only happened on the other side of the tracks. Or so people said."

"So, you divorced him?"

"Actually, he divorced me. There was a big scandal,

of course. Everyone thought I was a horrible, ungrateful wife."

"Ungrateful to leave a man who beat you?" scoffed Jenna.

"I hadn't told anyone about that. I couldn't. I was too embarrassed."

"So, you let him get away with it?"

Aunt Edie shrugged. "Things were different back then. Anyway, I just wanted to get out of the marriage and get away. He finally agreed to let me go, on one condition."

"That you not have him arrested," Jenna guessed.

"That I not tell our families why we were divorcing. Of course, this made things difficult because, when I was young, divorce wasn't quite so easy. There was no such thing as no-fault divorce. It was costly, and you had to prove that there was a reason your marriage couldn't work—adultery, cruelty, rape."

"Well, you had him on cruelty."

"I could have, but frankly I was too afraid of what he'd do if I told anyone, so I agreed to come out the bad one. He sent a friend over to deliver some flowers and then conveniently arrived to catch me 'in flagrante' with the man."

"Seriously? And it worked?"

Aunt Edie shrugged. "Back then couples created a fiction that their lawyers could present to the judge. That was what he came up with and I could take it or leave it, so I took it. We both got what we wanted. I got free and he kept his good reputation."

"A fake reputation," Jenna muttered. How could her aunt have let this man get away with that kind of dishonesty? "Aunt Edie, you left him to go on to abuse the next woman he married."

Aunt Edie dropped her gaze. "Yes, I suppose you could say I did, letting him go on record as the injured party. But once I was free of him I made sure word got out about his violent temper. I told a friend in the utmost confidence and, well, you know how that goes. Suddenly, he wasn't so welcome at parties anymore. No woman in town would have anything to do with him."

"What happened to him?"

"He moved away. He finally married again. I saw the announcement in the paper." One corner of Aunt Edie's mouth lifted. "He died only a few years into his second marriage. Food poisoning, so the story went. But we all knew the truth. His wife poisoned him. Sometimes I wish I'd had to nerve to do that. But in the end he got what he deserved. You know what they say. Every dog has his day."

Gram always said that, too. Jenna never had known exactly what it meant, but she'd gotten the gist of it. She hoped a certain dog up in Seattle had his day and soon.

"Anyway, things worked out. Along came my Ralph. I can tell you, everyone wondered what I saw in a rough old fisherman. I told them I saw a kind man with a big smile and a big heart. I saw how he treated his mother and his sisters and I knew he'd never raise his fist to me. And he didn't. He hardly ever even raised his voice, God bless him." She reached out and patted Jenna's arm. "That's how I know that things are going to work out fine for you, too, dear. You've had your struggles, but remember, every storm brings a rainbow."

"You sound like my mom," Jenna said, wiping a tear from the corner of her eye.

Aunt Edie grinned. "Who do you think she learned it from?"

"Oh, Aunt Edie, you're great," Jenna said, and hugged the old woman.

"No, I'm just a selfish old woman."

"No one would ever accuse you of being selfish," Jenna told her.

"I am, dragging you down here, uprooting your daughter..."

"She needed to be uprooted."

"All so I could keep this place going."

"You *should* keep it going," Jenna said firmly. Why give up on a dream that meant so much?

"A lot of people have made wonderful memories here over the years," said Aunt Edie. "Ralph and I built the place back in 1962. We made a good life in Moonlight Harbor. I thought you and your daughter could, too."

"We can," Jenna said, and patted her hand.

"I'm afraid the place needs a little work now."

A little? That was like saying the *Titanic* had a tiny leak. "We'll make it work," Jenna said. "It's probably going to cost a bit."

"Don't you worry about that. I have a little of Ralph's life insurance money left to live on and my social security. And I've got three thousand dollars in savings in a bank in Quinault that Sherwood Stern here at Harbor First National doesn't know about," Aunt Edie said with a firm nod of the head.

And Jenna had eight hundred and one dollars and fifty-two cents—couldn't forget that fifty-two cents— in the hidden account under her mom's name. Oh, yeah. They were rich. "We may need a little more than that. Maybe you could get a business loan."

"I did take out a loan, oh, let me see, I think it was a couple of years ago. Or was it three? I used it to do a few repairs."

*Where?* Jenna wondered.

"I'm afraid I've had a bit of a struggle paying it back."

With nothing but vacancies? What a surprise. "So, no chance of a loan from the bank?"

Aunt Edie's mouth drooped. "Probably not."

And here came the tic. *Blink, blink.*

"Well," Jenna said, determined not to spoil her first day by thinking about their lack of funds. "I'd better get the trailer unloaded and returned to the trailer rental place."

"And while you're doing that I'll put together some clam chowder for our dinner. If you need any help unloading, Pete can help you."

"Pete?" Had Aunt Edie hired someone?

"Pete Long. He's been here a couple of years now. He's my handyman."

Jenna thought of the pathetic fence around the pool, the dangling sign and the slanting steps. What exactly was he handy with?

"I let him stay in one of the rooms in exchange for working around the place."

"What kind of work does he do?" Jenna asked.

Aunt Edie shrugged. "Oh, this and that."

In other words, he was a loafer. Well, once she was settled in, Jenna would make sure he moved on down the road and found a new place to loaf and a new little old lady to take advantage of.

She hurried to her car under an assault of rain, opened the trailer and pulled out a box, trying not to look in the direction of the derelict pool. What had she gotten herself into?

She turned, box in hand, and nearly ran into a grizzled old man with a chin full of gray stubble. Tall and thin, with a long face, he looked to be somewhere in his seventies. He wore an old navy peacoat over tattered jeans and a hat on his head that could have been stolen from the Gorton's fisherman. Where had he come from? He looked like he'd popped out of a copy of *The Old Man and the Sea*.

He put his hands on his hips and scowled at her. "Who are you?"

"Who are you?" she countered.

"I'm Pete Long. I run this place."

"Ah. You're the handyman." Run this place indeed. "You work for my aunt."

The scowl got darker. "You're the niece nobody's seen in years."

Jenna pushed aside the guilt. "That's right. I've come here to help Aunt Edie." She shoved the box into his midsection, making him grunt. "She said you'd help me unload my things."

He took it grudgingly. "She doesn't need any help here. She's got me."

"And just by looking around I can see what a help you've been," Jenna said sweetly.

"We were doing all right," he informed her. "But your aunt's glad you're here, so I guess it's okay by me," he said, and walked off toward the house.

"So glad you gave your permission," Jenna muttered, and pulled out another box.

She followed Pete inside the house and set her box in the front hall. Aunt Edie was standing there now, along with Pete, who seemed in no hurry to make a trip back for more.

"I see you two have met," Aunt Edie said, smiling from one to the other.

"We have," Pete said, sounding like he'd just been forced to make nice with a cobra.

"I know we're all going to be a great team," Aunt Edie gushed.

Yes, as soon as Pete learned there was no "I" in Team. Jenna said nothing, just turned to go out for another box. As she went down the steps she heard Aunt Edie say to him, "You'll have dinner with us, won't you? I'm making clam chowder."

"You know I love your clam chowder, Edie," he said, the gruffness gone from his voice.

Oh, brother. What a suck-up. Not only was he getting a free room from her aunt, he was also getting free food. If this was how Aunt Edie ran things, no wonder she was in trouble.

Jenna spent the next forty minutes hauling in boxes, stowing them in her room and Sabrina's. Sabrina didn't offer to help and Jenna didn't ask. Better to let her daughter sit in the window seat like a sphinx until she calmed down, which would hopefully happen sometime in Jenna's lifetime.

She stowed her bike and massage table in Aunt Edie's garage, next to yet another gas-guzzling car leftover from an era before she'd been born, then went to the trailer rental place next to the gas station and returned the trailer. The semisupermarket was right across the street, so she dropped in and picked up a bottle of white wine to contribute to dinner and a bottle of root beer for the unhappy one. And a giant chocolate bar for herself.

"All the right food groups," the checker said to her with a smile. "Enjoy."

The store might not have been huge but what it lacked in size it obviously made up for in friendliness.

Since there was a Redbox right outside, Jenna also found a movie she thought Sabrina would enjoy. Ice cream, root beer, movies—what else could she bribe her daughter with? A promise to buy out every shop in town the following day? Right. Because she had money to burn. She was made of money. She was frowning when she walked back to her car.

Her mother called as she was pulling into the motel parking lot. "I wanted to see if you made it there safely," Mel said.

"We did." Jenna wished she had more to say, something positive. Nothing came to mind.

"How's Aunt Edie?"

Now, there was something positive. "She's as sweet as ever. But she's got quite a past. Did you know about it?"

"I did."

"How come you never told me?"

"I never thought to. Ancient history, dear. I mean, you don't want to be defined by your past mistakes, do you?"

"Good point. And I've got to admit, hearing about how she restarted her life gives me hope that I can, too."

"Of course you can," said Mel. "That's what we do when things take a turn for the worse. We move in a new direction."

"Is there any woman in our family who isn't a superhero?"

"We're all made of pretty sturdy cloth," Mel said. "Speaking of sturdy cloth, how does my darling granddaughter like Moonlight Harbor?"

"Well, the ice cream parlor was a hit. Nora Singleton's still there, dishing up the calories."

"Good old Nora, she's a treasure."

"Yes, she is, and stopping there got me points. Plus, we saw a deer and its fawn, which Sabrina thought was really cool. But then we hit Aunt Edie's. Oh, Mom, the place is a disaster. I don't blame Sabrina for being mad. And let me tell you, she was. She let me have it. Naturally, Aunt Edie had to overhear."

"I'm sorry. But it's only your first day. Things will get better," Mel predicted.

"I hope you're right. By the way, there's some old guy hanging around here who's supposed to be her handyman. He's about as useful as a tanning bed in a desert."

"Maybe there's a shortage of handymen down there," Mel said.

"Maybe. He's invited to dinner tonight."

"A regular dinner party."

Yes, wouldn't that be fun? Her, Aunt Edie, the grumpy handyman and her discontented daughter. She could hardly wait.

She ended the call and went inside, delivering the wine to the kitchen, where Aunt Edie was busy stirring a big pot of chowder. The aroma of garlic bread danced over from the oven to greet Jenna.

"It sure smells good in here," she told her aunt as she pulled the bottle from the bag.

"Let's hope everything will taste as good as it smells," said Aunt Edie. She caught sight of the wine. "Oh, aren't you a sweetie."

"You can't show up to dinner without bringing something," Jenna said.

"You can when you're family." Aunt Edie smiled at

her. "I can't begin to tell you how happy I am that you're here."

"It's good to be with you again," Jenna said. That much she could truthfully say. And she would have been ecstatic to be there in spite of the motel's run-down condition if only her daughter wasn't so unhappy.

"I'm glad you had a chance to meet Pete," Aunt Edie continued.

Yes, Pete. "What exactly does he do around here?" Jenna asked.

"Oh, he just helps keep things shipshape," Aunt Edie replied vaguely.

"But what specifically does he do?"

Aunt Edie became very focused on stirring her clam chowder. "He repairs things."

"He hasn't repaired your sign."

"He'll get to it," Aunt Edie said.

Sometime this decade? "So, how'd you come to hire him?"

"Well, we met quite by accident. I'd stepped over to the Seafood Shack for some popcorn shrimp and he was there drinking coffee. He was new in town and retired. It turned out he was looking for a room to rent and I told him since I had some rooms free at the motel he was welcome to stay in one. That was when he suggested we do some good, old-fashioned bartering."

Obviously, Pete had gotten the good end of that deal.

"That seems like only yesterday. But then so do those days when you were a little girl. My, how the time does fly by after seventy," Aunt Edie mused. She set down her spoon. "I think our dinner is just about ready. Why don't you fetch Sabrina, and I'll go find Pete?"

Jenna almost suggested Aunt Edie fetch Sabrina and

let her go find Pete. She didn't much like the guy, but she'd rather deal with him than her angry daughter. But she went up to the blue bedroom, resigned to more unpleasantness.

The door was now shut, a sure sign that she was still Poopy Mom. She steeled herself and knocked on it.

"Go away," came the muffled response.

She opened the door and poked her head inside. "It's time for dinner."

Sabrina was sitting on the bed, her knees pulled up, glaring out the window at the view. "I'm not hungry."

"You will be later if you don't eat. And this isn't a restaurant where you can get a meal whenever you want, so you need to come down."

Sabrina transferred the glare to her mom. "I don't want to."

Decision time. What to do? Wimp out and let her daughter have her way or insist she be polite and come down and eat?

Maybe letting her stay in her room and sulk wasn't such a bad idea. Sabrina loved her food too much to maintain a hunger strike for long. Jenna should let her suffer the consequences of her decision.

"Okay," she said. "If you're not hungry, you're not hungry. But there will be no more opportunities to eat after this and it's a long time until breakfast."

Sabrina shrugged and returned her attention to the view out the window.

"And I brought home a movie," Jenna added.

"She probably doesn't even have a DVD player," Sabrina said in disgust.

Maybe Aunt Edie didn't. "Suit yourself," Jenna said, and shut the door.

She went back downstairs and stopped in the living room again. The TV looked fairly new, but it appeared that Sabrina was right. There was no DVD player. There was an old VCR, though. Wow. Special. So it looked like there would be no visits to Redbox anytime in the near future.

Jenna went on into the kitchen to find that her aunt had emptied the grocery bag. The root beer was gone, along with the wine, probably both in the fridge, and the candy and movie were on the counter.

"I'm afraid I don't have one of those machines for playing that," Aunt Edie said, nodding to it.

"That's okay," Jenna said. "We can find plenty of other things to do."

"Well, I do have cable. And that's a smart TV, so we can always stream something."

Aunt Edie even knew what streaming was?

Jenna's surprise must have showed on her face because her great-aunt chuckled, then said, "I'm eighty-two dear, not dead. I've got a smartphone and an e-reader and an iPod where I listen to Adele and Lady GooGoo."

Jenna smiled at that. "You mean Lady GaGa?"

"Yes, her. I think she's very talented, and I always appreciate creativity."

Pete opened the kitchen door, stamping his feet on the mat and then stepped into the kitchen and brushed the rain off his coat. "It's coming down like crazy out there," he announced in case no one had looked out the window or just been out in the squall. "Supposed to get some sixty-mile-an-hour winds tonight. Make sure you batten down the hatches."

Batten down the hatches? Had Pete been a sailor? Maybe he was just a sailor wannabe. Who knew?

He removed his hat, showing wisps of hair over a shiny pink scalp, and walked over to the table, took off his wet coat and hung it over a chair, letting it drip on the floor. No, Pete couldn't have been a sailor. He'd been born in a barn.

Aunt Edie was now struggling to pour the contents of the pot into a soup tureen. "Let me do that," Jenna said, and jumped to the rescue.

"Oh, thank you, dear. I'm not used to having help."

"Well, you have help now," Jenna told her.

"You've had help all along," Pete muttered.

"Where's Sabrina?" Aunt Edie asked, looking around the kitchen as if expecting her to pop out from under the table.

"She's not hungry," Jenna said.

"She has to eat," protested Aunt Edie.

"She will. But not until breakfast."

"Hunger strike, huh?" Pete guessed. "In my day kids did what they were told. If you said come to supper they came to supper."

And who had asked him? "Oh, do you have kids, Pete?"

"Nope. Never had any."

Jenna nodded. "Ah." A real expert.

Suddenly, to Jenna's surprise, her daughter appeared in the doorway, looking sheepish. "I guess I'll eat something," she said.

Jenna nodded.

"I'm so glad," said Aunt Edie. "I know you'll love my clam chowder."

"I've never had clam chowder," Sabrina said.

Aunt Edie looked at her in shock. "Never had clam chowder? Oh, my, we definitely have to rectify that situ-

ation." She pulled on an oven mitt and took out a loaf of
foil-encased French bread. "Chowder and garlic bread,
the perfect meal for a stormy day."

Once the food was on the table and everyone was
seated, Aunt Edie smiled at Pete. "Pete, would you offer
up the blessing?"

Pete didn't look all that happy to be put in charge of
blessing the food, but he grunted and shut his eyes and
Jenna followed suit. "Thanks, God. Keep us going." And
that was it. "Let's eat," he said, and rubbed his hands
together.

Conversation didn't exactly flow at dinner. Roger,
freed from his cage, sat on his kitchen perch and chat-
tered, reminding everyone what a pretty bird he was.
Aunt Edie chatted about the joys of digging clams and
how the chowder was her own top-secret recipe. Then
she volunteered Pete to take Sabrina clam digging.

But since Sabrina had made a face with her first taste
of chowder he didn't appear too enthused at the prospect.
"The kid doesn't even like clams."

"No matter," Aunt Edie said easily. "It's still fun to
dig them. And clams are an acquired taste," she said
to Sabrina. "Would you like something else? A grilled
cheese sandwich, perhaps?"

"Oh, you don't have to go to all that trouble," Jenna
said, and earned a scowl from her daughter.

"It's no trouble," Aunt Edie assured her. "Your mother
always loved grilled cheese sandwiches when she was a
girl," she told Sabrina.

No way was Jenna going to let her aunt wait on them
hand and foot. "I'll do it," she said, getting up. "You stay
where you are."

Roger put in an order, too. "Give me whiskey, give me whiskey."

He was more talkative than Sabrina, who concentrated on looking at her plate and eating her sandwich.

"You don't say much, do you?" Pete said to her.

She bit her lip and shook her head. Then a moment later she asked to be excused.

"Yes, you may," Jenna said, resigned to letting her go back to her pout. Their first meal in their new home hadn't exactly been a success.

"Not a very friendly kid," Pete observed.

"She's unhappy," said Aunt Edie. "The poor child has been through a lot."

"Was she abused?" Pete asked.

"No," Jenna said, horrified.

"Beat up at school?"

"No."

"Has she got some disease?"

"No," Jenna said, exasperated.

"Then what's her problem?"

*You.* "If you must know, her father and I are divorced. She didn't want to move so far away from him. And she had to leave behind all her friends."

"Yeah, well, that's nothing. My mom went through two husbands after my dad died and they both beat me. Had to fight in 'Nam and saw my best buddy die before my eyes. Life is tough."

"Well, thank you for those encouraging words," Jenna said.

Her sarcasm was lost on Pete. "She'll be okay once she settles in," he added. "Just don't baby her."

This sage advice from the man who never had kids.

"Well," said Aunt Edie with forced cheer. "What

would you like to do after dinner, dear? We could play some Anagrams."

Another game Jenna had loved as a kid. Aunt Edie had an old trunk in the dining room where she kept her collection of games, including an old Folgers coffee can filled with small cardboard squares each with a letter of the alphabet on it. They would draw letters from that can and take turns making words, adding letters to existing words to make them bigger and steal back and forth.

But tonight Jenna was too pooped for that much brain work. "How about tomorrow night?" she said. "If you don't mind, I'll just go flop on my bed and read for a while."

"Oh, of course. You must be exhausted," said Aunt Edie. "What was I thinking?"

"You were thinking of me," Jenna said, and reached over and laid a hand on her arm. "Thank you."

After dinner, she left Aunt Edie and Pete to play Anagrams without her and went upstairs to her bedroom. She looked in on Sabrina, who was back to employing the silent treatment, kissed the top of her head and told her she loved her.

Then she went to her own room, where the dolls were waiting, and unpacked the Muriel Sterling book Mom had given her. *New Beginnings*. Well, that was appropriate, for sure. She opened to the first page and read the chapter title—"Death in Winter, Growth in Spring."

A garden is God's constant reminder to us that we live in a world of change, a world of birth, death and rebirth. What happens to us is often exactly like what happens in our gardens. Winter comes and the garden dies.

Cheery. Jenna frowned but read on.

> But in reality it's not dead. It's merely dormant, waiting for the warmth of a new spring to bring back to life those perennials we so enjoyed the year before.
>
> It's often the same with our lives. We plan for certain things and hope for positive outcomes, dream big dreams, only to see our plans crumble and our dreams die.

Jenna couldn't help but feel as though the woman had written this just for her. Was Muriel Sterling psychic?

> You may be mourning the death of a dream, but you don't have to mourn without hope. Like a flower in winter experiencing a period of dormancy, use this time to heal and gather strength for spring when a new dream will crop up.

Jenna hoped she could heal here at the ocean's edge. She read on, the book growing heavy in her hands, and soon her eyelids had fallen shut.

Next thing she knew, she was out in the ocean, paddling around desperately in the icy cold water, waves crashing over her and pushing her under. In the distance, she could see a fishing boat chugging away. There, in the stern, stood Damien and Sabrina. He had his arm around Sabrina's shoulders and was waving goodbye to Jenna.

"I told you I didn't want to stay," Sabrina called.

"Come back!" Jenna cried. "Somebody help me."

Oh, hallelujah, here came rescue—Pete in a little dingy. He stood up, a life preserver in his hand, and threw it to her. She reached out and caught it only to discover it was made of cement.

She awoke with a gurgle and a cough, her heart pounding as furiously as the waves on the beach. The rain was beating against her window. Great. Welcome to Moonlight Harbor.

# Chapter Five

*To Do:*
*Attend church*
*Check out town with Sabrina*
*Assess what needs to be done to get Driftwood Inn up*
*and running*
*Take deep breaths*

Sunday morning brought blue skies and sunshine and Jenna decided to take that as a good sign. Church on Sunday was a habit her mother had cultivated in both her and her sister, and while Celeste had drifted off toward Sunday morning sleep-ins, Jenna had kept it up. Back home, she and Sabrina had attended a small church with a large kid population. It was where Sabrina had first met her friend Marigold. Jenna had high hopes that maybe another good friend would be waiting at a church here at their new home.

She donned a sundress and sweater, then slipped into Sabrina's bedroom and woke her with a kiss. "Time to get up, sleepyhead."

Sabrina groaned and pulled the covers over her head.

"I smell breakfast," Jenna told her. "I bet Aunt Edie's making cinnamon rolls."

No sound from under the covers.

"Come on, baby girl. It's Sunday. Church day."

"I don't want to go to church," said the muffled voice.

"Staying home isn't an option," Jenna said firmly. She pulled the covers back and gave her daughter another kiss. "Come on. Breakfast and church and then we can check out the town and do some shopping."

*Shopping.* The magic word. Sabrina sat up and pushed the hair out of her eyes. She was frowning but at least she was upright.

"See you downstairs in twenty minutes," Jenna said, and exited before any whining could commence.

As she went downstairs the aroma of freshly baked rolls, sausage and coffee greeted her. It was a treat to have someone cook breakfast for her but she hoped Aunt Edie wasn't going to make a habit of it. She'd feel guilty having the old woman waiting on her all the time.

Her aunt was up and ready for the day, wearing coral-colored slacks and a sweatshirt, pink slippers on her feet. Roger was out of his cage and on his kitchen perch, keeping her company. She smiled at Jenna as she walked into the kitchen. "There you are. How did you sleep?"

Until her dream? "Great," Jenna lied.

"There's nothing like the sound of the waves to lull you to sleep," Aunt Edie said.

And nothing like worry to wake you up.

She studied Jenna. "You look tired, dear."

"I'm fine. And I'll be great once I have one of your cinnamon rolls," Jenna said, pointing to the plate in her aunt's hand.

"You always did love them," Aunt Edie said, placing it on the table. "Sit down, eat. I've got sausage and scrambled eggs coming, too."

The table was set for two, with orange juice already poured. "Aren't you eating?" Jenna asked as she slipped onto a seat.

"Oh, no. I was up ages ago. But I will join you for a cup of coffee." With Jenna's breakfast dished up, her aunt sat down, too. "What would you like to do today?"

"Well, first of all, I'm going to find a church."

Aunt Edie nodded. "There are plenty here. I don't go anymore. Too much trouble and too many hypocrites."

Jenna wasn't sure what to say to that. "Or maybe just people trying to get their act together."

"Maybe," Aunt Edie said with a shrug. "Anyway, the music's too loud. All those drums and guitars. In my day you had an organist."

"I guess times have changed," Jenna said.

"And not for the better." Aunt Edie pursed her lips in disapproval. Then changing times were forgotten as she returned to the subject of Jenna's itinerary. "And after church?"

"I thought it would be good to show Sabrina around."

Aunt Edie nodded her approval. "Excellent idea. Be sure to take her to the kite store. You loved to fly kites when you were a girl."

Sabrina chose that moment to make her entrance, wearing her favorite white cold shoulder dress and sandals.

"Don't you look adorable," gushed Aunt Edie. "My, oh, my. Fashions for girls are so cute. Makes me wish I was young again."

"My, oh, my," echoed Roger. "My, oh, my. Wish I was young."

Aunt Edie proceeded to fuss over Sabrina, making sure she not only had sausage and eggs but seconds on cinnamon rolls, and Jenna was pleased to see a smile finally surface on her daughter's face. She was even more pleased when Sabrina complimented Aunt Edie on her cinnamon rolls.

"They're one of my specialties," Aunt Edie said. "If you like, I'll teach you how to make them. And oatmeal muffins."

"That sounds good," Sabrina said, and Jenna took hope that maybe this would all turn out.

Until they got to Moonlight Harbor Evangelical Church. Not that she didn't get a friendly greeting from several people, and not that the pastor's sermon was boring. At least not to most of the single women in the congregation. He was a cutie, maybe midthirties, with sun-bleached hair and blue eyes and the face of an angel. No wedding ring, which made her wonder whether the women were giving their rapt attention to the sermon or the man.

The kids were another story. A boy came up and said hi to Sabrina almost as soon as they walked in the door, but the same two girls from the ice cream parlor were hanging around in the church foyer and they both glared in Sabrina's direction, which left her frowning through the entire service.

Afterward the older woman who'd been sitting in the row in back of them tapped Jenna on the shoulder and asked her if she was new in town. She was a beautiful woman, probably somewhere in her seventies, with snow-white hair and delicate features. She wore white slacks and a matching jacket over a mint-green top and had accented her outfit with a printed scarf in shades of pastel orange and green.

"I am," Jenna said. "I've come to live with my aunt."

"With Edie Patterson? You must be Jenna."

"I am."

"I'm Patricia Whiteside. I own the Oyster Inn."

"The Oyster Inn. I can't tell you how special it was to eat in your dining room when I was a girl." Jenna introduced Sabrina, who was fidgeting and anxious to escape. "I've told my daughter about how I had my first ever crab cocktail in your dining room."

"You bring her to see us and I'll give you both a crab cocktail on the house," Patricia said.

"All right. A crab cocktail on the house," Jenna said to Sabrina as soon as Patricia had turned to talk to someone else.

"Cool. Can we go now?"

It looked like they were leaving now. They started for the door, but two more people waylaid Jenna on the way. Sabrina didn't stick around to meet anyone else.

Jenna was about to chase her when a fortysomething black woman with dreadlocks, gorgeous big eyes and an impressive bustline stopped her. The woman wore a long top and flowing crocheted sweater over white leggings and sandals.

"Are you Jenna?" she asked. Jenna nodded and the woman said, "We've all been looking forward to meeting you. You're all Edie has talked about for the last three weeks. I'm Tyrella Lamb. I own Beach Lumber and Hardware here in town. I suspect I'll be seeing a lot of you."

"I suspect you will," Jenna agreed.

"I hope you're not too discouraged after seeing the place. Edie was afraid you'd take one look at it and turn tail and run."

At this point, Jenna wasn't sure where she'd run. "I'm here to stay," she said as much to herself as to Tyrella.

"Good. Because your aunt really needs you. And that place of hers may look like a wreck now, but the bones are good and it's still got life left in it. You know, my husband, Leroy, and I stayed there when we first came to town to check into buying the hardware store. It was awfully cute back then and Edie was so welcoming."

"No surprise there," Jenna said. "My aunt definitely has the gift of hospitality."

"Yes, she does. She always baked cookies for her guests and had them available in the lobby. Staying at the Driftwood Inn gave us a very good first impression of the town. Twenty years ago, there were only two choices for where to stay, the Driftwood or the Oyster Inn. Both did a very good business."

"I hope we can do a good business again," Jenna said.

"You will," Tyrella assured her. "I'll help you when you're ready. And if you need a listening ear, I'm pretty good at that, too."

Jenna thanked her, then made her way through the crowd of chatting people and back to the car where Sabrina sat scowling out the window. "I hate that church," she said, not mincing words.

"I thought the music was really good," Jenna offered.

"The kids are mean."

"Honey, this was only our first visit. You have to give it a chance."

"That's what you said about coming here!"

Sabrina was close to tears. This was not the time to continue a conversation about the church or life at the beach. "Come on. I'll buy you lunch at the Seafood Shack and then we'll go shopping."

"Okay."

It was said grudgingly, but Jenna wisely decided to ignore that.

The Seafood Shack was doing a brisk business, with young families and a smattering of seniors ordering fish and chips and fried clams and all manner of shakes. A couple in shorts and T-shirts lounged at one of the tables outside, digging into baskets of popcorn shrimp. The place smelled of fish and grease.

They ordered fish and chips and chocolate shakes and went outside to sit in the sun. The day was balmy with only a light breeze, and the food was…greasy. Sabrina licked up every little bit.

"Okay, what next?" she asked, sounding almost enthusiastic.

"How about checking out Something Fishy? We'll take your picture standing in the giant shark's mouth and you can send it to Daddy and the grandmas. How's that sound?"

It sounded good, and after the requisite photo op and buying T-shirts that said Moonstruck at Moonlight Harbor they moved on to Cindy's Candies, a little shop with giant suckers painted on the window, where they stocked up on saltwater taffy, licorice and jawbreakers. Sabrina's smile was getting bigger.

And Jenna's wallet was shrinking. She told herself this was an investment in the future. If her daughter had fun and fell in love with the town, life would be so much easier.

After that they hit Sunken Treasures Consignments where Jenna found a new top and Sabrina fell in love with a ceramic kitten. Then it was on to the cabana shops where Sabrina got bored looking at home decor, scented candles and gift items in the Beachcomber.

"Hey, look at this," Jenna said, picking up a cloth-bound journal decorated with a starfish.

Sabrina shrugged but reached for it.

"You can write all your great thoughts and poems in here," Jenna said. The only class Sabrina had enjoyed the past few months had been her English class, and she loved to write.

Sabrina looked it over with a frown. "I guess," she said, and let Jenna buy it for her.

She went from frowning to sneering when they entered Beach Babes. "They're all old lady clothes," she complained.

Jenna had to admit most of the clothes weren't exactly trendy, even the sweatshirts were nothing a fourteen-year-old would want to be caught wearing, and the sales-woman there, a striking thirtysomething who obviously wasn't wearing anything off the store racks, looked almost apologetic as they left. But the kite store was a winner and they came out with a single line kite decorated with a red octopus. Goodbye another thirty dollars. But now Sabrina was smiling again, and squeezing Jenna's arm and thanking her. Ah, yes, her daughter's moods matched the weather. Stick around a few minutes and it was bound to change.

Speaking of changing, the wind was picking up and Jenna could see gray clouds gathering out over the water.

"Can we fly the kite when we get back?" Sabrina asked.

"We can try," Jenna said, and hoped the rain held off.

They did a quick drive around town, Jenna pointing out the little bowling alley, the park and tennis courts and community pool hidden away on a side street. At least there'd be a pool somewhere for Sabrina to enjoy. Beans and Books, a combination coffee shop and bookstore, she knew would appeal to her daughter. "You can ride your bike there, get a smoothie, write in your journal." As Sabrina nodded agreement Jenna had a quick vision of dollar signs flying away. Hopping into the coffee shop for a treat on a regular basis could get expensive. "Or you can hang out at the beach," she added.

They ended their tour of the town's possible teen temptations checking out the arcade where there were kids Sabrina's age. All of them were with friends, though, and too engrossed in what they were doing to pay any attention to a new kid in town, even if she was cute. They didn't stay long.

By the time they came out it was raining. Once they reached the motel it was pouring.

"I'm not flying a kite in this," Sabrina said in disgust. "What else can we do?"

"Well, I actually have to check out the motel with Aunt Edie. You could read or watch something on TV."

"I guess," Sabrina said in a bored voice. Then added, "There's no one to hang out with here."

"There will be," Jenna assured her. *Please let that be true.*

Aunt Edie was ready for them with cookies and the promise of hot chocolate. "Did you girls have fun?" she asked.

Sabrina was now wet and her hair was dripping and she wasn't in quite such a happy mood. Jenna hurried to speak for her. "Oh, yes. And we have the stuff to prove it." She held up the Something Fishy bag that held her new T-shirt.

"Isn't that store fun?" Aunt Edie gushed.

"Fun, fun," echoed Roger, who was perched on her shoulder.

"They have baby sharks in a jar," Sabrina said in disgust.

"Boys like 'em," said Aunt Edie. She pointed to Sabrina's bag. "What did you get?"

"A T-shirt," Sabrina said, her voice lackluster.

"We have matching Moonlight Harbor T-shirts," said Jenna.

"Well, now you're truly one of us," Aunt Edie said with a smile. "What else did you girls find?"

"What didn't we?" Jenna said heartily, hoping to remind her daughter of the fun parts of the day. "We got candy from Cindy's."

"Saltwater taffy?" Aunt Edie guessed. "That's a must when you come to the beach."

"Sabrina's never had it," said Jenna.

"Oh, you'll love it."

Sabrina nodded politely.

"And we got a journal for Sabrina to write in," Jenna continued. "And a kite."

"Which we can't fly because it's raining," Sabrina grumped.

"Don't worry," Aunt Edie told her. "The weatherman's predicting nice weather for tomorrow."

"The weatherman, the weatherman," echoed Roger. "The weatherman's an idiot."

That made Jenna smile. She knew who'd taught Roger that—Uncle Ralph.

"Now, that's enough out of you," Aunt Edie said, and put the bird back in his cage.

Sabrina wasn't amused. "I'm going to my room," she announced, and disappeared up the stairs.

"I need hot chocolate," Jenna said, and went to the kitchen.

"It's a shame the weather's not cooperating," Aunt Edie said as she poured out a mug of her homemade hot chocolate for Jenna.

Even if the weather had cooperated, Jenna doubted her daughter would. She reminded herself that Sabrina had been slammed with a lot of change, none of which she'd asked for. *Thank you, Damien, for making our lives miserable.*

Except she'd chosen him, so who was really to blame? "Sometimes I wish I could restart my life as a grown-up," she said with a sigh.

"What part would you do differently?" asked her aunt.

"I'd choose someone other than my lame-o ex."

"Ah, but then you wouldn't have your sweet daughter."

"True." And, difficult as Sabrina was being at the moment, Jenna loved her with all her wounded heart. "She is sweet, really."

"Of course she is. She's just unhappy. That's allowed."

Jenna smiled at her aunt. "Thanks for being so understanding."

"Believe it or not, I was young once, too. I remember being unhappy with the grown-ups in my life. Then I grew up and realized it wasn't all that easy being an adult, either."

"You can say that again," Jenna said, and took a comforting sip of her hot chocolate.

"Things will work out. You'll see. Everyone loves the beach."

"I know Sabrina would. If only we were still a family."

"You are still a family," Aunt Edie reminded her. "Don't ever forget that."

Of course they were. Just like she and her mom and sister had been a family. "You're right."

Aunt Edie smiled. "I'm always right. That's what Ralph used to say."

The wind had picked up and the rain was beating on the kitchen window. Jenna felt like going to her room, too, and crawling under the covers. She took another fortifying drink of her cocoa, then said, "Well, let's go see what needs to be done at the Driftwood Inn."

They donned rain slickers and made the short walk from the house to the motel. Amazing how nippy the wind could be at the beach in June.

"It's going to be beautiful tomorrow," Aunt Edie predicted.

"I always liked it at the beach when it was stormy," Jenna said.

No lie. She'd had a friend who lived at the far end of town where the jetty was and had loved sitting warm and cozy inside the house and watching the waves crash into the rocks, sending a twenty-foot spray racing the length of them. She'd also enjoyed having what Aunt Edie called an at-home day, playing games at the kitchen table with her mom and sister and Aunt Edie and Uncle Ralph, or burrowing under a blanket on the couch, reading a Nancy Drew mystery. As she got older Carolyn Keene—who she'd been shocked to finally learn wasn't a woman but an entire team of hirelings—gave way to Debbie Macomber and Nora Roberts.

Oh, how she'd believed in happy endings back then. Did she still?

She wasn't so sure when they walked into the first

room. It smelled musty and looked terrible. The bed-spreads were ratty and tufted, the carpets worn and stained. And speaking of stains, one of the walls looked like it had some water damage. How many other walls in how many other rooms had similar stains?

"We've had a few leaks," Aunt Edie confessed when Jenna pointed it out.

Great. A leaking roof. She wasn't surprised though, considering what it looked like.

The other rooms were in just as bad a state as the first. Even the vinyl in the bathrooms would have to be replaced. Oh, boy. Fixing the motel was going to cost a fortune.

"Well," Jenna said as they walked back to the house, "we're not going to get any customers with the place looking this way. We'll have to repaint, replace the carpet and the bedspreads as well as fix the broken window. We'll need to get the pool up and running." That had been scary—half-drained with a crack on the bottom, it looked like an oversize petri dish growing heaven know what. She had no idea what all that would cost, and she wasn't sure she wanted to. "It's not going to be cheap."

"I did figure we'd have to get new bedspreads and carpet," Aunt Edie admitted.

"And we should replace the flooring in the bathrooms. We've got water damage on the walls, which means we're going to have to have the roof checked out. That's all going to cost money," she added. How much did it cost to replace the roof on a twenty-room motel? More than they had, for sure.

Aunt Edie gnawed on her lower lip. "We do have a challenge."

There was an understatement of tsunami proportions. They were in deep doo-doo.

"I guess we'll have to get some estimates and figure out where to go from here," Jenna said. And that was about as positive a spin as she could put on things.

Aunt Edie wasn't exactly looking positive. In fact, she looked close to tears.

"The good news is, now that Sabrina and I are here we can contribute a lot of sweat equity. I'm sure I can find a bargain on carpet somewhere." That coaxed a smile out of her aunt.

But no one was smiling at dinner when she talked up the joys of manual labor.

"We're going to work all summer?" Sabrina asked, horrified.

"Well, not twenty-four hours a day," Jenna said.

"I've got a bad back, you know," Pete informed her, and helped himself to a second hamburger.

"Look, everyone, we all need to pitch in if we're going to make this place ready to turn a profit." No one was saying, "Rah, rah," yet, so she continued. "We can make the Driftwood Inn really cute again. Just picture it with a fresh coat of blue paint, some netting on one corner with a couple of buoys, some driftwood outside the office. Sabrina, you've got a good artistic eye. You could find just the right piece of driftwood to put there."

Flattery didn't work. Sabrina scowled at her hamburger.

She did help clean up after dinner without grumbling, though. That was something. But after that, just as Aunt Edie was proposing a game of cards, she asked Jenna, "Mom, can I talk to you?" and tugged on Jenna's sweater sleeve.

Oh, boy. Jenna wished she could say, "No, you can't," but she followed her daughter out into the living room. "Okay," she said once they were out of earshot. "What's wrong?"

"I don't want to be here."

Hot news flash. "Sabrina, we've only been here a couple of days."

"I hate it. I miss Daddy."

"You've been texting him, right?"

Sabrina scowled. "He sucks at texting."

In other words, he was ignoring her.

"I want to go home. I want to live with Daddy for the summer."

This again. They were caught in some kind of time loop, doomed to have the same conversation over and over and over. "You know that's not how things have been set up." *And you can thank your shithead dad and his new woman for that.* "You're just going to have to try and be happy here. Look for the rainbow in the storm."

"That's such a stupid saying," Sabrina spat.

"But it's true. There's always something good you can focus on, something to be happy about," Jenna said as much to herself as her daughter, and reached to pull Sabrina into a hug.

She jerked away. "Not here. There's nothing good and I'm not happy and you don't care!"

"Of course I care. Good grief, Sabrina. Do you think I get up every morning thinking of ways to make your life miserable? I'm doing the best I can and I'd appreciate it if you'd make some small effort to be happy."

"I would be if you'd let me go live with Daddy. But you won't and I hate you!" Having sliced her mother's heart in two, Sabrina ran from the room and up the stairs.

Jenna shook off the shock and marched to the bottom of the stairs and hollered up, "Well, I love you!"

No response other than a slamming bedroom door.

"Even though right now you're not very lovable," she muttered. She sat down on the bottom stair and bit back the good cry she wanted to indulge in, wiped away the stinging tears. Darn it all. Why didn't anyone ever tell you how hard it was being a parent?

Simple answer there. No one would sign up for the job and the whole race would die out.

She had to force herself to go back into the kitchen, where Aunt Edie was scrubbing down the counter. Again. "Is everything all right?" she asked, not turning to look at Jenna.

"Yes, everything's fine," Jenna lied.

Aunt Edie turned to face her. "I really meant this to be a blessing for you," she said in a small voice.

And no good deed ever went unpunished. Her poor aunt. Poor her. Poor all of them.

She hurried over and gave the old woman a hug. "It is a blessing." A very well-disguised one. "And everything's going to work out." Who was she kidding?

"At least we have one reservation," Aunt Edie said. "He's arriving this week. That will get some money coming in."

Until he saw his room.

Hopefully, he was blind.

"Come on, let's forget our trouble and play cards," Aunt Edie said.

Her daughter didn't want to do anything with her, so Jenna settled at the kitchen table with her aunt for a game of Hands and Buns, Aunt Edie's all-time favorite.

Once upon a time Jenna used to love to play cards,

but at the moment it was hard to focus on the game when she felt like she'd landed in a sick version of a fairy tale. Cinderella arrives at the prince's castle only to discover she's gotten stuck with a ruin, and she's still expected to do the cleaning. Jenna's aunt was expecting her to somehow turn into a superhero and save the day, and her daughter thought she was a superloser and hated her. Who cared how many red canastas she got? Never mind canastas. She needed money.

By the time she finally went to join the dolls in her bedroom she was mentally exhausted and discouraged. She shed her clothes and slipped into her sleep tee, then went to the window. The wind had blown away the clouds and it was a clear night. You could see a million stars in the sky and a half-moon was shining over the water. She opened her window and the smell of clean air and kelp drifted in. She let the soft sounds of waves rolling onto the beach slip in to soothe her.

It was beautiful down here. Perfect. Timeless. She'd always loved the beach. She still did. She leaned against the window and thought about something Damien said once said to her when they were first together: "I'm your ticket to greatness."

He'd said it jokingly, but he'd meant it. Without him, he was sure Jenna and her little massage business and what he called her cute little crafts would never make much of contribution to the world. Okay, so maybe rehabbing a motel wouldn't make her famous. But it would make her and everyone who came to stay there happy.

This was where she belonged. This was home.

# Chapter Six

*To Do:*
*Go through the Driftwood's books and*
*assess financial situation*
*Organize office*
*Try to find the bright side so I can look on it*

Monday morning dawned sunny and perfect. The sky was blue and the water was sparkling and Jenna could hear the gulls playing. Ah, life was good at the beach.

She showered and dressed and read a little of Muriel Sterling's book on starting over for inspiration, then went to check on her daughter.

Sabrina was awake, sitting on her bed in her pj's and drawing in her sketchbook. She seemed to have set aside her hatred of the day before and was ready to fly her kite until Jenna reminded her that they needed wind.

"There's wind," Sabrina said, pointing out her bedroom window to where the grass on the dunes was barely moving.

"That won't take your kite very far."

Sabrina's mouth pinched tightly in irritation.

"Don't worry. We'll get some good kite flying weather," Jenna assured her.

"Yeah, when I'm three hundred years old," Sabrina grumbled. "What are we going to do today?"

"Well, one of 'we' has to go over to the motel and do some paperwork. But don't worry, we'll do something later," Jenna hurried on before her daughter could protest. "The wind usually picks up in the afternoon. So, while you're waiting for me to finish, maybe you can clean the upstairs bathroom for Aunt Edie." Knowing her daughter, that would take her at least an hour.

"I guess," Sabrina said with a sigh and a shrug.

At least there'd been no more talk of going home to Daddy. Jenna took that as a good sign. She was smiling when she went down to the kitchen to grab a cup of coffee.

Aunt Edie had beaten her there and was pulling a coffee cake out of the oven. Ah, the aroma.

*Eat, eat, eat!* cried Jenna's taste buds. *Give us a break,* begged her hips.

"You're just in time," Aunt Edie told her. "I've made blackberry coffee cake, your favorite."

"Everything you make is my favorite," Jenna said. "But just a cup of coffee for now. I want to get over to the office and start sorting through things."

Aunt Edie didn't look all that thrilled to have things sorted through. Jenna might as well have said, "I'm going to take you to the dentist and the gynecologist today. And when we're done I'll run over your foot with my car."

"We need to know where we stand," she reminded her aunt gently.

"I know," said Aunt Edie. "But remember, I have that money in savings."

"No worries," Jenna lied. She grabbed a mug of coffee, then took her laptop over to the motel office to work.

A calico cat sat outside the office, licking a paw. It stopped at the sight of Jenna and regarded her curiously. It had no collar but it looked well fed. Hardly surprising, considering that the Seafood Shack was right next door.

"Hey there, kitty," she said, and bent to pet it.

The cat pushed its head against her hand and mewed, then slid along her leg.

"Wouldn't my daughter love you? But I don't think Roger would."

*Okay, Jenna, you're stalling.* She gave the animal a final pat and went inside.

Her first order of business was to try and sort through the piles of paperwork that lay on her aunt's desk. Aunt Edie may have had an iPod and iPad and smart TV, but her record-keeping methods were stuck in the dark ages, with receipt pads from decades ago and records kept in notebooks and folders in an ancient metal filing cabinet. A phone as old as Jenna sat on the office desk along with an answering machine that belonged in an antique shop. Jenna found loan papers stuffed in the desk drawer and, after looking at the figures made her bilious, she shoved them back in and shut the drawer. Catalogs for everything from linens to home decor cluttered the desk, and Jenna set those aside and opened the reservation book. It was sparsely populated.

Actually, it hadn't been populated since the previous August. Hardly surprising considering the state of the place. She turned on her computer and checked the online reviews. They didn't exactly lure people in.

What a dump. I thought I was staying at the Bates Motel…

After one look at our room we decided not to stay. The crazy old woman running the place offered us a discount. She should have offered to pay us to stay…

I wouldn't put up my dog there let alone a person.

With such glowing recommendations, it was a wonder they even had one guest lined up for summer. Seth Waters. Was he clueless? Desperate? Broke? Aunt Edie had dutifully written down his contact information in her reservation book and Jenna decided to call him.

A deep voice that made Jenna think of Vikings or pirates answered on the second ring.

She cleared her throat. "Is this Seth Waters?"

"Yes," the voice answered suspiciously.

"Oh." Duh, of course it was. "Hi. I'm Jenna Jones and I'm calling from the Driftwood Inn."

"Is there a problem?" asked the voice.

"No, not at all. I'm just calling to confirm your reservation."

"I'll be there," said Voice, making Jenna's nerve endings thrum.

"I felt I should tell you that we're undergoing some renovations here." That was putting it mildly. Jenna's right eye began to twitch.

"That won't bother me."

"Your room is a little…" *Subpar, pathetic, disgusting.* "That is, well, it needs some work."

"That's not a problem. I'm not particular, and the price is right."

Okay, good news. The nervous tic settled down.

"I told whoever I talked to earlier that I don't know

how long I'll need it, probably for a few weeks. I'm starting a new business in town and I've got to get that going before I look for someplace to rent."

"Not a problem," Jenna said. "We can make room for you." *We have nothing but room.*

"Good," said Voice. "Thanks for calling."

"Thanks for choosing the Driftwood Inn," Jenna said, and ended the call. At least they'd have one paying customer. Maybe they could pay the electric bill. She decided to go to the local consignment store and see if she could pick up some cute bargain bedding for their guest's bed. At least the bed would look good. She sure hoped he'd meant what he said when he told her he wasn't particular about his lodging.

She sorted through more papers, looked at a pile of bills and decided it was time to meet with Aunt Edie's accountant. She wasn't sure what he'd be able to tell her that she hadn't already figured out, but she called for an appointment, anyway. Whitley Gruber could fit her in at eleven. Should she be happy or terrified?

She set aside the pile of papers and went back into the house in search of more coffee. Sabrina had come down now and Aunt Edie was plying her with hot chocolate and blackberry coffee cake. Pete was present, too, enjoying a generous slice of the treat.

"Are you ready for some of this now, dear?" Aunt Edie asked Jenna.

"No, but I'll take more coffee if there's some left," Jenna said, moving to the vintage coffeemaker. "I have a few more things I want to do in the office before I go see the accountant."

"You're going to see Whit?" Now Aunt Edie looked

as if Jenna had changed her mind about running over her foot and was upgrading to vehicular homicide.

"It will give me a clearer picture of where we stand." The picture was already ugly, but what the heck.

Aunt Edie scowled. "I hate talking with Whit. He's always nothing but doom and gloom."

"Yeah, but he saved you money on taxes last year," Pete said to her. "When you run a business, you got to have an accountant, Edie, old girl."

Pete, the fount of all wisdom. "So, Pete, what does Aunt Edie have on the agenda for you today?" Jenna asked.

He scratched the back of his head. "Well."

"How about fixing that broken sign out front," Jenna suggested.

"Oh, yes. Pete's been meaning to get to that," Aunt Edie said in the old loafer's defense. "Haven't you, Pete?"

"I have," he said.

"And then maybe you can fix the broken front porch step," Jenna added.

Pete glared at her. "What are you trying to do, kill me?"

They should be so lucky. "I think you can handle doing two things in an eight-hour period," Jenna said.

"More coffee cake, Pete?" Aunt Edie put in quickly.

Jenna shook her head and left. They'd be lucky if the sign even got fixed.

The office of Gruber Accounting was located in a small building pretentiously called the Moonlight Harbor Business Complex on Sand Dune Drive. It shared the building with other businesses such as Williams and Weaver, Attorneys at Law; Drew Anderson, Architect;

and Beach Dreams Realty. The landscaping was typical of the beach—pampas grass, river rock, shells.

Whitley Gruber was as plain as his office, a man somewhere in his sixties, with a high-tide hairline, glasses, a rail-thin body and an even thinner mouth that drooped at the corners, wearing black slacks and a white shirt complete with pocket protector.

He managed a smile for Jenna and shook hands with her, welcoming her to Moonlight Harbor. "I'm glad your aunt's finally got some help," he said as they settled at his desk.

"I'm not sure how much help I can be," Jenna said. "It looks like we've got a cash flow problem."

"You do. That's nothing new. I'm afraid Edie's had trouble managing since Ralph died." He shook his head. "I've advised her more than once to sell the place before it comes down around her ears. The land's valuable and if she sold it and invested the money she could live quite comfortably for the rest of her life."

"She doesn't want to sell," Jenna said.

Whit removed his glasses and cleaned them with a handkerchief. "I know she doesn't. Maybe you can talk some sense into her."

This wasn't how Jenna had wanted their meeting to go. Although, really, what had she come in expecting to hear?

"The good news is, right now she's got a tax write-off," he said.

"You can't live on a tax write-off."

"Talk to her. The Driftwood Inn has seen its day. She should move on."

Seen its day. How sad. It seemed that, eventually, everything unraveled. But if they pulled the plug on the

Driftwood Inn it would be the same as pulling the plug on Aunt Edie. The old place had potential. Surely there were still memories to be made there.

Jenna sighed, thanked Whit for his time and left, discouraged but determined.

Not watching where she was going, she found herself colliding with a tall man with a broad chest tucked inside an expensive shirt. The slacks and shoes didn't look cheap, either. Hair bleached blond from the sun, tanned firm skin, baby-blue eyes with only a few crinkles at the edges, probably somewhere in his forties. He smelled like expensive aftershave and success.

"Sorry," she said.

"My bad. I wasn't watching where I was going."

"I wasn't, either."

He nodded at Whitley Gruber's door. "Meeting with your accountant can do that to you. Are you new in town?"

"I am," Jenna said, and introduced herself.

"Ah, the amazing niece has arrived," the man said with a smile. "I'm Brody Green. I own Beach Dreams Realty. We make your dreams a reality," he added with a grin.

If only he could do that for her and Aunt Edie. "Nice slogan," she said.

"Thought it up myself. It came to me in a dream."

"Really?"

He chuckled. "No, but it sounds good. So, how long have you been in town?"

"Just got here on Saturday."

"Ah," he said with a nod. "Then you probably haven't had a chance to enjoy any of our fabulous restaurants. How about lunch?"

Newly divorced and going out to lunch with a good-looking man. Was this wise?

Probably not. "I've got a lot to do," she hedged.

"Me, too. But hey, we've got to eat, right? How about it?"

She threw caution to the beach breeze. "All right. Why not?"

"Good. How about the Porthole?"

"Sounds great. I haven't been there in years."

"Come on," he said, "we can take my car."

She'd as soon follow him in case she wanted to make a fast escape, but he was already walking out the door so what the heck. Once she saw him opening the door on a late-model red Mustang convertible she decided she'd made the right decision. A good-looking man who had a great car and probably plenty of money to fill it with gas, as well as money for incidentals like lunches out. Ha! Take that, Damien.

"Edie tells me you spent a lot of time down here as a kid," Brody said as they roared off down the street.

"I did."

"My family came down here a lot, too. Funny we never ran into each other."

"Who'd remember someone you saw on the beach as a kid?" Jenna said.

He shot her a grin. "As pretty as you are now, you had to have been cute. I'd have remembered."

*Oh, yes. Flattery will get you everywhere.* "Is this how you sell houses, by flattering your clients?" Jenna teased.

"No, I sell houses by showing people great places to live. It's not hard. Who doesn't want to live at the beach?"

"For sure. I always loved it here. It's good to be back." And it felt good to be zipping down the road in a nice car with the wind whipping her hair and the sun on her face. Ah, this was the life.

Jenna and Sabrina had passed the Porthole coming in. Its location between the Best Western and the Quality Inn made it popular with visitors to town and the food made it popular with locals. In addition to good food, it offered a view of the dunes and the water beyond from the second story, which was where the fine dining area was situated. They passed the café and bar down below and went up the rough-hewn wooden steps to the main restaurant. Brody obviously knew the skinny woman with jet-black hair and red lipstick standing at the hostess podium.

"Brody," she purred. "I didn't know you were coming in today." This was accompanied by a not quite so welcoming once-over of Jenna.

"I wanted our newest citizen to see our best restaurant," said Brody the schmoozer. "Can you squeeze us in by a window, Laurel?"

The restaurant was nearly full, but Laurel managed to get them a table in a far corner where they could watch the surf roll in.

"This is Jenna Jones, by the way," Brody said. "Edie's niece."

"I heard you were coming," Laurel said to Jenna. "Good thing. Old Edie could use some help over there."

That was putting it mildly.

"So, what are your plans for the old place?" Brody asked after their waitress had taken their orders for shrimp sandwiches and tossed salad.

"We're going to try to get it up and running again."

"Good luck with that," said Brody. Their waitress returned with iced tea and he dumped a bunch of sugar in his and gave it a thoughtful stir. "You know, even though the motel's got issues, that property's really valuable. If Edie sold it she'd make a nice bundle."

This was the second person in an hour who'd told her that. The accountant had no hidden agenda. Jenna had to wonder about Brody. If he handled the sale he'd make a fat commission.

"Have you talked with my aunt about this?"

"Oh, yeah. She's attached to the place, which is understandable. But sometimes you have to let go of things."

Like bad marriages. But, unlike a bad marriage, the Driftwood Inn could be saved. "Sometimes you have to fight for things, too."

He smiled. "A woman with drive. I like that."

"A woman who's not looking to get involved with anyone," Jenna warned him.

"And why is that? I thought your aunt said you're divorced."

"Just barely. Not in a hurry to jump into anything new."

Brody nodded. "I get that. I'm divorced myself." He picked up his iced tea and shook his head. "Eighteen years down the tube."

"Have you got children?"

"A boy and girl, both in high school. College right around the corner."

And wouldn't it be nice if he could convince Aunt Edie to sell the Driftwood Inn? That commission would help with the college tuition.

*You're being cynical*, Jenna scolded herself. Still, she couldn't resist saying, "I guess you'll have to sell a lot of beach homes."

He shrugged. "Not that many. My boy's looking good

for a football scholarship and my daughter's a killer on the basketball court. I think she'll probably get some kind of scholarship money, too." He leaned back in his chair. "So, no pressure beyond the usual paying whatever the ex can suck out of me." His cheeks suddenly flushed. "Oh, sorry."

"Don't be. My ex is sucking me dry."

He cocked an eyebrow. "Wait a minute. Didn't your aunt say you've got a kid?"

"I do. And an ex who's an artist. I was the main earner, so I'm the one paying spousal support until he can get on his feet. He can't even support himself right now, let alone our child." *But who's bitter?* She ripped open a sugar packet and dumped its contents into her tea.

"Well, equal rights, I guess," Brody said dubiously.

"He shouldn't have any rights. He's a bum and rat and doesn't deserve anything," Jenna snapped. Way to make a good impression. "Sorry," she muttered. "I'm still adjusting."

"I get it," Brody said. "I put my ex's picture on a dartboard and used it every day for the first six months after we split."

That made her smile. "Is it still there?"

"Nah. I moved on. You'll get there," he added.

"The sooner, the better."

Their sandwiches arrived and they left behind the unpleasant topic of exes, focusing instead on the future, mainly Jenna's.

"You really should try to talk your aunt into selling the place," Brody said, making Jenna suspicious of his friendliness all over again. Until he added, "But if you're determined to make a go of it, I can recommend a roofer. It needs a new roof," he added, just in case she hadn't noticed the missing shingles, water stains and musty carpets in the rooms.

"I figured as much," she said. "I wonder what that will cost."

"Well, fortunately for you, the motel's not that big. Maybe you could get by for forty or fifty K."

"Fifty thousand dollars," Jenna repeated weakly. So much for Aunt Edie's three thousand and her eight hundred. That was just the roof. It didn't count new paint and carpet and all the other needed improvements. Quicksand. They were in quicksand. Was there a way she could make blue tarp attractive?

Jenna suddenly wasn't hungry.

"Eat up," Brody encouraged her. "You're going to need your strength."

"I need more than strength," she said. "Maybe I should try and find an investor." She looked at him hopefully. Maybe Brody Green would like to invest in a motel.

He didn't take the bait. He was too busy digging into his sandwich. "You don't have to do everything all at once," he said around a mouthful of shrimp. "Take it in stages. Get one of those Pardon Our Dust signs. People will understand." He motioned to her untouched sandwich. "Try it. It's really good."

She did. It was.

She ate the whole thing while Brody filled her in on the nightlife in Moonlight Harbor. In short, there wasn't much of one.

"The Drunken Sailor is still the favorite hangout at night," he said. "They've got line dancing there on Sunday nights. Austin Banks, who owns the kite shop, teaches it. She's from Texas. If you couldn't tell by the name you sure could by the accent. Her husband, Roy, does the music for it."

"That sounds fun," Jenna said. She'd always thought she'd like to take up line dancing. Maybe she would. She could do anything she wanted now. As long as it didn't cost money.

"I'll take you sometime if you like," he offered. "Introduce you around."

"Thanks. That's sweet of you."

"Hey, we like to make the newcomers feel welcome. This is a friendly town."

"Yes, it is," Jenna agreed. "So, what else is there to do?"

"We've got a movie-plex with four whole theaters. The community club sponsors bingo once a month and we've got a bowling alley, which is great if you like playing on lanes that never get oiled. There's a group of old guys who play tennis over on the courts three times a week." Brody shook his head. "I played with them once. Thought they'd be easy pickings. They kicked my butt."

"I'm not very sporty," Jenna confessed.

"Well, if you like to read, the library sponsors a book club. And a bunch of the women hang out at your aunt's place every Friday night. You'll meet a lot of our movers and shakers there. You know, your aunt's been a fixture here for as long as I can remember. Everybody loves her."

Was there somebody who loved her enough to float her a loan? Probably not. All those movers and shakers had their own businesses to keep afloat. Business at the beach was seasonal and Jenna suspected that some people barely hung on from season to season.

Could she and Aunt Edie hang on? Once again, her appetite evaporated.

She passed on the offer of dessert, so Brody called for the check and they zipped back to the Moonlight Harbor Business Complex. The wind was still playing with Jenna's hair and the sun was still warm on her face, but reality had doused her earlier feeling of euphoria.

"Don't get discouraged," Brody said, reading her worried mind. "Things always work out somehow."

Yes, they did. And if worse came to worst, good old Brody would be right there to help her sell the Driftwood Inn. *Sigh.*

She returned home to find Aunt Edie on the living room couch, crocheting, Jolly Roger perched on the back, looking over her shoulder.

"No solicitors!" he greeted her.

Aunt Edie looked up with a worried smile. "You were with Whit a long time."

"Actually, I wasn't with him the whole time," Jenna said, plopping onto her favorite seashell chair. "I met Brody Green and he took me out to lunch."

The smile got sunnier. "Brody is a sweetie. He's single, you know," Aunt Edie added oh-so-casually.

"Yes, so he said."

"Nice man. Oodles of money."

"Aunt Edie," Jenna chided. "You're not suggesting I go after a man for his money."

"Oh no, of course not. But money is always a nice bonus. It greases the wheels."

And heaven knew, their wheels could use some greasing. Still. "I'm not in the market for a man. I just got rid of one."

"Well, he was a poor excuse for a man," Aunt Edie said. "Sometimes the first try doesn't work out but you can strike gold on the second. I certainly did with Ralph."

"Yes, you did," Jenna agreed. "I don't think I ever want to try again, though."

"You're much too young to be saying things like that."

"I don't feel young." In fact, she was sure she'd aged ten years in the last hour.

"You need to get out and have some fun, and Brody's just the man to do it with."

*Do it.* It would be nice to have sex again sometime in her lifetime. But celibacy was safer. In so many ways.

"First things first. Maybe I'll have time for a man after we get this place whipped into shape."

Maybe.

Or not.

"I wouldn't wait that long," cautioned Aunt Edie. "Life's too short."

"Life's too short," Roger agreed. He and Aunt Edie must have had many a philosophical discussion.

"Where's Sabrina?" Jenna asked, changing the subject.

"She's cleaning the upstairs bathroom. Isn't that sweet of her? I didn't even ask her—she did it all by herself."

Yes, all by herself. With a little nudge from Mom. But at least she was doing it.

Doing it. Do it. *Sex.*

*Stop it, Jenna! Focus.*

Focusing on everything they had to do was enough to give her a headache. She took two ibuprofens, and then spent the afternoon beachcombing with Sabrina. They didn't get enough wind to fly the kite but they did find an agate, which helped Sabrina temporarily forget her hatred for her mean mom who had ruined her life.

Time on the beach with her daughter was good medicine, and by the time they returned Jenna was feeling much better.

Until she saw that Pete still hadn't fixed the sign or the broken step. They were no closer to getting the Driftwood Inn in shape and that dangling sign mocked her.

With a growl, she went in search of Uncle Ralph's old toolbox. If you wanted anything done you had to do it yourself.

Half an hour later the sign was properly hung and swinging in the breeze. There. Now they were one step closer to having the old place up and running.

Hahahahahahaha.

# Chapter Seven

*To Do:*
*Price paint and carpet*
*Check out bedding suppliers*
*Clean bathroom in reserved unit*
*Pray for money to fall from heaven*

After breakfast Jenna found someone to take care of the boarded-up window, then left Sabrina busy texting with Marigold about how bored she was and drove to Beach Lumber and Hardware to price paint. She figured her top priority was probably to get the roof checked, but the potential cost of that was overwhelming so she decided to start with something she knew they could handle.

The place was busy. An old geezer in a baseball cap with Beach Lumber printed on it was ringing up a sale. A middle-aged couple was waiting to buy a clam gun, and several men were wandering through the store holding plastic pipe or bags of nails.

One woman wheeled past Jenna with a cart filled with lavender starts. "It's one of the few things the deer don't eat," she explained.

Jenna spotted Tyrella Lamb, who was advising a woman on hinges. She gave Jenna a cheerful nod and promised to be with her in a minute, and Jenna nodded back and went to the paint section. So many shades of blue—how could she choose?

A moment later, Tyrella was standing by her side. "Paint for the inn?"

"Yes. I need something to match the blue tarp we're probably going to have to put on the roof."

Tyrella smiled at that. She picked up a sample card. "This one's very popular down here."

It was a pretty shade—not too pale but not too dark, either. "Summer Sky," Jenna read. "I like that."

"I think your motel would look great that color," said Tyrella. "And white for the trim." She handed Jenna another sample card. This one was labeled Summer Cloud.

Blue with white trim. Perfect. She could already envision the Driftwood looking fresh and pretty and ready for business. "I love it. How much do I need?"

"Well, let's see." Tyrella pulled a small tablet and pencil from her carpenter's apron and began to scribble. "Your place is about two hundred feet long."

"Two hundred feet. That's not bad."

"Don't forget, you've got a front and a back, and two sides. Your building is about ten feet high, give or take. That's probably around forty-four-hundred square feet. So, I'd say you'll need fifteen gallons. Oh, then there's paint for the window and door trim, and your doors. And, of course, you'll need paint for your rooms. You'll want to figure two gallons for each room. You'll probably want forty gallons to be safe."

"That much more paint for the rooms?"

"Four walls, ceilings."

Expense.

"And if you paint the bathrooms..."

"Oh, boy," Jenna said faintly. She looked at the escalating price and gulped. There went more than a third of Aunt Edie's stash just on paint. But it had to be done.

"I'll give you a ten percent welcome to Moonlight Harbor discount," Tyrella said.

"Thank you." It would help. "Will that be okay with your husband?"

"Leroy? I doubt he cares. He passed on four years ago."

"Oh, I didn't realize. When you mentioned him…"

"I should have said that he's in heaven now," Tyrella said. "But it always sounds so stuffy and old lady to say 'my late husband,' and just calling him my dead husband sounds creepy. Anyway, my late, dead, gone husband was a generous man, and he'd approve of me helping another member of the community. You've got a lot on your plate, so if I can help make your life a little easier, I'm glad to do it. Everyone's excited that you've come to help Edie. We all love her."

"I'm excited to be here," Jenna said. And she was… except for when she was worrying about her daughter or wondering where the money was going to come from to fix the place.

"What are you doing for lunch today?"

Who had time to eat? "Tuna fish sandwich probably."

"How about a salmon Cobb, my treat?"

"That's awfully nice of you, but—"

"Oh, not really. I want you to come to the chamber of commerce meeting with me. Lunch at noon at Sandy's. The schmoozing starts at eleven-thirty."

"Chamber of commerce?" Jenna repeated. "Isn't that for business owners?"

"You're managing your aunt's motel, aren't you? And,

trust me, it's no secret that Edie's leaving it to you. You qualify as a local business owner. And it never hurts to network."

"I was going to go to Quinault and price carpet this morning."

"Go to Ben Samuels over at the Carpet Guys. He'll give you a square deal. There," Tyrella added with a grin. "Now you won't have to run all over the place looking. I just saved you a good hour."

"Well, when you put it that way," Jenna said, smiling at her. She looked down at her jeans and T-shirt. "Guess I should go home and put on something more professional looking."

"Business casual is fine."

So Jenna went home, donned a sundress, sweater and sandals and then drove down Harbor Boulevard to Sandy's, a restaurant that offered casual dining. What they lacked in a view they made up for in decor. The small space outside the restaurant had been turned into a tiny beach, complete with sand and shells, a small lime-green lifeguard chair planted in it. Inside, a net was hung on one wall, holding a starfish and a turquoise glass float. The smell of cooking fish told her what was popular on the menu.

She heard the chatter of voices all the way down the hall, and she arrived at the meeting room to find it packed with men and women of all ages. She caught sight of Patricia Whiteside, who owned the Oyster Inn, and the woman from the kite shop. The kite lady's hair was long and perfectly styled and she wore a sleeveless top with fringe along the neckline over skinny jeans. Her earrings were glittery little lavender cowgirl hats. That had to be

Austin Banks, who Brody had told her about. And there was Brody himself, busy talking to Whit Gruber.

She quickly spotted Tyrella, who had ditched the carpenter's apron and was wearing a coral top over her slacks. She was chatting with two middle-aged men. Jenna suspected that if Tyrella wanted to replace Leroy she'd have no trouble.

She saw Jenna, waved and hurried over. "I'm glad you made it. You're going to love this bunch. They know how to keep it real." Brody turned and saw Jenna and made a beeline for her. "Here comes Brody Green. He's the broker at Beach Dreams Realty," Tyrella said. "Don't be surprised if he hits on you."

"He already has."

Tyrella shook her head and chuckled. "Leave it to Brody to zero in on the new single woman in town."

"Pretty single woman," Brody corrected, coming up in time to hear her.

"Don't you go breakin' this sweet young thing's heart," Tyrella scolded him.

Brody put a hand to his chest. "Tyrella, you wound me deeply."

Tyrella rolled her eyes. "Since you've already met Jenna, you just move on out of the way and let me introduce her to everyone else."

"Only if you promise to let me sit with you two," he said, and smiled at Jenna. The man had quite a smile.

"Come on. Before this boy sucks you in like an undertow," Tyrella said, taking Jenna's arm and leading her away.

She first introduced Jenna to one of the men she'd been talking to earlier. His name was Ellis West and he looked to be somewhere in his fifties and was a husky man with a jaw the size of a boulder. Jenna caught a whiff of cigar.

"You need to know this man," Tyrella told her. "He owns the Seafood Shack."

"My daughter and I were just in your place Sunday," Jenna told him.

"I thought I recognized you. Welcome to Moonlight Harbor," he said, and held out a large paw.

Jenna made the mistake of putting her hand in it. Ellis West had a crushing handshake.

"Glad you're here. Now Edie will have help and the old Driftwood will get spruced up like it oughta be."

And that would mean more business for him.

"Let me know if you need help with anything."

Money help? Would Ellis West be willing to make her a personal loan?

"I swing a mean paintbrush," he said.

So maybe not money, but a kind offer all the same. "Thanks. I appreciate that."

Next Tyrella introduced Jenna to Sherwood Stern, president of Harbor First National Bank. He gave Jenna a quick smile and even quicker welcome and then excused himself to go talk to someone else. That didn't bode well for hitting up good old Sherwood for more money.

Cindy Redmond was next on Tyrella's list of people to introduce Jenna to. She was thin in the hips and legs but full in the bust and she had a round, pink face and red hair. Looking at her, Jenna couldn't help but think of a Tootsie Roll pop. She owned Cindy's Candies along with her husband, Bruce, who was minding the shop.

"We take turns coming to the meetings. Can't leave the candy unguarded," she joked.

There were so many people to meet. Jenna managed

to shake hands with about half of them, including Austin Banks, who invited her to come join her gang of line dancers on Sunday nights.

"Good fun," she drawled. "Get out there and shake your booty to the only music worth listening to. It's a great way to shed your troubles."

Did she know Jenna had troubles?

She had eyes. She'd seen the Driftwood Inn.

Whit Gruber said hello to her, and Alex and Natalie Bell, who owned Beachside Burgers and Doggy's Hot Dogs, invited her to stop by and have a hot dog on the house. Rita Rutledge, close to Jenna's age and thin enough to blow away in a strong wind, owned Beans and Books, the combination coffee shop and bookstore, and offered to give her a free latte.

"Everyone's so generous," she said to Tyrella.

"Good people here," Tyrella said.

It sure looked that way.

The preluncheon chitchat ended promptly at noon when Brody, who was the president of the chamber, herded everyone to their seats, making sure he got one next to Jenna.

"What do you think so far of our business community?" he asked her.

"They all seem really nice."

"That's because they are. And they believe in this town, want to really put it on the map. You know, way back in the sixties, when developers first started building down here, they thought it was going to turn out like Vegas or some California beach town."

"They didn't reckon with the weather," Tyrella put in. "Don't get me wrong. In July, when the sun is out, it's heaven. And in August a lot of people come down here from the city to cool off. Fall can be nice, too, but winter is rainy and windy and sometimes stays that way clear into June. Not exactly what people want when they come to the beach."

"Still, we're working at making the place more attractive to year-round visitors," Brody put in. "We've got the razor clam festival in March and people come down in droves to dig clams. A lot of people come down for Labor Day weekend, too. Then we've got the Sand and Surf Festival end of June. And people always come here for the Fourth. The best fireworks show in all of Washington takes place right here on our beach. And, thanks to all the people who bring their fireworks, the city doesn't have to pay for it. Well, other than overtime for our firemen. We can't have the dune grasses catching fire."

"Those are summer draws," Tyrella reminded him. "We need to find a way to bring people here year-round."

"You don't have a convention center here, do you?" Jenna said thoughtfully. "With something like that you could put on events all year long."

Brody rubbed his fingers together. "Money."

"Well, if you had plans for one and presented it to voters…"

"They'd vote it down," he said. "We've got a lot of retirees down here living on limited incomes."

"Yes, but you also have a lot of business owners and working families. Something like that would really help the local economy."

"Or break the city," Brody said.

Their servers had arrived by then with salads and fish and chips and that ended all talk of a possible convention center. Probably a dumb idea, anyway, Jenna thought.

What did she know about stuff like that? She didn't even know how to rehab a motel.

Still, if the movers and shakers here at the beach wanted to give their town a popularity boost, it seemed like they'd have to do something. She'd noticed a large chunk of vacant property on the north end of town when she was driving around with Sabrina. Not a bad location for a convention center.

*Never mind that*, she told herself. *You've got your hands full with the Driftwood.*

And her daughter, who was probably going stir-crazy by now. Jenna vowed to play a game with her as soon as she'd priced carpet. Life was so much easier when Sabrina was smiling.

Speaking of smiling—or not—who was that woman on the other side of the table with the taupe hair and dark roots and cat-eye eyeliner? She was young, thin and hot. And she looked like she'd rather skewer Jenna than get to know her.

Tyrella followed Jenna's gaze. "That's Rian LaShell. She owns Sandy Claws—pet toys and supplies." Tyrella lowered her voice. "I think she and Brody might have had a thing once. And based on the looks she's giving you, she probably sees you as competition."

"Probably every single woman in town is competition," Jenna murmured, making Tyrella chuckle.

"He does appreciate women. Especially good-looking ones," Tyrella added, giving Jenna a nudge.

Yeah, that was what she needed, another potential cheater. Not.

Once lunch was half-eaten, Brody called their meeting to order. "For those of you who haven't met our guest today, this is Jenna Jones, Edie Patterson's niece. She's going to be managing the Driftwood Inn."

"About time somebody did something with that dump," muttered a thin, middle-aged woman in slacks and a pink blouse.

Her hair was as thin as the rest of her and she had frown lines carved into the sides of her mouth. Who the heck was she? Who cared? She wouldn't be anyone Jenna wanted to hang out with, obviously.

Brody cleared his throat and moved on. "Can our secretary read the minutes from our last meeting?"

Cindy Redmond had her iPad ready and began to read. As she did, Tyrella leaned over and whispered, "Don't pay any attention to Susan Frank. She's a pill."

"What business does she own?" Jenna whispered back.

"Beach Babes."

No wonder she was cranky. That store was an embarrassment to clothing stores.

Cindy finished reading the minutes from the last meeting and the treasurer, Ellis West, gave his report.

Brody thanked him and then, after old business had been covered, it was time to discuss the upcoming event, the Sand and Surf Festival, which took place at the end of the month.

"We've got all our vendors in place," reported a stylishly dressed older woman named Wilma Spike, who owned the consignment store.

"But we'll need to get a handle on the garbage thing," put in the frowning Susan. "All those out-of-towners are going to spread litter everywhere."

"I think we'll need to do what we do on the Fourth of

July and get volunteers to go along the beach and pass out garbage bags," said Nora Singleton, who'd slipped in late.

Susan shook her head in disgust. "People are so inconsiderate. How would they like it if we went up to their towns and littered everywhere?"

This was obviously a rhetorical question, and discussion continued, with members reporting in on everything from reserved porta-potties to who would be judging the sand castle contest.

"It sounds like fun," Jenna said to Tyrella.

"It is. Your daughter will love it."

"I hope so." At least that was something Sabrina could look forward to.

The meeting broke up and, after a little more chitchat, the members began to scatter, heading back to their various businesses.

"Don't forget to come in for your free latte," Rita said to Jenna.

"That's how she gets you hooked," Nora teased. "I'm glad you came today," she told Jenna. "Don't know why I didn't think to invite you myself. Good for you for thinking to," she said to Tyrella.

"We can always use fresh blood," Tyrella said.

"Yes, we can. I hope you're going to join."

Nora was looking expectantly at Jenna. "Well," she hedged.

"I know. You're still finding your feet," Nora said.

"We'll give you one more meeting," Tyrella told her, and grinned. "Then we'll reel you in. It's only forty dollars to join."

Jenna needed to hang on to every dollar she had. She nodded politely.

"I'll pay your membership for this year," Nora said
to her.

She may have been poor, but she wasn't a mooch.
"No, no. I'll pay."

"You can pay next year, after the motel's up and running."

Jenna hoped they could stay afloat until the next
year. She thanked Nora, said goodbye to Tyrella, skirted
around crabby Susan and then left to go see what kind
of bargain she could find on carpet.

Ben Samuels, the head carpet guy, was a good-
looking middle-aged man with the kind of muscles
that could probably lift a roll of carpet as easily as if
it were a roll of paper. He had a friendly smile when
Jenna introduced herself, which she hoped was a symp-
tom of a big heart.

"Actually, I got a call from Brody. I've been expecting you to drop by. Got some remnants I think might
work for you."

"Great," she said, and followed him past several aisles
of carpet rolls and vinyl and laminate samples.

"I don't think I've got enough of the same for all
of your rooms, though," he added, and her heart sank.
"But," he continued, "I do have an idea."

"I'm open to ideas."

He took her over to an area where the size of the carpet rolls were considerably smaller, unwinding one in
brown. "Can't go wrong with Stainmaster," he said. "And
brown won't show the dirt." Then he turned to another
hunk of carpet. This one was blue. Dark blue. Very, very
blue. "This one's not bad, either," he said.

It sounded to Jenna as if he was trying to convince
himself as much as her.

And then there was… "Yikes." Not the most diplomatic reaction, but it just slipped out of her. "Sorry. I didn't even know they made orange carpet anymore."

"Yeah, I know," said Ben. "And we've got some black."

Black and blue, brown and—ugh!—orange.

"So, here's my thought. You could do the rooms in different colors, and have different themes. Some could be your Sunrise rooms."

Jenna had to smile. "Don't tell me, let me guess. That would be the orange carpet."

He smiled back and shrugged. "You've got the Sandy Shores rooms with your brown, the Seaside rooms with the blue."

"And the black?"

Ben grunted and rubbed his chin. "Maybe we got enough of the other colors that you won't need it."

"Otherwise, the rooms with that will have to be the Stormy Sky rooms," she joked. But it was a good idea. "I could decorate to match the carpets. Maybe a framed picture of a sunrise in the Sunrise rooms, hang some starfish in the Sandy Shores rooms."

"You get a lot of good home decor at garage sales down there—people are always selling off lamps filled with shells and clocks shaped like boats."

"It's a great idea," she said with a smile. Then her smile faded a little. "But how much?"

"Come on, let's go back to the counter and do some calculating," he said.

Once he'd finished, she found herself wishing he had a different calculator. She could barely afford paint. How was she going to pay for this carpet?

He must have seen her chewing her lip because he

said, "Why don't we set you up with a payment plan? Give me a couple hundred down to seal the deal."

"Oh, God bless you. That would be great."

"Hey, I'm happy to help. We get a lot of business from all of you down there and I want to see you all succeed. We can cut labor costs if you take up the old carpet yourself and haul it away."

Twenty rooms worth of old carpet. By the time she was done she'd be as buff as Ben. She nodded. "I can do that." She could do anything if it meant saving money.

She left the carpet store armed with determination and excited by the challenge. Making each room unique would be fun. And a great way to express her creativity. Sabrina would probably enjoy helping her with that, and it would give her something to do.

Her carpet and decor plan met with her aunt's approval when she shared it at dinner that evening. "What a cute idea!"

Even Sabrina looked pleased when Jenna offered the use of her old digital camera and suggested she take some pictures for them to use. She wasn't smiling when Jenna got down to the how-tos of room transformation, though, looking at her mother as if she was nuts as Jenna went on to talk about moving out the furniture and pulling up carpet.

"Gross," she said in disgust.

Pete, who, as usual, had joined them for dinner and was enjoying Aunt Edie's shrimp casserole, wasn't any happier. "I've got a bad back, you know."

"I've got a bad back," Jolly Roger repeated from his kitchen perch. "Give me whiskey, give me whiskey."

"Don't worry," Jenna said to Pete. "I've got plenty of Advil."

Both Pete and Sabrina pouted.

"Come on, guys, how about some team spirit? We can do this. And think how much fun we'll have decorating and how cute the rooms will all look when we're done."

"I'll be dead by the time you're done," Pete muttered.

"It has to be done," Jenna said firmly, making herself ever so popular with her fellow diners.

"Who's for ice cream?" asked Aunt Edie, a determined smile on her face.

Poor Aunt Edie. She probably felt guilty.

Sure enough, later that night, after Pete had wandered off and Sabrina had gone to the beach to take pictures, she came to Jenna's room where Jenna was reading Muriel Sterling's book and half wishing she could smack the ever-positive author with it.

"I shouldn't have done this to you," Aunt Edie said, joining the dolls on the window seat.

She looked tired and sad, and frail and ready to crumble. Aunt Edie had always been so full of life, so…timeless. When had time caught up with her?

"You didn't do this *to* me, you did it *for* me."

"I really did want to help you. But truth be told, I did what I did as much for myself as you. I know the Driftwood Inn is no Hilton, but the memories it holds are priceless. And even though it's getting old, just like me, I know the place still has some life left in it. I can't let it go, Jenna. I want it to stay in our family. I want the place to have a future. A good one, with you."

"It will," Jenna assured her. It was what Muriel Sterling would have said.

"Well, I'm going to help you tomorrow."

Jenna had a vision of Aunt Edie keeling over with a

heart attack after her first tug on the carpet. "The best way you can help is by keeping us supplied with food."

Aunt Edie gave her a knowing look. "You're just trying to get me out of the way. But I can still strip a bed."

"I'd rather have you bake me cookies."

"I'll do both," said her aunt, suddenly energized. She hopped up from the window seat and came over and gave Jenna a hug and a kiss. "Bless you, dear child."

Jenna hugged her back, told her she loved her, and when Aunt Edie left she'd gained a smile and shed ten years.

"You'd better know what you're talking about," she informed the absent Muriel Sterling. "This new beginning needs to work out."

The next morning Jenna rented a truck and mobilized the troops. Fortified with omelets and cinnamon rolls, they stripped the bed in the first room and began to move out the furniture. They'd barely gotten the box spring mattress out when Pete announced that he'd pulled something.

Jenna took a small bottle of ibuprofen from the back pocket of her skinny jeans and handed it over. "Here you go. Eat up."

He glared at her, shook out two pills and downed them with a swig from his water bottle.

"Think how fit you'll be by the time we're done," she told him.

"You're trying to kill me," he said, in no mood to consider his future fitness.

She smiled and walked back into the bedroom, passing her daughter, who was coming out with a lamp, on her way to the office where they were going to stack and store everything until the new carpet could be laid. When they ran out of space there they'd have to use Aunt Edie's garage.

Ellis West left the grill at the Seafood Shack and, along with one of his workers, lent a hand. But even with extra help, moving furniture took all morning.

After lunch (goodies from the Seafood Shack—thank you, Ellis!) Jenna gave Pete and his bad back the afternoon off. She sent Sabrina to the Laundromat with Aunt Edie to wash bedclothes while she started tackling pulling up carpet.

She tugged and grunted, turning the air as blue as some of the carpet remnant she'd bought. She'd just tugged hard enough to send her flying onto her backside and let loose with a word that would have inspired her mom to wash out her mouth with soap when a male voice from the doorway asked, "Having fun?"

She turned to see Brody Green leaning against the doorjamb. She was a sweaty mess with her makeup long gone. He looked like he'd just stepped out of the pages of *GQ*.

"Yeah, tons of fun. Want to join me?"

"I'd love to."

"Liar."

"I'm on my way to meet a client. Thought I'd stop by to see how you're doing."

"Good. We've got paint and we've got carpet."

"You need a roof," he said.

"I know. But right now all I can afford is paint and carpet. Anyway, it's summer."

"And you know what comes after summer."

She frowned. "Thanks for the reminder. Say, you

wouldn't like to invest in a nice motel with lots of potential, would you?"

He made a face and shook his head. "Sell the dump, Jenna. The value's in the land."

"Money isn't the only value we're talking about here," she said. "We're going to make a go of this place. You'll see."

"I hope you prove me wrong. I really do. But you've got a big job ahead of you."

"Tell me about it." She went back to uprooting dead carpet. "Would love to chat, but I've got work to do."

"And I've got money to make. Try not to kill yourself," he said cheerfully. "And when you're ready, Top Dog Roofing is your best bet," he added, and left.

He probably got a kickback for recommending them, Jenna thought cynically.

Her cynicism left her when, an hour and a half later, Brody returned, this time wearing jeans and a black T-shirt with a pirate flag on it.

"What are you doing back here?"

"Saving you from getting blisters."

She held up her palm. "Too late."

He shook his head and got to work.

"I didn't really mean what I said about you helping," she told him, feeling suddenly guilty. She barely knew the guy. He didn't owe her anything.

"I know," he said. "But I can spare a couple hours. This looked like more fun than going to the gym."

"Oh, it is," she said, straight-faced.

"And the company's prettier."

Brody Green was a flatterer. But he was also a nice guy.

"Besides," he added, "your aunt and I are buds."

"So even though you think she should sell, here you are helping me renovate?"

"If you're determined to bungee jump over the cliff, someone ought to make sure your cord's in good working condition. Anyway, I figure this will score me some points with Edie's pretty niece."

"Ah, now we come to the true motive," Jenna teased.

"Seems like it might be worth dinner out on Saturday."

"Maybe," she said. "Unless Aunt Edie offers me a hot card game."

He chuckled and gave the carpet a yank.

They were just carrying it out of the room when a well-worn truck pulled into the parking lot. "Did you hire help?" Brody asked.

"No. That must be our one paying guest," Jenna said with a grunt as they heaved the carpet into the U-Haul.

"You actually got someone willing to stay here?" Brody sounded incredulous.

"He's moving into town and needs a place to stay while he starts his new business."

"Yeah?" Brody gave the truck an assessing stare. "What kind of business?"

"I don't know."

"Probably handyman or lawn care," he said, sounding slightly snobbish. "I might be able to throw some business his way."

He looked a little less inclined to be helpful once the stranger got out of his truck. He wasn't quite as tall as Brody, but he had twice the muscles. In fact, he looked like he had muscles growing on his muscles. He had dark hair and brown eyes and swarthy skin and he made Jenna think of pirates. Gorgeous, sexy. He walked with a swagger. Dangerous?

Why, oh, why did he have to show up when she was all sweaty? She pushed a lock of hair out of her face and called a cheerful hello.

He nodded and said nothing until he was standing in front of her. "I'm Seth Waters. Are you the woman I talked to the other day?"

The dumpy-looking woman. "I am. You got here earlier than I expected." *And you're so gorgeous.* Was there drool on her chin?

An eyebrow shot up and he checked his phone. "It's four. I thought check-in's at three."

"It's four? Already?" Jenna was suddenly aware of Brody standing next to her. His friendly air had evaporated. "I lost track of time. As you can see, we've been busy with our renovations."

The newcomer took it in and nodded. Didn't say anything else.

"This is Brody Green," Jenna said. "He's a real estate broker. He might be able to help you when you're ready to find a place to live."

"I don't deal in rentals," Brody said rudely, and it was all Jenna could do not to kick him.

"That's okay. I'm not in a hurry," said Seth Waters, pirate.

"Jenna says you're here to start a new business."

Now it sounded like she'd been gossiping about him. "I did happen to mention we had a guest arriving." Where was a fire extinguisher when you needed one? Her whole face was burning. Looking at Seth Waters the rest of her was heating up pretty quickly, too.

"I treat houses. Mold removal."

"There's sure a need for that here on the water. Everyone battles it," Jenna said. Brody didn't say anything encouraging, and she felt the need to put out the welcome mat. "You probably won't have trouble finding customers—seniors, house flippers, Realtors."

"We could probably use you," Brody deigned to admit.

Seth Waters nodded in Brody's direction. Then he smiled at Jenna. Call the fire department!

She cleared her throat. "Well, let's get you checked in."

"I've got to be going, anyway," Brody said. "See you later," he said to Jenna, as if they were an item. Were they?

No, no, no. It was too early to be an item. And besides, she didn't want to be an item with anybody—not Brody Green or pirate Seth Waters.

Brody drove off and she led Seth to the office. Halfway there she realized they'd have to make their way through a mattress canyon. "Sorry," she muttered as they clambered over furniture. "Like I said on the phone..."

"Renovations. I get it."

She had to climb over two dressers to get to the cash register, giving him a view of her dusty bottom. She managed to lose her balance and fall behind the desk rather than land gracefully as originally intended, hitting the floor with an "Oomph." She righted herself and pushed her hair out of her face and apologized again.

He was smiling now, mocking her.

She frowned. "Credit card?"

"I prefer to pay cash."

Cash? Cash, cash, cash! She forced herself not to jump up and down and pump air. "All right. Cash. In that case, I'll need you to pay in advance."

"No problem. How about I pay for the first week?"

Seed money! "That will be fine." She took his money,

wrote out a receipt and handed over a room key. No key cards for the Driftwood Inn. Her aunt preferred to do things the old-fashioned way. She also probably preferred to not have to spend the money updating their security system. "You're in room number two."

Pete had the first room on the far end, and had complained mightily about having to make do with an army cot instead of a bed.

Bed. Furniture. Oh, no! Jenna's right eye began to twitch and her face was on fire again. "There's just one little problem."

"Let me guess. You moved the furniture out of it."

*Blink, blink.* "I'm afraid so. And the carpet." *Blink, blink, blink.* "We have new carpet coming in just a few days." New carpet. There. Wasn't that worth sticking around for and sleeping on the bare floor. "I'll give you a discount."

"How about a free night?" he countered.

She frowned.

"You don't have a bed in the room," he pointed out.

"Fine," she said grudgingly. "One night free."

"How about every night I don't have a bed free?"

When was that carpet coming? She hesitated.

"I was kind of looking forward to having a bed."

There was that mocking smile again. If he hadn't been a paying customer she'd have slapped him.

No, no, no. No slapping. No violence.

No income if he went somewhere else. Someplace with a bed.

"Okay, deal," she said. "And I am sorry we're not more prepared for you."

"No worries," he said. "I don't need a lot."

She had to smile in spite of her irritation. "But I guess a bed would be nice."

"It would," he agreed, and this time his smile was genuine.

"I'm sorry the room's not in great condition yet." What were they thinking, anyway? Letting someone stay in the place when it was such a disaster area.

"It's okay. I've been in worse."

Jenna wondered what that meant. Had he been in some special forces unit in a Middle Eastern desert?

He didn't elaborate and she didn't ask. Instead, she said, "Thanks for being so understanding. The place really is going to be nice when we get done with it."

"I believe you." He put out a hand. "Would you like help getting back out?"

Oh, yeah. That. "I can manage," she said with as much dignity as she could muster.

"Okay." He turned and started to make his way back through the mattress canyon.

"Do you need me to find a cot or something for you?" she offered.

"No. I've got a sleeping bag. I'll be fine on the floor."

He'd be fine anywhere.

*Oh, no,* Jenna scolded herself. *Don't go there. Don't even think about it. You are so through with men.*

Hmm. Maybe she was just through with artists.

# Chapter Eight

*To Do:*
*Pull up more carpet*
*Buy a case of pain reliever cream*

"We're half done," Jenna announced at breakfast, forcing energy and good cheer into her voice. It wasn't easy since she felt like she'd been run over by an entire convoy of trucks. Carrying cows. And lumber. Bricks. Manure. And today she got to do it all over again.

But after today the old carpet would, hopefully, be gone, and they'd be ready to start transforming the rooms.

"I don't know if I can help," said Pete. "My back's in pretty bad shape."

He'd looked fine when he walked in to scrounge coffee and French toast. "Come on, Pete. You can do it. Don't poop out on me now."

He frowned. "I can probably manage for a while. But don't expect me to work as long as I did yesterday."

*Yeah, it would be awful if you had to put in two four-hour days in a row.*

"What about your kid?" he asked as Aunt Edie poured him more coffee. "Is she helping?"

"Yes. Once she gets up she and Aunt Edie will be back at the Laundromat, washing the last of the linens."

"You should have her help us. She's still got a good back."

"And I want to keep it that way. Besides, she's only fourteen."

"When I was fourteen I was pitching hay on my uncle's farm," Pete said.

Good for him. "Which is why you're so strong now," Jenna said in response. She downed the last of her coffee and stood. "Okay, let's go."

"I was going to have another piece of toast," he protested.

"You can have an extra sandwich at lunch," Jenna told him. And boy, was she going to make sure he earned it.

She left Aunt Edie with instructions to haul Sabrina and the rest of the laundry to the Laundromat as soon as her daughter had eaten, and then dragged Pete out the door, with him grumbling all the way.

She caught sight of their new guest as they walked to their first room of the day. Seth Waters had obviously been out running. He was wearing some baggy shorts and a faded T-shirt dotted with sweat. He sure filled out a T-shirt nicely. She gave him a casual wave and he waved back and kept on going to his room.

"That's who's staying here, huh?" said Pete. "Reminds me of myself when I was young. I was pretty buff back then."

"I can imagine," Jenna lied. Then, to inspire him, stretched the lie a little further. "You're still pretty buff."

He looked at her suspiciously. "Not really."

But he did make it through the morning before he claimed to be on the verge of collapse.

"You should probably rest," Aunt Edie told him as he inhaled a grilled cheese sandwich and half the bowl of fruit salad she'd made. How was her aunt managing to afford feeding this two-legged locust?

"Yeah, I'm pretty beat," he said. "Your niece is killing me."

"I'm not asking you to do anything I wouldn't do myself," Jenna said.

"You should take it easy, too, dear," said her aunt, looking at her in concern.

"I'm fine. Anyway, we need to get this done. I don't want to have to pay another day on the rental truck. Did you and Sabrina finish the laundry?"

"Oh, yes. It's all clean and ready to go."

"Where's Sabrina?" She loved grilled cheese sandwiches. She should have been there at the table, chowing down.

"She already ate," said Aunt Edie.

"So she's up in her room?"

"No, she went outside."

"To the beach?"

"I think so."

She had to be at the beach. She knew to let her mother know where she was going, so surely she would have reported in if she was planning to ride her bike somewhere. *She's fine*, Jenna told herself. She was probably taking more pictures to turn into art for the rooms.

And speaking of rooms... "I'd better get back to the motel."

"Oh, dear, I do worry about you," Aunt Edie said, looking at her in concern.

"I'll be fine."

"She's young and tough," put in Pete, not moving from the table.

Jenna shook her head and left. At least he'd put in a morning's worth of work. In fact, he'd probably done more work in the last two days than he'd done in the last two years. Sheesh.

She could hardly blame Pete for not wanting to do any more. She didn't want to, either. But there was no one else. She sure couldn't ask Aunt Edie.

She was crossing the parking lot to room eleven when Seth Waters drove in. He pulled a minicooler out of his truck and started for his room. "How's it going?" she called.

"Good," he called back, and kept going to his room, toting his cooler. Poor guy, he didn't even have a mini-fridge in the room.

Of course, he wouldn't have had one even if the rooms were refurbished. Jenna wasn't sure Aunt Edie even knew what a minifridge was. They'd have to add those in the future. People liked having a place to store their restaurant leftovers.

Room eleven smelled especially musty, and it was one of the ones with the worst water damage on the wall. It was a painful reminder of the looming large expense. Jenna found herself standing in the middle of the room, looking around, wishing everything was already done. What she'd give to be able to take a beach towel and spend an afternoon simply lying on the sand with a good book. Not Muriel Sterling's.

"A big job," said a deep voice, making her jump.

She turned to see Seth Waters standing in back of her. He'd exchanged the slacks and shirt he'd been in a moment ago for jeans and that same old T-shirt. He smelled like soap.

"Sorry. Didn't mean to scare you," he said.

*Nothing scares me as much as looking at this mess.* "That's okay. I just wasn't expecting anyone."

"No help today?"

"He has a bad back." *And a lazy butt.*

"He looked pretty fit to me," said Seth.

"Oh, you're talking about Brody. He just stopped in for a while. We do have a handyman—Pete. You may have seen him around."

"Old dude, not into shaving?"

"Not into working, either," Jenna muttered.

Seth nodded, taking that in. "A broomer."

"Broomer?"

"You know, a guy who stands around leaning on his broom while everybody else is working."

"That would be Pete."

"So, want help?"

"From you?" Well, duh. Who did she think he was talking about? "You're a guest."

"Guests help out, that's what my mom always said."

"Not paying ones."

He pointed in the direction of the other rooms. "You still got a lot of carpet left to pull."

Jenna's shoulders slumped. "Thanks for the reminder."

"How about this? I'll help you with your remodeling in exchange for a free room."

She already had one handyman getting a free room. Except he wasn't very handy and she wasn't getting much work out of him.

"I have to work on my own business but I'm going to have some free time while I'm getting it off the ground.

How about I give you my afternoons in exchange for the room for the rest of the summer?"

Jenna still had carpet to pull up and a motel to paint, inside and out. She did some quick calculations, weighing the pittance they'd get from the room rental against the cost of labor.

Before she could answer, he sweetened the pot. "You can keep the money I already paid up front."

All this in exchange for a room that didn't have carpet and was missing its furniture. "Deal," she said.

He nodded and pulled some work gloves from his back pocket. "Okay, let's get started."

And so they did. Seth worked hard and fast and it gave Jenna hope that they'd be done by the end of the day and she could haul her carpet to the dump and return the rental. He didn't seem to be much of a talker, though, other than to observe that she had taken on a pretty big project.

"Bigger than I thought it would be," she confessed. "I'm new to this sort of thing." *And don't have a clue what I'm doing.*

"They say the best way to learn is by doing. I bet you always wanted to learn how to tear up carpet."

"Oh, yeah."

And then that was it. Okay, fine. Jenna could live with that.

For about fifteen minutes. Then her curiosity got the better of her. Hey, they were going to be working together a lot. Couldn't hurt to find out a little about each other. Right? And didn't most people chitchat a little when they were working side by side?

"Where's home for you?" she asked as they tugged carpet across a floor.

"Here."

"No, I mean before here."

"I've been around."

"So, no family around here?"

"Got a brother in Tacoma."

"Maybe he'll want to come visit you while you're down here."

"Maybe."

And that was the end of that conversation. Okay, so not all men were big talkers. She got that. But this was like working with the Sphinx.

She tried again when they moved to the next room. "So, what did you do before you decided to start your business?" she asked as she knelt next to him. He smelled like sweat and aftershave. Eau de man.

"This and that," he answered. Seeing her looking expectantly at him, he added, "I used to be in construction."

"I'm not surprised to hear that. I can't picture you behind a desk."

"If I'm going to be sitting around I'd rather be reading a book or watching a game on TV than staring at a computer."

"Why'd you quit construction?"

He frowned. "Do you always ask your renters so many questions?"

She blinked and her face flamed. "No. I'm just making conversation."

"Well, how about we make conversation about something else?" he said shortly.

"Sorry," she muttered, and gave her section of carpet a tug.

He softened his voice. "Let's talk about you instead. I suspect you're a lot more interesting than me."

"Not really."

"Let's find out. Where's home for you?"

"Lynwood."

"How'd you end up here?"

"My aunt asked me to come. She needed help running the place."

"So, what's a pretty woman like you doing alone?"

"Do you always ask your landlord so many questions?"

That got half a smile from him. "Just making conversation."

"I'm divorced, that's what I'm doing alone." Just a little bitterness bleeding into the voice.

"Don't tell me, let me guess. Your ex is a shit."

"As a matter of fact, yes. How'd you know?"

"Because every woman's ex is a shit."

"Well, that's a little biased. Are you someone's shit?"

"Nope," he said, and yanked up a corner of carpet.

"Then why are you so cynical?"

"I'm not cynical. I'm an observer of life."

The carpet-pulling philosopher. "Well, for your information, I'm not just some unreasonably bitter ex-wife. To show his gratitude for me supporting him all those years, Damien cheated on me. And I'm paying for the privilege of being rid of him. Literally. Tar and feathers would be too good for him."

"Whoa, a little anger there."

"Wouldn't you be pissed?"

"Yeah, I would."

"I swear, if I was a braver woman I'd…"

"What? Shoot him? Shoot her?"

"Maybe."

"No, you wouldn't. That sort of thing always backfires. Anyway, living well is the best revenge."

Hadn't she told herself that at one point? "I guess," she said. "Still, it makes me mad."

"Obviously, since you just spilled your guts to a stranger."

Jenna sat back on her heels and sighed. "I did, didn't I? I'm a mess."

"It's okay," he said, walking the musty carpet back on itself. "I'm a good listener."

"You are. But that's enough of my ugly past. Let's talk about something else."

"Okay, how about your future?"

"That will be fabulous," she said as much to herself as him. "We're going to get this place fixed up and business will be booming. My aunt will be thrilled and my daughter and I will live happily-ever-after."

"Sounds like a plan," he said. "And what about what's-his-name?"

"Pete?" Jenna rolled her eyes.

"No, the tall dude who was with you yesterday. Where does he fit in the picture?"

Who knew? Jenna shrugged. She was through with men, after all. Why didn't she come right out and say that to Seth Waters?

"Still gun-shy, huh?"

"There's an understatement."

"Eventually, you got to get out there and start living."

"I'm living just fine now."

He looked over his shoulder at her with a mocking smile. "Yeah?"

"Yeah," she said with an insistent nod.

"Most people don't do well in solitary."

"I'm hardly solitary," she informed him. "I've got my family in Lynwood and down here. I've got friends."

"No friends with benefits."

"Yeah, well, sex is overrated." Had she just said that out loud?

He snickered. "Yep, still bitter. You'll get past it."

She was trying to think of a reply to that when Brody knocked on the doorframe. "Just stopping by to see how you're doing," he said with a smile for Jenna. And a frown for Seth.

"I'm doing great," she said, standing and pushing back her hair. "I got help."

"I can see that." And he didn't look all that happy about it. "Where's Pete?"

"He gave himself the afternoon off."

"There's a surprise," Brody said. "Thought I'd see if you want to go to the Lighthouse for fish and chips later."

For a moment, Seth hesitated in his carpet yanking, as if waiting to hear her answer, and she felt suddenly awkward. She commanded her eye not to twitch. "I think I'm going to be too pooped to do anything tonight."

Brody took the refusal in stride. "Okay. See you Saturday, then."

She nodded and he left.

"Looks like things are moving along with the house peddler."

"We're just friends," Jenna said. Although the idea of becoming more with Brody was tempting. Rich, nice-looking, easygoing.

Popular with the ladies. Maybe not.

Conversation stalled out after Brody's visit and Jenna and Seth worked on in silence for another couple of hours. At last they were done. Yes! Progress.

"I can hardly wait to see these rooms with new carpet," she said.

"You'd better paint before you put in the carpet," cautioned Seth.

Of course. That made sense. "Good point." And if she'd known what she was doing she'd have thought of it herself.

"And looks like you've had some water damage. Have you had someone out to check your roof?"

There it was again, the pesky roof. "Not yet. But I will."

"I wouldn't put that off too long if I were you."

"I don't intend to. But I do need an infusion of cash for that."

He nodded. "Well, maybe once you get the rooms done and the furniture back in you can start making some money."

"I sure hope so."

"I'd get some tarp on that roof though," he added.

Blue tarp, what every well-dressed dump would be wearing for summer. Ugh.

She nodded. "Thanks for all your help today."

"No problem," he said. "See you tomorrow."

Jenna watched as he sauntered off. The man was a walking work of art and she'd have liked nothing better than to run her hands over all those gorgeous muscles.

No, no. One didn't touch works of art. And one didn't get involved with men.

"You're working too hard," Aunt Edie fretted when she returned to the house to shower.

"Don't worry," Jenna told her. "I've brought in some muscle. I made a deal with our new resident. He's going to help with our renovation part-time while he works on getting his business up and running."

"Splendid," Aunt Edie said with a smile. "Is he single?"

Jenna pointed a teasing finger at her. "Don't be getting any ideas. Pete would be jealous."

"Jenna Jones, you are a terrible tease," Aunt Edie said, but she got the message and dropped the subject.

Hopefully she wouldn't pick it up again anytime soon. She seemed anxious for Jenna to find a Prince Charming. But after Prince Poop Jenna was in no hurry.

"What's Sabrina up to now?" she asked.

"I gave her some money to go get an ice cream," Aunt Edie said. "I hope that was all right."

"Of course it was. But she's supposed to let me know where she's going. How long ago was that?"

Aunt Edie looked suddenly guilty and concerned. "It was about two hours ago. She said she was bored so I suggested she ride her bike down to Nora's place."

She was going to be more than bored when Jenna found her. She was going to be dead. "It doesn't take two hours to get ice cream."

Fuming, Jenna marched to her car and drove down Harbor Boulevard. There was no bike parked in front of the ice cream parlor. She went to the cabana shops and looked around. No sign of Sabrina or her bike. No sign of her at the bakery or Beans and Books. Okay, she was fine. She was…somewhere. But where? The more Jenna searched with no positive results the more worried she became.

She was ready to call the police when she finally spotted the cute little body wearing shorts and a tank top racing down the road from Beachside Burgers, light red hair flying. Okay, she was probably on her way home.

But that didn't get her off the hook for not letting her mother know where she was. Jenna pulled past her, checking in the rearview mirror as she passed. Sabrina had recognized the car, and the expression on her face told Jenna she knew she was in trouble. She doubled down and pedaled faster.

Jenna beat her back, pulled the car into the driveway and then leaned against the back of the car to wait.

Sabrina pulled in, opting for cheerful ignorance over contrition. "Hi, Mom," she called as she rode up the driveway.

Jenna let her dismount and walk her bike up to the garage before laying into her. "Where have you been?"

"I just went to the ice cream parlor. Jeez, Mom."

"All day? You've been gone all afternoon."

"I went to the beach, too."

"We have beach right here, in back of the motel, in case you didn't notice."

"I wanted to see a different beach. Okay?"

The snotty voice didn't win her any points. "No. Not okay. I didn't know where you were."

"So what? You keep telling me what a great town this is and talking about all the time you spent on the beach."

"It is a great town. And yes, I spent a lot of time on the beach. But I told my mom what beach I was on. I never went wandering off."

"Well, I'm back now," Sabrina informed her, and tried to flounce past.

"Not so fast." Jenna caught her arm. "You can't be making a habit of this."

"Why not? I'm fourteen."

The perfect age for some pervert to grab her and drive off to parts unknown. "You need to let me know where you are so I don't worry," Jenna insisted.

Sabrina rolled her eyes. "You don't care, anyway."

"Of course I care."

The eye-rolling upgraded to a glare. "If you really cared we wouldn't be here. I hate it here!"

Said the girl who'd spent the day at the ice cream parlor, the beach and probably the arcade.

Jenna was about to go into her give-it-a-chance routine, but Sabrina didn't wait. "You're the meanest mom in the world," she cried, and stamped off to the house.

Jenna let her go and fell back against the car to collect herself. From across the parking lot she saw Seth Waters leaning against his truck, one foot crossed over the other, drinking a beer. Probably enjoying the show. She gave him a shrug and wandered over in his direction.

"Pretty fun being a parent, huh?" he greeted her.

"It's taking my daughter a while to adjust."

"I thought kids loved the beach," he said. "There seems to be a lot to do here."

"There is. But Sabrina wants someone to do things *with*. We left her best friend behind. And she misses her dad."

"Ah, so at least he was a good dad," Seth said, and took another swig from his bottle.

"No. But she misses him all the same."

"I get that. Kids love their parents no matter what."

"Do you have kids?"

"Nope." Another swig. "Known some pretty big losers who did, though. The kids didn't seem to care. Dad's their dad no matter what."

Jenna sighed. "And Mom gets to be the bad guy."

"I guess somebody has to." He nodded in the direction of the house. "She reminds me of my little sister at that age. Monica was always in a snit about something one minute, then happy the next. Is that a chick thing?"

"Hormones," Jenna said.

He grinned. "Oh, yeah. Those. Well, you've got some fun years ahead of you."

"Thanks for the warning," she said with a frown, and left him.

So, Seth Waters had a sister. One more bit of information pulled out of him. No kids, though. No woman? He was too good-looking not to at least have a girlfriend. What was his story?

Whatever it was, she'd pry it out of him eventually. It wasn't fair that he was learning so much about her and she still knew so little about him.

"You're a blabbermouth," she scolded herself.

But no wonder. With everything going on in her life she needed a shrink. Or at least a listening ear. Seth may not have been all that great at talking but he was good at listening.

She was sure Aunt Edie had dinner ready but she opted not to go in the house. Instead, she headed for the beach and some downtime. Being at the water's edge was so calming, better than drugs. Not that she'd ever taken drugs, but still.

She walked along the sand and watched as the tide came in. Someone had left behind a sand castle, and the waves were slowly eating it. A couple of middle-aged women passed her with smiles and nods. Farther down the beach a pair of young marrieds strolled, holding hands, completely into each other. The view was wasted on them. Jenna frowned.

"Don't be jealous," she scolded herself. She had a new start and beautiful setting to do it in. She had a dinner date for Saturday and her daughter was safe. She found a log and sat, watching the sunlight dance on the water. A flock of sanderlings were playing tag with the surf, running up to the edge and then racing away when the tide came after them. A gull flew overhead. She took a deep breath and closed her eyes, letting the early-evening sun settle on her shoulders. Her life wasn't perfect, but at least she had a beautiful place to do her worrying.

After a while the temperature dropped and she ambled back to the house. She found her daughter seated at the kitchen table with her aunt, playing cards.

"Where were you?" Sabrina greeted her. "Aunt Edie was worried."

"Oh no, I knew you were fine," protested Aunt Edie.

"You should tell people where you're going," Sabrina taunted.

"I have hamburger casserole left in the oven," said Aunt Edie, determined to stay neutral in a possible mother-daughter skirmish.

"It's really good," Sabrina added. She laid down her cards and cried, "Gin! I got you, Aunt Edie."

"You surely did," said Aunt Edie.

"Call the cops!" suggested Roger from his kitchen perch.

Jenna shook her head. There it was, a scene of domestic bliss. One would never guess that only a little while ago her daughter was having a hate affair with her new home. Yep, those moods were like the weather at the beach, highly changeable.

Maybe, if Jenna was lucky, that good mood would last for a while. Maybe they were in for some sunny weather. A mom could hope.

# Chapter Nine

*To Do:*
*Order business cards*
*Set up spare bedroom for massage*
*Put on makeup!*

Thursday morning was rainy, so Jenna opted to give her muscles a break and work on getting her business up and running, ordering business cards online and setting up her massage room in the spare downstairs bedroom that had been Uncle Ralph's den.

Of course, at breakfast Sabrina wanted to know what they were going to do that day. As in fun and games. She'd been itching to get out with her kite but not in the rain, and now she was frustrated and in need of a social director.

"I thought it was supposed to be sunny at the beach," she grumbled.

"It should be nicer tomorrow," predicted Jenna the weather girl.

Sabrina wasn't impressed with her weather forecast.

Aunt Edie came to the rescue with plans for baking cookies that met with Sabrina's approval. "And then maybe you can help me clean Roger's cage." Sabrina hadn't looked quite so excited about that, but she politely agreed, and when Aunt Edie promised to teach her how to play canasta afterward, she perked up.

"First, though, you can help me carry in my massage things from the garage," Jenna said.

"And then we'll bake our cookies," Aunt Edie added, sensing a mutiny.

Sabrina heaved a long-suffering sigh and followed Jenna to the garage.

"My, there is a lot," Aunt Edie observed as Jenna set up her equipment. She pointed to Jenna's old turkey roaster, which had been a garage sale find, and the ancient microwave sitting next to it on the repurposed bookcase. "Are you going to be cooking?"

"No. I use the microwave to warm up my damp towels, and the turkey roaster serves as my stone warmer. The real deal costs a couple hundred bucks. And as for the towels, well, Mom's old microwave was a lot cheaper than a towel cabi."

"You are so resourceful," Aunt Edie said.

"I don't know if I'd go that far."

"I'm certainly impressed."

Jenna smiled at her. "You impress easily."

"Not really. You are a wonderful girl, darling one."

If only Damien had felt the same way. They could have all been down here at the beach, starting this new adventure together.

Jenna shrugged off the moment of sadness. She was having enough adventure without him. She didn't need the cheater.

She stood back and admired her handiwork. In addition to her warming equipment, blankets and towels, she had her CD player for relaxing music, her aromatherapy oils and her massage oils. Her little desk looked cute in the corner with a vase of silk daisies sitting on it. Another small bookcase held her copies of *Massage Therapy Journal* along with a box of tissues for the inevitable runny nose clients would get while lying on their tummies.

"Now I just need a sign to hang outside the house," she said. "Maybe Seth can make me one."

"Seth?"

"Our new resident handyman," Jenna reminded her.

"Oh, yes. I caught a glimpse of him this morning when I went out to get the paper. A very nice-looking young man," Aunt Edie added, and watched for Jenna's reaction. Yep, back in Cupid mode.

"He's okay," Jenna said, keeping her expression neutral.

"I'd like to meet him. Maybe we could invite him over for dinner," Aunt Edie added slyly.

"I'll make sure you meet him," Jenna promised. "But we're already feeding Pete all the time. We don't need any more mouths to feed." Although the idea of spending more time getting to know the mysterious Seth Waters was tempting.

The mention of Pete's mooching made Aunt Edie frown. "I'd better get Sabrina started on those cookies," she said, and disappeared before the topic of Pete could be further discussed.

Jenna shook her head and got to work designing some flyers on her computer. Like rust and mold, Pete was an inescapable irritation here at the beach.

Soon the aroma of baking chocolate drifted in to her. *Stay put*, she commanded herself. *Don't go into Tempta-*

*tion Land.* If she even set a toe in the kitchen she'd wind up inhaling chocolate chip cookies.

She was about to cave right when Sabrina entered her office bearing a dessert plate with one lone cookie on it. "I brought you a sample," she said, setting it on the desk.

"Aww, that was sweet," Jenna said. Yes, those moments when she wasn't the hated, meanest mom in the world were worth more than sunken treasure.

"Aunt Edie wanted me to put more on the plate but I knew you'd only want one," Sabrina added.

"You did good," Jenna said. Then, as her daughter was standing there, waiting for her verdict, she took a bite. "Yum."

Sabrina beamed and went back to the kitchen, and Jenna went back to work smiling. Yes, life was getting better.

The morning slipped by on that nice, even keel as Jenna worked on odds and ends of paperwork. She was posting her new location on her business Facebook page when a shriek from her daughter had her racing into the kitchen. Roger's cage sat on the kitchen table and Roger was on his perch, walking back and forth, feathers ruffled. Sabrina was holding her bleeding hand and howling and Aunt Edie was trying to attend to it with a wet paper towel.

"What happened?" Jenna asked, hurrying over.

"He bit me!" Sabrina cried, tears in her eyes. "I just wanted to pet him and he bit me."

"I'm so sorry," fretted Aunt Edie. "I should have warned her about fast movements. She startled him."

"My finger's bleeding," wailed Sabrina.

"It'll be okay," Jenna said, putting an arm around her.

"I hate that bird!"

"He was only protecting himself," Jenna said as Aunt Edie rushed off in search of hydrogen peroxide, her cure-all for every wound.

"He's mean."

"He's really not. Aunt Edie will show you how to work with him."

"I don't want to know how to work with him. I hate him! And I hate it here!"

She began to cry in earnest. Jenna pulled her into a hug and assured her everything would be okay. She realized she meant those words as much for herself as for Sabrina.

Aunt Edie dressed the wound and Jenna found aspirin. Then Sabrina was seated at the kitchen table with ice and a plate of the cookies she and Aunt Edie had baked while Aunt Edie hurried to fetch the canasta deck. Another crisis survived.

With her daughter settled down, Jenna went to check on how the motel was surviving the rain. Some damp drizzles on the walls of several rooms told her she was going to have to invest in tarp for the roof sooner than later, and she drove to Beach Lumber and Hardware to stock up and pick up paint.

She was on her way to her car when her mom called to check in. "Thought I'd give you a quick call while I'm on my lunch break," Mel said. "How's it going down there?"

"Well, let's see. Jolly Roger bit Sabrina and she hates it here. And the motel roof is leaking like a sieve. I'm on my way to the hardware store to buy tarp."

"Adventures in Paradise," Mel murmured.

"Something like that."

"How are you holding up?"

"Okay. The place really does have potential. I just

have to figure out where I'm going to get the money to do all the work."

"How much do you need?"

"We're probably going to need fifty thousand dollars."

There was a moment of silence on the other end of the call. Then, "Oh."

"Yeah. Oh. But don't worry. I'll work something out. It's summer. I won't have to deal with the roof until September." And of course, by then, money would have magically fallen from heaven.

"Maybe we can all chip in," said her mother.

After their conversation the previous month, Jenna wasn't holding her breath. "It'll work out." She believed that. Yes, she did. *If you build it they will come...all good things come to she who waits... Somewhere over the rainbow...* Jenna frowned, told her mom she had to go and ended the call.

She detoured by city hall on her way and forked out fifty bucks for a business license. She hated to spend even fifty dollars of her hard-saved funds, but this was seed money. She'd make it back with one massage. Heaven knew they needed to make money somewhere.

"How's it going over there?" Tyrella asked her when she finally entered the hardware store. Today Tyrella had her hair up in a colorful headscarf and had accented her jeans and carpenter's apron with a chunky bead necklace and beachy charm bracelet dangling little seashells and coral-colored beads.

"All the old carpet is gone. Painting is next. But first I have to cover our leaky roof. Please tell me you've got enough tarp to do the job."

"I do. I'll give you a twenty percent discount."

Jenna smiled at her. "You're the best."

"No, if I was the best I'd be giving it to you for free. Come on, let's get you set up."

Half an hour later Jenna was ready to roll, her charge card maxed out and every corner of her car filled with tarp and five-gallon buckets of paint. There went Aunt Edie's money and hers and then some. She encouraged herself as she drove back to the motel by envisioning it all prettied up and decorated and filled with lodgers.

She saw Seth's truck parked in the parking lot when she pulled in. Now was as good a time as any to see if he could make her some sort of sign. She knocked on his door.

It opened to reveal a mussed sleeping bag on the floor, his cooler and a small pile of books. He had one in hand.

"Were you busy?" she asked, feeling guilty for bothering him. Except why was she feeling guilty? They had a deal. He worked in exchange for…a bare floor.

"Just killing time till you came back. I went over to the house and met your aunt. She said you were out getting paint. Need some help unloading?"

"That would be great."

"So, what have you got for me today?" he asked as they walked to her car.

"Well, actually, I was hoping you could make me a sign. For my business."

His brows dipped. "I thought this place was your business."

"It is, but I'm also a licensed massage therapist. We need an income flow while I'm getting the inn renovated and I've gotten set up in my aunt's spare room."

He nodded thoughtfully. "A massage therapist, huh? I'll have to keep that in mind for the future."

That comment produced an image of Seth Waters all

oiled up, her running her hands over his back. *No, no, no. Don't go there.*

"What's the name of your business and what do you want the sign to look like?"

"It's Healing Hands Massage. I just need a simple plaque with that on it. Can you help me out?"

"Sure. I'll have it for you tomorrow."

"Great." The sooner, the better. "Then tomorrow we should be ready to paint."

"You'd better let me pressure wash the outside and treat the mold before you paint the outside," he said.

"I thought I'd start with the inside and do the outside later when the weather's a little more dependable."

"Good idea. Let me know when you're ready."

"I will. And, about the sign, I'll pay for the cost of your materials."

"It's not that much. Don't worry about it," he said.

With that, the topic of the to-do list was exhausted. But she was curious about the book he was holding. She pointed to it. "What are you reading?" He held it up for her inspection. "*The Complete Works of William Shakespeare*? I never figured you for a Shakespeare kind of guy."

He shrugged. "Just furthering my education. Never finished college."

"I never started," Jenna confessed. Did that make her sound stupid? "I like to read, though," she said. Not Shakespeare, but she decided not to share that. "Once I discovered massage it was all I wanted to do, so I went to massage therapy school instead."

"At least you went to school for something."

He sounded wistful. She was about to ask why he

didn't finish when he said, "Well, see you tomorrow, then."

"Yeah, tomorrow." And that signaled the end of the chitchat for the day.

Seth Waters sure wasn't much of a talker. Sometimes, the way he looked at her with those dark pirate eyes, she could swear he was interested, but unlike Brody, he hadn't put the moves on her, so maybe she'd imagined that interest.

Oh, well. Her first love was now the Driftwood Inn. It really was going to be cute once it was all done.

"Yes, it is," Aunt Edie agreed as they sat around the dinner table that evening downing hot dogs and Aunt Edie's potato salad.

She'd also made one of her standbys, a salad with strawberry gelatin, cream cheese, frozen strawberries and a crust made with pretzel crumbs. If you asked Jenna, it was more dessert than salad. Not that she was complaining. Sabrina, who was on her second helping, sure wasn't.

"The first thing we have to do tomorrow is get that roof covered," Jenna said.

"Don't look at me," Pete told her, dishing himself up more potato salad. "At my age, I could fall and break a hip."

"I can help," Sabrina offered, making her mother immensely proud of her.

"That's sweet of you, but no, I don't want you up on the roof. I'll do it." She wouldn't cry buckets if Pete fell. Her daughter, however, was another matter.

"But you're afraid of heights," Sabrina reminded her. "Even the little-kid roller coaster at Enchanted Village used to scare you."

On the other hand, Sabrina was afraid of nothing. All the more reason why Jenna wasn't letting her up on the roof.

"This roof's not that high." She could do it.

"Okay," Sabrina said doubtfully, giving Jenna doubts, as well.

"I hate to think of you up on that roof," Aunt Edie fretted. "Why don't you let that nice young man help you?"

Jenna already had more than enough for Seth to do to earn his stay at the fabulous Driftwood Inn. She'd planned on getting Pete to help her. But really, it probably wasn't a good idea to send the old guy up on the roof with his brittle bones. So, this would be a job for Super Jenna.

"I'll be fine," she assured both her aunt and herself.

And she was. The next day, wearing the tool belt Tyrella had loaned her, which was stocked with nails and Uncle Ralph's old hammer, she managed to get a roll of tarp up on the edge of the roof and herself, as well. After several deep breaths.

Oh, man, it was high up here. And in bad condition. Some of the shingles were missing, probably blown away by high winter winds. She could get blown away!

"Don't be stupid," she scolded herself. The sun was out and there was no wind.

Yet.

She took another deep breath, and inched farther up the roof. What if she dropped her tarp?

Never mind the tarp. What if she dropped herself?

More deep breaths. The roof wasn't steeply pitched and she managed to make it to the peak where, gripping tightly with one hand, she squeezed her eyes shut and unfurled the tarp with the other. There. Good for her.

But now she had blue tarp in one hand and was holding onto the cap of the roof with the other. How was she going to get to her hammer?

With a whimper, she stretched out over the peak like a giant taco shell in the making and then reached out a foot to hold down the tarp. Getting out her hammer had her breathing hard but she managed. Now, a nail. Oh, Lord, she was going to die. She kept herself spread-eagle over the roof and managed to dig out a nail. Then scooted around so she could hammer while lying down, scraping her elbow in the process. Boy, was this fun.

But with her first corner nailed down she felt like she'd won gold in the Olympic Games. She could do this!

Once she got busy rolling out and nailing down tarp she was almost able to forget where she was. Until it came time to go down the ladder for more.

Her eye began to twitch. *Don't be such a sissy*, she told herself. *You can do this. Just turn around, put your foot on the ladder.* She reached out a foot…into empty space. Eeek. She pulled it back in, looked over the edge of the roof. It wasn't that long of a way down.

Oh, yes, it was. She edged away from the ladder, digging her hands into the crumbly shingles. Helicopter rescue, that was what she needed. "Help!" she hollered, hoping Pete was somewhere around to hear.

He wasn't. And while there were customers at the Seafood Shack across the parking lot, they were coming and going, talking and playing their car radios so loud no one would have heard her even if she'd had a bullhorn.

The sun began to beat down on her, frying her shoulders. She wished she'd put a little bottle of water in one of her apron pockets. No, she wished she'd never gotten on this roof.

Maybe someone would get the idea if she waved. She tried to stand to make the time-honored "help me" wave of the stranded, had a panic attack and sat back down, heart thumping. Never mind. She didn't want help that badly.

Her stomach began to rumble. It had to be getting close to lunchtime. That meant Aunt Edie would send Sabrina out with food. Then she could have her daughter call the fire department and they'd bring out a ladder truck and rescue her. And she'd look like the idiot of Moonlight Harbor.

Like she cared at this point? She just wanted off this roof.

A million years passed until, finally, Seth's truck came into sight. Help at last. And just in time. In addition to her whining stomach, Jenna's bladder was beginning to think fondly of a bathroom visit.

He got out and came to stand at the base of the ladder. "Checking out the view?" he called up.

"Something like that. Can you call the fire department?"

"Are you on fire?"

"I need someone to get me down."

"I think they only rescue cats."

"Ha, ha," Jenna said sourly.

"You're afraid of heights, huh?"

She scowled at him. "Can you just call someone?"

"No. I'll get you down." He started up the ladder, running up it with the agility of the fearless. Once at the top, he held out a hand. "Come on. Scoot down here where I can reach you."

"Oh," Jenna whimpered.

"You can do it. You got up there."

"Getting up and getting down are two different things," she informed him.

"Don't be a wuss," he said, his hand still out.

She sucked in a breath and scooted half an inch, the hot shingles burning her bottom as she went.

"You probably should let somebody else do this if you're afraid of heights," he said.

"Well, I didn't get any takers last night," she snapped.

"You didn't ask everyone. Come on, come down a little closer."

Another whimper, another six inches.

"You can do it," he said.

*Dear Lord, get me off this roof and I'll never be stupid again.* Jenna scooted down some more until, at last, she was back at the ladder.

"Good," he said encouragingly. "Now, stand up and turn around. I'll guide your foot."

"What if I fall?"

"I'll catch you."

"Yeah, but who'll catch you?"

"Come on. Don't think like that. Get up."

Jenna managed to get almost up and turned around. *Blink, blink.*

She commanded her eyes to stop twitching. She needed to watch what she was doing.

But she didn't want to see where she was falling. Maybe she should shut them.

"Okay, now grab the ends of the ladder."

*And fall.* Jenna was practically hyperventilating now.

"You can do it. Come on."

She swallowed hard, opened one eye and grabbed the ladder. Then she swung out a foot. Immediately, his hand clamped over her ankle, guiding her foot to the first rung.

"Okay. First rung's the hardest. After this it will be a piece of cake. Let's get your other foot on the ladder."

She had to stick out another foot! *Blink, blink. Blink, blink, blink, blink, blink.*

"Give me your damn foot," Seth growled.

His impatience galvanized her and she stuck out her foot. With a whimper.

That also was guided to the ladder, which she was now gripping with all her sweaty might.

"The hard part's over," he assured her, his tone softening. "Come on. Next rung."

Several eye twitches and another whimper and she managed another rung. And then another. Step by step, he walked her down until she was finally on solid ground. She was a sweaty mess and her heart was pounding as if she'd run a marathon.

She let out her breath. "Thanks."

"You're welcome. How long have you been up there, anyway?"

"Forever." And even though she'd put on makeup that morning, her lipstick had long worn off and she was grimy, slimy and sweaty. Someday this man would see her at her best. Maybe.

Not that it mattered since she was done with men.

"You'd better let me finish for you," he said.

She nodded. Fine with her. "Thanks. I need to go…" Well, she needed to go.

"Wait a minute." He ran to his truck, pulled a slab of wood from the front seat and returned with it. "Here's your sign."

He'd painted her company name on it and on the side had managed to carve in a hand holding a seashell. He'd screwed two hooks on the top so she could hang it up.

"I can put in a post so you've got someplace to hang it," he offered.

"Thanks. It's perfect. How did you do the hands?"

"I've got a Dremel. No big deal."

It was to her. "Give me the bill for your materials and I'll reimburse you."

"It wasn't that much."

But it was yet another thing she'd asked him to do. Was she asking this guy to do too much? In light of the poor excuse for a room she was giving him, absolutely. "I think I'm getting the better end of our bargain."

He shrugged. "I like to keep busy and I like being outside. Not enough business yet so I don't mind having things to do around here." He nodded in the direction of the roof. "I'll put up the rest of your tarp."

"Thanks," she said. Then, "I think I'll get inside. I need water."

"Better put something on your face," he advised. "Looks like you got a burn going."

There was an understatement, she thought once she looked in the bathroom mirror. She looked like Lobster Girl. *Note to self: don't work on a roof in a sleeveless top. Correction: don't work on a roof at all.*

"Can we fly my kite now?" Sabrina asked once Jenna had finished smearing every inch of available skin with aloe vera cream.

Just what she wanted, more sun. "Can we do that tomorrow?"

Sabrina frowned. "I guess." She wrinkled her nose. "You do look kind of sunburned."

"I am kind of sunburned. How about we play some cards with Aunt Edie instead?"

"Okay," Sabrina said in resigned tones.

"First, let's make a run to the store for some root beer. We can make floats."

That met with her daughter's approval, and they made their way to the grocery store. "What did you do all day while I was up on the roof?" Jenna asked.

"Nothing," Sabrina said with a pout.

"Nothing at all? You just sat like a rock all day."

"I did some sketching. And I wrote in my journal."

She didn't volunteer what she wrote and Jenna didn't ask. She didn't think she wanted to know.

"And I took some pictures."

Ah, something positive to focus on. "Did you get some good ones we can hang in the rooms?"

"I guess," Sabrina said, refusing to reward her mom with any kind of positive attitude.

"Great. You'll have to show them to me when we get back."

Sabrina just gave her another shrug, her reward for being a neglectful mom.

Beachside Grocery was busy when they walked in, with both locals and tourists in town for the weekend, all picking up supplies. They snagged the last gallon of vanilla ice cream and a bottle of root beer and made their way to one of the lines of people waiting for access to a checker.

In the process, they ran into Brody. He was looking handsome and polished as usual, wearing a blue shirt that matched those baby-blue eyes.

"Well, hey there," he greeted Jenna. "Hi there, kiddo," he added, smiling at Sabrina.

She frowned and muttered a hello.

Brody was impervious to teen girl disapproval.

"Stocking up on food for the chick gathering tonight?" he asked Jenna.

"No. Getting ready to play some cards and we need sustenance."

"Poker?" he teased as their goodies rode up the belt and the checker began ringing up the purchase.

"I'm not a gambler," Jenna informed him. Except she was taking the biggest gamble of her life with the Driftwood Inn. "We're playing Hands and Buns."

"Hands and Buns?" he repeated as if she'd said something naughty.

"It's a card game."

Sabrina grabbed the bag. "Mom, our ice cream's melting."

"Oh." Jenna pulled out a bill, paid up and got change.

"Have fun," Brody said. "See you tomorrow."

"You're going out with him?" Sabrina demanded as they crossed the parking lot.

"Just having dinner."

"Jeez, Mom, he's such a yuck. He called me *kiddo*."

"He was only being friendly."

"I'm not a kiddo," Sabrina said, her voice charged with umbrage. "Anyway, you and Daddy are barely divorced."

"And Daddy's already with someone else," Jenna reminded her, which made Sabrina scowl.

Jenna sighed inwardly. Wrong thing to say. As if her daughter wanted reminding that her father was moving on and leaving them in the dust. And now, Jenna was shaking things up just when Sabrina craved security.

She put an arm around her daughter. "I'm not getting involved with anyone."

"Not him, please," Sabrina added in disgust. "Anyway, I bet Daddy's not going to stay with Aurora forever. He'll start missing us and come back."

And fish would walk. But what if he did come to his senses and ask her to take him back? Would she?

Never. He'd hurt her too badly.

Sabrina was quiet on the ride home, but once they started playing Hands and Buns, she reanimated and even crowed when she won. And Jenna felt less like a neglectful mother. How did other single moms manage that delicate balancing act between work and family without falling into guilt?

She asked her mother that when she called her after dinner to report on her big roof adventure.

"You remind yourself that you're doing what you have to do," Mel said. "It's that simple. And that difficult."

"Sometimes I feel like such a failure," Jenna confessed.

"It wasn't you who failed. Don't take on the burden of your husband's bad behavior."

But maybe he wouldn't have behaved badly if Jenna had admitted defeat, acknowledged that they were two mismatched people pulling in different directions instead of together and set them both free. Too late to relive that part of her life. All she had was the present.

But she wasn't sure she was managing that so well. She heaved a sigh. "I know I'm not spending enough time with Sabrina. And she hasn't made any friends here."

"Things will sort themselves out and you two will be fine," Mel said.

"I hope so. I don't want to ruin her life." Aunt Edie's offer had looked like such a godsend at first. But now that Jenna was up to her eyeballs in the mess of trying to revive the motel it felt more like some sick cosmic joke.

"You're not. A little adversity is good for all of us."

"That which doesn't kill me makes me stronger?" Jenna said with a frown.

"Something like that. It seems like most of us build up fortitude only by wading through rough waters."

"I don't mind wading. I just don't want to drown."

Mel chuckled. "You won't. Trust me on that."

And, after what her mom had gone through, she should know.

They said their goodbyes, and Jenna went to help her aunt get ready for her Friday night gathering of friends. The fare was simple: shrimp dip and crackers, a cheeseball that looked radioactive and cubed watermelon.

"The girls always bring wine," Aunt Edie said as they pulled out wineglasses. Aunt Edie had a variety—everything from polka dots to turquoise swirls. Even one with a face complete with false eyelashes and earrings in the glass ears. "I collect them," she said.

There was an idea to hang on to for Christmas.

"Who all is coming tonight?" Jenna asked, bringing herself back into the present.

"Let's see. Nora Singleton, for one. You've met Nora. She's a doll, and she and Bill have been so supportive ever since I lost Ralph. And, of course, my old friend Patricia Whiteside. Sometimes I wish I'd thought big like Patricia and made this place larger."

Then they'd have had an even bigger headache trying to remodel. "It's perfect the way it is," Jenna assured her, and Aunt Edie gave her a grateful smile. "Who else?"

"Let's see. Tyrella, who you've met. We've done business for years. Cindy Redmond. She's just as sweet as the candy she sells. Then there's Courtney Moore, who works at Beach Babes. Nora invited her to join us. That girl has a flair for designing clothes. If Susan Frank would give her a chance she could bring in some wonderful distinctive pieces to Beach Babes."

Jenna remembered Susan from the chamber of commerce meeting, she of the frown and the grumpy comments.

"But you can't tell Susan anything," Aunt Edie continued. "Then there's Courtney's friend Annie Albright." Aunt Edie shook her head. "There's a gal who needs to hit Restart. Her husband is a drunken lout. Works on and off as a handyman. Drinks away most of his paycheck. Verbally abusive."

"Why doesn't she leave him?" Jenna asked.

"She keeps hoping he'll change. They've got a little girl. I think she's eight."

"Does Annie work?"

"She's a waitress at Sandy's, works the morning shift. She's quite the cook, and she'd love to have a little food truck someday. I don't know if she'll ever be able to make that happen, not with the man she's tied to."

"This almost sounds like a support group," Jenna joked.

"In a way, it is. They're all lovely women. I know you're going to enjoy them."

The women started arriving at a little before seven. Nora and Tyrella were the first, and came bearing wine.

They were followed by Cindy Redmond. "You can't have a Friday night without chocolate," she said, laying down a plate of chocolate truffles.

"It pays to know people," Tyrella said, plucking one from the plate. "Lord love you, Cindy. What would we do without you?"

"We'd be a lot skinnier," said Nora.

"You're one to talk, Ice Cream Queen," Cindy shot back good-naturedly.

Sabrina stuck around long enough to be fussed over and snag a chocolate treat, then disappeared into her room to text with Marigold, and Jenna vowed to invite the bff down to visit as soon as they got things more squared away.

"She's adorable," said Tyrella, who was already digging into the toxic cheese ball.

"She can be," Jenna said.

"Girls," Cindy said, shaking her head. "They're enough to drive you to sugar. I have two, twins. They're off to college in the fall, thank God."

"Remind me again. How old is your daughter?" Nora asked Jenna.

"Fourteen."

Nora gave a knowing nod. "The right age to start driving you nuts. That was when my daughter became a handful. And the boys." She rolled her eyes. "Once the testosterone kicked in they were always at each other's throats. They're the best of friends now, though, and I don't know what I'd do without them to run the go-carts and arcade and golf."

"What is it about teenagers, anyway?" put in Cindy.

"Aliens," Nora said. "When they hit adolescence, aliens come and take over their bodies. Once they hit their twenties the aliens return to the mother ship and your kid becomes human again."

There were smiles, nods and chuckles to confirm the truth of Nora's statement.

"I think my little alien would be happier here if she had a friend," Jenna said. "She's lonely. And I'm not spending as much time with her as I'd like."

"Kids need to have friends to hang out with," Nora acknowledged. "My granddaughter Caroline is the same age, and she's coming for a visit later this month. Maybe they can hang out together."

"That would be great," Jenna said. Any granddaughter of Nora's had to be a good kid.

"I wish my daughter was old enough to keep her company," said Annie, who had arrived with some chips and dip. "But she's still playing with dolls."

"Encourage her to enjoy that as long as possible," Nora told her. "Kids these days grow up way too fast."

Annie nodded, and her smile looked sad. How fast was her little girl growing up in a home with an alcoholic dad?

Of course, everyone wanted to hear all about Jenna, and the room was full of praise for her boldness in leaving her husband—as if she'd had a choice—and her kindness for coming to help their pal Edie. Hardly surprising, in light of the fact that Edie made her sound like a cross between Mother Teresa and Joan of Arc.

She was impressed with them, too. Courtney was striking, tall and willowy with dark hair, strong features and a flair for dress that declared her an artist. She had a fancy mani and pedi, with both her fingernails and toenails dotted with tiny seashells, and wore a necklace of silver mermaids and sand dollars. She was a gum chewer, taking her gum out to enjoy treats and perching it on the edge of her wineglass.

"Tacky, I know," she said to Jenna. "But it's either this or smoking."

Jenna couldn't help admiring her cold shoulder top with the lace-trimmed bottom that she wore over her tight jeans, which were decorated with lace seashells.

She smiled down at it. "It's one of my designs."

"It's gorgeous."

"It would look great on you," Courtney said. "One of these days, I'm going to have my own clothing line and put on a fashion show at the Porthole. Maybe you and your daughter will be models for me in exchange for getting to keep the clothes?"

"No maybe about it," Jenna said. "That would be a for sure."

Courtney's friend Annie was as shy and quiet as Courtney was outgoing. She was a pretty brunette, clad simply in white jeggings and a faded T-shirt printed with a picture of a smiling quarter moon. No fancy manicure for her.

As the evening wore on Jenna noticed her rubbing her right shoulder a lot. She moved over to sit next to Annie on the couch. "Is your shoulder bothering you?"

Annie blushed and waved away Jenna's concern. "It's nothing."

"I'm a massage therapist. Let me see if I can work out some of the kinks." Annie's protests were weak enough to convince Jenna the woman was only being polite, so she moved behind her and went to work.

"Oh, my gosh, that hurts so good," Annie said with a groan.

"Whoa, what's this?" demanded Courtney.

"Oh, I forgot to tell you all. Jenna's a massage therapist," said Aunt Edie. "She's going to set up business right here at the house."

"I'll be your first customer," Tyrella said.

"Then I'll be your second," said Cindy.

Jenna smiled. Good. She could use all the business she could get.

"Your traps are a little tight," she told Annie. "Are you under any stress?" She had to be with the man she was married to.

"No more than anyone else, I guess," Annie replied.

Courtney gave a snort. "Yeah, right. She may as well know right off what the rest of us know. Your husband's a shit."

Annie's muscles bunched under Jenna's fingers. "I get it," Jenna assured her. She found a rhomboid and worked it.

"Oh, my," Annie yelped. "That goes all the way up my neck."

"You get trigger points where the neck is knotted," Jenna explained. "It refers pain to other parts of the body. This one in your shoulder is referring right up your neck."

"In other words, her husband is a pain in the neck," Courtney said.

"Maybe," Jenna said.

Courtney was trying to drive home a point, but in light of what Jenna had gone through and what Annie was going through, it wasn't funny. And nobody laughed.

"I guess that was tacky, huh?" Courtney muttered.

"Just a little," Cindy said. "Greg's not going to change," she told Annie. "You should kick him out."

Annie sighed. "I can't afford to. Anyway, he's fine when he's not drinking."

Courtney gave a disapproving frown. "And when is that?"

"He's started AA. Things are going to improve."

"He's started AA before," Courtney reminded her.

"I'm trying to keep us a family, for Emma's sake."

"Yeah, but what kind of example are you setting for

Emma?" Courtney argued, making Annie tense up all over again.

Jenna suspected these two had had this conversation before. She didn't blame Courtney for wanting to help her friend, but what to do with a problem husband was a very personal decision. Was Courtney married? Did she understand the whole family dynamic dilemma thing?

"I know, I know. I don't have a kid," Courtney said as if reading Jenna's mind. "But I had a loser husband, and I don't regret cutting him out of my life."

"It's different when you have a child," Annie said softly.

Jenna sighed. Yes, it was.

"Well, we'll just keep praying for him," Tyrella said firmly. "Pray that demon alcohol right out of him."

"I say we beat it out of him," Courtney muttered.

"I say we change the subject," Nora said, and after that the evening's conversation turned to lighter subjects— what new books the women were reading, whether or not the latest movie showing at Seaside Cinema was worth seeing, who was dieting, who had given up.

At one point there was a discussion about the upcoming festival and the hope that it would bring in some new visitors.

"And some return visitors," Cindy said.

"I'm sure it will," Nora told her. "I hear we're supposed to have a hot summer, which will be good for tourism."

"I hope so. We need to bring in more business than we did last summer if we're going to make it through the winter," Cindy confessed.

Her words sent a cold shiver down Jenna's spine. She wasn't sure they were going to make much money at the inn before winter. She hoped between her massage business and Aunt Edie's social security they could hang on until the next summer.

"Okay, ladies, let's make sure we all buy a ton of chocolate," Nora said, and the others smiled and nodded.

"It'll be tough to force myself to eat more chocolate but I'll try," Courtney joked.

"Don't worry, we'll get you through winter," Tyrella promised, demonstrating the commitment the people of the little beachside community had for each other.

"It's got to be hard to keep going when the bulk of your business is seasonal," Jenna said, hoping someone would contradict her.

"It is," Nora admitted. "But we're all here because we love Moonlight Harbor."

"Life's good at the beach," Courtney said, "as long as you can pay the bills."

"We just need to keep working on ways to bring people into town," Nora said. "We're not that far from Seattle, and Olympia's only an hour away."

"Our mayor keeps talking about making things happen," Tyrella said, "but so far we're not seeing much."

"We do have those way finders now," Nora said.

Tyrella made a face. "Street signs shaped like giant shells. That will bring the tourists."

"Change takes time," Nora reminded her. "Anyway, it's a beginning." Obviously, she was a fan of the mayor.

Time. How much time did Jenna have?

The evening ended around ten, with hugs for all, and Jenna went up to her bedroom, feeling like she'd put down some good roots in the sandy soil of Moonlight Harbor. Now, if they could just find a friend for Sabrina, life at the beach would be really good.

She checked in on her daughter, who was still texting away, and ordered a switch to a book so she could settle down for sleep. It wasn't too hard to persuade Sabrina to do that as she loved to read and was caught up in a dystopian tale of a mutant teen girl with superpowers.

Jenna wished she had superpowers. If she did she could find a way to use them to make a huge pile of money for the motel. Except superheroes never used their powers for ignoble and boring things like money.

She flopped on her bed and began texting her sister about her adventures.

I'm so jealous, Celeste texted. You get to live down at the beach.

You did look at the pictures I sent, right?

That can all be fixed, Celeste texted back breezily. It's all cosmetic.

Cosmetics for hotels don't come cheap. I need a new roof. No $.

We'll think of something.

Maybe Celeste would. Her sister was the creative one. When they were kids she could craft circles around Jenna and specialized in turning clamshells and beach pebbles into charming characters complete with eyelashes and beach hats. When she wasn't doing that she was often curled up in a corner with a notepad, scribbling stories. She had enough imagination for ten people.

After hearing about the mysterious Seth Waters she'd decided he was either a burned-out navy SEAL or one of America's most wanted criminals come to the beach to hide out.

Maybe he was. Of course, he could also be the type of man who didn't like to talk about himself. Who knew? Jenna wished she did. There was something fascinating about the man that pulled her like the moon pulled the tide.

Or maybe she was just sex starved, because Brody managed a pretty good pull, too.

What was the deal with Seth?

So, anything happening with Sethalicious?

Her sister was a mind reader.

Not interested.

She'd been fascinated by Damien, too, and look where that had gotten her.

You can't give up on love.

Oh, yes, she could.

I want to come down and meet everyone, texted Celeste. Hook me up with Seth if you don't want him. He sounds like a hunk.

What about the new Mr. Wonderful?

Hee, hee. Yeah, him. He's great. Sooo sexy. And fun.

And responsible? You did say he has a job, right?

Of course he has a job. He's a cop. It doesn't get any better than that.

Has he used his handcuffs on you yet?

What do you think?

A noise downstairs caught Jenna's attention. Aunt Edie had gone to bed. Sabrina was reading about the end of the world.

You there? prompted Celeste.

Yeah. Thought I heard something.

What?

Nothing. Just my imagination.

But there went her imagination again. It sounded like someone was in the kitchen. There it goes again. And there went her heart rate, picking up.

Call 911!

It's probably the wind.

But the wind didn't open cupboard doors. Now Jenna's right eye was twitching. She'd locked both the front and back doors.

Who would break into Aunt Edie's house? It didn't exactly look like Millionaire Acres.

I'd better go see who's down there. *Or maybe I'd better hide under the bed.*

Jenna told herself to stop being such a baby. She had to be imagining things.

Oh, boy. There went her imagination again.

Call the cops!

I'll be back, Jenna texted, then slipped off the bed and tiptoed to her bedroom door. She opened it a crack and listened. Was someone moving around down there? What did she have for a weapon?

She remembered the pepper spray she'd always carried in her purse when she'd gone for walks after work in case of rape or mad dog attack. Good thing she never cleaned her purse. She fished out the can and tiptoed back to the door. She'd never used the stuff, wasn't even sure it worked, but it was better than nothing. Unless the intruder had a gun. She swallowed and tiptoed across the landing, heart thumping, eye twitching.

Maybe she should call the cops. *Blink, blink, blink. Thump, thump, thump.*

She started down the stairs. Just like the idiots in movies who went into the dark basement all by themselves and then got their throats slit.

That was her. Idiot Girl.

There was someone in the house. The kitchen light was on. What kind of dumb crook turned on the light?

"I've got a gun," Jenna yelled. "And I've called the police."

"What?" replied the burglar.

The kitchen door opened and Jenna grabbed her pepper spray and aimed. And got a nice dose in the face.

# Chapter Ten

To Do:
*Paint rooms*
*Fly kite with Sabrina*
*Get eye drops*

Pain, horror, misery! With a screech, she bolted into the kitchen, knocking over the burglar, and ricocheting off the table, groping for the sink. Her face was on fire. Her eyeballs were going to melt.

"What the hell are you doing?" demanded the burglar from behind her.

Pete? What was Pete doing in the kitchen this time of night?

"You could have broken my hip."

"Never mind your hip. My eyes," Jenna cried, fumbling for the faucet.

Pete turned it on and shoved her head underneath the water. "Of all the dumb things to do."

First, he'd scared the snot out of her, now he was practically drowning her. She shoved his hand away, and positioned her eyes under the cool water. Misery, torture.

"You shouldn't have that stuff if you don't know how to use it," he scolded.

"I never had to use it. And I was scared. What are you doing in here, anyway?"

He shoved something into her field of vision. Through the curtain of water it looked like a jar of mayonnaise. "I was making a sandwich."

"At eleven at night?"

"I got hungry. So sue me."

"How did you even get in?"

"I have a key."

Were her eyes ever going to stop burning? She rubbed them and whimpered.

"Water alone isn't gonna do it," Pete said. "Hold out your hand." Jenna held out her hand and he squirted dish soap into it. "You gotta wash out the oils."

Jenna soaped up her eyes and let out a screech.

"Keep washing," he instructed.

"How do you know this, anyway?" He was probably simply trying to torture her, the old goat.

"I demonstrated in the sixties."

Never mind his political beliefs. "What were you doing with a key to the house?"

"Your aunt gave me one," he replied, sounding offended. "In case she fell or something."

"Or in case you get the munchies in the middle of the night?" Talk about taking advantage.

"I earn my keep," he muttered.

Yes, she'd seen how he'd earned his keep before she arrived. She held out her hand again. "You don't need a key anymore. I'm here."

"You don't own this place yet."

"Pete, give me the key. You're not going to be coming in at all hours scaring the tar out of us." It was hard to look authoritative when you had your head stuck under a faucet.

He stood there for a moment, then finally slapped the key in her hand. "I'm gonna talk to your aunt," he threatened.

"So am I," she shot back.

From outside a siren sounded. "Did you call the cops?" he demanded.

"No."

"Well, they're here," he snapped, and to prove it there was a banging on the front door.

"Give me a towel," Jenna demanded.

"Get one yourself," he said, leaving Jenna to fumble for a kitchen towel and stomping off toward the back door. He opened it to find a police officer standing there.

The officer was short and husky with a receding hairline and a bulbous nose, and he looked about as intimidating as a mushroom. "Put your hands on your head and step back," he said.

Rule follower that she was, Jenna obeyed immediately.

"Not you, miss," said the cop. "I can tell you're not a perp."

"I'm not a perp," Pete growled as he put up his hands. "I live here."

The banging on the front door continued and the officer lifted his shoulder and spoke to it.

"I'll go let your partner in," Jenna said, and hurried down the hall, wiping at her stinging eyes as she went.

The officer at the front door was much better looking than his partner, probably thirtysomething, with sandy-colored hair and hazel eyes. He wasn't much taller than his partner but he sure filled out his uniform well.

He took in Jenna's pink Old Navy camisole and her

sleep shorts and blushed. "Are you all right, ma'am?" he asked as she let him in.

"Yes, I'm fine. I didn't call the police."

The officer nodded. "I know. Your sister did. She said she was on the phone with you when you had an intruder."

"My intruder turned out to be our handyman," Jenna said, leading him down the hall. "I'm so sorry we bothered you."

"No bother. That's what we're here for."

He had a nice, rumbly voice. She hadn't seen a ring on his finger. For such a small, sleepy town there sure seemed to be plenty of single men around.

"Will you tell him I'm not a burglar?" Pete demanded when she returned to the kitchen with her police escort. He was still standing in the middle of the room with his hands up and looking none too happy about it.

"He's not," Jenna said as she wiped her poor watering eyes. "This is our handyman. I didn't know he had a key to the house."

The short officer looked him up and down. "Where did you get the key, sir?"

"Edie gave it to me," Pete snarled.

The officer frowned and nodded.

"I'm sorry we bothered you," Jenna added. "This was all a big misunderstanding. I was on the phone with my sister and made the mistake of telling her I heard a noise."

"It's better to be safe than sorry," said Officer Mushroom.

"Says who?" Pete demanded.

She walked the two officers to the door and thanked them for coming.

"Are you sure you're all right?" asked the tall one.

She would be after she'd poured another ten gallons of water over her face. She wiped at her eyes. "I'm fine. I just accidentally sprayed myself with pepper spray."

"Keep washing your eyes," advised Officer Mushroom.

She nodded and opened the door.

"And call us anytime," he added as they walked out. "We're not busy."

That was comforting. She didn't think she'd want to live in a community where the police were busy all the time. She waved goodbye to the officers, then went back to the kitchen to deal with Pete. She found him putting together a bologna sandwich.

His cheeks turned russet under her disgusted gaze, but he braved it out, calmly returning the mayo and bologna to the fridge. Then he picked up his sandwich and started for the door. "I could have had a heart attack, you know."

They should be so lucky. "Well, you didn't. You'll live to mooch off my aunt another day," she retorted.

"You should talk," he shot back, and left, slamming the door behind him.

"Hey, I'm family," she called after him. "What's your excuse?"

No response.

"Bon appétit," she muttered, and stuck her head under the faucet again.

The next morning, she had a little talk with Aunt Edie before Sabrina came down and before Pete the mooch showed up, and explained what had happened.

"Oh, my! I didn't hear a thing," Aunt Edie said. "I took out my hearing aids and was dead to the world."

"If he had been a burglar, you could have been dead, period," Jenna scolded.

Aunt Edie waved that concern away. "Nonsense. Pete wouldn't hurt a fly."

"That's not the point," said Jenna. "We can't be giving out house keys right and left. And why does Pete need a key?"

"In case of emergency," Aunt Edie said.

"Was that his suggestion?" Jenna probed.

Her aunt got suddenly very busy making coffee.

"So, it was."

"I was in perfect agreement. We've become good friends and we've been helping each other."

It appeared the one getting most of the help had been Pete. If there was one thing Jenna was becoming an expert on, it was men who were users.

"And it made sense for him to have a key. I was here alone."

Guilt popped up and bit Jenna in the behind. "I know," she said, and moved to put an arm around her aunt. "But I'm here now, so he doesn't need a key anymore. Besides, he takes advantage of you. Do you know that I caught him making himself a sandwich? He already eats three meals a day thanks to your generosity and does practically nothing to earn them, plus he's got a room he's not paying rent for."

"With no furniture in it," Aunt Edie pointed out.

"Beggars can't be choosers. Besides, I walked by the other day when his room door was open and saw he's put an army cot in there. So he's fine. And really, considering how little he does around here he should be grateful he even gets a bare room."

The subject of their conversation walked into the kitchen at that moment. Of course, Aunt Edie had already unlocked the back door for him.

He scowled at Jenna. "Did she tell you she called the cops on me last night?" he said to Aunt Edie.

"Call the cops," suggested Jolly Roger, who was stationed at his kitchen perch.

"I thought you were a burglar," Jenna said. And her eyes were still smarting from the experience.

"A burglar who turns on the light?" Pete scoffed.

"How do I know what burglars do? Anyway, it was Celeste who called the cops."

Aunt Edie's brows shot up. "Your sister?"

"I was texting her and told her I heard a noise. She panicked." And she hadn't been the only one. Thank God Sabrina, who would sleep through an earthquake, had missed the whole thing. She'd have been terrified.

"I almost got arrested," Pete continued, looking accusingly at Jenna.

"Well, I got pepper spray in my eyes, so let's call it even."

"She took my key," Pete tattled.

Jenna spoke before her aunt could cave and insist on giving back the key along with free access to the fridge. "She knows. We've talked about this. It's just not good to have keys out there all over the place."

Pete's eyebrows dipped. "I'm not all over the place. And I've been here with your aunt, watching over her and—"

"I know. And I do appreciate that," Jenna added, trying for some level of diplomacy. "But really, Pete, it's best that only the family have keys. Anyway, the door's unlocked all day long. It's only locked after we turn in for the night. Surely there's no reason you need to be in here in the middle of the night, right? I mean, what reason could you possibly have?" *Other than to gobble up more food you didn't pay for.*

He frowned and grunted, but dropped the subject when Aunt Edie said, "Poached eggs for breakfast."

"That sounds good," he said, and plunked himself down at the table as if he belonged there.

Maybe, after all this time, he did. But not in the middle of the night.

"Now, what's on the agenda for today?" Aunt Edie asked, obviously determined to steer them away from any further conversation about the night before.

"We need to start painting the rooms," Jenna said, and Pete scowled.

"Well, I think I'll make some beach sandies," said Aunt Edie. "Your favorite," she added, smiling at him.

*Sure, reward his bad behavior.* Honestly, it was a good thing Aunt Edie never had kids.

The promise of his favorite cookie coaxed a smile from Pete, and by the time they were done eating, he was almost in a cheerful mood.

Until Jenna stood and said, "We'd better get to work. Come on, Pete. If Sabrina wants she can help you make cookies," Jenna said to Aunt Edie. "Tell her if she comes help paint we'll fly her kite this afternoon."

It would mean an afternoon of work lost, but mother-daughter bonding time gained. It was a good trade-off. No, better than good.

Sabrina did show up to help and worked hard, and Jenna was happy to reward her. They hit the beach after lunch.

They had just assembled her kite when Seth Waters came walking up the beach. He was barefoot, in jeans and a gray T-shirt, and he looked like a cover model on his way to a shoot.

"Great. Now you're gonna stand around and talk," Sabrina grumbled.

"Be nice," Jenna said, and waved at him.

"Your aunt said you were out here. I just came to check and see if you wanted some help painting."

"Actually, we've quit for the day. We're taking the afternoon off to play. Aren't we, Sabrina?"

Sabrina nodded. "Can we start?"

"Sure," Jenna said, and handed over the kite.

Sabrina took it and began to run down the beach. She failed to catch the breeze and the kite trailed after her halfheartedly.

"First time?" Seth asked.

"Yes. I guess I should have given her a little more instruction. It's been too many years since I've done this."

Sabrina came back. "This kite is lame."

"Here." Seth took the kite from her hands. "You hold the string."

Sabrina's brows knit. "He's walking off with my kite."

"He's going to help you launch it," Jenna told her.

"Okay, I'm gonna let go," he called. "Tighten your string a little when I do."

He let go and the wind caught the kite, taking it into the air. The octopus on it began to dip and bow with the currents, the kite tail dancing.

Sabrina concentrated on keeping the string tight, her top teeth clamped on her mouth.

"All right. You've got liftoff," Jenna said to her.

"Now what do I do?"

"You can unspool the string and let it go higher. Keep your back to the wind."

Sabrina smiled. "It's so pretty!"

So was her daughter, with the wind blowing her hair, her eyes shining with the joy of a new experience. Jenna pulled her phone from her pocket and snapped a picture.

Seth was back with them now. "Here, let me get one of both of you."

Sabrina was busy concentrating on keeping her kite in the air, so Jenna stepped next to her and smiled.

"Nice," he said, and handed the phone back.

She checked out the picture. Yes, it was nice. They both looked relaxed and happy. Caption this *A good day at the beach*.

"Who knew you were an expert at kite flying," Jenna said to him as Sabrina worked on becoming one with the wind and the octopus.

"I used to like to fly kites as a kid." He watched Sabrina and smiled. "Being out here brings back good memories."

Something in his voice made her wonder if he'd racked up some not so good memories since then, but she refrained from asking him. He wouldn't appreciate it.

"If you don't need me, I think I'll go work on drumming up some business," he said.

She kind of hated to see him go, but the man did have a life. "Maybe you could help me Monday afternoon?" A few hours painting together would be the perfect opportunity to get to know her new handyman better. Okay, to be nosy.

"Sure," he said. "See you around."

She watched him walk away. The man had a beautiful butt. So, maybe she liked to see him go, after all.

Kite flying followed by a cookie break left her daughter in a happy mood, which put Jenna in a good mood, as well. Sabrina's mood wasn't quite so happy when Jenna started getting ready to go out with Brody.

"I don't see why you have to go out," she muttered. "You don't spend any time with me."

Oh, boy. Guilt trip time. "Oh my gosh, was that your

clone I was out with this afternoon?" Jenna asked in mock horror.

"Funny, Mom," Sabrina said sourly. "You're going out to have fun and leaving me here."

"To have pot pie and play Monopoly with Aunt Edie."

"I don't need a babysitter," said Princess Thundercloud.

"No, you don't. But she needs company. She's been lonely down here. Maybe you haven't noticed how much she's enjoying having you helping her in the kitchen."

"Yeah," Sabrina said with a half shrug.

"And she's looking forward to you spending some time with her tonight."

Sabrina pursed her lips. "I guess I could do that."

Jenna rewarded her with a smile and a kiss. "Good."

"What are we going to do tomorrow?" she asked when Jenna went back to putting on her mascara.

"Church, for starters."

"Yuck," Sabrina said, falling against the doorjamb. "Those kids are mean."

"They can't all be mean." Well, maybe they could. "We'll do something fun after church. I think Tyrella's going to have us over for dinner."

"She doesn't have any kids," Sabrina grumped.

"Yes, but Mrs. Singleton has a granddaughter your age and she'll be down here soon."

"She's probably mean."

Ah, yes, the glass was half-empty.

"How's it going?" Brody asked as he drove Jenna to Sandy's.

"I'm loving it. My daughter, not so much."

"Kids adapt," he said.

"Do they? I wonder."

It seemed like most of her life there'd been a daddy-shaped hole in her heart no one could really fill. Although heaven knew the grandpas and Uncle Ralph had done a good job of taking up a lot of space. And what about Sabrina? What was going to fill that hole that Damien had left when he chucked them for the Disney princess with the big boobs?

"They do," said Brody. "My kids turned out fine. They come down here with all their friends, windsurf, tear around on mopeds, party and eat me out of house and home. Hit me up for money."

"And then leave again. Don't you miss them when they're gone?"

"Are you nuts? My place is a madhouse when they're here. Love it when they come, love it when they go." He smiled at Jenna. "Don't worry. Your girl's going to be fine."

She hoped so.

They pulled up in front of the restaurant. "Come on, let's go in and wash away your worries with some wine. You need to try their coconut shrimp. It's the best."

By the time she'd sipped some wine and eaten some coconut shrimp and let Brody regale her with tales of life at the beach she was feeling much better.

"Of course," he concluded after his last story, "no one ever let poor Bruce live down the fact that he'd spent all that money on clam guns and shovels and the bucket and collecting net and then forgot to get boots. We nicknamed him Mud Man."

Jenna giggled and had some more wine. It was her second glass and she was definitely getting giggly. Was it her imagination or did she have trouble holding her liquor?

After wine, coconut shrimp, followed by prime rib and baked potatoes the size of small boats, she was feeling stuffed. But Brody convinced her she had to try the coconut cream pie.

"I'll split it with you," he said.

One bite and she pulled the plate away. "Sorry. It's too good. I can't share."

"I figured as much," he said, and signaled the waitress for another piece.

By the time they left, though, she was wishing she had shared. "I shouldn't have been such a pig," she groaned. "I'm going to explode."

"Please wait till you get home. I don't want a mess in my car," he teased.

But he didn't take her right home. Instead, he drove out onto the beach where they watched the waves throw themselves onto the sand and the sky start to turn rosy as summer twilight turned to sunset.

"It's so beautiful," she said, laying her head back against the seat.

"So are you," he murmured.

She turned her head and smiled at him. "My ex found someone prettier."

"I can't even imagine." He smiled and leaned in, and the next thing she knew, he was kissing her.

It had been way too long since someone kissed her with such…appreciation, and for a moment, she lapped it up like a cat, letting him have at it and threading her hands through all that beach-boy blond hair.

But then she came to her senses and pulled away. "This is not a good idea."

"Really? I thought it was a great idea."

"Brody Green, I've got you figured out. You're the playboy of Moonlight Harbor."

He pouted. "You wound me."

"Oh? You take in even more territory?"

"I'm not a shallow ladies' man."

"You may not be shallow," Jenna conceded, "but it doesn't matter because I'm not in the market. Remember?"

"You don't want to be alone all your life," he told her.

"Maybe not. But I do want to be alone for the next year. Well, not alone," she amended. It was nice going out to dinner with someone with a low voice and different body parts. It was nice to be wanted. "Just not involved."

"You're right. I'm a shit," Brody said, moving back behind the wheel. "You're still reeling from your divorce. The wound's still fresh. I remember that feeling."

"Yeah?"

"Oh, yeah. I went through a phase, believe me. Every woman was a user." He shrugged. "Sometimes I wonder if there's really not some truth to that. Present company excepted," he quickly added. "A lot of the ones I met were. I don't want to be somebody's ticket to the pot of gold at the end of the rainbow."

Yep, there'd be no hitting Brody up for a loan.

He smiled at Jenna. "You're different, Jenna. There's something so…honest and vulnerable about you. You're like a movie heroine trying to make a go of something that doesn't want to go."

"I will make a go of that place," she said as much to herself as him.

"I hope you can," he said, and started the car.

Back home she gave him a smile and a heartfelt thank-you for a nice time. And her phone number. ("Not that I don't mind stopping by, but it would be handy to have," he'd said.)

But no kiss. One had been one too many. Kisses on a beach at twilight were how a woman lost all perspective. Not to mention control.

Would she ever lose control with a man again?

Maybe in her dreams.

She came dangerously close when Seth Waters invaded those dreams. There she was, bobbing happily on the water in a little dinghy, and a giant pirate ship pulled up next to her. He stood at the bow of the boat, his feet firmly planted, his chest bare and glistening. He'd grown his hair and it hung under his pirate hat in dark dreadlocks. He'd grown a moustache, too, and he looked like Johnny Depp's Jack Sparrow from all those *Pirates of the Caribbean* movies she'd loved to watch when she was a sweet, young (horny) thing.

"Come with me," he said in that deep voice of his, and held out a hand to her. "We'll sail off to the Caribbean and make love on the beach."

How could she resist? She let him pull her up onto the boat and against his broad—oh, baby!—chest. "I've wanted you ever since I first saw you," he whispered in her ear.

"Well, here I am," she told him.

"Just a minute!" She turned and saw Brody Green striding toward them. He, too, was dressed like a pirate. Only, unlike Seth, his clothes were clean. "She's already kissed me," he informed Seth.

"Poor her," Seth sneered.

Brody grabbed her arm and pulled her away. "Come with me. I've got more money."

"I've got more sex appeal," shot back Seth, taking the other arm and pulling.

"I've got a sore arm," she protested.

Neither man listened. In fact, they became so intent on fighting over her that she got shoved aside. The next thing she knew she was pitching overboard and falling. Here came the waters, which had gone from sparkling blue to inky black. And what was that rising from the waves? Some sort of giant squid, wearing a T-shirt that said Damien.

And it could talk. "Oh, boy. Dinner!"

Jenna awoke with a yelp.

She pushed her hair out of her face and shook her head. "Dream on," she told herself. "We're not going there."

Brody and Seth and the squid would have to carry on without her because she was sticking to her no-man vow.

She settled back down into the pillows. Still…where were those two pirates? Could she find them again?

# Chapter Eleven

*To Do:*
*Call Top Dog Roofing*
*Start painting rooms*
*Convince daughter this will be fun*

Jenna's mom checked in when Jenna was getting ready for church. "I'm glad you're settling in down there," she said to Jenna.

"Well, one of us is settling in," Jenna said, twisting her hair into a knot. It was a good thing that ombré highlights were in style because her roots were taking over. "Sabrina's still not happy in Wonderland. And she's really not looking forward to church. The kids haven't exactly been welcoming. I'm probably going to have to pry her out of bed with a crowbar."

"Jealous girls?" Mel guessed.

"You got it."

"Don't give up. There's bound to be a nice one in there somewhere."

"I wish she'd show up pretty soon."

"So, our baby's not enjoying herself at all?"

"Oh, she is. As long as I'm spending money on her or doing something to keep her entertained. She's not enjoying helping with cleanup. She'd as soon go live with Damien as stay here with me." Jenna sighed. "If he wanted her…" Would she be able to part with her daughter if it made her happy? Yes, if that was what it took. The very thought made tears rush to her eyes.

"That's a moot point, since he doesn't have custody."

He'd claimed he wanted to be able to spend time with his daughter, even made sure the court entitled him to do so, but his actions didn't exactly speak louder than his words. She should give him the opportunity to prove it, call him and see if he could take Sabrina for a weekend visit. He could certainly manage that.

"Anyway, don't give up," Mel said. "She'll adjust."

"I wish I could make her transition easier."

"It would be easier if she fixed her attitude. Maybe, instead of trying to make her happy, you suggest she try and make herself happy and then offer a bribe. Try to have a good attitude and I'll…"

"Let you live another day?"

"That, too. Seriously, what's she been wanting that you could dangle in front of her?"

As if Mom didn't know. "Mom, she's too young."

"Honey, she's fourteen."

"Barely."

"Barely counts. Anyway, there's no school right now. You don't have to worry about earning the PTO stamp of approval. Let her color her hair."

"I don't know," said Jenna.

"Remember your twelfth birthday?"

"I know. You didn't want me to get my ears pierced."

"But we did it. You'd done all your chores without complaining for the whole month. It made a great reward and a perfect birthday present."

That had been a memorable day of mother-daughter fun. Her mom had taken her to lunch at Red Robin first, and after the big ear-piercing event, they'd gone shopping for some pretty earrings with her birthstone. It had probably blown her mother's budget for the month but the time together had been priceless.

"Ask Sabrina to try and be a cheerful helper for a week. If she can keep a smile on her face you'll turn her hair purple. Or green. Or whatever."

"Pink."

"Oh, yes. Pink. Pink is nice. Think pink, pretty in pink, in the pink."

"You're right," Jenna conceded. What did it matter if her daughter had pink hair for the summer?

"It's a bargaining chip," Mel said.

And Jenna could use all the bargaining chips she could get her hands on.

They chatted a few more minutes, then ended the call so each could get ready for the day.

Jenna finished putting on her makeup, mulling over behavior modification and bargaining chips. Hair was a good one, but the best reward of all would be a visit to Daddy. In fact, that shouldn't be something to be earned; it should be something to be expected. Of course, when it came to Damien, expecting and getting were two different things. Still...

On impulse, Jenna put in a call to him. Spending time together would be as good for him as it would for Sabrina, and maybe if he began to act the part of good Dad he truly would become one.

It took several rings for him to answer with a sleepy hello.

Jenna didn't bother with niceties like, "Did I wake

you?" Instead, she plunged right in. "Sabrina misses you. Can we set up a weekend visit?"

"What? When?" He sounded panicked.

"Next weekend." Why not? "I'll bring her up." She had a ton of things to do, but she'd carve out the time. A visit with her family and friends would do her good.

"I can't."

Balking, of course. She frowned. "Do you have an art show or something? She could come, you know."

"No. But you know where I'm living." He made it sound as if it were her fault he'd wound up in his parents' basement...which had a bedroom, bathroom, mini-kitchen, TV, couch and pool table. Poor baby.

"There's no place for her here."

"Your parents have a spare room."

"It's being used."

Probably as his mom's sewing room. What a flimsy excuse.

"Jenna, it won't work right now. I want to see her but I need time to pull my life together."

Ironic, considering he was the one who'd pulled it apart. Jenna felt her temper rising like the tide. "How much time do you need? When are you planning on seeing your daughter?"

"I'd have been able to see her anytime I wanted if you hadn't moved to the other end of the world."

Oh, yes. It was all her fault. She forced herself to calm down and stay on point. "I can bring her up anytime. We can stay at Mom's and you can pick her up there and go do something."

"Good idea. Later this summer. Okay? After I get settled."

Who knew when that would be. "She misses you, Damien."

"And I miss her."

Yeah, Jenna could tell.

"But I'm in the middle of some things right now. I got a commission."

Here was a surprise. "You did?"

"A new theater is opening up in Icicle Falls and they want something for the lobby."

Icicle Falls was a cute German town in the Cascades. Were they aware of Damien's medium? Was he going to make them something out of lederhosen and old tires?

Okay, she could be gracious. "That's great." And if he started getting enough commissions for his art maybe he could become self-sufficient and she could renegotiate the maintenance settlement. Go, Damien.

"Yeah, it is. My reputation is spreading."

"I'm glad for you." Sort of. Almost. "So, what can I tell Sabrina?"

"Hmm?"

He'd checked out of the conversation, moved on to envisioning himself as the next Dale Chihuly. "Your daughter," she prompted.

"I know, I know. Just give me some time to adjust."

He had to be kidding. What was he adjusting to besides having no responsibility? "I'm still adjusting, too, Damien," she said irritably.

Wrong thing to say. "I'll take her when I'm ready. Quit pushing."

"I shouldn't have to push."

"And quit trying to guilt me into doing what you want. We're not married anymore and I don't have to put up with your bullshit." And on that pleasant note he ended the call.

*Bullshit!* Really? How was it pushing trying to pin down a time for him to see his own daughter?

Jenna scowled at her phone. Any time she tried to get him to act like a grown-up he accused her of making him feel guilty. When he wasn't accusing her of that he was complaining that she didn't understand him, didn't believe in him.

Okay, so maybe after a while she had stopped believing. Or maybe she'd simply gotten tired of being the only grown-up in the relationship. Obviously, he'd gotten tired of that, which was where Aurora had come in. Peter Pan had needed a new Wendy. No, Wendy had been responsible. He'd wanted a Tinkerbell and that was what he'd gotten. More like Tinkerboob. Tinkerboob and Peter Poop, Jenna thought in disgust.

What was she going to tell Sabrina next time she talked about wanting to see Daddy? Not the truth, that was for sure.

With a sigh, she made her way to her daughter's room to see if Sabrina had managed to haul herself out of bed yet.

She hadn't. In fact, she'd slipped farther under the covers and pulled them over her head.

"Come on, lazy daisy, time to get up," Jenna said, forcing mommy good cheer into her voice. She pulled the covers from her daughter's head and kissed her.

"I don't want to get up." Sabrina groaned. "I don't want to go to church." She'd said the same thing about school when she was eight and struggling with math.

"I know. But this isn't optional."

"You are *so mean*," Sabrina informed her, pulling the covers back over her head.

"It's in my job description."

Jenna weighed her options. Be mean and drag the child out of bed. Threaten her with...what? No ice cream for a week? There would be no promise of a visit to Daddy to motivate an attitude adjustment. Okay, that left pink hair.

She sat on the edge of her daughter's bed. "It's a shame you're not being more cooperative. I was thinking if you tried to be more positive I'd let you color your hair."

Sabrina flung off the covers and sat up, her eyes bright. "Really?"

"I'm not wild about you doing this. Your hair is already gorgeous," Jenna began, making her daughter's mouth dip down at the corners. "But if you could work on improving your attitude...a little less complaining—"

"I can!"

"No complaints about going to church."

For a moment, Sabrina looked dubious. But then she came to a decision and nodded. "Okay."

"All right, then. Let's see if you can make good on that promise."

"I will! When can we do it?"

"When I see a change in your attitude."

Sabrina frowned. "But when? Tomorrow?"

"Let's give it a few days. This is a big deal, Sabrina. I want you to earn it."

"Okay. You're the best mom ever!" Sabrina cried, and hugged Jenna.

Yep, the best mom ever. For about two minutes.

Sabrina was true to her word. She was all smiles at breakfast, and set the table without being asked.

"What are you so happy about?" Pete asked her as they dug into pancakes.

"Mom's gonna let me dye my hair."

Pete rolled his eyes. "Why do women do that?"

"To look good, of course," Aunt Edie told him.

"Men don't care about stuff like that," Pete said.

"Oh? Ever hear the saying 'Gentlemen prefer blondes' or 'Blondes have more fun'?" Aunt Edie replied. "You don't think Marilyn Monroe was born with that hair color, do you? Anyway, it's fun. An artistic expression." She smiled at Sabrina. "What color are you thinking of?"

"Pink."

"Pink? You'll look like you got cotton candy on your head," Pete said in disgust. "Who dyes their hair pink?"

"Lots of girls these days," Jenna said, coming to her daughter's defense. Or maybe she was coming to her own. Good moms let their daughters go pink. Well, why not? Maybe she'd put some fun color in her hair...and embarrass her child.

"I think it's great that your mother's letting you do that," said Aunt Edie, who had obviously gotten the bribe-the-kid memo.

"But remember, you have to hold up your end of the bargain," Jenna reminded Sabrina.

"What's that?" Pete wanted to know.

"She's going to work on improving her attitude," Jenna told him, making Sabrina blush and frown at her. Okay, she shouldn't have shared.

"Ha! Good luck with that," Pete said, and shoveled in another mouthful of pancake.

"Why'd you have to tell him?" Sabrina demanded once they were on their way to church.

"You're right. My bad. Our deal was none of his business."

"I don't like him."

"He's a little lacking in social skills," Jenna said.

"A little?"

"Okay, a lot. And just between us, I'm not real fond of him, either. But he's been kind to Aunt Edie and she likes him, so let's try to find the best in him."

"Good luck with that," Sabrina said.

And good luck with her daughter making any effort to make friends. She didn't hang out in the foyer with Jenna, preferring to duck into the sanctuary and hide. Jenna watched her go with a sigh.

"It will get better," Tyrella assured her.

"Only if you can birth an instant fourteen-year-old for her to hang out with."

"She'll find her feet. Transitions are tough on kids. It takes a while."

"It's my fault she's here."

"No, it's thanks to you that she's here. This will turn out to be a good thing for both of you. Wait and see."

"How long do I have to wait?"

"For as long as it takes. Come on, let's go in and keep her company."

Pastor Paul Welch was in fine form that morning, and Jenna wished her daughter was paying attention. Even though Jenna had a no-iPod-in-church rule to cut down on distraction, she knew from experience that a kid could tune out adult talk even without the aid of technology.

"And so," concluded Pastor, "if Abraham could strike out and leave behind his family and friends and way of life, surely we can be brave enough to tackle whatever challenge we're being called to meet."

Hmm. Had Pastor Paul read Muriel Sterling's new-beginnings book?

"I think God gave Pastor that message just for you girls," Tyrella said when the service was over and the congregation began to leave the sanctuary. "What do you think, Sabrina?"

Sabrina blushed, evidence that she hadn't been listening. "I guess," she said, not meeting Tyrella's eye.

Tyrella chuckled. "Run home and collect your aunt," she told Jenna. "Then you girls come on over to my place. I've got fried chicken, macaroni salad, green beans, and a key lime pie that will make you think you died and went to heaven."

"Sounds great. What can I bring?" Jenna asked.

"Just your sweet little aunt and a big appetite," Tyrella said. "And, of course, your darling girl," she added, and gave Sabrina's cheek a pat.

"Hear that?" Jenna said to Sabrina as they left. "You're a darling."

"I'm *your* darling," Sabrina said, and linked arms with her.

With the promise of pink hair dancing on the horizon, yes. For the moment. No. Always, no matter what.

Tyrella's snug little bungalow was a two-story affair with lots of windows and a long front porch. It was painted the same Creamsicle orange that was popular with some of the shops and other houses around town. Clumps of daisies and lavender hugged the porch and the front walk, and a big rhododendron with purple flowers made its presence known at one corner of the house. Wind chimes created from shells and beach glass and tiny bits of driftwood tinkled a welcome.

"Isn't this adorable?" Aunt Edie gushed as they made their way to the front door. "Tyrella has such flair."

"It makes me think of fairy tales," Sabrina observed.

Her daughter was right. Jenna could almost imagine pixies hiding under the rhodie or envision Snow White inside, tidying up before the dwarfs came home. Tyrella did, indeed, have flair. "Welcome, ladies," she said, throwing wide the door.

"This is really sweet of you to have us," Jenna told her.

"I love having people over for Sunday dinner," she said.

Obviously. They entered to discover they weren't her only dinner guests. Tyrella had also invited the pastor. "I thought you two should get to know each other," she said to Jenna and Pastor Paul. "Seeing as how you're new in town and all, Jenna," she hastily added.

Too late. She'd already betrayed her ulterior motive. But seriously? As if the pastor would be interested in someone newly divorced. Or divorced at all. Pastors were supposed to have it together. The same thing held true for their wives. Jenna doubted she'd qualify, even if she wanted to.

"Nice to see you again," he said politely after Tyrella had introduced everyone. "This was your second Sunday with us, wasn't it?"

"As a matter of fact, it was," Jenna said.

"I hope everyone's making you both feel welcome," he said.

Most everyone. "Yes," Jenna answered for herself and her daughter.

"You're not going to see me in church," Aunt Edie informed him. "All the churches these days play the music way too loud."

He took the scold with a good-natured smile. "I know."

"But I think Jenna's enjoying it," Aunt Edie continued.

"Your sermon sure fit my life right now," Jenna told him.

"I'm glad," he said with a nod. "I just say what I think God wants me to say. So," he continued, still smiling, "is your husband going to be coming down with you?"

Awkward as a fart in church. Silence, a pout from Sabrina, a flush across Jenna's face and an uh-oh look on the pastor's.

"They're divorced," Aunt Edie said.

"Oh. I'm sorry."

"These things happen," Aunt Edie said. "Tyrella, can we help you?"

Tyrella, who had been standing frozen, came to life. "You sure can. Sabrina, are you any good at cutting French bread?"

"I don't know," Sabrina said, still frowning.

"Come on. Let's find out," Tyrella said, and she and Aunt Edie escaped, herding Sabrina into the kitchen, leaving Jenna and Paul standing in the living room. He motioned to the sofa and she sat down.

He took a chair opposite. "I'm sorry I stepped in it just now. Tyrella didn't tell me."

"I guess she figured you'd find out. Anyway, it's all good." Or it would be. Eventually.

"You couldn't pick a better place to hit Restart," said Paul.

"You're right, and I'm ready to. It wasn't my idea to get divorced," she couldn't help adding. *I'm not the sinner here.*

"Things happen," he said.

"Other women happen." She felt her cheeks heating. "Sorry. I guess I'm still working through things."

"I guess that's all right," he said, giving her a sympathetic nod.

Tyrella was putting food on the table now, and the aroma of chicken wafted over to Jenna. "That smells great," she said, drifting over to the table. Paul, too, followed his nose, and smiled appreciatively at the large platter. A huge bowl of macaroni salad enhanced with crab and shrimp followed, along with French bread, green beans and a spinach salad.

"This was Leroy's favorite Sunday dinner," Tyrella told everyone after she'd had Paul say grace and the food had been passed around. "The only thing he liked better than having company was eating."

"It helps when you're married to a good cook," Paul said to her.

She pointed a chicken leg at him. "You need to find yourself a good cook." Subtle. Very subtle.

They had just started their pie when he got a call. "I'd better take this," he said after checking his phone's caller ID. "It's Janice Walters."

"Of course. Her mother's in the hospital, not doing well," Tyrella explained as Paul left the table, phone to his ear.

"He seems like a nice young man," Aunt Edie said.

"He is," Tyrella assured her, and they both looked expectantly at Jenna.

She smiled and kept her mouth shut. Except to insert more key lime pie.

"This is really good," Sabrina said.

"It's real easy to make," Tyrella said. "I'll give you all the recipe."

Paul was off the phone now. "Sorry, I'm going to have to leave. Janice's mom just passed, and I need to get to the Aberdeen hospital."

"Oh, I'm sorry," said Tyrella. "You want me to call around and start arranging for meals?"

"That would be great. Good to meet you all," he said, not singling Jenna out in any way.

Which was fine with her. She didn't need to add any more men to her collection.

The women passed the rest of the afternoon teaching Sabrina how to play Triominos, and she was in a happy mood when they finally left. And that made Jenna happy.

Sabrina got even happier when they arrived home and Aunt Edie proposed a movie marathon. "I think every girl should get to watch the Alfred Hitchcock classics," Aunt Edie said, pulling out an old video cassette of *Rear Window*. "This movie had me on the edge of my seat when I first watched it. But that was nothing compared to *The Birds*."

"A movie about birds?" Sabrina asked dubiously.

"A horror movie about birds."

Horror movie, the magic words. "Let's watch that one!" Sabrina said.

"Oh, I don't know if your mother would want you watching that," Aunt Edie said, looking to Jenna.

"Her father's let her watch worse, believe me," Jenna said.

"Well, all right, then," Aunt Edie said, digging around in the cabinet where she kept her outdated technology. "That will be our encore movie. You know, I have almost every movie Alfred Hitchcock ever did. He was a genius."

They settled in with popcorn and root beer and

watched Jimmy Stewart spy on his neighbors. "That was pretty good," Sabrina said when it was done. "Grace Kelly sure was pretty."

"No prettier than your own lovely mother," Aunt Edie said. "She could have been a movie star."

"The one who could have done that was Celeste. She was the ham," said Jenna.

"You could totally have been a movie star, Mom," Sabrina said, and Jenna was touched by the compliment.

They were about to move on to the invasion of the birds and Jenna was in the kitchen in search of a pop refill when Courtney called the house, looking for her.

"You up for going to the Drunken Sailor for some line dancing?" she asked.

"Oh, I don't know," said Jenna. "I'm not too into country music." Although the idea of line dancing appealed to her.

"But do you like to dance?"

"Who doesn't like to dance?" Jenna replied.

"If you have a chance to go out, don't feel you have to stay here with us," said Aunt Edie, who'd come to the kitchen in search of cookies for the next movie course.

"They have a lesson at seven where they teach you a couple of dances before it starts," Courtney said. "And besides, unless you're into playing pool this is about as good as the nightlife down here gets."

Why not? Jenna put on some jeans and a pair of flats and slipped away, leaving Aunt Edie and Sabrina to watch the birds peck out people's eyes. At least after that Sabrina couldn't complain about not getting to watch any horror films.

The Drunken Sailor had a good crowd of landlubbers perched on bar stools, playing darts or pool and hanging out at the edge of the small dance floor. In fact, it looked like just about every single person in town under the age of fifty was there, including Brody, who sauntered over to say hi as soon as he caught sight of her.

He was wearing jeans and a black T-shirt that showed off well-toned pecs and biceps. Brody Green sauntered well.

Not that she was interested. It was just an observation.

"I see you decided to give line dancing a try," he said.

"Aunt Edie and Sabrina are watching *The Birds*. I decided this was better for my psyche. I want to be able to walk on the beach without fearing a seagull attack."

"They will dive-bomb you when they're nesting," he warned.

"Just so they don't peck out my eyes. Anyway, nothing's going to happen to me in here."

"Sprained ankle," he teased.

"You going to risk spraining your ankle?"

"Not me. I'm here to watch." He held up a bottle of Hale's ale. "And drink."

"You should try it, Brody," Courtney said. "I bet you'd be great."

"That's okay. I'd rather watch you girls, anyway," he said with a grin.

More people were drifting over to the dance floor, including one of the cops who'd come to rescue Jenna from her faux burglar. He came over to say hi to Jenna.

"You know Vic?" Courtney asked, looking from one to another.

"Not really," he said. "Victor King."

"King of my heart," teased Courtney, making him blush. "So how do you guys know each other?"

"I thought we had a burglar. He came to check it

out," Jenna explained. "So embarrassing," she said with a shake of her head. "It turned out to be Aunt Edie's handyman, Pete. He'd sneaked into the house to make himself a sandwich."

Courtney snickered. "Still, you'd rather have that than the real thing. Not that we have that many burglars down here," she quickly added.

"Nope," Vic said. "It gets a little boring."

"I'd rather have you bored than me scared," Courtney told him.

Jenna caught sight of Austin Banks in the corner, talking with a man in his fifties who had long hair, a beard and a beer belly. He was setting up their sound system for the night.

"If you haven't met her yet, that's Austin Banks," Courtney explained. "Her husband, Roy, runs the music for us."

A moment later Austin was taking the floor, calling, "Come on, y'all. Let's get goin'."

The dancers began to form lines in back of her and Jenna followed Courtney onto the floor and placed herself next to her. Vic placed himself next to Jenna.

Austin pointed at her. "Well, you came out! Good for you. Hey, ya'll, this is Jenna Jones. She's runnin' the Driftwood Inn now."

Several women murmured hello, and a couple of men looked her way eagerly.

"I got a new dance to teach you tonight. It's called the Twisted Pony."

*More like twisted feet*, Jenna thought as she tried to keep up with the various step patterns.

"And a grapevine and a hitch," Austin said, and demonstrated.

"I thought you said this was easy," Jenna said to Courtney.

"You'll catch on," Courtney assured her.

They went through the whole song without music and then, just as Jenna thought she had the steps down, Austin called to her husband, "Okay, Roy, give us some music," and everything went into fast motion.

Half the time Jenna found herself either doing the wrong step or facing the wrong way.

Great. And she'd thought it would be fun to do this? She hated looking stupid and she could feel her cheeks sizzling.

But nobody seemed to care. A couple of times Vic caught her by the shoulders and gently turned her the right direction. "You'll catch on," he said after the dance ended. Then he called to Austin. "Hey, Austin, how about something easy for the newcomer?"

"Sure," Austin said.

"Let's do 'Footloose,'" somebody called.

A fast song? "Oh, boy," Jenna said under her breath.

"No, let's give her something real easy," said Vic.

Austin nodded. "We'll do the Electric Slide."

"That old song?" groaned a twentysomething redhead.

"Just to get her started. Then we'll do 'Footloose' and 'Drunken Dreams.'"

Jenna was beginning to think she needed a drink.

But the Electric Slide turned out to be easy, and it gave her enough confidence to stick around for another dance. Pretty soon she was kicking and flicking with the best of them.

"Okay, that is fun," she said to Courtney as they went to the bar to order soft drinks.

"You looked good out there," Brody told her as they joined him.

"You should come dance with us, you big chicken," she teased.

"Maybe next time."

"Right. That's what he says every Sunday night," Courtney said.

Jenna laughed, took a sip of her drink and looked around, checking out the rest of the patrons. That was when she saw Seth Waters. He was standing at a pool table in the corner, leaning on his pool cue and watching a blonde in tight jeans and a low-cut top take a shot.

It looked like Seth Waters was making new friends. Well, good for him.

Jenna left after a couple more dances. Nothing to do with Seth, of course. She had to get up in the morning.

Sabrina was still in a good mood the next morning. Jenna came in from a beach walk to find her in the kitchen, helping Aunt Edie make oatmeal muffins. Her expression wasn't quite so sunny when Jenna mentioned their painting job. Obviously, painting didn't hold the same excitement as walking around on a roof.

It only took one word to motivate her: hair.

"Okay," she said with a sigh.

Pete was no more excited than Sabrina, and, as they worked, he groaned every time he bent to dip his roller in the paint tray. They were covering the walls a light brown shade, aptly named Sandy Beach. She only hoped the tarp would keep the roof dry enough to save them from getting a river running down her sandy beach wall.

Finally, by noon, Pete was done groaning. He was

done. Period. "That's enough for one day," he informed Jenna.

"Can I quit, too, Mom?" Sabrina asked.

"Yes. You worked hard. Good job," Jenna said, making her smile. "How about you go help Aunt Edie make lunch? Bring me back a tuna sandwich."

Sabrina nodded and was gone. Then it was just Jenna and her paint roller, singing "Stand by You" along with Rachel Platten, who was serenading her from her iPad. The song had such a great beat, before she knew it she was dancing as well as singing.

Her performance ended to applause, and she whirled around to see Seth Waters leaning against the door. "You missed your calling."

She was blushing; she knew it. "You have a way of sneaking up on people. You know that?"

He smiled and pushed away from the door. "All your helpers on lunch break?"

"No, done for the day."

"Not you, though, huh?"

"It has to get finished."

At that moment, Sabrina returned with a sandwich on paper plate and a glass of lavender lemonade.

"Do you want a sandwich?" Jenna offered. The calico cat that Jenna had seen hanging around before approached, lured by the smell of tuna. She broke off a piece and absently handed it over and the cat took it, dropped it on the ground and hunkered down to enjoy its snack.

Seth wasn't interested. He shook his head and picked up an abandoned paint roller. "I'm good."

She'd just bet he was.

"Can I go get an ice cream?" Sabrina asked.

"Yes. But don't go anywhere else without letting us know where you are. Got it?"

Sabrina nodded vigorously and vanished.

"She seems like a good kid," Seth said as he began work on the wall opposite Jenna's.

"She is, for the most part."

"Reminds me of my little sister," he said.

"Where does she live?"

"California. Both my sisters are there, and my mom."

"You wound up a long way from home."

"Guess so, but so did my brother."

"How come you didn't wind up in Tacoma with him?"

"I like the beach."

She'd buy that. "Me, too," she said. Still, she didn't think she'd want to wind up someplace by herself. "So, you don't know anybody around here?"

He shrugged. "You."

"I mean anybody else?"

"Nope."

"You just came here without knowing anyone?"

"I came here because it looked like a good place to start a business."

"Especially the business you're starting. Looked like you made a new friend at the Drunken Sailor," she couldn't resist adding, and looked out of the corner of her eye to see his reaction.

His smile was downright cocky. "Were you watching me?"

"No," she insisted, wishing she didn't blush so easily.

He chuckled. "I was watching you. You looked pretty good out there on the dance floor."

"How come you weren't out there?"

"I was later. You and the house peddler had both left by then."

"We didn't come together," she said. Somehow, it seemed important for Seth to know that. "There were plenty of women left to keep you company," she added, shifting the spotlight back on Seth.

"Yeah," he agreed, not offering any further information.

She frowned. "I can't believe there's no one special in your life."

"No chance to find someone," he said.

"Been too busy?"

"Something like that."

"Well, there seem to be plenty of women around here," Jenna said casually.

"Are you a matchmaker in your spare time?" he teased.

"All women are matchmakers in their spare time."

"You're probably right about that. So, what about you? There's plenty of guys in this town. Looks like the house peddler's already found you."

"We're just friends."

He grunted. "The F word."

"I know, guys hate that. Almost as much as women hate hearing, 'It didn't mean a thing.'"

If only Damien had said that to her. But he hadn't. His affair with Aurora had meant something. Jenna scowled at her Sandy Beach. "Why can't men be faithful?"

"Some can."

"You ought to wear badges or something. That way we'd know."

"Love's a crap shoot," he said. "Hell, all of life's a crap shoot."

Jenna wished he'd say more on that topic. What roll of the dice had affected his life? Who was Seth Waters, really?

Even though they spent three hours together painting, she didn't learn much more beyond the fact that he liked nachos, thought boy bands were stupid and loved a good cage fight. She tried to pry more information out of him about his family, but failed. Instead, he would turn the table on her, asking about her family.

"I think you know my whole life history now," she said as they cleaned up the brushes and rollers, "but I hardly know anything about you."

"My life's not that interesting," he said.

Which, she strongly suspected, was a big, fat lie.

What was the story with Seth Waters? "I'll find out," she murmured as he drove off in his truck, headed for who knew where. *I'll find out.*

# Chapter Twelve

*To Do:*
*Paint*
*Paint*
*Paint*
*Try to be a good mother*

Tuesday brought more painting, and while Sabrina didn't complain, she didn't exactly smile over the prospect.

"Remember, attitude," Jenna prompted.

"I'm doing it, Mom, that should count for something," Sabrina said.

Jenna let the pissy tone of voice slide, deciding to blame it on those aliens Nora had talked about at the women's gathering the Friday before.

Once they got started on the painting, the alien took a rest. Pete was working in the next room, so it gave Jenna and Sabrina time for some mother-daughter visiting. Although the visiting appeared to have a hidden agenda.

"A new boy moved in next door to Marigold," Sabrina informed Jenna, filling her in on the perfect world of home.

"Lucky her. Is he cute?"

"Yeah." Said with a tinge of jealousy.

"You'll meet cute boys down here."

"I'm never going to meet anybody down here," said the little prophetess of doom. Then she slid into a new topic. "Marigold's dad is taking them to a Mariners game."

Marigold's dad was very involved with his kids. Marigold's mommy had chosen more wisely than Sabrina's mommy.

Sabrina was quiet a moment, focusing on her paint roller. Jenna braced herself for what was coming next.

Sure enough. "Can we go back and visit Grandma this weekend? I want to see Daddy."

But Daddy wasn't in a hurry to see her. He'd made that clear enough. "Honey, I'd love that, but I've already got massage clients lined up for Saturday." Not that she wouldn't have canceled every one if Damien had cooperated. "And we've got too much to do here," she added for good measure. "It's going to be a little while before we can get back."

"But Daddy misses me."

Jenna felt sick at heart. If only. "I'm sure he does, but that's the beauty of technology. You can Skype. And text. That's why you've got an iPod."

"It's not the same," Sabrina grumbled.

"Honey, Daddy's a little busy sorting out his life, too, just like we are." *And we're not part of it.*

"Okay, then, can Marigold come here? You said she could come for a visit."

"As soon as we get the Driftwood up and running," Jenna promised. "So, the sooner we get the work done, the sooner we can play."

Sabrina put in an extra hour.

She was just leaving to take pictures when Seth showed up.

"Good job, high flyer," he told her.

Jenna looked to see how her daughter would take that nickname. She hadn't appreciated being called kiddo by Brody.

She was smiling. "Thanks."

"She's about to go take some more beach pictures. We're going to frame the best ones and hang them on the walls in the rooms," Jenna said.

"Cool," Seth said, and Sabrina left looking happy.

"She's in a good mood," he observed.

"We're working on attitude improvement. I promised her she could have her friend down once we get some of the work done here. And that she could dye her hair."

"Then life is good," he said, and picked up a paint roller.

"Yes, it is," Jenna agreed. "My business cards came this morning."

"Got any customers lined up?"

"Clients," she corrected him.

"Ah. Clients," he said, his tone of voice mocking her.

"As a matter of fact, I do. One of them happens to be the mayor."

"Whoa, I guess this means you've made it."

"Don't be mocking me. The mayor can open a lot of doors."

"Oh? Who told you that?"

"No one," Jenna admitted. "I just know it helps to know people."

"Yeah, I guess."

"How's your business coming along?" *Any better than mine, smart guy?*

"I picked up three new *clients* this morning."

Seth Waters was a smart mouth. But an ambitious one.

"I figure by September I'll be going full-time."

Okay, that was impressive. She hoped she could get the motel whipped into shape half that quickly. At the rate Seth's business was picking up she'd be lucky if she could. The window of time when she'd have his afternoon help was quickly shrinking. Not a good thing considering who her other laborers were.

"I'd better take advantage of you while I can," she said. Hmm. That hadn't come out right.

"I'm all for women taking advantage of me."

He probably didn't have any trouble finding ones to do it, either.

They worked on companionably, accompanied by the various singers on the playlist on Jenna's vintage iPad. Seth Waters was easy to be around. Hotter than jalapeños, hardworking, certainly not hard to please considering the subpar living conditions she'd offered him. Attentive and interested in her, asking questions about her family and her life—even if the motivation for that might be to deflect from having to answer any questions himself. She liked his sense of humor and quick wit. Most of all, she liked the fact that he didn't discourage her from bringing the Driftwood back to life and she said as much.

"I think you should be going for it. This is a cool old place. You gotta go for your dreams, Jenna. Life's too short not to."

A man who listened and who was supportive—you didn't see that every day. You hardly ever saw it at all. Why was he single? It seemed like he ought to have a girlfriend.

"I just don't get it," she said later when they were cleaning up.

"Don't get what?"

"Why you don't have a girlfriend."

"I'm alone right now because that's how I like it," he said. "Same as you." And that ended that particular conversation.

But it didn't stop her from mulling over the mystery of his private life.

Until Herbie from Top Dog Roofing showed up to give her an estimate on fixing the roof.

"Not sure how you expect someone to be able to tell with that blue tarp up there," he said to her, and scratched his massive chest.

"I had to do something. The roof leaks."

He nodded. "I know. Actually, your aunt had me out about a year ago."

"She did?" This was the first Jenna had heard of it. And why didn't he say so when she first talked to him? "Did you give her an estimate?"

"I told her it would probably be about sixty K."

Jenna swallowed. That was even worse than what Brody had guessed. "Sixty thousand?"

"Give or take. We never got as far as a written estimate."

She could see why. "How much would you charge to just patch the bad spots?"

Herbie was shaking his head before she even finished with her question. "I wouldn't advise that, not with all the patching this place needs. You may as well replace the whole roof with the investment you'd have to make in all those patches."

No problem. She'd just go to her safety deposit box

and pull out a few wads of bills. She felt her throat tightening and the tear spigot turning on.

"Want me to give you a written estimate?"

"Sure," she managed. Although what was the point?

"Okay, I'll get it to you as soon as I can."

"Take your time." It would be a million years before she could afford to hire him. Which meant it would be a million years before the motel could start earning its keep.

"You're smart to get on this right away," Herbie told her. "You don't want to let it go another winter."

She nodded, and stayed put until he got in his truck and drove off, then she, too, took off to indulge in a good cry, leaving Seth to deal with the last of the cleanup. She heard him call her name, but she kept going, picking up her pace. She was late for a pity party.

She threaded her way through the beach grass and over sand dunes until she arrived at the shore. The sun was out, the sky was blue, and she was under the world's biggest black cloud. She plopped on a giant piece of driftwood, bent over and let the tears fall. This was hopeless.

A hand on her shoulder had her about jumping out of her skin. "Hey, there, no crying allowed on a nice day."

"You scared the tar out of me," she accused, taking a swipe at her eyes. "And it's not a nice day."

Seth settled next to her. "How much did he think it was going to cost?"

"Sixty thousand. Right now I don't even have sixty dollars." Or she wouldn't once she finished paying for all the things she'd already ordered for the Driftwood.

"That is tough," Seth agreed.

Jenna gave a bitter chuckle. "It's not tough. It's the end. No way are we going to be able to get this place renovated."

"So you're going to give up, just like that."

She scowled at him. "What would you do?"

"Keep fighting." He picked up a rock and gave it a toss.

"Easy for you to say. Your business is all coming together." That sounded lovely. She gave a disgusted grunt. "Sorry. Crab in the pot syndrome."

"What's that?"

"You know, you're boiling the crab, they're all going to die. One tries to climb out but the others pull him back in. 'If we can't get out, neither can you.'"

"Ah." He nodded.

"I'm being a jerk," she admitted. "I'm just tired of getting dumped on. First Damien, now all this. My mom says every storm has a rainbow. I'm having trouble finding mine."

"You will." He edged closer and put an arm around her.

Probably to comfort her, but it did more than that. She could smell the musky scent of a hardworking man. His thigh was touching hers, all manly and muscly. She got a sudden case of arrhythmia.

"It could be worse. As long as you're not in prison, life is good."

"Well, that's a little extreme."

He shrugged. "Still."

"Right now prison doesn't sound so bad. Free room and board."

His arm disappeared from around her shoulders. "Stuff like that's not funny."

"I thought it was."

"That's because you've never been in prison."

"Oh, and you have?"

He was silent a moment, then said, "I knew someone who was. It about ruined his life."

"Someone in your family?"

"It doesn't matter. My point is you need to put things in perspective. Don't give up, Jenna. Rebuilding is hard, but it beats going nowhere." With that, he gave her shoulder a squeeze and left.

His pep talk hadn't so much encouraged her as consumed her with curiosity. Who was Seth talking about? Had someone in his family gone to prison? He'd been pretty evasive. In fact, he'd been evasive ever since he arrived.

A feeling of foreboding crept over her. Who was he talking about, really? She pulled her phone out of her pants pocket and began to surf the internet. She started her search with the name Seth Waters. There were tons of Seth Waterses, including an up-and-coming country singer. Okay, narrow the search. She began hooking his name with charming words like *prison* and *sentencing*.

And then she found him. In an article from the *Los Angeles Times*. Not front page news but it was there all the same. She read the headline and terror cloaked her.

Seth Waters Sentenced.

As she continued to read, her eyes got wider and wider. Oh, no. Oh, no. They were harboring a criminal. *Former criminal*, she corrected herself.

Was there such a thing?

She left the beach, hurrying back to the motel to… what? Ask Seth to leave?

Yes. For sure.

She got back to discover that he'd finished cleaning up for her. A considerate criminal.

Former criminal.

Criminal.

His truck was still in the parking lot, which meant he was in his room. By the time she approached his door her heart was hammering so hard she was sure it was going to explode. Should she confront him all by herself? Wasn't this just as stupid as what she'd done the other night, going downstairs in a dark house to catch a burglar with her tiny can of pepper spray? Idiot Girl 2.

She'd barely knocked before he opened the door. "I wondered how long it would take you," he greeted her.

"What?"

He pointed to the cell phone in her trembling hand.

She stuffed the phone in her back pocket and bit on her lip.

"I'd ask you to come in but I suspect you're afraid."

"I'm not afraid," she lied, and stepped inside.

He leaned against the wall, crossed his arms. "So."

"So, what happened?"

"You just read what happened."

"I want you to tell me. Did you shoot the man on purpose?"

His brows dipped. "Of course on purpose."

It was suddenly very cold in Seth Waters's room. Jenna rubbed her arms, trying to warm up.

"That son of a bitch drug dealer got my little sister hooked on heroine."

There was something that hadn't been mentioned in the article she'd read.

Still, he'd shot a man. She opened her mouth to speak but nothing came out. She had no idea what to say. What to do.

"I know. That makes me look like a real badass."

That was putting it mildly. All Jenna could do was nod.

"More like a dumb ass." He shook his head. "I had a

good job working in construction. Almost had enough money saved to go back to school and finish up my degree. Everything was looking good. But after what he did to Monica… I found out where the rat bastard lived and went to his place and shot him as soon as he opened his door. Got him in the shoulder."

Her hands were still shaking. She was shaking all over. She shoved them in her back pockets to steady them. She had to have looked as shocked as she felt.

"I guess I'd watched too many Vin Diesel and Clint Eastwood movies," he said. "Somehow, I thought I could ride in, take out the bad guy and everything would be okay. You'd think by twenty-seven I'd have known better. I was convicted. Assault with a deadly weapon is a felony."

He'd tried to kill someone. Jenna was finding it difficult to breathe. She'd seen those action movies, too. In the movies it seemed so right when the hero took matters into his own hands and took out the bad guy. But this was real life.

It was hard to speak, hard to think even. She found herself sliding down the wall to sit on the floor. He sat down next to her, shoulder to shoulder, but didn't look at her. An eternity of silence passed before she finally asked, "What happened to the drug dealer?"

Seth gave a snort. "No idea. For all I know, he's still out there somewhere, responsible for God knows how many deaths."

Jenna nodded, taking that in, trying to process it all. "If you could have a do-over, would you do it again?"

He focused on the wall opposite and let out his breath. "I've asked myself that a million times. Each time the answer is different. I know nobody has the right to take another person's life." He shook his head. "But it was my little sister. My dad wasn't in the picture. It was just me, my younger brother and sister and Monica, the baby. I guess I felt like, as the oldest, I needed to make things right."

"How did the rest of your family feel?"

His jaw tightened. "Pissed. I wasn't a hero to them. I was a fool. An embarrassment. I broke my mom's heart. She already had her hands full with Monica and then I had to go and do what I did. I just wanted that bastard to pay."

"He will. Someday."

"Do you believe that?"

"I do," Jenna said. "I think. I hope."

"Vengeance is mine, sayeth the Lord?"

"Yeah. Something like that."

"Well, I guess I wanted to be the tool God used. I was a tool, all right."

"What happened with your family?"

"My mom came to see me every week. My sisters wrote me. I kicked around for a while, trying to figure out what to do. My brother finally loaned me the money to start this business."

"Your life's been like—"

"A bad movie," he finished for her.

The question that had been plaguing her ever since she did her internet search demanded to be asked. "So, are you a violent man?" Well, duh. He'd shot someone.

He looked at her and it was hard to decipher what she was seeing written on his face. "What do you think, Jenna?"

"I don't know. I don't know anything about you."

"You know more than most people ever will. All I can tell you is I've never in my life hit a woman. I always tried to protect my sisters. I've never kicked a dog or put my fist through a wall." His smile was bitter. "I've shaken my fist at heaven a few times, though."

"What happened to you wasn't God's fault," Jenna said, feeling that God, somehow, needed defending.

"You're right. Neither was what happened to my sister. We all make our choices. She made some bad ones. Still, that loser who got her hooked..."

Jenna could feel him tensing next to her. "You would do it again."

He relaxed. "No, I don't think so. I might dream about it, but no. Like I said before, life's too short. I already lost enough years of mine." He smiled at her, this one free of bitterness. "The past is long gone. There's only one way to go and that's forward. Don't worry," he added, "I'll leave tonight."

Yes, a good idea. He should leave. She had a child to protect. And an old lady.

He got back up, smiled sadly down at her and held out his hand to help her up, and she let him pull her to her feet. He didn't talk like a criminal. Or act like a criminal.

As if she knew what a criminal acted like. What if he was conning her? What if he was just telling her what she wanted to hear? Maybe he was the one who'd been the drug dealer.

Or maybe he was a man who'd done a terrible thing and had paid for it and was trying to rebuild his life. People did dumb things. People did wrong things. You couldn't hold a person's past against him when he was trying to start over.

You sure couldn't fall for him, though. And you couldn't let him stay.

All she could say before she left was "I'm sorry."

# *Chapter Thirteen*

*To Do:*
*Paint*
*Go to bank*
*Pray hard and cross fingers and toes before*
*going to bank*

Jenna didn't go into the house right away. Instead, she plopped down on Aunt Edie's front porch and did some more internet surfing, trying to figure out Seth Waters. One article backed up his story about the man he shot being a drug dealer. It played on the human-interest aspect of the story. A quote in that article jumped out at her. It was from his sister Monica, she of the drug problem.

The Waters family all broke down when the judge delivered his sentence this morning. Waters's youngest sister appeared to be the most shaken, crying over and over, "He shouldn't have done it. I shouldn't have let him." The family offered no further comment.

*I shouldn't have let him.* Like she could stop her brother hunting someone down and shooting him? Like she'd have known?

Had she known?

Seth's words came back at her. *I found out where the rat bastard lived, went to his place and shot him as soon as he opened his front door.*

He went to kill a man, got close and personal on his front porch and only managed to shoot him in the shoulder? Surely he could have done better at such close range. Okay, something was off here.

She looked across the parking lot. Seth was throwing his sleeping bag and cooler in the back of his truck, where he kept his power-washing equipment. She watched as he walked back into his room for the rest of his things. Was he a thug or a hero?

*I shouldn't have let him.* Shouldn't have *let* him shoot the man? Wrong, wrong, something was wrong.

He came back out, carrying his duffel bag. Another minute and he'd be gone.

Jenna bolted down the porch steps and raced across the parking lot. "Seth!"

He either didn't hear her or was ignoring her. He walked around to the cab and got in. Jenna hadn't run so fast in years. He'd started the engine by the time she grabbed the passenger door and climbed into the cab.

His eyebrows shot up. "What are you doing?"

"I want to talk to you."

He kept his gaze straight ahead. "There's nothing to talk about."

"I think there is."

"Trust me, there's not. Now, if you don't mind, I'd like to get going."

"Where are you going to go?"

His lips clamped shut. She could see the muscles bunching in his jaw.

"You just got here."

"And now I'm just leaving."

She took a shot in the dark, testing her theory. "You didn't do it, did you?"

He looked at her as if she were nuts. "What?"

"Oh, no." She shook her head. "Don't play dumb."

"I don't know what you're talking about. Would you mind getting out of my truck?"

"Actually, I would."

He heaved a sigh and looked heavenward. "Jenna."

"You can find anything online, you know. Recipes, old friends, old news stories."

He made no reply.

She pressed on. "What your sister said—'I shouldn't have let him do it'—she wasn't talking about you shooting the man. She was talking about you taking the blame for what she did. You took the fall for your little sister, didn't you?"

He glared at her. "The hell I did, and don't you ever say that to anyone. You hear me?"

Now he did look like a criminal, threatening and dangerous. Jenna scooted up against the door, but she kept going. "She was already on a bad path. How did it start, with some gateway drug?" His breath came out in an angry hiss, but she persisted. "Where was she getting the money for drugs? Shoplifting? Stealing from family and friends? Dealing?"

"Get out."

She was right. He wouldn't be reacting the way he was otherwise. She jutted out her chin. "No. Not until you promise to stay."

His jaw was clenched so tightly she thought he might break it.

"Hey," she said softly. "If you want the whole world to think you're a badass that's fine with me."

"I don't care what the whole world thinks. I don't care what anyone thinks about me."

"Even if they think that was a pretty noble thing you did?" Jenna asked softly.

He turned his head away and looked out the window. "I told you what I did."

"And isn't it interesting that the police believed your stupid story?"

He turned back and glared at her. "It wasn't stupid. It was true. What do you think, the guy shot himself?"

"No. Where'd you get the gun?"

"My dad had one. He left it behind when he split."

"So, you took your dad's gun, walked up on a man's porch and, standing right in front of him, aimed to kill."

"Damn right I did."

"And missed?"

He let out a breath. "Okay, so I chickened out at the last minute and couldn't do it. So, sue me."

"Or how about this? Your sister took Daddy's gun and went over there to get her fix. Maybe she was out of money and hoped to rob the guy. Whatever. The gun went off and she called big brother. You came running and took over from there. Who called the cops? The dealer? What kind of deal did you make with him? Not to rat him out if he didn't press charges against your sister?"

"You don't know what you're talking about," Seth growled. "You don't know anything."

"Okay, then. How did it go down?"

"It went down the way I said it did."

"Right. The cops had you, they had the gun, they had a confession. Everybody won."

His jaws were clenched again.

"Except you."

"I came out fine. And my sister's fine now. That's what matters."

"How many years of your life did you lose?"

"It doesn't matter. What matters is that my sister's okay."

"Maybe it matters that you get to be okay now, too." She reached over and laid a hand on his arm. "Don't leave us, Seth. I won't tell. Your secret's safe with me."

He shook his head.

"I need help. I'll never get this place in shape without you. Please."

"You don't need a jailbird."

"You're not a jailbird anymore, and you've got a chance for a good life here. Don't blow that just because I got nosy." She wasn't sure why she was arguing so hard. Maybe she felt guilty for opening Pandora's box. Maybe it was something else. Maybe it didn't matter why.

He took a deep breath. "I shouldn't stay."

"You can't keep running every time someone learns about your past. Didn't you tell me only a few minutes ago to keep fighting, that the only way to go is forward? So, let's go forward. Put your cooler back in your room and come over to the house. Aunt Edie's making a tuna casserole." He still hesitated, so she added, "I promise I won't say anything to anyone about your bad aim."

"Ha, ha."

"You have to start over somewhere. It may as well be here. And besides, you can't outrun the internet."

She kept talking, kept pressing, until he finally said, "Okay, stop already. I give up."

"Good. See you at dinner."

She walked back to the house smiling, glad his past was out in the open, glad she'd gotten to the heart of the man. In a way they were kindred souls, each trying to make a new start, trying to get over the mistakes of their pasts.

What lay out there in the future? What was going to happen to her? It wasn't prison, that much she knew. Seth was right. Things could always be worse.

The next day Jenna paid a visit to the bank to see if she could find a way to get more money.

Sherwood Stern, the bank manager, was a master at the regretful smile. He reminded her of the wizard in the old movie *The Wizard of Oz*. The great and powerful Oz.

Except Sherwood wasn't acting very great and powerful. "I'm afraid your aunt's been having trouble paying back the loan I already made to her."

"Yes, but this wouldn't be to my aunt. This would be to me," Jenna told him.

"What collateral would you offer?"

He looked almost hopeful until she said, "The Driftwood Inn?"

He pursed his lips and shook his head. "I'm afraid Edie already put that up as collateral."

"Isn't there such a thing as a second—"

"Mortgage? That doesn't apply here."

"Perhaps we could add on a little more to the loan."

"I'd like to help you," Sherwood said. "Really, I would. But I don't think that would be wise, considering the current situation."

"Another sixty thousand…" Okay, there would be other expenses. "Seventy," Jenna corrected herself, "and we'd have the place up and running and would be in a position to pay back what we owe."

He was shaking his head.

"How about this? Could we refinance? You could charge us more interest," she added recklessly, hoping to sweeten the pot.

"I'm afraid your aunt's credit score is too low. The bank won't take the risk. Unless you yourself have something you could put up as collateral? Some property?"

"I have a business," Jenna said.

"Then you have some assets?" he asked hopefully.

"Well, I don't own a building."

"Inventory?"

A massage table, stone warmer, desk and oils and towels and blankets wouldn't exactly impress Sherwood. "Nothing worth more than a few hundred," she confessed.

He looked so regretful. He probably practiced that expression in the mirror. "Ms. Jones, I would love to help you and your aunt, I really would."

She doubted it.

"But I can't take the risk. I have a board of directors to answer to."

"But surely your board of directors all know my aunt. She's been a member of this community since the sixties. Staying in business that long should count for something."

"Her current situation is too big a problem."

"But that's why we come to banks, when we're having a cash-flow problem."

"I'm sorry. I truly am."

Just not sorry enough. Jenna returned home feeling even more discouraged than she'd been the day before.

All well and good to talk about keeping on fighting, but how could you do that when nobody even let you in the ring?

One look at Jenna's face when she walked into the kitchen was enough to make Aunt Edie's hopeful expression die a quick death. "That penny-pincher Sherwood," she said in disgust. "And to think I gave him a special discount when he and his wife honeymooned here."

They were going to have to have a serious discussion about what to do with the Driftwood Inn. "Aunt Edie, I don't know what else to do," Jenna began.

She had no idea how to rehab a motel. She'd jumped in with no clue and been in over her head from the beginning. Now she was going under and taking her poor aunt with her.

Aunt Edie quickly turned and pulled a casserole dish from the oven. "Don't you worry, dear. We'll think of something. Meanwhile, tonight we're going to forget our troubles and have a bonfire on the beach. I went to the store and picked up marshmallows and chocolate and graham crackers for s'mores. And we have hot dogs and my best ever beans to go with them. I got root beer for Sabrina and some of those wine coolers all you young people like for us grown-ups. Pete's already making the fire and I sent Sabrina and that nice young man Seth down with the cooler. All we have to do is bring the bean dish."

*Eat, drink and be merry, for tomorrow we die.* Jenna sighed. Well, what the heck. They should probably enjoy the beach as much as they could. Who knew how much longer they'd be able to stay?

She resigned herself to having fun whether she wanted to or not, and escorted her aunt over the dunes, balancing baked beans in one hand and Aunt Edie in the other.

"I haven't done this in years," Aunt Edie said, sounding as excited as a child. "It does bring back such memories."

It did for Jenna, too. All those evenings around the campfire, roasting hot dogs, listening to Uncle Ralph go through his repertoire of ghost stories—"The Man with the Golden Arm" and "Johnny, I Want My Liver Back" never failed to send shivers down her spine. And then, of course, there'd been all the silly songs, from "Ninety-nine Bottles of Beer on the Wall" to "Found a Peanut." Maybe she'd teach Sabrina some songs tonight. Maybe it would be good to forget her troubles for a little while.

The men had the fire roaring and Seth was helping Sabrina launch her kite.

"It's a perfect night for a beach fire," Aunt Edie said happily, settling on a log.

"I got a good blaze going for you," Pete told her, as if he'd single-handedly collected the driftwood and started the fire, something Jenna highly doubted.

But, oh well. There would be no quarrels with Pete tonight. No frowns, no worries. Tonight she would hide from the ugly future.

She set the beans on a makeshift table the men had set up on a piece of driftwood and fell onto the blanket laid out on the sand. The sun was still high in the sky, the late-afternoon air was warm and the breeze was gentle. Her daughter was letting out more string on her kite and laughing as it dipped and soared. It was a perfect moment. She was going to stay in it and enjoy it.

Pete broke into the wine coolers and gave one to both Aunt Edie and Jenna.

"Don't let me have more than one," Aunt Edie cautioned. "I don't want to be a bad example for Sabrina."

"Aunt Edie, I never figured you for a wine cooler kind of woman," Jenna said after they'd toasted each other.

"I really prefer iced tea to alcohol, but once in a while it's fun to splurge. Party hearty, as they say. And at my age, you don't know how many years you have left so you need to make the most of them."

"You've got lots of years left," Jenna assured her, and hoped she was right. It had felt so good to reconnect with her great-aunt. She wanted to be able to enjoy that connection for as long as possible.

Sabrina finally abandoned her kite in favor of hot dogs and s'mores and Seth pulled a beat-up guitar case from behind a huge piece of driftwood and began to play, his fingers flying over the frets.

"Wow," Jenna said. "Where'd you learn to play like that?" Crap. Probably in prison. That would be the last thing he'd want to be reminded of.

"I had a band when I was in high school," he said, and she relaxed.

Of course he did, with teenage girls standing in front of the stage drooling. He had to have been a cute teenager.

"Any requests?" he asked.

"'Harbor Lights,'" said Aunt Edie.

"I'm afraid I don't know that one," he said.

"Of course not," she said, shaking her head. "It would have been way before your time."

"Sing a few bars," he said.

"Oh, I couldn't," she protested.

"Come on, Aunt Edie," Jenna coaxed. "You used to have a great voice."

"I still do," her aunt informed her, and began to sing. Her voice had gotten thready, but she could still carry a tune, and Seth picked up on the melody quickly and began to accompany her.

Jenna leaned back against a log, shut her eyes and let herself drift back in time. She was a kid again, hanging out with the grown-ups, no worries, no need for money. No need for anything but to enjoy life.

Aunt Edie and Seth finished, and Pete applauded. "That was real pretty."

"Yes, it was," Jenna said.

"Okay, what else?" Seth asked.

"'Found a Peanut,'" Jenna requested. "It's time Sabrina learned some classics."

With Seth accompanying, she taught her daughter all the silly campfire songs she'd sung as a kid, including a few of her favorite *Veggie Tales* ditties. Pete knew some of the same ghost stories as Uncle Ralph had told, and regaled everyone with them as the twilight began to loosen its hold on the day. Then, once it became dark, Seth brought out some fireworks and set them off.

"Oh, this is fun," Aunt Edie said, clapping her hands. "But you just wait until the Fourth of July," she told Sabrina. "People from all over come to set off their fireworks here on Moonlight Beach. Miles and miles of fireworks going off—it's lovely."

Sabrina had been smiling up until then. "We always go to Green Lake with Grandma to watch the fireworks. We are going back for the Fourth, aren't we?" She looked to Jenna in concern.

"Well." No, Jenna hadn't planned on it, not after her conversation with Damien. "I was thinking maybe we'd see if Grandma wanted to come down here. And Aunt Celeste."

The plan didn't meet with her daughter's approval. "But I want to go home. I want to see Daddy."

Him again. "We will."

"When?"

"Soon." As soon as Jenna could convince him to grow up.

Sabrina frowned at the fire and fell silent. Minutes later she stood and said, "I'm going back to the house."

"Maybe you wouldn't mind walking me back," Aunt Edie said to her. "This log is getting a little hard on my bony old bottom."

Jenna suspected the last thing Sabrina wanted to do was to be polite and escort her great-great-aunt back, but she bit her lip and nodded, and a moment later they were gone.

"I think I've had enough, too," Pete said. "These girlie drinks aren't doing it for me." He followed them back through the beach grass.

"I guess we're in charge of putting out the fire," Seth said to Jenna, and came to sit next to her on the blanket.

Putting out the fire? With him sitting so close? Not likely.

He turned to her. The firelight danced on his face and she thought of pirates and buried treasure. Sex on the beach.

"No regrets about my staying?"

Those eyes. She felt like a marshmallow in the flame. Her throat was suddenly dry. She swallowed. "Why should I? We both know the truth."

"The truth is what you read in the paper," he said sternly.

"Right. Whatever. Anyway, we need the help around here."

"You've got Pete."

"Yes, and we both know how helpful he is. I'm glad you stayed."

"Yeah?" He was looking at her lips. Then he was looking lower and she felt like Lois Lane with Superman checking out her boobs with his X-ray vision. If she moved one inch closer...

She made herself stay rooted right where she was.

He got the message and looked back into the fire. "Yeah, you're right. Probably not a good idea. You can do better."

Pity flooded her heart. Once upon a time this man had plans for his life. Now here he was, staying in a dump, sleeping on the floor and reading Shakespeare. "I didn't say that."

"You didn't have to."

Okay, now he was feeling rejected. Next he'd get up and leave. She didn't want him to.

"What did you want to get your degree in when you were saving to go back to school?" she asked.

"I was going to major in English lit. I'd have gone back as a junior. Planned to get a teaching certificate, maybe a master's." He took a deep breath. "I won't be teaching kids now, not with my background." He gave a bitter laugh.

"Maybe what happened to your family is a way of teaching, too."

"I'm not broadcasting my past, Jenna. I hope you won't, either."

"Of course not," she said, shocked that he'd even think her capable of doing that.

"Don't look so outraged. People gossip. Things slip out."

"Well, not from me," she said, and took another draw on her wine cooler.

"I wish I'd met you fifteen years ago," he said softly.

For a moment, so did she. And for another minute she thought maybe now was the perfect time to meet. They could both make a new start together.

She had a pleasant buzz going from her wine cooler, and her hormones had an equally pleasant buzz going from such close proximity to him. She was beginning to feel a little off balance. She started to list in his direction.

This time he was the one who put on the brakes. He tapped her on the nose. "That stuff's going to your head. Come on, time to pack it in."

He hauled her to her feet and together they doused the beach fire and covered it with sand, effectively smothering it.

That only took care of one fire. She was still smoldering when she went to bed.

Brody stopped by on Thursday to see if Jenna wanted to go to lunch. A shrimp Louie at the Porthole sounded a heck of a lot better than the tuna sandwich she'd just sent her daughter to the house to fetch. But she was a mess—sweaty and dotted with paint, in faded sweats and a T-shirt.

"I'm a disaster," she said, wiping at her damp forehead.

"Even as a disaster you look good," he said. "But go ahead and get cleaned up. I can visit with Edie while I'm waiting. Anyway, you deserve a break."

Yes, she did. She decided to ignore the fact that she'd have to get right back into her gunky clothes and start painting again once she returned. The sun was out, the day was pretty and the view from the Porthole would be more than worth changing clothes.

"You talked me into it."

They were leaving when Seth pulled up in his truck. Ready to work. With Jenna. She felt suddenly guilty and self-conscious with Brody next to her.

"I'd better tell Seth I'm leaving," she said.

"You have to ask his permission?" Brody taunted. "You're the owner. You get to go to lunch whenever you want."

"I know. But we've been working on the rooms together. I want him to know I'm coming back."

"Whatever," Brody said, and leaned against the building, crossing one ankle over another. He looked like a misplaced model in his Dockers and blue polo shirt. Was he aware how well that color set off his eyes? Probably.

"Hi," she greeted Seth as he sauntered up to them. Her cheeks were hot. Why was she blushing? What did she have to blush about? "I'm going out to lunch, so how about we start work around one?"

"Better make it one-thirty," put in Brody. "It can get busy at the Porthole."

And he could always get a table. She suspected he was angling for more time, and felt both flattered and embarrassed. Oh, if Damien could see her now.

"No problem," Seth said. "I'll go ahead and start on my own."

"You don't need to," she said.

He shrugged. "I don't mind."

Great. "I feel guilty," she said as she and Brody made their way to the house.

"Because you're taking time for lunch? Come on, Jenna, as hard as you're working, it's allowed."

"I guess." Still, it didn't seem right that she was skipping off and leaving Seth to do everything on his own.

She was the one with skin in the game. She should be working every moment.

"So, how's it going with the handyman?" Brody asked as they went up the steps to Aunt Edie's house."

"Pete? He's not quite as useless as he first was."

"I meant your other handyman. The mold guy."

Mold guy, there was a flattering nickname. Of course, Seth hadn't been much more complimentary of Brody the house peddler.

"Seth's great." He was more than great. He was noble.

Brody frowned. "Just how great is he?"

"He's a hard worker and he's really helping out." *And no, he hasn't kissed me. Darn.*

Brody gave a grunt. "There's something about that guy."

There sure was.

"You don't know him very well."

She knew him better than Brody could even begin to imagine. "When it comes right down to it, I don't know you very well, either," Jenna pointed out.

"I'm working on changing that," he said with a smile. Brody Green had a gorgeous smile.

They entered the house as Sabrina was coming out of it with Jenna's sandwich.

"Hi there, kiddo," Brody greeted her.

"My name's Sabrina," she said, filled with umbrage.

"Sorry. Sabrina," Brody corrected himself.

She ignored both him and her mother's scolding look, holding the plate out to Jenna. "I made your sandwich."

"Thanks," Jenna said. "I'll have it a little later. I'm going to run out for a bite."

"Together?" Sabrina managed to look both shocked and displeased at once.

"Yes, together. Put it in the fridge for me, please."

"Fine. I don't know why you had me bother to make it if you weren't going to eat it," Sabrina grumbled as she turned back to the kitchen.

"Sorry," Jenna said to Brody. "She's a little grumpy today." There would be a talk about manners a little later and a reminder that pink hair was on the line.

Or maybe she'd let this one slide. Both she and Damien had put their daughter through so many changes she probably had emotional whiplash. So maybe she was allowed some grumpiness.

Anyway, Brody didn't seem to be offended. "It's okay," he said easily. "I've got a girl. Remember?"

Aunt Edie hurried out of the kitchen now, wiping her hands on her apron. "Brody, how nice of you to stop by and take Jenna out to lunch. Would you like some iced tea while you wait for her to freshen up?"

"No, I'm fine."

Yes, he was.

"Well, sit down and make yourself at home," said Aunt Edie, gesturing to Uncle Ralph's old recliner.

Jenna needed more work than a simple freshening up, but she promised not to be long.

"Take your time," Brody told her. "Edie and I can catch up on what's been going on around here."

They caught up, all right. Jenna came back downstairs dressed for lunch just in time to hear him say, "If worse comes to worst, I can help."

And she knew exactly how he wanted to help. The skunk! The minute her back was turned, there he was, working on Aunt Edie, trying to convince her to sell.

"Were you just trying to talk my aunt into selling the Driftwood?" she demanded as soon as they were out the door.

He held out both hands in a gesture of innocence. "I was only reminding her that it was an option."

Jenna developed sudden amnesia regarding that huge chunk of money she didn't have. "It's not," she said firmly. "And now I can't help but wonder if there's another reason you're being so nice to us."

"Oh, come on. Seriously?"

"Yes, seriously."

"Jenna…" he began.

She didn't let him get any further. "You just don't get it, do you? This place is important to us."

"Of course it is. And I do get it. But sometimes you have to be practical and face reality." He pointed to the roof, all dressed up in blue tarp. "You're going to have to do something about that roof. And what about the mattresses for all those beds? What kind of condition are those in?"

"I know we need to do some work."

"And that takes money. If you've got it, great. Go for it."

The drive to the restaurant wasn't exactly a companionable one, and Jenna failed to dredge up a smile as Laurel the hostess seated them. But then Laurel wasn't smiling, either. *You can have him*, thought Jenna.

"Look, I'm sorry I brought it up," Brody said after their waitress had taken their orders and left. "I just hate to see you guys go under and lose the opportunity to come out well-off."

"We wouldn't go under if we could get an infusion of cash."

She must have been looking at him speculatively, because he frowned and said, "My money's all tied up in other real estate here around town. I can't afford to take on a money pit like the Driftwood."

Neither could she. She sighed.

He reached across the table and laid a hand on her arm. "I'm sorry, Jenna. Sorry your aunt got you into this. Edie's a doll, but she's not very practical."

He was right. Uncle Ralph had been the practical one, the one who kept things maintained, paid the bills. The condition of both the motel and Aunt Edie's bank account were proof that her talents lay in a different direction.

"I know she's not. But she's got vision. You know, the Driftwood was one of the first motels down here. She saw what the town could become. And she sees what the old place could be again with just a little loving care."

"And a lot of money."

"I'll have to find a way to get it."

"I like you a lot, Jenna, but I'm not driving the getaway car if you rob the bank," Brody said, making her smile. "But if you need more help around there let me know. I'll come swing a hammer anytime."

And since he'd helped before, she knew she could count on him to do it again. "I'm sorry I reacted the way I did back at the house," she said once their food had arrived. Her shrimp Louie did look good. Maybe if she could clear the air with Brody she'd actually enjoy it.

"No worries," he told her.

"I thought…"

"I know. Hidden agenda. Except, that agenda is pretty much out in the open. If you decide you need to sell, I'll help you. And I'll kick over my commission to your aunt."

She set down her fork and gaped at him.

"Oh, come, Jenna, do you think I'm such a greedy bastard that I wouldn't want to help a sweet little old lady like Edie?"

"Well…" It had crossed her mind.

"I only have one other thing on my agenda," he continued.

"What's that?"

"You," he said with a grin that made her cheeks sizzle and her heart rate pick up.

"Of course, I like to make money as much as the next guy," he confessed. "It comes in pretty handy when you're paying child support."

Or spousal support. There went Jenna's appetite.

She managed a couple of bites, then gave up and let the waitress box her salad and had Brody take her back to the motel. She felt like she had a giant hourglass strapped to her back, with sand quickly running out. She had to find a way to make money and fast. And she had to get as much done on the motel as soon as possible. If she could get everything done but the roof…

She'd still have a problem.

She could hear voices in the kitchen. Aunt Edie probably had Sabrina busy with some culinary creation. Which was good, as Jenna didn't particularly want Aunt Edie asking what she and Brody had talked about at lunch.

She slipped upstairs, put on her grubby paint clothes and hurried back to work.

Seth had painted an entire room in her absence and started on the next. She was both grateful and mortified. "I'm sorry I left you on your own," she said as she joined him.

"Don't be. I don't need supervision."

"No, it's not that. It's that this is my place. I shouldn't have other people doing my work."

"Nobody with eyes could accuse you of that." He stopped and studied her. "What's got you wound so tight?"

"Nothing," she said, dipping her roller in the paint tray.

"Okay. If you say so."

She managed to go a whole five minutes before saying, "We should sell this place."

"I wonder where you got that idea."

She frowned at him. "Brody's not trying to make me sell. It's just that…"

"I know. You're up against it."

"Where am I supposed to come up with the money to replace that roof? I can't have people staying here and putting out buckets to catch the rain."

"So maybe you just patch the roof this year."

"The roofer said the whole thing needs replacing."

"That's what roofers say."

"We need mattresses and bedding and…" Her eye was twitching.

"Hey, hey, deep breath," he said gently. "Didn't your mother ever tell you how to eat an elephant?"

She frowned at him. "No."

"Well, that's your problem."

"Okay, how do you eat an elephant?"

"One bite at a time. Let's get these rooms painted and your furniture back in them. That's a big enough bite for right now, don't ya think?"

She took a deep breath. "Yeah, I guess it is."

They got two more rooms painted that afternoon and Jenna found she was actually smiling by the time they were done. She managed to give Aunt Edie a vague answer at dinner, and she did manage to have a talk with her daughter and reassure her that she wasn't importing a new man into their life.

That didn't mean she couldn't dream, but dreaming was as far as her wounded heart was willing to go.

An occasional hiccup or two aside, Sabrina did manage to find a better attitude, so Friday afternoon, after Jenna had painted another two rooms, they made a run into nearby Quinault, where they found a beauty supply store and a clerk who was happy to sell them everything they needed for Sabrina's new look and to give Jenna several tips, as well.

"Start with something temporary until you find the color you really like," she advised. "Then once you do, you can go with—

"Not something totally permanent," said Jenna, making her daughter scowl.

"A demi perm is good," the woman said. "That will last twenty to thirty washes. Oh, and speaking of washing, don't wash your hair the day you're going to dye it," she advised Sabrina. "That will strip all the oils you need to protect your scalp from irritation."

The products began to mount up. They needed to bleach Sabrina's hair first, then they needed a purple toner to ensure a perfect pink. Dyes, bleach, cape... money. Yikes!

But Sabrina was beaming when they left the shop. "I can hardly wait till tomorrow," she said.

"Tomorrow afternoon," Jenna reminded her. "I have to work in the morning."

"I know," Sabrina said, resigned but happy.


"I hear you're going to get all gorgeous," Tyrella said to her later when the women started arriving for their Friday night gathering.

Sabrina nodded eagerly. "Mom's doing it tomorrow. It's gonna be awesome."

"I'll bet it is," Tyrella said, smiling at Jenna. "Good for you," she added, once Sabrina had disappeared upstairs with some of the cheese and crackers Nora had brought and saltwater taffy from Cindy. "You're a sport."

"Hair grows," Jenna said, quoting her mom. Mom was right. Pink hair would be fun. In fact, she wished she was brave enough to do something crazy with her hair. But all her bravery was needed for pulling the Driftwood together.

"Caroline is bound to be impressed," said Nora. "She arrives tomorrow. Maybe we can get the girls together for a visit on Sunday."

"Good idea," Jenna said. Her daughter finding someone to hang out with would take one big worry off her mind.

Chitchat and fun eventually turned to sharing and dreams. It started with much raving over Courtney's latest design, a dress with a vintage flair and a scalloped neckline.

"How I wish I was young again," Aunt Edie said. "I would certainly wear something like that."

"I'd wear it now," Annie said, looking longingly at it.

"I'm glad to hear it, because guess what you're getting for your birthday," Courtney told her.

"Really?" Annie was practically glowing.

"You need to hurry up and go into business for yourself," Tyrella said to Courtney.

"Once I get some more money together." She frowned. "Coming down here after my divorce was the right thing to do, I know. I've felt so free ever since. But staying… I'm not exactly getting rich at Beach Babes. I'd talked with Susan when she first hired me about maybe selling some of my designs, but that never seems to get off the ground. Maybe I should go back to Seattle and get a job in an office somewhere. Or at Nordstrom's."

"It costs a lot more to live in Seattle than it does here," Nora said.

"Yeah, but I'd make more."

"But you'd lose all of us," Annie reminded her.

"True. And when it comes right down to it, friends are worth more than any amount of money. Still," she added wistfully, "I'd sure like to have both. Maybe I should play the lottery."

"There's a good way to throw away your money," Tyrella said in disgust.

"Oh, but if I won... Mega Millions is up to fifty-two million, but I'd settle for Lotto. That's up to eight."

"I'd settle for a million," said Annie.

"What would you do with that million?" Patricia Whiteside asked her. Patricia, herself, was looking elegant in white slacks, wedge sandals and a red top accented with a red-and-white polka-dot scarf. Patricia didn't need to win the lottery. She was doing fine.

"I'd buy myself a food truck and sell wraps and croissant sandwiches and cookies," Annie said.

"And I'd give you the recipe for my oatmeal ones," Aunt Edie told her.

"I'd quit dishing up ice cream and make wind chimes and cute ice cream dishes decorated with shells," Nora said, "and hit all the arts and crafts stores from here to Seattle."

"You love your ice cream business," Edie said in surprise.

"Yes, I do," Nora admitted. "But I'm tired of being on my feet all the time, and I want more time to be creative. In fact, maybe I won't wait to win that million. Maybe I'll turn the business over to the boys and let them get plantar fasciitis. Beau and Beck are already managing the fun-plex. They could handle the parlor, too."

"You could open up an arts and crafts store here," Jenna said. "I'd sure love to do something like that. In addition to managing the Driftwood," she quickly added lest her aunt worry she was planning on defecting.

"Is that what you'd do with a million?" Courtney asked her.

Jenna shook her head. "I don't know what I'd do with a million. In fact, I don't know if I'd even want a million. But I'd love to come up with enough money to put a roof on our motel. If I could find money for that and a few other things we need I'd be one happy camper."

"You will," Tyrella assured her. "I'm praying about it. That money's gonna come. I don't know from where, but it's gonna come just when you need it."

"Can you pray me a big win in the lottery while you're at it?" Courtney asked, making Tyrella frown and shake her head. Tyrella obviously didn't believe in gambling.

The party broke up around ten and Jenna spent the next hour chatting with her sister via text, then went to bed. The next morning the sun was shining and she could see blue waves curling their way to the beach. Her first client—the mayor!—was coming at ten. She had time for a beach walk.

She donned shorts and flip-flops and made her way through the beach grass to the sandy shore. The air was so clean down here. She greedily gulped it in, then took off her flip-flops and started down the beach barefoot. What a gorgeous morning! What a beautiful scene! How could a woman not feel positive, hopeful even, on a day like this?

Speaking of beautiful, here came Seth, jogging her

way. He was something to watch, those leg muscles flexing, arms pumping. Not a spec of fat on the man.

He slowed down at the sight of her, a sure sign he was going to stop and say hello. "Don't stop on my account," she called.

"Not planning on it," he called back. He caught up with her, turned her around and started moving her his direction. "Run with me."

"I don't run," she explained as her klutzy feet struggled to keep up. That afternoon in the parking lot had been an exception.

"Sure you do. Everybody runs. You ran as a kid, right?"

"Yeah, playing tag. But that was a long time ago," she said, gasping for breath.

He on the other hand was having no trouble breathing. "Gets your heart pounding."

"It's pounding." Right about out of her chest. She pulled up, bent over and sucked in more air to her poor, starving lungs.

He, too, stopped. "After all the work you've been doing I'd think you'd be in great shape."

"I guess you'd be wrong," she said. "The only way I ever plan to run is if a bear is chasing me."

"I heard someone spotted one over on Razor Clam last week," he said. "Better stay in shape," he added with a wink.

"I'll stay in shape my way. You stay in shape yours," she said.

"Okay, suit yourself. But there's nothing like a morning run on the beach."

"Or a walk," she said. "And don't come haunting me if you keel over dead."

He chuckled, then was off again.

She stood for a moment, watching him go. Yep, the beach was sure beautiful in the morning.

By the time Jenna had finished her walk and showered Aunt Edie had bacon and eggs frying on the stove. Sabrina was nowhere in sight. No surprise. Teenagers excelled in sleeping away a morning.

Once Jenna was showered and dressed, she did check in on her girl, kneeling by the bed and giving her a kiss on the cheek.

"What time is it?" Sabrina mumbled. She was splayed out across the bed, one foot sticking out from under the covers.

"Almost ten. Are you planning on getting up anytime soon?"

"There's nothing to do."

"The library will be open in an hour. Or you could do some sketching at the beach."

"When are we going to dye my hair?"

"This afternoon, after I've finished with my clients. Meanwhile, see if you can find something to do besides lying here like something dead washed up on shore."

"You're always wanting me to *do* things," Sabrina complained.

"That's because there's so much to do in life. You don't want to miss out on anything."

Sabrina grabbed her pillow and pulled it over her head. "I won't cuz there's nothing to do here."

Jenna wished she could have a moment with nothing to do. "Well, I can think of something. You could pick up your room, Miss Piggy."

Sabrina clamped the pillow more securely over her ears. Jenna gave her foot a playful tickle, then left to start her day.

She'd gotten the massage table warmed up and her towels ready to go when her first customer, Parker Thorne, the mayor of Moonlight Harbor, arrived.

Parker was a compact woman who looked to be in her early sixties. No hint of gray in the mayor's brown hair, though, and it was cut short and stylish. She had a toned body that proclaimed her a devotee of the gym, and a kind of friendliness that felt a little on the slick side.

"We're all so happy that Edie has help now," she said to Jenna. "It will be wonderful to see her little place all fixed up again."

"We hope to get there," Jenna said as she worked on Parker's shoulder.

"I'm sure you will, and that will be a boon for both yourselves and the community. It's nice when everything looks shiny penny pretty," Parker continued.

Shiny penny pretty?

"It leaves a good impression on our visitors."

Ah, and right now the Driftwood Inn was looking more like a penny someone had set on the railroad track to get squished by a train. Jenna frowned and concentrated on not letting her hands dig too deeply into the mayor's oh-so-trim, shiny-penny-pretty bod.

But she couldn't resist saying, "I can see how it might be a challenge for some of the businesses to stay shiny penny pretty when it's hard to get a loan." Hmm. Maybe the mayor could talk to good old Sherwood at the bank.

"Yes, that is a challenge. Some of our businesses struggle. It's difficult when so many visitors are seasonal."

"Maybe we should try and find a way to get them to come down more throughout the year," Jenna suggested.

"Oh, we're working on that," Parker said breezily.

"Yeah? What's being done?"

"We have all kinds of plans in the works."

Very comforting. And very evasive. Jenna wasn't so impressed with the mayor of Moonlight Harbor.

But she liked getting paid, and she was happy to take the woman's money.

She was also happy to take money from one of the cops who'd come to rescue her from her fake burglar. It turned out Officer Mushroom's name was Frank Stubbs. Poor man. At all of five-five, he probably took plenty of teasing over that.

It turned out Frank was single. "Been on my own for the last three years, ever since the wife and me split," he said, and groaned as Jenna worked a knot out of his back. "Man, you're good."

"Thank you," she murmured. Then, before he could get any further into discussing his single state, or hers, she asked, "How long have you been on the force down here?"

"Too long. I'm ready to hang up my handcuffs and spend my days fishing. Well, on second thought, maybe I'll keep the handcuffs," he added with a chuckle.

Oh, yes, Frank was a witty one.

"Sounds like a great life. Fishing, that is," Jenna added.

"It is. You can't go wrong living at the beach. But my old place gets lonely. It needs a woman's touch."

And here it came. Jenna braced herself.

Sure enough. "Are you seeing anyone?"

Jenna was spared answering by a screech coming from the living room. "Get out!" cried Aunt Edie. "Get out, you horrible thing! Help! Help!"

Jenna tore out of the room, leaving Frank to fumble for his pants. "I'm coming, Aunt Edie!" Why, oh, why had she tossed that pepper spray?

# Chapter Fourteen

*To Do:*
*Attend church*
*Take Aunt Edie to Beach Babes*
*Have Nora and Caroline over*
*Put up a No Cats Allowed sign*

Jenna arrived in the living room to see Roger flying for his life just as the same cat she'd seen hanging around outside leaped for him. Aunt Edie was in hot pursuit, trying to whack the cat with a pillow. A lamp had already been overturned. Roger flew off through the open door into the kitchen, squawking all the way with the cat in hot pursuit.

"Stop that beast!" cried Aunt Edie.

"Come here, kitty," Jenna called.

Kitty paid her no attention. Who wanted to bother with humans when you could catch a parrot?

Jenna had barely gained the kitchen after the cat when Roger saw it coming and flew back into the living room again, nearly taking off Jenna's face in his attempt to escape.

She dove for the cat and missed, and it hissed at her and ran for the living room.

Frank had donned his pants and was in the room. "I'll

get it," he said, and tried to snatch the cat. It ducked under the couch and Frank tripped over a footstool.

"Call the cops!" Roger squawked. "Call the cops." He was on top of his cage now, and he used his beak to climb inside. "Call the cops! Call the cops!"

Jenna rushed to shut the cage door and collided with Frank in the process. Chest bump. Both landed on the couch.

"Sorry," he muttered, and bounded back up, trying to get to the cat. Jenna hurried to the cage and shut Roger in.

Meanwhile, Aunt Edie was back with the broom. She took a swing at the invader and caught Frank on the side of the head just as he was reaching for it, which landed him on the floor again.

Finally, Jenna managed to grab the cat. It wasn't happy and squirmed to get away, scratching her in the process. She let out a yelp and dropped it, but by that time Frank was on the job and succeeded in catching the animal and getting it out the door.

The enemy vanquished and Roger safe, they all three collapsed on the couch, Frank wiping his brow, Jenna trying to get her breath and Aunt Edie sitting with a hand to her chest.

"Aunt Edie, are you all right?" Jenna asked. Why was she holding her chest?

She nodded. "I'm fine. It just gave me such a scare. I don't know how that animal got in."

"I've seen it hanging around," Jenna said. *I fed it some tuna fish.* She decided not to offer any extra unnecessary information.

"It didn't have a collar," Frank said. "Probably a stray. Sometimes people dump their animals and leave," he added in disgust.

"How did it get in?" Aunt Edie asked, her voice tremulous.

Jenna was sure she'd seen the back door open when she'd been in hot pursuit in the kitchen. She went and checked. Sure enough, it was still open, letting in a nice ocean breeze. Someone, probably Pete, hadn't closed it properly and the wind had blown it open.

"The back door was open," she reported when she returned. "Pete—" she began.

"Oh no. I shut the door after Pete when he was done with breakfast," Aunt Edie said.

That left only one culprit. Sabrina tended to be a little casual about things like closing doors and picking up after herself. That was going to have to come to an end, especially the door neglect.

"Glad we got rid of the thing," said Frank. "I hate cats. They're sneaky."

Jenna liked cats, but there would be no kitty in residence at the Driftwood Inn, not as long as Roger was alive.

She thanked Frank for saving the day, then saw him to the door. He launched into an invite to the Drunken Sailor, but she cut him off, claiming the need to make sure Aunt Edie was okay.

It was hardly a manufactured need. She returned to where her aunt sat, twisting the agate ring on her finger, watching Roger, who was pacing back and forth on the perch in his cage muttering about whiskey and cops. "Ralph, Ralph. Where are you?"

"Poor Roger. He's so upset," her aunt fretted.

Aunt Edie didn't seem to be doing too well, either. "Let me make you a cup of tea," Jenna offered.

"That would be lovely. And please cover the cage. I think Roger needs a rest."

So did Aunt Edie. Heck, so did Jenna. She covered the cage, then hurried to the kitchen, nuked a mug of hot water in the microwave, then stuck in a tea bag of chamomile.

"Thank you," Aunt Edie said when she returned. She reached to take it and Jenna saw that her hand was shaking. "I know he's just a silly old bird," she said in a small voice, "but he means a lot to me. Ralph got him for me as an anniversary present for our fiftieth wedding anniversary. He's—"

"I know," Jenna said, patting her shoulder. "He's your baby. Don't worry. We'll make sure the doors are closed from now on. And I'll see if I can find out who owns that cat."

"People shouldn't let their animals wander around loose," Aunt Edie said with a frown.

"I know." Boy, was she going to have a talk with Sabrina when she showed up.

Which she did, ten minutes later, ready to turn her hair pink.

"First, we need to have a talk," Jenna said, leading the way to her room.

"What did I do?" Sabrina asked as they walked up the stairs. "You knew where I was going. You said I could go to the library."

"Yes, I did. And you're not in trouble."

"Then why do we have to go up here and talk?" Sabrina protested, following Jenna to her bedroom.

*So if you throw a fit you can do it without upsetting Aunt Edie.* "I just wanted a moment of privacy."

"Great, I'm in trouble," Sabrina muttered. "I don't even know what I did wrong." She plopped on the bed and scowled.

"I wanted to talk to you about making sure you shut the door when you go out."

Sabrina didn't deny her carelessness. "Sorry. But what's the big deal?"

"The big deal is that a cat got in and tried to eat Roger."

"Good. I hate that bird. He's stupid."

"Sabrina," Jenna chided.

"Well, he is. And he's mean." She gnawed her lower lip. "Does this mean we don't get to dye my hair?"

Was there any creature on the planet more self-centered than a teenage girl? "No, we'll still do your hair. I promised we would and I'm not going back on my word. But I'm a little disappointed in your attitude."

"I can't help it if I don't like Roger. He bit me!"

"I know you don't like Roger. But you do like Aunt Edie, don't you?"

Sabrina caught her lower lip with her teeth again and nodded.

"She loves Roger, and she was really upset when the cat tried to get him. She was almost in tears," Jenna added. A little guilt once in a while never hurt, right?

Sabrina's eyes suddenly misted. "I'm sorry. I didn't do it on purpose."

"I know. If you had you'd really be in trouble. And if something had happened to Roger Aunt Edie would have been heartbroken."

For all her grumbling and complaining and snotty moments, Sabrina still had a tender heart. "I'm sorry," she said, and began to cry.

Jenna sat down on the bed and hugged her. "I know, sweetie. Just be more careful in the future. Okay?"

Sabrina sniffed and nodded.

"Now, let's go make you look awesome."

Awesome took the rest of the afternoon and by the time they were done Jenna was thanking her lucky stars that she'd never opted for beauty school. Good grief, what a lot of work.

Sabrina was thrilled, though, and Aunt Edie, who'd been watching the process, complimented her on how pretty she looked. "Isn't she pretty, Roger?" she asked the bird, who'd recovered enough from his ordeal to sit on his kitchen perch.

"Roger's a pretty bird," he replied. "Give me whiskey."

Sabrina, happy with her new look and the world in general, even Roger, giggled.

"No whiskey for you," Aunt Edie told him. "But I'd better get some dinner going for us. Just look at the time."

"I think, after your stressful day, you should let Sabrina and me make dinner," Jenna told her. She turned to Sabrina. "So, how about we run to the grocery store and pick up a frozen pizza and some salad in a bag?"

Sabrina thought it an excellent idea, and preened her way up and down the grocery store aisles. She checked herself out in the visor mirror so many times on the way back that Jenna teasingly threatened to nickname her Narcissus.

Sabrina frowned. "I know who that is."

Jenna smiled and said nothing more.

Pete had plenty to say at dinner. "You look like you've got cotton candy on your head," he informed her.

"Oh, Pete, you know nothing about fashion," Aunt Edie said, coming to Sabrina's rescue. "You look adorable, dear," she assured Sabrina.

"Yes, you do," Jenna agreed.

"It looks goofy if you ask me," Pete said, reaching for another piece of pizza.

"Pete, I don't think anyone's going recruit you to join the fashion police," Jenna told him.

That made him frown and Sabrina snicker.

The night ended well, with a movie on TV, popcorn and root beer floats. Life was looking up on the home front at last. And the following day Sabrina would be meeting Nora's granddaughter. Thank God her daughter would have one of her own kind to hang with. Jenna would soon have one less thing to worry about.

The next morning it looked like Aunt Edie was recovered from the trauma of the day before. She'd made a French toast casserole for breakfast and was dressed in her favorite jeans with the elastic waistband and a pink sweatshirt about the color of Sabrina's hair.

"Beach Babes is having a sale today," she said as she and Jenna drank their morning coffee together. "I thought you might like to go."

Not particularly, but Jenna knew her aunt would, so she said, "That sounds like fun. Nora's coming over with her granddaughter later so how about we go right after lunch?"

"That will be lovely. I'd like to get a new sun hat."

And so, after lunch, Jenna and her aunt wandered into the shop in search of the perfect hat. In spite of the lure of an offer of twenty-five percent off on all merchandise, the shop wasn't exactly packed. One window-shopper was just leaving, empty-handed, as they came in and a couple of older women stood in a corner by the window, checking out sweatshirts with cats on them. Aunt Edie wouldn't be buying one of those.

She forgot her quest for a hat and drifted over to a sale rack hung with pastel slacks, all with elastic waists.

Jenna decided to go say hi to Courtney, who was at the cash register at the back of the store.

She stopped halfway when she realized Courtney was having a discussion with her boss, Susan Frank.

"I've asked you before and I don't want to have to ask again," Susan said sternly. "I need you to wear some of the things we sell here. I don't understand why it's so hard to comply with that request when I give you an employee discount."

"I'm sorry, Susan," Courtney said.

If Jenna hadn't seen her she wouldn't have believed it was Courtney talking. Courtney hadn't struck her as a meek woman.

"At least wear a scarf," Susan continued. "Go pick one out. And try to talk up those beach bags. We need to move them."

"Yes, Susan."

Courtney started for the scarves and caught sight of Jenna gawking. A flood of red crept up her neck and onto her cheeks. "Hi, Jenna. Can I help you find something?"

"Aunt Edie's looking for a hat over in the slacks section," Jenna said in an attempt to lighten the moment. "I'm thinking I need a scarf." She needed to buy something.

Courtney nodded and led her over to the scarves while Susan, who had seen Edie, was now busy selling her on a pair of slacks. "Does that happen a lot?" Jenna asked in a low voice.

"Often enough." Courtney frowned. "What circle of hell is it where you have to wear the ugly clothes your boss sells? I hate working here."

"Maybe you should quit," Jenna suggested.

"I can't afford to. I'm stuck."

Ironic that Courtney was always after Annie to leave her husband yet she couldn't leave her job.

Jenna bought a scarf.

Nora came over late that afternoon with her granddaughter Caroline, and bearing ice cream and hot-fudge sauce and a can of whipped cream. "I can have ice cream anytime I want," Caroline bragged to Sabrina as they settled around the kitchen table with their treats.

"That has its drawbacks," Nora said. "I'm walking proof. Remember when I was skinny?" she said to Aunt Edie.

"You were too thin," Aunt Edie informed her.

"No danger of that now," Nora joked.

"I'm never getting fat," Caroline announced. She pulled out a cell phone and took a picture of her sundae. "Ice cream whenever I want. My friends are going to be so jealous."

Then, with that out of the way, she turned her attention to Sabrina. "I like your hair." Oh, yes. These two were going to be good friends.

"We just did it yesterday," Sabrina said.

"I want to dye my hair but my mom says dark hair doesn't dye very well." Caroline scowled at her ice cream. "I think I will, anyway."

"Not until you check with your mother," said Nora.

Caroline shrugged. "She won't care." She shoved aside her half-consumed sundae and said to Sabrina, "Come on. Let's go up to your room."

"Okay," Sabrina said, and they vanished.

"What a waste of ice cream," Nora said. She pulled her granddaughter's bowl over and began to eat it. "I know," she said between mouthfuls. "I'm an addict."

"I can think of worse things to be addicted to," Aunt Edie told her.

"Me, too," Jenna said as Seth's little sister came to mind. "Thanks for bringing it," she added. "My hips thank you, too. Not."

"I know. I couldn't resist. It looks like the girls have hit it off."

"Yes, it does. Thank heaven. Maybe now I won't have to hear about how bored Sabrina is and how much she misses her father."

"Girls and their daddies," Nora said.

"This daddy doesn't deserve her," Jenna said. No way did he deserve to have anyone think he was a loving father. "He's balked at the idea of me bringing her up to visit. And he sure hasn't said anything about coming down here to see her."

"The man's a disgrace," put in Aunt Edie.

"But her mom more than makes up for it," Nora said, putting them back in positive conversational territory.

"I'm trying," Jenna said. "I really want her to be happy here."

"You have to have gotten major mommy points with the hair," Nora said to her.

"Oh, yes. And I have to admit, it is cute. And I'd rather her have that than gauges in her ears."

"That will be next," Nora predicted. "Or at least a nose ring."

"I'll probably let her do that down the road, but right now she's too young." She was too young for a lot of things, including taking a bus all the way to Seattle to see her dad, which was her latest plan. Barely fourteen, going on twenty.

Was Jenna being too overprotective? She didn't think

so. Surely with kidnappers, perverts and terrorists everywhere there was no such thing.

Nora checked her watch. "I should dash back and see how everything's going at the parlor. Want me to leave Caroline here for a while?"

"Great idea," Jenna said.

"I'm sure they're both enjoying time together on their devices," Nora said with a grin and a shake of her head.

"Probably," Jenna agreed.

"We're going to dinner at the Porthole at six. How about I pick her up a little before?"

"Sounds good."

Nora left, Aunt Edie decided to relax with her latest gory mystery novel and Jenna, with some free time, headed for the beach.

She found Seth at the water's edge, a bucket by his side and a fishing pole in the water.

"Catch anything?" she called as she walked up to him.

"Crab in a pot." He gestured to the plastic bucket next to him.

Sure enough, there was a crab trying to make its way out. "I've never seen anyone fishing for crab," she said.

"You can buy a collapsible trap to put on the end of a pole," he said. "Gonna build a fire and cook me some crab. Want to join me?"

"I never turn down free crab. How about I start the fire?"

"Deal."

An hour later he had two crabs killed and cleaned and they were dipping cooked crab in butter melted in an old iron pot at the edge of the fire. "I never get tired of being out in the open air," he said, looking out to sea.

She could only imagine what that felt like after having

been deprived of his freedom for so many years. "You're doing a good job of making up for lost time."

"I'm trying." He pulled some more meat from a shell, leaned over and dredged it through the butter, then popped it in his mouth with a satisfied sigh. "When I was in high school a couple of buds and I would go north and camp at the beach. Dig clams, catch crab. Good times." His smile faded.

"Have you heard from them since...high school?" She already knew the answer.

He shrugged. "Nope. Haven't heard from any of my old friends. Guys aren't like women. They don't keep in touch."

Especially when one of them was alleged to have shot someone.

"New town, new friends," he said.

"New start," she added, thinking of her own life. "Do you ever think about making up for lost time by finding someone and settling down?"

"I was 'settled down' for a lot of years. Anyway, how'd that marriage thing work for you?" She made a face at him and he chuckled. "I rest my case." He sobered. "There's more than one kind of prison, Jenna."

She made a mental note later as she walked back to the house not to fall for Seth Waters. He was not in the market.

Brody probably was. And she had to admit she was drawn to him, as well.

*Don't fall for any man*, she lectured herself. There was a reason she wasn't in the market, either. These days the man market was full of cheats and liars. It was no place for a nice (not to mention dumb and trusting) girl like her.

# Chapter Fifteen

*To Do:*
*Install new carpet*
*Get pictures made into canvas prints for rooms*
*Stop by Sunken Treasures*
*See Tyrella for massage at four (wish somebody*
*could give me one)*
*Pick up Caroline*

Life at the beach was getting busy. The rooms at the Driftwood Inn were finally all painted and carpet installation happened on Monday. While the carpet man worked on installing, Jenna dropped off a thumb drive with some of her favorite pictures that Sabrina had taken at Beach Memories Pictures and Framing. Then she made a run to Sunken Treasures Consignments, where she did, indeed, find a lot of treasures—a couple of glass lamps stuffed with seashells, a lamp shaped like a lighthouse, another with a base shaped like a blue crab that was so pretty she hated to not keep it for herself. She snapped up a few framed posters from past Sand and Surf festivals and she also found a couple of nautical-themed queen-size bedspreads as well as a couple of sets of sheets, which would save her a little money on linens.

(Surely every little drop in the proverbial bucket added up.) The rooms were going to be funky and cute by the time she was done decorating them. She left the shop feeling downright excited.

Until she drove into the parking lot and the blue tarp roof greeted her. Sigh.

"I have got to find a way to get that gone," she said to Tyrella when she came in later for a massage.

"You will," Tyrella assured her. "Something's going to break for you, I just know it. I've been praying. And, girlfriend, when I pray things happen."

As if in cue, right after Tyrella left, Celeste called. "Stock up on the chocolate. Vanita and I are coming down for the weekend and we're going to get you the money you need for your new roof."

"Oh? How are you going to do that?"

"You'll see."

Oh, boy. What crazy scheme had her sister cooked up?

"Anyway, this is the Sand and Surf Festival, right? I haven't been to that in years. We can build a sand castle and find a pirate for Vanita."

"No pirate for you?" Jenna teased.

"No. You can't top a sexy cop who likes to dance."

"I'm surprised you're not busy with him this weekend."

"He had to work. Anyway, even if he didn't, I was coming down. I need a sister fix."

So did Jenna. It would be great to see her sister and one of her girlfriends and introduce them to the new friends she was making at the beach. "Make sure you get down here by seven so you can come hang out with the gang. We're painting tiles."

"Ooh, fun."

Yes, it would be. "Speaking of fun, I have to go pick up Sabrina's new beach buddy."

"She found a friend? Yay."

Yay was right. Jenna said goodbye to her sister and went to Nora's house to pick up Caroline, who was coming for dinner.

It was quarter after five when she got to Nora's house, a few minutes later than she'd intended.

Caroline met her at the door. "You're late."

Getting scolded by a fourteen-year-old was a little off-putting, but the kid was right. "Yes, I am," Jenna admitted.

"Oh, well. My mom's always late, too. I'm used to it," Caroline said, and breezed past her.

"How are you enjoying Moonlight Harbor?" Jenna asked as they drove to the house.

"It's okay. My grandma made me help dish up ice cream at the parlor today."

A regular teenage workaholic. "So, you didn't get to ride the go-carts or play in the arcade?"

"Oh, yeah. That was okay."

Damning with faint praise. "You'll have to visit Something Fishy."

"We do that every time we come here," said Caroline, and might as well have added, "Ho-hum."

Jenna tried again. "Well, you can't go wrong going to the beach."

"I guess." They pulled into the parking lot and Caroline pointed to the blue tarp on the roof. "That looks like the part of town where all the mobile homes are. My dad calls it Blue Tarp City."

Blue Tarp City. Charming. "It's temporary, until we can get the roof repaired."

"Yeah, it's kind of an old place. I bet it's got lots of leaks," Caroline said, and hopped out of the car.

Honesty was a good thing, Jenna reminded herself. But a girl could get too much of a good thing.

As soon as they were in the house, Caroline disappeared upstairs to hang out with Sabrina, and Jenna went to the kitchen to see if she could help Aunt Edie.

"Is our guest here?" Aunt Edie asked.

"Yes, she's upstairs with Sabrina."

"I'm so glad Sabrina has someone to keep her company," Aunt Edie said.

"Me, too," said Jenna. *I think.*

Pete had grilled burgers on Aunt Edie's ancient barbecue out on the back porch, and Aunt Edie had made potato salad, deviled eggs, and cooked up some corn on the cob. Caroline wrinkled her nose at the sight of the platter of burgers. "I'm a vegetarian."

"Oh, brother," Pete said, shaking his head.

Caroline frowned at him. "Eating dead animals is gross. I mean, you wouldn't want to eat your bird," she informed Aunt Edie.

"Eew," said Sabrina, and Roger, who was on his kitchen perch, supervising the meal as usual, began his request for whiskey. Jenna didn't blame him.

"Do you have any veggie burgers?" Caroline asked Aunt Edie.

"Sorry," Pete said before Aunt Edie could offer to make up a special order. "We're into dead animals here. Have some potato salad."

Caroline shrugged and helped herself to a large serving, along with several deviled eggs.

"Can you eat those?" Jenna asked.

"I don't want to be rude."

"Too late," Pete said, frowning at her. Ah, yes, the old pot calling the kettle black.

"How about a PBJ?" Jenna offered.

Caroline wrinkled her nose. "No, thanks. I haven't eaten those since I was a kid."

Jenna gave up and decided their guest would have to be happy with potato salad.

Caroline directed the conversation at dinner, telling everyone about her parents' cool house on Lake Tapps and regaling them with her family's vacation plans. "Mom and Dad are coming down here for the Fourth of July. They always do. Mom says my grandma expects it, so we have to."

"Being here for the Fourth of July is a treat," said Aunt Edie. "Picnics, beach fires, fireworks. Uncle Ralph loved his fireworks," she said to Jenna.

"Yes, he did," Jenna agreed, thinking fondly of those childhood holiday celebrations.

Caroline didn't appear that impressed. "After that we're going to Disneyland."

"I've never been to Disneyland," Sabrina said wistfully, and Jenna vowed to find a way to get her there before she graduated. Maybe a high school graduation present? Could she save enough money by then?

"You've never been to Disneyland? Seriously?" Caroline was shocked.

"Big deal," Pete sneered. "It's all fake. Fake castles, fake jungle. A big, expensive rip-off."

Caroline started at him as if he'd just uttered blasphemy.

Aunt Edie, always the diplomat, said, "Well, I think it's time for some dessert. Who'd like chocolate chip cookies?"

Cookies were consumed and then Aunt Edie suggested a game of cards. "Good idea," Jenna said. "Let's get the table cleared."

Sabrina got up and began to collect plates. Caroline stayed put and sipped on her lemonade.

"Aren't you going to help?" Sabrina asked her.

"I'm company. I don't have to," Caroline replied, further endearing herself to Jenna.

"Well, we like our company to feel right at home," Jenna said with a smile, and handed her a plate.

Caroline didn't smile back, but she got the message and got busy helping clear the table. As soon as the dishes were stowed in the dishwasher she said to Sabrina, "Come on. Let's go up to your room," and the two girls vacated the kitchen.

Aunt Edie looked disappointed. "I thought they'd like to play a game."

"You know teenage girls," Jenna said. "They like to be by themselves."

"You never did," Aunt Edie said. "You and your sister liked to do things with the grown-ups."

"I still do," Jenna said, putting an arm around her. "Let's play some canasta."

That perked her aunt up, and the rest of the evening went pleasantly.

"How was she?" Nora asked when she arrived at nine to pick up her granddaughter.

"She was fine," Jenna lied.

"No sign of those aliens?"

"Well…"

Nora shook her head. "She was such a sweet little girl. Oh, well. If we can get her to twenty without killing her we'll be fine."

Jenna smiled at that and called up the stairs for Caroline, which brought both girls bouncing down.

"See you tomorrow," Caroline said to Sabrina.

"We're going to the beach," Sabrina explained.

Instant friendship. Jenna had wanted her daughter to find someone to hang out with. She only wished she could have found one with better manners.

Caroline did thank Jenna for having her over, though, and without prompting, which made her grandmother smile. Maybe the aliens hadn't quite taken over yet.

With a friend to hang out with, Sabrina seemed happier. She even pitched in without complaining when they started moving furniture back into the rooms the next day.

Which was more than Jenna could say for Pete, who made mention of elder abuse more than once. "You're gonna kill me," he informed Jenna.

"You're too tough to die," she said. "Come on, pick up your corner of the mattress and let's get moving."

After lunch Sabrina disappeared and, not surprisingly, Pete did, too.

"The guy's useless," Seth said later as he and Jenna walked to the office to fetch a bed frame. "How did you end up with him, anyway?"

"Aunt Edie adopted him."

"Is there something between them?"

"Aunt Edie and Pete? At their age?" Oh, there was an image she'd never get out of her mind. "She's got to be ten years older than him."

"After a certain point age doesn't matter."

Did Aunt Edie have the hots for Pete? It would certainly explain how well she treated him. And the fact that he'd had a key. But... "No. If there was something between them he'd be living in the house instead of one of the rooms."

"Maybe. Or maybe your aunt didn't want you to know she was fooling around. Maybe she didn't want anyone to know."

Jenna frowned at him. "You've got a sick mind. You know that?"

He chuckled and shrugged. "Hey, you'd be surprised how many of my grandma's friends are shacking up. That way they each get to keep their social security benefits."

"Aunt Edie would never do that," Jenna informed him. "Uncle Ralph was the love of her life."

"And he's been dead how long?"

"No way would she be with Pete. She's got better taste than that."

"With women, you never know. You're not half as picky as men."

"If you mean we don't look on the outside the way you do, then true." Well, theoretically, anyway. Nothing wrong with a nice set of pecs and a six-pack.

He grunted. "Plus, you're all too trusting."

He was right there. She'd trusted Damien, believed him when he said he was out looking for materials for his sculptures. He'd been out looking, all right.

"Oh, well," said Seth. "The old guy isn't much help, anyway."

"Not with his bad back. He wrenched it when we were moving a mattress and now he won't be able to move for a week. I'm sure he'll recover enough to be able to get to the house for dinner tonight, though."

Sure enough. He showed up just as Aunt Edie was putting on some hot dogs to boil. Groaning and moaning from his morning's labors, of course.

Jenna was too tired to groan and moan. She ate a hot dog, took a hot bath and climbed into bed to read more advice from Muriel Sterling.

*Starting over can be hard work*, Muriel wrote. *But, in the end, it always pays off.*

"You'd better be right," Jenna muttered. She tossed the book aside and managed to turn off her bedside lamp with only a small groan.

No dreams for her that night. No pirates fighting over her. Just as well. She was too tired to entertain.

The next couple of days were filled with working on putting things to rights in the motel, and Jenna was pleased with how the rooms were turning out. Yes, most of the bedspreads were still a disgrace to bedspreads, but the new carpet and paint went a long way toward making everything look better. She'd have to order more bedding before they opened for business, and get the pool functional. And down the road she'd need to upgrade the flooring in the bathrooms, but for the moment she'd have to be content with what she'd managed.

She avoided looking at the roof on Friday afternoon when she made her way back to the house to shower. She'd already had enough ugly for one day when she'd written out Damien's check that morning. She wasn't going to add to it by thinking about that four-letter word *roof*, not with her sister and friend due to arrive soon. She was going to have fun and enjoy her weekend, and Herbie's written estimate could stay in her desk drawer where she'd stuck it.

Once she'd cleaned up she made some brownies for the evening's entertainment. "Those sure smell good," said Pete, who'd followed his nose to the kitchen shortly after she'd taken them out. That was what she got for not locking the back door.

Much as Pete irritated her, she didn't have the heart to deny him a brownie. She cut one off and handed it to him on a napkin. Good grief. She was turning into Aunt Edie.

He frowned. "Only one?"

"These are for the women tonight."

"They're probably all on diets," he said.

She caved and gave him another small one. "No more," she said in her firm mommy voice.

"Fine," he muttered, and helped himself to some milk.

If Pete deserved brownies, so did the man who was doing most of the work around there. She cut two generous pieces for Seth and put them on a paper plate.

"Who are those for?" Pete demanded.

"Seth."

"How come he gets such big pieces?"

"Because he does most of the work. And don't you be sneaking into those while I'm gone," she said as she left the kitchen.

She caught Seth just leaving his room, all showered up and wearing jeans and a shirt rolled up at the sleeves, flip-flops on his feet. He smelled spicy and yummy.

"Looks like you're ready for a night on the town," she said.

"Got a pool game at the Drunken Sailor." He pointed to the plate. "What's this?"

"Your reward for going the extra mile and helping me. I'd have brought more but I have to save something for when Aunt Edie's friends show up."

"This is enough." He took the plate, picked up a brownie and bit into it. "Good," he said around a mouthful.

"Thanks. It's a family recipe."

"Haven't had home baking in years," he said, and popped the rest in his mouth.

Poor Seth. He'd paid in so many ways for his little sister's crime.

"I'd better get back," she said. "My sister's coming in with one of my friends and they should be here any minute."

He nodded in the direction of a white Prius pulling into the parking lot. "Looks like any minute's here."

Jenna had missed seeing her sister, but she didn't realize how much until she saw Celeste's car pull in. Celeste screeched the car to a halt, then hopped out and, with a squeal, ran for Jenna. As always, she looked adorable wearing a flirty sundress that showed off her curves, her hair and makeup perfect. Jenna found herself wishing she'd at least done something with her nails. She was a mess.

Celeste didn't seem to notice. "You look superbuff," she said after they'd hugged.

"Hulking around mattresses and dressers and pulling up carpet will do that," Jenna said. "But this is the man who's been doing most of the heavy lifting."

"Not really," Seth said, and introduced himself. Vanita had joined them now, too, and she was looking at Seth the way he'd looked at Jenna's brownies.

"Jenna told me she had a new handyman," Celeste said, giving him one of her famous flirty smiles.

"Counting Pete, that brings me up to one and a half," Jenna said.

"I could always use a handyman," said Vanita. "Do you come as far as Lynwood?"

"Afraid not," he said.

"He's only helping out until he gets his business off the ground," Jenna explained.

"Oh, what's that?" Vanita asked.

"Mold removal," said Seth. "The houses down here at the water battle it a lot."

"And no, you don't have mold," Celeste said to Vanita, which made her frown.

"I could find some," she said.

"Sorry," Jenna said to Seth. "We don't let her out of her cage very often."

Vanita stuck out her tongue at Jenna.

"Good to meet you," he said. "You all have fun tonight." Then, with a polite smile and a nod, he left them.

"Wow," Celeste said, watching his truck drive off. "You weren't kidding when you said he's gorgeous."

"Probably taken, anyway. The good ones always are," Vanita grumbled.

Jenna started for the car. "Come on, let's get your stuff unloaded." And they had plenty to unload. "Good Lord, how many clothes did you need for a weekend?" she asked as she helped them carry in their things.

"There's more than our clothes in here." Celeste held up a beach bag with a wine bottle peeking out the top. "We brought chocolate, wine, chips and a makeover kit for you."

Jenna looked at her suspiciously. "What do you mean?"

"Have you looked at your eyebrows recently?"

Okay, so her sister had noticed.

"We're doing your hair and your nails tomorrow," said Vanita. "And I'm giving you my fabulous egg facial."

"I thought you two wanted to go to the festival."

"We do. But we're not taking you anywhere looking

like you've been shipwrecked for months," Celeste said. "You need rehabbing even more than the Driftwood."

"And what about this plan to make me a ton of money?"

"We'll get to that," Celeste said breezily as they entered the house. "Aunt Edie, we're here!"

There was no more talk of money-making schemes after that. Aunt Edie had to find out all about Vanita and get caught up on Celeste's life and latest this-is-it love.

Celeste produced a picture on her phone. "This is what I'm giving up for you and my sissy this weekend."

"He is handsome," said Aunt Edie.

He was every bit as hot as Seth. "That was a sacrifice," Jenna admitted.

"But you're both worth it," Celeste said, and hugged her aunt.

"I'm so glad you came down," Aunt Edie said. "It's like old times, having both you girls here. And lovely that you brought along a friend," she added, with a smile for Vanita.

"We did come with a purpose in mind," Celeste said. "We're going to kidnap Jenna tomorrow and take her to the casino."

"The casino?"

"Where else are you going to get your hands on a big bundle of money interest-free?"

Jenna blinked. "That's your big plan for getting money to fix the Driftwood?"

"Don't knock it," Celeste said. "One of the teachers at my school just won twenty thousand at the Silver Wings."

"Yeah, but how often does that happen?" Jenna argued. "The odds are always in favor of the house."

"Not always," Celeste insisted. "Anyway, all you've

been doing is working. You could use an evening out with the girls. Couldn't she, Aunt Edie?"

"Yes, indeed," said Aunt Edie. "I think you should go out and have some fun, dear."

"Speaking of fun, where's my favorite niece?" Celeste asked.

"She's out in the kitchen, putting together a special appetizer for you," Aunt Edie said. "She's becoming quite the queen of the kitchen."

"All right. Let's go see what she's making and get this wine chilling," Celeste said, and started for the kitchen.

"Sounds good to me," Vanita said, and followed her, leaving Jenna to trail behind.

The casino. That was the big idea. Great. She'd just wind up throwing away ten bucks. Which was all she had in her purse. If Celeste and Vanita wanted to eat dinner there she hoped one of them was footing the bill.

Sabrina was making shrimp dip to go with the crackers she'd set out on a platter. At the sight of Celeste, she abandoned her mixing bowl and ran to hug her.

"So, you've missed your favorite aunt?" Celeste teased. "The one who always brings you chocolate-covered sunflower seeds?"

Sabrina's eyes got big. "Did you?"

"Of course." Celeste held up her beach bag of goodies. She grinned at Jenna. "And I brought…"

"Fritos," Jenna said, her mouth watering as her sister pulled out the bag.

"Yes, because you can't go to the beach…"

"And not have Fritos," Jenna finished with her.

"Ah, traditions," Vanita said with a smile.

"Are you going to the Sand and Surf Festival with us tomorrow?" Sabrina asked. "My friend Caroline and me—"

"And I," Jenna corrected.

"And I are entering the sand castle contest."

"Well, then, we'll have to go and take tons of pictures," said Celeste. "Meanwhile, give me some of that shrimp dip. I'm dying to try it."

Shrimp dip was followed by pulled pork sandwiches. Of course, Pete joined the women for dinner, and was happy to let them know that he worked like a slave to help Edie and Jenna. "Even though I've got a bad back," he said. "But you gotta keep moving."

He certainly did that, usually as far away from a job as he could get.

"So, that's Pete, huh?" Celeste said later as they set up an extra cot in Jenna's room for Vanita. "He's a character. Do you think Aunt Edie's got the hots for him?"

"You're the second person who's asked that. But no. Eww."

"Hey, even old people need love," said Vanita.

"Aunt Edie's not that desperate," Jenna assured both them and herself.

"Let's hope not," said Celeste.

"Speaking of men, is your handyman taken?" Vanita asked. "He's gorgeous."

"I think you scared him," Jenna said to her.

"Hey, I was only being friendly."

"More like scary," Celeste teased.

"I think you'd have to fight Jenna for him," Celeste said, eyeing her sister.

Oh boy, warm cheeks. That meant a blush was forming. Jenna turned away, busy with stuffing a pillow in a pillowcase. "Nothing happening there."

"Yet," said Celeste. "But hey, if you don't want him, gosh, he is tempting."

"What happened to Mr. Perfect?" Jenna demanded.

"If things don't work out it's good to have a backup plan."

"He's not your type," Jenna said. Who was she kidding? Every man was her adorable little sister's type.

"Never mind him," Vanita said. "I want to see that Realtor who's been taking you to lunch. If you don't want him I wouldn't mind doing some house hunting down here."

Vanita and Brody? Oh, they wouldn't be a match. She was…funny and sweet and, well, who wanted someone funny and sweet these days?

Good grief. When had Jenna turned into Miss Piggy?

"I don't think she wants to share," teased Celeste the mind reader.

"I don't have a collar on anyone," Jenna said quickly. "And I'm through with men."

"Man," corrected both Celeste and Vanita.

"Anyway, we're just teasin'," Vanita said. "We wouldn't poach on your territory. Girlfriend code."

"Well," Celeste said, pretending to consider the idea.

The doorbell rang, signaling the arrival of the first guest of the evening. "Come on, you wild things. Let me introduce you to my new posse."

"Who can never take the place of your old posse," Vanita told her as they followed her out of the bedroom.

"Of course not," she said with a smile.

"By the way, Brittany would have come, too," Celeste said, "but she had to go to her cousin's wedding in Yakima. She says to let her know when you have your grand opening and she'll come down for it. Mom wants to come down, too."

If there ever was a grand opening.

Jenna pushed the ugly thought away and shifted into party gear, introducing Vanita and Celeste to Courtney and Annie, who had come bearing diet pop and some of Annie's caramel corn.

"This is amazing," Celeste told Annie, sampling some as soon as she'd set the bowl on the coffee table next to Sabrina's shrimp dip. "You could sell it."

"Maybe someday I will," Annie said.

Nora was the next to arrive, with Caroline, and she and Sabrina disappeared to the beach. But not before Nora gave them strict instructions to be back in the house by dark.

Tyrella and Patricia arrived, one right after the other, and once everyone was settled with drinks and had gotten a chance to meet the visitors, Nora produced their evening's entertainment. "Clear the coffee table and bring out those old TV trays of yours, Edie," she said. "And, Jenna, get that old drop cloth I asked you to dig out and newspapers. Tonight we're painting coasters with alcohol ink."

Celeste's eyes lit up. Like Jenna, she loved anything having to do with arts and crafts.

The project turned out to be fun. Nora had provided everything necessary, including aprons for everyone so nobody's clothes would get wrecked.

Jenna wound up making a set of tiles to use as coasters, done in shades of blue—a couple of seascapes showing the ocean at night under a full moon to represent her new home and a couple with trees in full bloom, bathed in moonlight.

"Those are lovely," Aunt Edie said. "You do have such flair."

Flair. Ha! Take that, Damien. "I think I'll give them to Mom for Christmas," Jenna decided.

"She'll love them," said her aunt.

"I suck at this," Vanita said, looking at her bleeding blobs of color in disgust.

Celeste looked over her shoulder. "Modern art."

"Mess," Vanita corrected.

"I'm not very good, either," said Annie.

"That's because you use all your genius in the kitchen," Courtney told her. "Someday she's going to have her own restaurant," she said to Vanita and Celeste.

"I just want my food truck," said Annie.

"Lose the creep and maybe someday you'll get it," Courtney said, and snapped her gum.

Annie bit her lip and stared at her tile. "I can't."

"Yes, you can. You can move in with the Gerards. Emma's over there most of the time, anyway."

"Okay, I'll leave my husband when you leave your job," Annie replied with a flare of uncharacteristic fire, and Courtney blushed and shut up.

"How's he doing?" Nora asked Annie.

"He missed his last two AA meetings," Annie said with a sigh.

"There's your proof he really doesn't want to change," Courtney told her.

"Did I mention that this is often a therapy session?" Tyrella said to Vanita.

"Girlfriends are the best therapy," Vanita said. "And they usually have really good advice."

"Honey, your man's no good," Tyrella told Annie. "That's no shame on you. It's just the truth."

"I understand your wanting to stay," Patricia said. "As women, we take our marriages seriously."

"Are you suggesting she stay with him?" Courtney looked outraged.

"No. I do understand her reluctance to leave, though. It's hard to let go. And scary."

"But if you leave maybe a new door can open up somewhere else," Jenna said. *And then you walk through it and fall through the rotten floorboards.*

"Everyone has to make their own decision when it comes to their personal life," Aunt Edie said later when the women had left and it was just her, Jenna, Celeste and Vanita. "You can't force people to do what's right for them. And chances are you don't even know what's right for them. That's something everyone has to figure out for herself."

Too bad you couldn't force people to make wise decisions. If you could, then both Mom and Gram would have saved Jenna from marrying Damien. But then she wouldn't have had Sabrina. Anyway, the past was the past.

What about the decisions she was making now? Had it been wise to come here? Was she crazy to keep trying to pull together her aunt's dream, even when it was looking more and more impossible? But it was her dream, too, now, and she wanted it to come true.

She was still awake long after Celeste and Vanita were happily snoring. She slipped out of bed, leaving Celeste to instantly spread out and take over her side, and walked to the window. The night was dark and still. The moon was casting the dune grass in a soft glow. She caught the flicker of a fire on the beach and had a strong suspicion who was out there.

She couldn't sleep. Everyone else was asleep. So, of

course, it was only natural she take a little midnight stroll. Right?

She pulled on some sweatpants, grabbed her flip-flops and slipped out of the room. She grabbed her fleece jacket from the downstairs closet and made her way over the dunes to where Seth sat propped against a log, legs stretched out toward the fire, drinking beer.

"Want company?" she asked, then joined him without waiting for an answer.

"I guess I do. I thought you and your sister would still be up yakking."

"She had one too many glasses of wine. It puts her out like a light. She approves of my hunky handyman, by the way."

"Hunky?"

Uh-oh. Had she just said that?

"You told her I was hunky?"

"Well, you are and you know it."

He chuckled. "So, you've been talking about me."

"I've been telling her about everyone down here."

"Oh." No more chuckling. "The house peddler, too, I guess."

"Yes. My friend Vanita wants to meet him. She claims she's looking for a rich man."

"How about you, Jenna? You looking for a rich man? It'd come in pretty handy right about now, wouldn't it?"

He sounded almost surly. "How much have you had to drink?"

"Not nearly enough." He took a final swig and crushed the can, tossing it aside.

"I hope you're going to pick up after yourself," she said primly.

"Of course I am. I never leave a mess. Only in my personal life," he added sourly, and grabbed another can.

Yes, he'd been drinking too much.

"How was the hen session?"

"You're good with the flattery tonight, aren't you?"

"That's me. I guess I'm a little jealous. Nice to have friends. Women are good at that kind of thing."

"We are more communal than you men," she said.

"So, how's the commune?"

"Good. We're trying to convince one of our members to leave her husband."

"I'm sure he'll appreciate that."

"He's abusive."

Seth popped the tab on his beer. "If he is, then she should get out of there. I met enough of those assholes in the joint."

"Maybe you should talk to her," Jenna suggested, suddenly inspired. "Give her a man's perspective."

"She doesn't have any other men in her life? No dad? No brothers?"

"I don't know."

"She probably does. She's just not ready to listen."

Jenna frowned into the fire. "Aunt Edie said as much."

"Your aunt's a smart woman."

"Most of the women in my family are."

"But not you?"

"Not always."

"Well, I'm not one to talk," he said.

"You were young." And noble.

"And dumb. And impulsive. Being impulsive gets you nowhere."

She found herself wishing he'd be impulsive and kiss her.

He shifted his gaze from the fire to her face. "I've

learned a thing or two about not giving in to every crazy thought that comes into my head."

She was having a crazy thought right now. "Yeah?"

"Yeah. What are you doing out here, Jenna?"

She realized she'd been leaning in toward him. She seemed to be making a habit of that lately. She pulled back. "I couldn't sleep."

"I hear warm milk's good for that."

"I don't like warm milk."

"What do you like?" His voice was soft.

She liked slow dancing and soft kisses on her neck, gentle fingers on her skin. Her eyes drifted shut.

She felt his breath on her cheek. Then he was whispering in her ear. "Go to bed."

No kiss. Instead, he stood and poured his beer out on the fire, making it hiss. "It's getting late."

# Chapter Sixteen

*To Do:*
*Party with the girls*
*Don't go crazy on the slots*

Sabrina was off to the beach right after breakfast to start work on her castle with Caroline, but Celeste decreed that there would be no castle visiting until her sister had been turned into a living work of art.

"You're getting awfully bossy in your old age," Jenna teased her. "Who's the older sister here?"

Celeste grinned. "It's my turn to be bossy. You bossed me around enough when we were kids." She sobered. "You also watched out for me. I used to have nightmares," she explained to Vanita. "She always let me sleep in her bed when that happened."

"That was no big deal," Jenna said, shrugging off the cloak of nobility. Noble was taking the fall when your sister shot someone.

"She was always helping me," Celeste continued. "Taking on mean girls who picked on me, helping me with my homework."

"Yelling at you when you read my journal," Jenna added.

"Okay, so it wasn't all perfect. But close enough. Now, quit stalling and let's get those brows waxed."

The eyebrows were waxed, the nails got painted and the hair color updated. Then out came the eggs and lemon juice for Vanita's egg facial.

"My face is set in cement," Jenna complained, trying to move her mouth.

"She can still talk. Put on more," teased Celeste.

At last Jenna was prettied up, painted up and had slipped into shorts, a nice top and sandals. "Oh, yeah. There's the sister I know and love," Celeste said, giving an approving nod.

The Sand and Surf Festival was a big deal with what seemed like every foot of beach occupied by a team of builders erecting some sort of sand creation, and people from all over the county present to enjoy the spectacle. In addition to all manner of traditional castles, there were other creations, too—Neptune's Court, complete with mermaids and starfish; a farm sporting a pig, a horse and a farmer and his wife and sand cornstalks; a sand submarine; trolls; and sand sea monsters galore. Jenna's favorite was a sandscape labeled Reverse Safari that had jungle animals in a jeep checking out the humans' campsite.

The revelers strolled among the various creations, enjoying everything from cotton candy to shaved ice. At the water's edge, children and dogs raced back and forth, playing tag with the tide. Several people had set up campsites and were enjoying picnic lunches or a beach fire.

"This is too cool," Vanita said, looking around. "I want to move to the beach. Maybe I'll open up a little shop down here."

"Or write that novel you keep talking about writing," said Celeste.

"Next summer I'll come down and spend my whole vacation," Vanita vowed. "I'll stay at the Driftwood Inn and write. Fresh air, walks on the beach. No office drama. This is the life," she said to Jenna.

"Oh, yeah. No drama here," Jenna said, thinking of everything she still had to pull together if she and her daughter and Aunt Edie were going to survive.

They'd all gotten corn dogs and were watching Sabrina and Caroline try to keep their castle walls from collapsing when Brody found them. He was wearing shorts, a T-shirt and sandals and Ray-Bans. Oh, he did fill out a T-shirt nicely.

"Who's that?" Vanita asked as he waved to Jenna and started walking toward them.

"I bet that's the Realtor," Celeste said, checking him out over the top of her sunglasses. "You sure are getting a nice man collection, big sister."

"I'm not collecting," Jenna replied. No, sir. Not her.

Introductions were made and plans shared. "The casino, huh? I didn't know you were a high roller," Brody said to Jenna.

"I'm not. I'm not even a low roller. This is my sister's crazy idea. She's sure I'll win big and live happily-ever-after."

"You could land in that lucky five percent," Brody said. "But I wouldn't hold my breath."

"Oh, well. It will be fun, anyway," Celeste said.

"They've got a good restaurant there. How about I take you ladies to dinner?" Brody offered.

"Great idea," Celeste said before Jenna could answer. "That way you'll have more money to invest in the slot machines, sis."

Invest, right. "I'm only taking ten dollars," Jenna said.

"In that case we may as well have dinner late, because you won't be staying long afterward," Brody said.

"Fine with me." Okay, that made her sound like a party pooper. "But it'll be fun to go out to dinner."

"Are you sure you want to pay for all of us?" she asked Brody later as Celeste and Vanita helped the girls with their sand castle.

"Absolutely. I'm looking forward to hanging out with three beautiful women. Anyway, it's been a while since I've been to the casino. Should be fun."

It probably would. With Sabrina spending the night at Nora's house, Jenna was free of responsibility. And Aunt Edie was currently engrossed in a gory murder mystery, so she didn't have to feel guilty for leaving her alone.

Well, not too guilty, anyway. She suspected that her aunt would have loved to tag along and get some cheap thrills watching her lose her ten dollars, but Brody was already paying for dinner for three women. She didn't want to add another meal to the tab.

The Sea Winds Resort and Casino was a mile outside of town, set back from the highway and perched on the shore. Much of the area had once been marsh. Now it was all landscaped, with smooth, paved road.

"Check out the speed limit," Brody said.

"Twenty-one miles an hour? That's weird," said Celeste.

"Twenty-one. Oh, I get it," said Vanita. "Like the card game. Pretty clever."

And just plain pretty, Jenna thought as they drove over a pond thick with lily pads.

The resort hotel was big and impressive, and the restaurant provided a million-dollar view. Being at the beach, it also offered plenty of seafood, including salmon, crab cakes, crab legs and shrimp scampi. The women all ordered crab legs. Brody opted for steak.

"I so need to move to the beach," Vanita said after she'd popped the last bit of crab in her mouth.

"I can make that happen," Brody told her.

"Maybe you'll win big tonight and come up with a down payment," Celeste said. "Speaking of winning, let's hurry up and finish so we can get to the casino."

*And say goodbye to our money*, thought Jenna. But, oh, well. What was ten dollars when she needed thousands?

They finished the meal with chocolate lava cake and coffee, then made their way to the other end of the resort.

The casino area of the resort was one gigantic playland of brightly lit machines and people happily pushing buttons on them. Zips and whirs greeted Jenna as she and her posse and their escort walked in. This was the goofiest idea her little sister had come up with since the time she begged Jenna to go into Seattle and audition for *America's Got Talent*. Jenna had refused to wear a giant yellow duck costume and sing "Rubber Ducky," and Celeste had pouted for a week.

At least Celeste wasn't asking her to make a fool of herself publicly. And all those big, grown-up toys did look fun.

"It has kind of a carnival air, doesn't it?" she said to Brody.

"Yeah. It does. And it can be exciting. But you can lose on carny games, so I never spend beyond what I've set as my limit for the night."

"Well, mine's ten dollars," Jenna told him.

"Twenty," Celeste corrected her, handing over a ten. "It's the least I can do to help Aunt Edie. If you win big, I'd better get a free room for life."

"I'm not sure how big you're going to win on twenty bucks," Brody cautioned. He dug out his wallet and took out a twenty. "So I'll contribute something to the cause."

"Me, too," said Vanita, pulling out another ten.

"Guys, I don't want to take your money," Jenna protested.

"Never turn down free money," Celeste told her.

"We'll all split it if I win," Jenna promised. As if she would. Everything she knew about gambling wouldn't even fill a shot glass.

"Nah. You keep it all. You need it," Brody said.

"Can I get that in writing?" she teased.

"Hey, I'm a man of my word."

"Now, come on, let's see if you get lucky," Celeste said, moving her toward the back of the room where the dollar machines were.

They passed a machine with a pretty picture of perfume on it. "Parfume Adore," she read, and started for it.

"No, that's only a penny slot," Celeste said, pulling her away. "We want a bigger jackpot."

"Oh, look, there's Willy Wonka."

"Keep moving, high roller," said Brody. "We want the dollar slots."

At last they were to the big-money machines. "If you're going to win anything you're probably going to win it on the mega slot," he said.

"I had no idea you were such a big gambler," she said to him.

He shrugged. "I come in once in a while and drop a few dollars here or at the card table."

The slot machine he and Celeste positioned her in front of wasn't as cute as the one with the perfume bottle on it, but once she started playing it was certainly as much fun as the other machine had looked.

"Hit the max button," Brody instructed her. "It's going to cost you more but the payout is better."

Gambling 101. "Okay," Jenna said, ready to try.

The numbers on the right-hand side of the machine began to climb.

"Whoa, you're already up to a hundred and seventy bucks!" cried Vanita.

Small potatoes. She needed more than that. Jenna kept playing.

"Two-hundred and eighty," Vanita reported. Then, "Oh, no. It went down."

Jenna pulled away her hand. "I should stop."

"Keep playing," Celeste commaded. "Go big or go home."

The numbers began to climb again, the machine partying with every match of the bars, serenading them with synthetic drums and violins. Jenna's rooting section began to go crazy and that brought some observers.

"You know, I won nineteen thousand dollars just last week," a woman reported.

The numbers continued to go up, right along with Jenna's heart rate. This was insane. She should quit before she lost everything she'd won. She could envision a little Tyrella sitting on her shoulder, saying, "No good can come of this. Gambling is dangerous."

Well, all of life was a gamble.

"Oh my gosh, look what she's up to!" Vanita squealed.

The pressure! Jenna was going to pass out any minute. Or have a heart attack. Or both.

"Quit while you're ahead," advised one woman.

"No," said the nineteen-thousand-dollar winner. "You're on a roll."

"Winner, winner, chicken dinner," Celeste said. "And a new roof."

Jenna hit the max button again.

Finally, to her astonishment, she did hit it big. Eighty thousand dollars. The machine lit up like the Fourth of July and locked. Jenna gasped.

"You just won eighty thousand dollars!" Celeste shrieked, and grabbed her and hugged her as their crowd of onlookers hooted and applauded.

"I can't believe it," Jenna said. "Somebody pinch me."

"Don't tempt me," Brody said with a grin.

"Thank you!" Jenna said to Celeste and Vanita. She was laughing and crying. Then she was jumping up and down.

"We did it!" Celeste cried, and she and Vanita hugged Jenna and they all jumped up and down together.

Then Jenna turned to Brody. "Thank you!" she cried, and kissed him. It was a quick kiss but it packed a wallop. Whether that was because she was high from having won a bundle or because she'd just kissed a handsome man was hard to tell. Either way it was quite a kiss.

"No, thank *you*," he said, still grinning.

"What happens now?" she asked him.

"Security's been verifying your win. You'll probably see them any minute."

Sure enough. Two security guards appeared bearing a bucket of ice with a bottle of champagne in it. "Congratulations," one of them said to Jenna.

"I won," Jenna said to her. As if she couldn't see for herself. Well, Jenna was seeing for herself and she still couldn't believe it."

"What happens next?" Vanita asked the guard.

"I get a new roof," Jenna crowed. "A roof, a roof. I get a roof!"

"We have a form for you to fill out," said the guard. "We'll need your social security number and your address."

"Millionaire Acres," Celeste cracked, and she and Jenna hugged each other again.

Not only were there papers to be filled out, there were pictures to be taken. And Facebook announcements to be posted. Winner, winner, chicken dinner, Celeste typed under the selfie of all of them that she posted on Jenna's page. Guess who's buying margaritas for everyone?

Margaritas, nachos, more dessert, they had it all. The food was on the house, thanks to the casino host, who was Jenna's new best friend. Jenna opted to pick up a check the next morning rather than leave the casino with that much loot in cash, even though a security guard would have escorted them to their car.

"Anyway, that way when I come back tomorrow I'll know I didn't just dream this all," she said when they finally walked back to Brody's car. "Are you guys sure you don't want some? You all contributed to the cause."

"I don't need any," Brody said.

"It's yours," Celeste said to her. "That's why we came down. Remember?"

"I know, but I feel guilty."

"You shouldn't," Vanita said. "It's not like you're spending it on yourself."

"Well, in a way I am."

"Investing in your business," Vanita reminded her. "You're not going to buy a car or a boat."

"Although a boat would be nice," said Celeste.

"And it seems like a lot," Brody said, "but the tax man is taking a big chunk."

Oh, yeah. Him.

Still, she'd have enough money left to save the Drift-wood Inn, and that was all she cared about.

Brody dropped them off, Celeste and Vanita singing the Velvet Revolver version of "Money," complete with bass riff, Jenna giggling and turning in circles.

"We'd better be quiet," Jenna said as they made their way up the front steps. "We don't want to wake Aunt Edie."

Aunt Edie was asleep, but she hadn't gone to bed. They spotted her in the living room, in Uncle Ralph's recliner, an afghan over her lap, the TV playing some ancient movie.

"Should we tell her now?" Celeste whispered to Jenna.

"Maybe we'd better wait until morning," Jenna whispered back. "The excitement might be too much for her. She'll never get to sleep."

As it turned out the excitement was too much for Jenna. No beach fires that night, so she had to content herself with lying in bed, planning the grand reopening of the Driftwood Inn.

The first rays of sunlight were drifting into the room when she finally fell asleep and it was nearly nine in the morning before the smell of coffee woke her. "I smell breakfast," she mumbled.

"Good," Celeste mumbled back from her side of the bed. "Go have some for me."

"You don't want to be there when I give Aunt Edie the good news?"

"Okay. Give me a minute to pry my eyes open."

They showered and dressed and left Vanita still dead to the world, hurrying downstairs as if it were Christmas morning. In a way, it was.

Pete was lounging at the kitchen table, inhaling a cinnamon roll and Sabrina was at the stove, stirring a batch of Aunt Edie's made-from-scratch hot chocolate, and Roger was supervising from his perch and begging for whiskey.

"My, you girls had a late night," Aunt Edie greeted them. "Did you have fun?"

"You're not going to believe what happened," Celeste said.

"Aunt Edie, I think you'd better sit down," Jenna said, and led her aunt to the kitchen table.

Aunt Edie looked suddenly worried. "Jenna, you didn't lose a lot of money, did you?"

"Just the opposite. I won."

Aunt Edie was beginning to connect the dots. Sit down…won. "How much did you win?" she asked, her voice tremulous.

"Eighty thousand dollars," Jenna said, and the excitement of the night before came bubbling up again.

"Holy crap," Pete said, setting down his coffee mug to gape at her. "Who wins that much at the casino?"

"Me," Jenna said. She'd have to tell Tyrella all her praying had worked.

"We're rich!" Sabrina exclaimed. "Can I have a cell phone?"

"We'll see," Jenna said.

"I am fourteen. And we can afford it now."

"Yes, we can." Which didn't mean her daughter would be getting one. Not until she was driving and really needed one.

"I can't believe it," Aunt Edie said, shaking her head. "It seems too good to be true." And then she began to cry.

Jenna rushed to kneel in front of her. "Don't cry, Auntie. It's all working out."

"I know. Oh, Jenna, there are so many things you could do with that money."

"I want to help you," Jenna said. "I want to bring the Driftwood Inn back to life."

"You dear girl," Aunt Edie said, and hugged her.

"Now we can go home and visit Daddy," Sabrina said, joining them at the kitchen table with her mug of hot chocolate.

Oh, boy. This again. How long was she going to have to cover for Damien?

"As soon as we get the motel up and running," Jenna promised. Surely after a few more weeks Damien would be missing his daughter enough to grant a visit.

Sabrina frowned. "I only want to go home for a weekend."

"We'll talk about it later," Jenna said.

"I could go back with Aunt Celeste," Sabrina said, looking brightly at Celeste, who wisely kept her mouth shut.

"We'll see," said Jenna.

Sabrina scowled. "I know what that means. It means no."

"It means we'll see," Jenna said, her patience leaking.

"Fine," Sabrina snapped. She set her mug on the table with a thump and stamped out of the room.

"Pretty is as pretty does," Jenna called after her, quoting one of her mother's favorite sayings.

"You're so mean," her daughter's voice echoed back at her.

"You can take a weekend off and go home," Aunt Edie said to Jenna.

"This is my home now," Jenna told her. "And we'll go back to visit her lame-o father when we have things squared away here and not before."

So there. Winner, winner, chicken dinner.

# *Chapter Seventeen*

*To Do:*
*Buy thank-you gifts for Celeste, Vanita and Brody*
*Call Top Dog Roofing*
*Pinch myself!*

Jenna still could hardly believe her good luck of the night before. Was it really true or had she dreamed it?

No, it was true. When she went back to the casino there was the check, waiting for her. She went straight to the bank on Monday, waved it under Sherwood Stern's nose and deposited it in Aunt Edie's business account, to which they'd added Jenna's name.

Old Sherwood was suddenly so helpful. "Anything you need, just let us know."

What she'd needed he hadn't been willing to give. "I think we're fine now," she said.

"Well, we're here for you," he told her.

Right.

She met Tyrella going into the bank as she was coming out, and shared her good news.

Tyrella wasn't quite so jubilant.

"You don't sound very excited for us," Jenna said in surprise.

"Of course I'm happy for you. I'm just not a big fan of gambling, is all. I remember when that fancy resort was nothing more than a Quonset hut on the beach. Now look at it. How do you think they got their money? You were lucky you didn't lose a fortune."

"But that's just it," Jenna said happily. "I didn't. You did say you were going to pray. And you said you had no idea how the money was going to come."

"You've got me there, sister. I'm glad for you. But take my advice and stay out of the casino from now on."

"I will," Jenna said, and crossed her fingers behind her back.

Then she skipped off to call Top Dog Roofing and do some shopping. Her fellow gamblers had all been insistent they didn't want a share of her winnings, but that didn't mean she couldn't buy them all thank-you gifts.

At the Beachcomber, she picked up goodies for her sister and friend—candles embedded with tiny starfish and shells, necklaces with a silver shell dangling from them and matching earrings.

Her next stop was Cindy's Candies, where Cindy Redmond was happy to guide her in her choice. "Brody is crazy for saltwater taffy," she said, handing Jenna a little wooden basket to fill with taffy from the huge bin in the center of the shop.

Jenna walked around it, reading the flavors in the various sections. "Peppermint, buttered popcorn, coconut, lime, orange, huckleberry, chocolate. This is overwhelming."

"He likes them all, but I know for a fact he's partial to coconut," said Cindy. "Fill a basket for yourself, too, so you can celebrate your big win. On the house."

Jenna filled a basket for Brody, then took a small

amount for herself, not wanting to take advantage of Cindy's kindness. She vowed to pass the goodies on to her daughter so she wouldn't give in to temptation and eat them. In addition to taffy, she also purchased chocolates in the shape of clamshells for Celeste and Vanita.

At In the Suds she bought them fancy soap and scented oil, and picked up a couple of T-shirts from Something Fishy sporting a crab. The slogan over it said Never Crabby at the Beach. That was for sure. Not anymore.

She decided to round out her goody collection with gift cards from Beans and Books for the next time Celeste and company came down.

Rita Rutledge gave her a warm welcome when she walked in. Rita was only a couple of years older than Jenna, a casual dresser, happy to wear jeans and a Beans and Books T-shirt with her logo of an open book and a cup of coffee. She was divorced with a son in college and waiting for her dream man to walk through her doors, someone who was a reader and a coffee addict, she'd informed Jenna at the chamber meeting.

"Did you come in for your free latte?" she asked.

"That, too," Jenna said. "Actually, I also want to get a couple of gift cards. Thank-yous for my sister and girlfriend. And Brody." Brody liked coffee. She'd get him some champagne, too.

"Brody, huh? Well, well. You move fast."

"It's not what you think," Jenna said. "They all bankrolled me at the casino last night and I won big."

"You did?"

Jenna nodded. "Enough to get a new roof for the Driftwood."

"Wow. That is truly amazing." Rita turned to the Gen-X man in the jeans and casual shirt and flip-flops.

"Did you hear that, Aaron? This sounds like a story for the *Beach Times*."

He looked up from his phone, where he'd been busily texting. "What?"

"Jenna, this is Aaron Baumgarten. He's the star reporter at our local paper."

"The overworked reporter," he amended. "There's just me to do local and sports and Piper Lee, who handles the home and garden stuff."

"And who writes the advice column. She writes as Dear Miss Know-It-All, and her identity's supposed to be top secret," Rita said. "But we all know it's Piper."

"How much did you win?" Aaron asked. Jenna told him and he let out a whistle. "That's a nice chunk of change. What are you gonna do with it?"

"I'm going to finish renovating the Driftwood Inn."

"She's Edie's niece," Rita added. "She's come down to help run the place. This would be a nice human interest story."

"You're right. Plus, it would be the biggest news since Clem Jackson got stranded on Pebble Point at high tide. How about we do a story on you? We could get a picture of you standing in front of the Driftwood along with your aunt."

"That would be great," Jenna said. A good way to get the news out that the old Driftwood would soon be back in business. And Aunt Edie would probably love having her picture in the paper.

"How would this afternoon work for you?" Aaron asked.

"Fine." She could hardly wait to get home and tell Aunt Edie that they were about to be famous.

Before she went home to share the news, she stopped

by the drugstore for gift bags and tissue paper and assembled her thank-you gifts. On her way back, she bought champagne and delivered it and his other gifts to Brody at his office.

"You didn't have to do that," he said, but she could tell by his smile and the way his eyes lit up when he saw the expensive bottle and the taffy that he was pleased nonetheless.

"And you didn't have to give me money or pass up the chance to take your share of the winnings," she said. "I owe you a lot more than champagne."

"Yeah?" He gave her a lecherous grin. "Like what?"

"Like lifelong gratitude."

"That'll do for a start. How about dinner out?"

"If you let me pay."

"If you think I'm going to turn down dinner with a beautiful woman just because she's offering to pay, you can think again," he joked. He held up the champagne. "Maybe I'll save this to drink on the beach after."

Which would mean there were more tipsy kisses in her future. Brody Green and a moonlight beach. Danger, Will Robinson. Danger.

"You don't want to have to share that. Go ahead and drink it all," she said lightly, then laughed at his phony disappointed expression.

Back at the house, Celeste and Vanita were thrilled with their gifts and Aunt Edie was delighted to get in the paper. "I'd better go put my face on."

"You look great," Jenna told her.

"Oh, no. I need more lipstick," she said. "And I can't be caught in this old sweatshirt."

"She's so cute," Vanita said as Aunt Edie went up the stairs to get gorgeous.

"She's a treasure," said Celeste. "She and Uncle Ralph were one of the best parts of our childhood." She popped one of Cindy's chocolates in her mouth. "Oh, I'm in heaven."

"You didn't need to do this," Vanita said to Jenna as she, too, raided her little box of chocolate shells.

"Oh, yeah, she did," Celeste said, pulling out another chocolate.

"Where's Sabrina?" Jenna asked. "I've got goodies for her, too."

"She's on the beach with Caroline. I heard something about taking selfies in their bathing suits."

"Oh, boy," Jenna said, thinking of inappropriate Facebook posts.

"Don't worry," Celeste said. "We already warned her to keep her bathing suit on. By the way, she's been working on me to take her with us when we go back tomorrow."

"Pass me that chocolate," Jenna said, and sunk onto the seashell chair.

"Give me whiskey," said Roger from his cage.

"That, too," Jenna said. "I swear, she never gives up."

"Determination is a good thing," Vanita said.

Jenna sighed. "Not when it comes to seeing her dad. He's not interested."

Celeste's brows drew together. "Seriously?"

"Don't look so surprised," said Jenna. "You know what he is." Self-absorbed and immature.

"But that's a new low."

"He claims he can't take her right now. He needs time to…whatever."

"I take it Sabrina doesn't know."

Jenna shook her head. "I keep putting her off. At some

point he is going to want to see her. He's a jerk but he's not totally heartless. Anyway, what did you tell her?"

"I told her no," said Celeste. "It really wouldn't work out this time. Somebody would need to bring her back and Mom's working. Once we get home I'm taking off for two weeks in Icicle Falls."

"And it's not with me," put in Vanita. "I'll give you three guesses who she's going with."

"The cop?" Jenna guessed.

"That would be the one. I think this is it," Celeste added. "He's so...strong. He's going to teach me how to shoot a gun," she added.

Jenna remembered her encounter with the pepper spray. "You're liable to shoot yourself in the foot."

Celeste made a face. "Very funny."

"I wasn't joking." Jenna regarded her sister. Celeste was cute and fun and bubbly. And she tended to rush into things. "Isn't this moving along kind of fast? I mean, you haven't been going out all that long."

"Long enough," Celeste said.

Jenna couldn't help thinking about how quickly she'd rushed into marrying Damien.

"You sound like Mom," her sister added, which told Jenna that their mother had reservations, too.

"I just don't want to see you get hurt." *Learn from me, little sister.*

"Don't worry. I'm not planning on racing down the aisle."

That didn't mean she couldn't get her heart broken.

"I really think I love him," Celeste said softly.

"As long as he loves you back," Jenna told her.

"What's not to love about her?" Vanita put in.

True. Celeste was all heart. Jenna hoped this latest romance bloomed into something serious. It would be nice if at least one of them could find true love.

Aunt Edie came back down the stairs, resplendent in a black dress spattered with big, red roses that she'd accented with a red scarf and red flip-flops adorned with a miniature red bouquet of silk red carnations that covered most of her slightly crooked toes.

"How do I look?" she asked.

"Hot," Celeste said. "You look smokin', Aunt Edie."

She did look cute, like the kind of little old lady you'd want to hang out with. Which, of course, was exactly what she was.

Aaron showed up shortly after, along with the paper's photographer. He had plenty of questions for Jenna. How long had she been in Moonlight Harbor? What had brought her down?

*I needed a life.* "I had a chance to come and help my aunt bring this wonderful, old motel back to its former glory.

"What makes the Driftwood Inn so special?" Aaron asked.

*My aunt.*

"We were one of the first ones here," Aunt Edie said, answering for her. "There's a lot of history here. A lot of people have made happy memories at the Driftwood Inn."

"And we want to make more," put in Jenna.

"What are you going to do with your winnings?"

"We're going to finish renovating, starting with a new roof," Jenna said. *And we're going to finally get to stop worrying.*

"You're pretty lucky," Aaron said. "Winning all that money."

Jenna looked at her sweet aunt, her sister and good friend, thought of her wonderful mom and grandparents, of the great life she'd had growing up. All those blessings far outweighed the bump in the road that was Damien.

"Yes, I am," she said.

"Okay," Aaron said at last, "how about a picture of you and your aunt in front of the motel?"

"I'm ready," Aunt Edie told him.

Next to her aunt, Jenna looked boring in her denim skirt and black top. But that was okay. She had no problem with her aunt outshining her. This was Aunt Edie's moment.

They were saying goodbye to Aaron and the photographer when Seth arrived. "You look nice, Mrs. Patterson," he complimented Aunt Edie as he got out of his truck.

"Thank you," she said. "We just had our picture taken for the paper. They're going to do an article about Jenna. She won eighty thousand dollars at the casino last night."

Seth's eyes popped wide. "No shit. Oh, sorry, Mrs. Patterson."

"Don't be," she said. "And yes, no shit."

"Looks like you can get a new roof now," he said to Jenna.

"And maybe even a few other things we need," she added. Oh, yes, she was one lucky duck.

"I guess I'd better get busy and power wash the place, then, so we can start painting," he said. "Paint and a new roof and you're good to go."

"And new mattresses for the beds and new linens and probably some new flooring in the worst of the bathrooms," Jenna said. Everything had seemed so overwhelmingly impossible only two days ago. Now the sky was the limit. Well, sort of. They still had a bank loan to pay off and a petri dish swimming pool to fix. But this unexpected infusion of cash would get them started in the right direction.

"It'll get there," Seth assured her.

"Meanwhile, we need to celebrate," Aunt Edie said. "Let's have a beach fire before Celeste and Vanita have to leave tomorrow. Seth, you can join us, can't you?"

"Thanks for the offer, but I can't. You have fun, though."

"Well, next time, then," Aunt Edie said. "I'm going to go inside and bake some cupcakes," she said to Jenna, and hurried across the parking lot to the house.

"Your aunt's stoked," he observed.

"The place means so much to her," Jenna said. "Now it's going to finally get fixed up again. Uncle Ralph would have been happy, too."

"Pretty unusual, winning all that money."

"Which means it was meant to be."

"I guess you're right," he said.

"You're going to be missing a major party tonight," Jenna told him. "Whoever she is, she must be something special to keep you away." Was she fishing for deets? No. Yes.

He made a face. "Yeah, right."

"So you didn't have plans for tonight?"

"I have plans to not crash your family party."

"You think it will be only family? I can guarantee you, Aunt Edie's going to invite half of Moonlight Harbor."

He shook his head. "Family and old friends, that's how it should be."

"New friends don't count?"

He turned and started for his room. "See you later, Jenna."

"Celeste and Vanita will be disappointed with no eye candy there."

"Invite the house peddler," he called over his shoulder.

"Maybe I will," she called back.

In fact, maybe she should. She pulled out her cell phone and made the call.

"Sounds fun," Brody said. "I'll be there to feed you s'mores."

Not only was Brody there. So was Pete, Tyrella and Nora, along with her husband and Caroline. Naturally, everyone brought something to contribute to the feast. Brody brought wine coolers, Nora brought the makings for s'mores, Tyrella brought chips and pop and Pete… brought himself.

The men built a bonfire that was a pyromaniac's dream and, as everyone roasted hot dogs, Aunt Edie reminisced about the past. "You know, Ralph didn't know a thing about building when we first came down here, but he figured he could learn. We both did. I helped put on the roof, and I got pretty good with a hammer. We had so much fun painting the place and ordering all the linens. And let me tell you, we were so excited when our first guests pulled in. It was a mother and father and two little boys. And you know, they came back every year until the father got a job in Nebraska. I even got a Christmas card from them that first year. Then there was the professional wrestler. He showed your Uncle Ralph a few moves. It was all fun and games until Ralph broke his nose."

"Good old Ralph," said Bill. "He was a character."

"Yes, he was," Edie said, and her smile turned wistful.

"Who else stayed here?" Jenna asked, wanting to turn her aunt's thoughts in a happier direction.

"Let me think. Oh, yes, there was the bride who

locked herself in the bathroom on her wedding night. The poor thing."

"Why did she do that?" Sabrina asked.

"You'll have to ask your mother later," Aunt Edie said.

"Oh. She was afraid to have sex," Caroline said knowingly. "I'm not going to be afraid. I'm going to have sex on my sixteenth birthday."

"We'll see about that," Nora told her, and Jenna determined to find a friend for her daughter who would be a better influence even if she had to put an ad in the paper.

"You know, Pat Boone came to town several times to play golf," Aunt Edie continued.

"Did he stay here?" Jenna asked.

"He did, one night. I got his autograph."

"Who's Pat Boone?" Caroline asked.

"He was a crooner," Aunt Edie said. "Such a handsome man." She sighed happily. "Who knows who we'll have to come stay with us once we're ready for business again. I can hardly wait to find out."

"Well," Brody said, raising his bottle, "here's to the future. Hope you get lots of movie stars and singers."

"I just want lots of paying customers," Jenna said. She didn't care how their guests earned their money just so long as they shared it with the Driftwood Inn.

The party finally broke up at ten-thirty. "I have to open the store at eight," Tyrella said, standing and stretching. "That means bed for me."

"We should go, too," Nora said to Bill, and he nodded.

"Do we have to, Grammy? Can't I spend the night?" Caroline begged. "Sabrina can loan me her toothbrush."

Jenna wasn't all that excited for Caroline to stay, but Aunt Edie said, "We've got extra toothbrushes."

"All right," Nora said. "If it's not an imposition."

"Not at all," Aunt Edie said cheerfully, ever the good hostess.

Jenna vowed to have a talk with her later and explain about the birds and the bees and fourteen-year-olds.

"Come on, girls. I'll help you get settled. My old bones have had enough of sitting on logs for the night," Aunt Edie said, "and it's getting past my bedtime, anyway."

Pete, too, decided he'd had enough, and gallantly offered Aunt Edie the use of his arm for balance.

Brody made no mention of leaving, so Celeste and Vanita, Cupid's little helpers, decided they, too, needed to go in, following the others off through the dune grasses. Then it was just Jenna and Brody.

"Is it past your bedtime, too?" he asked.

"Almost."

He scooted closer to her on the blanket. "Stay out a little longer." He pointed to the sky. "We've got a full moon. I can stir up the fire."

He already was. Which meant it was time to go in. "Oh, I don't think—"

"Come on, Jenna, hang out a while. Give me a chance to seduce you."

His voice was teasing but she knew he was serious. "You're a heartbreaker, Brody Green."

"Who keeps telling you this stuff?"

"As if someone had to tell me?"

"You've got to have figured out that I've got feelings for you."

"And you know I'm not going to rush into anything." No matter how tempting. If she kept saying that to herself long enough, hopefully she could stick to it.

"Who's rushing?" he said, and nuzzled her neck.

"Am I interrupting something?"

The deep voice behind them made Jenna jump away from Brody with a squeak.

He frowned at Seth Waters, who stepped over a log and settled on it. "As a matter of fact, you are."

"Sorry. Saw the fire and figured the party was still going. Jenna invited me."

"The party's over," Brody told him.

"Yes, it is," Jenna said, standing up. "Will you two douse what's left of the fire?"

"There's not much left," Brody said, sounding grumpy, and Jenna had to chuckle. "So, how about that dinner you promised," he asked.

Nothing like making a statement to the other guy. And putting her on the spot. "How about tomorrow night?" she offered.

"Sounds good," he said.

She nodded and then scooted off to the house, anxious to get away from an embarrassing situation.

"I thought you'd be out a lot longer," Celeste said when she came into the bedroom.

Celeste and Vanita were sitting on her bed, playing a game of pig with a pair of Aunt Edie's dice.

"Seth came out."

"Two good-looking men wanted to hang out and you just left?" Vanita rolled her eyes. "Honestly, all that pretty is wasted on you."

"It was awkward." Jenna plopped on the bed next to her sister. "Can I play?"

"Have you got some quarters?"

"You're playing for money?"

"That's how you play the game. Remember? Anyway, you just won eighty thousand dollars. Can't you spare a few quarters?" Celeste teased.

Jenna went to her purse and dug out three quarters. "This is all I have."

"The way your luck's been running, it's all you'll need," Celeste said.

She was wrong. Jenna lost her quarters in the first five minutes. "Looks like my luck has turned." She wouldn't be going back to the casino anytime soon.

"It's turned in a good way when it comes to men," said Celeste. "You've got sexy man overload."

"They both seem really nice," said Vanita.

"They are."

"So, which one are you going to pick?" Celeste asked.

"Neither. I think one heartbreak in a lifetime is enough."

"You can't give up on love, sissy," Celeste said to her. "One of those men could be the perfect man for you, your chance to be happy again. And I want that for you."

"We both do," Vanita added.

"I know. Don't worry. I'm going to be happy." And the best way to do that was to protect her heart.

"At least go out with them a bit, have some fun," Celeste said. "You can do that. And who knows where it will lead?"

Surely not where things had eventually led with Damien. Except Brody was a player. She'd figured that out early on. And Seth?

*There's more than one kind of prison.*

Seth's words came back to remind her that he wasn't in the market for a serious relationship. He was probably damaged for life, and any woman who fell for him would wind up damaged, too.

*Don't worry, heart. I'll watch out for you.*

She hoped she could keep that promise.

# Chapter Eighteen

*To Do:*
*Pick up extra copies of the paper*
*Pay bills*
*Pinch myself again*

Celeste and Vanita left Tuesday morning, Vanita needing to get back to work the following day and Celeste anxious to get ready for her trip with her new man. Sabrina watched them go with a frown.

"I could have gone back with Aunt Celeste and Grandma or Daddy would have brought me back," she said to Jenna, her tone accusing.

Of course it was Jenna's fault that this latest plan had fallen through. "We'll get back. Don't worry."

"We won't," Sabrina predicted. "We're gonna be stuck here forever."

"Yes, they'll find our sun-bleached bones on Moonlight Beach."

Her daughter saw no humor in that remark and flounced back into the house, probably to eat more of Aunt Edie's coffee cake.

Jenna sighed. She didn't blame Sabrina for getting impatient. This was getting ridiculous.

What was she waiting for, darn it all? She'd get the roofers started and then she and Sabrina would go back to Lynwood for a visit. And if Damien wanted his next check he could come pick it up…from his daughter.

She pulled out her phone, looked up the number for Top Dog Roofing and gave Herbie a call. "How soon can you start?"

"A couple of weeks," said Mr. Top Dog.

"That long?" Somehow, she'd envisioned him and his crew coming right over with their nails and shingles.

"We're busy in the summer. Everybody wants to get their roofs fixed before winter sets in. Don't worry, though. We'll make sure you get the Driftwood watertight before the next big storm," he promised.

Okay, roof repair scheduled. She gave herself permission to take a break. She'd surprise Sabrina and take her back home for the Fourth of July. They could leave early in the morning and stay clear through the weekend. After that afternoon, she didn't have any massages lined up for the rest of the week, anyway. She smiled at the thought. Come morning she'd be Good Mommy, the best mom in the world.

Until the next time her daughter was mad at her.

She did some bookwork, made some calls. Once she finally came in for lunch it was to find her daughter long gone. "She said she was going over to Caroline's," Aunt Edie reported.

"At least she's telling people where she's going now," Jenna said. "I hope she can find some other friends to hang out with soon, though."

"Yes, I agree," said Aunt Edie. "That one's a little…"

"Yes," said Jenna.

"Nora's girls were so sweet. This next generation,

they're all rude and spoiled. Not Sabrina, though," she quickly added.

"No, she only wants to be spoiled," Jenna said. "Oh, well. At least she's got something to do today. I think, if you don't mind, tomorrow I'm going to run her back to Lynwood so she can see her dad and her best friend. And the new boy in the old neighborhood, which is probably another reason she wants to go back."

"Boys, they are a powerful magnet," Aunt Edie said.

"Yes, they are," Jenna said, remembering Johnny Milton, the boy of her dreams when she was twelve. Johnny had been Sabrina's age, tall and scrawny with sea-blue eyes and blond hair like Brody's. Maybe that was part of Brody's attraction. He was like a grown-up, filled-out Johnny Milton. "Anyway, I think a visit will do us both good." Jenna was ready for some mommy time of her own.

"It will. You've been working awfully hard."

Yes, the more Jenna thought about it, the better she liked the idea of taking a break. Meanwhile, though, she had massages scheduled and a dinner date.

Patricia Whiteside was her first client, and she came bearing a copy of the paper with the article featuring Jenna, Aunt Edie and the Driftwood. "I thought Edie would want an extra copy," she explained. "I'm so happy for you," she continued after Jenna had thanked her, conveniently neglecting to share that she'd already picked up half a dozen copies herself. "It's been a struggle for Edie these past few years and I'm glad to see the cavalry has arrived."

Jenna smiled as she laid a warm towel on Patricia's back.

"Oh, that feels good. I'm liking this already. You know, I've never in my life had a massage."

"Then I'd say it's past time," Jenna told her. "Your body will thank you for it."

Patricia's body did thank her, and she, in turn, thanked Jenna by giving her a generous tip on top of her fee.

"You don't need to do that," Jenna protested.

"I know. Now that you've won all that money, you're feeling very rich. But trust me, it goes quickly when you're in the hospitality business. You can always use extra cash."

Jenna would use this little chunk of change to gas up her car for her trip home.

Her next client was Laurel, the hostess from the Porthole, who had called out of the blue that morning. "Standing on my feet all day kills my back," she'd explained. "Although now that you've won all that money maybe you won't be in business anymore."

It seemed that everyone in town read the *Beach Times*. "All that money has to be invested in the motel," Jenna explained. "I'll still be doing massage." She had bills to pay. Besides, she liked doing massage, loved helping people feel better.

As Laurel lay on the table, Jenna working on her legs and back, the real reason she'd come leaked out. "It was nice of Brody to bring you into the restaurant the other day. How do you know him?"

Of course. Checking out the competition. "We met by accident."

"He's the president of the chamber of commerce," Laurel explained. "He likes to get new people involved."

And he liked to get involved with new people.

"Brody and I have gone out off and on for the last year," Laurel continued.

It looked like they were currently off.

"We took a little break."

Uh-huh. *Little* being the operative word. "Sometimes that's a good idea," Jenna said, and hoped Laurel wasn't working a nightshift at the Porthole that night. Maybe they'd go to Sandy's.

"I think we're going to be getting back together, though."

Definitely they'd go to Sandy's. Judging from Brody's behavior, only one of them was thinking of getting back together, and it wasn't him.

"So, tell me, how long have you lived here?" Jenna asked, hoping to move the conversation in a new direction.

"Three years. I'd been in a long-term relationship and I was pretty broken up when it ended. Brody saved my sanity."

Back to Brody again.

"I hear you're divorced," Laurel added casually.

Underlying question: And in need of having your sanity saved? Jenna could feel the woman's muscles tightening under her hands.

"Pretty recently. I'm in no hurry to jump into anything."

Laurel relaxed. "That's smart."

But when Frank, Officer Mushroom, came in for a late-afternoon massage and asked her to go out with him afterward for some fish and chips she gave him a different story. "I'm sorry, Frank. I'm seeing someone."

"Oh." He took a moment to digest that. "Who?"

"Brody Green."

Frank gave a disgusted grunt. "The guy's got bucks to throw around. No point trying to compete with him."

"Honestly, I'm not interested in dating anyone seriously," she said, lest word suddenly get back to Laurel.

"Yeah, I get it. Love's a crap shoot. Hey, speaking of craps, I heard you won big at the casino."

By now everyone in town seemed to know, whether they'd read the paper or not. "I did."

"Pretty cool," he said. "You oughta do something fun with the money. I mean, I know the article said you want to fix up your aunt's place, but you oughta save out some—take a trip, buy a car. Something."

"By the time we put a roof on the place, that will eat up most of the money," Jenna said.

"Eighty K for a roof? Man, that's grim."

"Not quite, but close. Plus I do have to pay taxes on all that money."

"Yeah, good old Uncle Sam. Oh, well. I'm glad you won. The money will be going to a good cause. Your aunt's lucky to have you here."

"And I'm lucky to be in such a great town," she said. "Everyone here is so nice."

How nice would Laurel be once she learned Jenna and Brody had gone out to dinner? She'd probably hear of it somehow, no matter where they went. That was how small towns worked.

Once Jenna got Frank out the door, she got herself ready to go. "Is Sabrina still over at Nora's with Caroline?" she asked her aunt.

"She must be," Aunt Edie said. "I haven't seen hide nor hair of her. If she calls and asks to stay to dinner what should I say?"

"Say yes. I'll pick her up on my way back." And give her the good news about going to Mom's.

Seth was power washing the motel when she walked out to her car. She waved at him and he turned off his machine and sauntered over.

"You look good," he said, taking in her little black dress and sandals.

He looked pretty darned good himself, standing there in jeans and flip-flops. Considerate of him to lose his shirt. So many men shaved their chest, but not Seth, and that tasteful amount of dark chest hair was like frosting on a cake.

"Thanks," she said, and restrained herself from saying anything lustful and tacky.

"Going out to dinner?"

As if he didn't know. "It's a thank-you dinner."

"Looked like you were already thanking him pretty good last night."

"Are you jealous?" she teased.

"I don't do jealous."

"There's nothing to be jealous of, anyway," she said with a shrug. "This is just dinner. He gave me some gambling money and this is payback."

"Generous of him. So, out gambling together, huh?"

"My sister and Vanita and I were going. He invited himself along. He wouldn't take any of my winnings, so this was the least I could do. I owe him."

"You don't owe that guy anything," Seth informed her. "And he's not after a free dinner."

She knew what Brody was after but she played dumb. "Oh, and what would that be?"

"You know," Seth said with a frown. "Just because he gave you a few bucks it doesn't mean you have to sleep with him."

Could he have put it any more bluntly? "That would make me, what? Oh, yeah. A hooker." She frowned at him.

His cheeks flushed. "That's not what I meant."

"Well, I'd love to stand around and try to figure out what you meant, but I need to go," she said, giving his arm a condescending pat. "Thanks for the insight."

"Hey, I didn't mean to insult you," he said as she walked away.

The only reply she gave him was a wave of her hand. But he did get her thinking. It was hard to be friends with men, especially good-looking ones like Brody. He obviously wanted more.

What if she gave him more? Then what? Brody was divorced, probably not in the market to get married again. Neither was she, but if they got involved, well, she'd get involved. She'd invest her heart and then when the love market crashed, there she'd be, jumping off the Moonlight Harbor pier.

"Keep your boundaries," she told herself as she drove to the address he'd given her.

Brody's house was a two-story dream right on the beach, painted a dark gray with white trim; it had a crenelated roof and a wraparound porch.

"Nice house," she said as he climbed into her trusty old car. It was hardly the same as his slick ride but she'd insisted on picking him up as well as paying for dinner.

"It'll do," he said.

"Fake modesty," she teased.

"Yeah, it's a great house. We always hold the Beach Dreams summer party in it. Good view from the balcony. I'll have to show you later."

"I've seen the ocean."

"Not from my house," he said with a smile. "You know, you didn't have to do this."

"Just like you didn't have to turn down my offer to share my winnings. Are you okay with Sandy's? I know it's not as expensive as the Porthole, but I figured it was safer."

"Safer?"

"If Laurel's working tonight she might grab a steak knife and stab one of us. Preferably you."

"Ah. So, you think there's something between Laurel and me."

"Laurel thinks there's something between Laurel and you. She came in for a massage today. I guess you two used to be an item?"

"For a while."

"She's under the impression that you're getting back together again."

"We're not."

"I wonder where she got that idea?" Jenna mused.

"We went out a couple of times before you came to town." He turned in his seat. "Look, Jenna, I've lived here a few years. I've dated people. But there's no one I'm serious with, and there's only one woman I'm seriously interested in."

"Laurel will be glad to hear that."

"And it's not her."

"Don't make it me, either, Brody, okay? I've had enough hurt to last a lifetime."

"I have no intention of hurting you," he said softly.

"Sometimes people get hurt whether you intend it or not."

"I'm not like your ex. I never cheated on my wife."

"What did happen?"

"She got tired of me working so much. So I worked less, and then I made less, and then she got tired of that. Then she got tired of me. Found herself a man who'd already made his fortune."

"She dumped you for another man."

He shrugged. "She dumped me first, then found another man. It's a small distinction but an important one.

I came here to the beach, slowed down a little and lived a little more. Dated some nice women and proved to myself that the problem in the marriage hadn't been me."

"Now that you've decided that, what's next?"

"Whatever happens," he said. "I'm open to the possibilities. I hope, at some point, you will be, too."

"I tell you what I'm open to," she said. "I'm open to proving to my ex that I matter, that I'm not something you use and then throw away. I'm open to making life better than it was six months ago."

Brody smiled. "I'd say you've made a good start on that."

She smiled, too, thinking of her plump bank account. "I'd say so, too."

Dinner was pleasant—steamed clams and salad for her and prime rib for him. He had wine; she stuck with water.

"I'm driving," she said.

"That's just your excuse. You don't want to get tipsy and find yourself in my arms under a full moon," he said with a wink.

She could think of worse places to be, for sure.

"Don't you want to come in for dessert?" he offered once they got back to his place.

"You bake?"

"No, but I've got ice cream. And a nice, comfy couch." To stretch out on.

"What do you say?" He slipped a hand up and gave her neck a friendly little rub.

"I say you should take up massage therapy. You're pretty good."

"I'm good with my hands."

Oh, yes, he was. And he was just getting warmed up. "Not interested. Remember?" But he was sure making it hard for her to remember.

"Yet. You forgot to add *yet*. Did I mention I'm irre-sistible?"

"You didn't need to. But I really do need to get going. I'm taking Sabrina to see my mom tomorrow and I've got a few things to do."

"Gotcha. Well, then, thanks for the meal."

"Thanks for making me rich, even if it's only temporary."

"Glad to help." His hand still on her neck, he nudged her toward him. "A lot of guys don't kiss on the first date but I'm not one of them."

What the heck. What was a kiss or two between friends?

She let him kiss her. And kiss her again. And play with her hair. *Boundaries, Jenna. Boundaries.*

That was the only body part he was going to get to play with. Even though what they were doing was way better than ice cream, she pulled away. Forced herself not to lick her lips.

"You're easy," she teased.

"I can be easier."

"I bet you can. Good night."

He chuckled and tapped her on the nose. "I can also be patient. Good night."

Once he was out of the car, she allowed herself to touch her fingers to her lips in an effort to recreate those kisses. Brody Green knew how to kiss a woman.

He probably knew how to do all kinds of things. Sigh.

She was still buzzing when she pulled up in front of Nora's house. Her husband, Bill, answered the door. She could hear the TV in the background.

"I just stopped by to pick up Sabrina," she said.

He looked puzzled. "She's not here."

"Oh. Did Nora take her home already?"

"I guess. Caroline was the only one here when I got home at five."

"But I left at five and Sabrina was here. Aunt Edie said she came over this afternoon."

"Let's ask Nora. Nora!"

A moment later Nora came out of the living room, looking relaxed in shorts and a top, a glass of lemonade in her hand. "Oh, hi, Jenna. This is a nice surprise."

"I actually was looking for Sabrina."

"She went home hours ago," Nora said. "The girls were in for ice cream and then Sabrina was going to go back…" Her words fell away right along with every ounce of blood from Jenna's face.

"She didn't come home?" Bill guessed.

Jenna shook her head. She suddenly couldn't breathe.

"She's probably home right now," Nora said. "Let's call and check with Edie."

"You'd better come in and sit down," said Bill.

Jenna felt suddenly light-headed. She staggered into the living room and fell onto the couch and watched as Nora called her aunt.

"Hi, Edie. Is Sabrina there?"

Jenna knew by the expression on her friend's face what the answer was. Terror gripped her. "Oh, no."

"Don't worry," Bill told her, and went to the kitchen.

"No, we're just trying to figure out where she is. Don't worry," Nora said into her phone. "Jenna? She's here with me. Don't you worry. We'll get this sorted out."

Jenna bit her lip hard, trying not to cry. Bill returned with a glass of water and handed it to her. She thanked him and set it aside.

"Don't panic yet," Nora said. "Let's see what Caroline knows."

Caroline was summoned to the living room, and from the smirk on her face it was evident she knew something. "I haven't seen her since this afternoon. She wasn't happy," Caroline informed Jenna.

"What did she say?" Nora asked sharply.

Caroline shrugged. "Just that her mom's mean."

"Was she running away?" Jenna asked. She could hardly get the words out without choking.

Here came another shrug. "I would."

"If you know something you need to tell us," said her grandfather.

"Why would I know something?" the girl hedged.

"Caroline Anne, you tell us right now what you know or I'm calling your mother to come get you."

"Fine with me. It's boring here."

"Yeah, ice cream, free play on the arcade games and the bumper cars," Bill said in disgust.

"Mom's taking me to Disneyland," Caroline retorted.

"She needs to take you to juvie," Bill growled. "Get on up to your room."

Caroline treated them to one final shrug and left.

"Where could she be?" Jenna cried, tears running down her cheeks.

"Don't worry. We'll find her," Nora said. She grabbed her phone and made another call.

Ten minutes later, a policeman was at the door. This was a new one Jenna hadn't met and he introduced himself as Officer Fleming. A fatherly looking man with salt-and-pepper hair, he was kind and reassuring but Jenna wasn't fooled. She knew what happened when young girls disappeared.

"When did you last see her?" he asked.

"This morning," Jenna said, and burst into sobs. Now maybe she'd never see her daughter again. If only she'd let her stay behind with Mom. If only she could turn back time. If only, if only.

"Okay. Any other place she could possibly be?"

At seven-thirty at night? She should have been home, playing cards with Aunt Edie or scribbling in her journal. Her journal! Maybe that held a clue.

Jenna gave the officer the picture she had of Sabrina in her wallet and an Amber alert was put out. Then she broke the sound barrier getting back to the house.

"Did you find her?" Aunt Edie called as Jenna raced up the stairs.

"Not yet," Jenna called back. *Please, God, let us find her. Let her be okay.*

Sabrina had left behind her journal. There it sat on her dresser. Jenna had never been one to snoop through her daughter's things. Maybe she should have.

She turned to the last page and read.

My mom is the most selfish person in the universe. She could have let me go back with Aunt Celeste and then come and gotten me later whenever she wanted. Grandma wouldn't care how long I stayed. I know Aunt Celeste would have taken me. She was just afraid to say yes cuz of Mom. It's not fair. I want to go see Marigold. I want to see Daddy. Caroline says I shouldn't sit around and feel sorry for myself. I should do something. I'm going to.

Oh, Lord. Jenna bolted off the bed and ran back down the stairs.

"Where are you going?" Aunt Edie called.

"To find Sabrina. Don't worry!" As if telling someone not to worry ever worked. Especially when a child's safety was at stake.

A few moments later she was back at Nora's house. Nora answered the door. "Did you find her?"

"No, but I have a strong suspicion of where she's gone. I need to talk to Caroline again."

Caroline was called back down. The smirk was gone now and she was looking sullen. Jenna guessed the threatened phone call had been made and the child was getting shipped off. Good. Even if she weren't, there would be no more Caroline encounters at the beach for Sabrina. Ever.

If Jenna could find her.

She fought back a wave of nausea and forced herself to be patient. She sat on the sofa and beckoned Caroline over.

The girl sat on the edge of the sofa and looked at her warily.

"Caroline, I know you don't want to rat out Sabrina, but I need to make sure she's safe," Jenna said, forcing herself to sound calm. "Can you just tell me, did she go back to her dad?"

The sullen look was now replaced with something akin to pity. "She misses him. She wanted to go back."

"I know. I was actually going to surprise her and take her tomorrow."

"You were?"

"I was. Did you girls by any chance walk down to the bus stop toward the end of town?"

Caroline bit her lip.

It was all the answer Jenna needed. She reached out

and touched the girl's arm. "It's okay. You kept her secret. But you know what would have been even better? To tell me what she was planning. Now we don't know if she's safe."

Caroline's eyes filled with tears and she nodded. "I'm sorry," she whispered. Then she turned and ran back up the stairs to her room.

"Good," Nora said, watching her go. "Maybe she's learned a valuable lesson today."

Jenna knew *she* had. She should have done a better job of meeting her daughter's needs.

Her phone rang. "Bad Boys," Damien's ringtone. She didn't give him time to say anything. "Is Sabrina with you?"

"Yeah, we're driving to your mom's place right now. What the hell were you thinking, Jenna?" he demanded.

"She ran away. Didn't she tell you that?"

"What? Sabrina, were you out of your mind?"

"She missed you and she wanted to see you," Jenna said. "I've been making excuses for you and she finally got tired of being put off. I should have told her the truth. She'd never have run away if she'd known what a selfish shit you are, that you don't want to see her."

"I never said that. Don't put words in my mouth."

"Let me talk to her," Jenna demanded.

"I don't think so. She's upset."

"What do you know or care about our daughter's feelings?" Jenna yelled. But no one was there to yell at. He'd ended the call.

"Is she okay?" Nora asked.

"Yeah. My ex has got her. They're on their way to my mom's." Jenna let out her breath and allowed her heart to slow down. She felt a million years old. She called her aunt to let her know Jenna had been found; then, after thanking Nora for her support, returned to the house.

Aunt Edie looked like she, too, had aged in just one hour. "Thank God nothing happened to her," she said after Jenna had filled her in.

"I swear, I'd put her on restriction for life if I didn't feel so guilty," Jenna said.

"Young girls don't always think things through," Aunt Edie said in Sabrina's defense. "Their brains are still developing."

"And while her brain is developing I'm developing an ulcer," Jenna said, leaning back against the sofa cushions.

An hour later her mother called. "I wanted you to know that our girl is now in bed, recovering from her big adventure."

"I'm not sure *I'll* ever recover," Jenna said.

"I guess she had one harrowing moment. It certainly scared me hearing about it. Some old guy tried to pick her up in Quinault where she had to change buses, but a woman took her under her wing and helped her transfer to the right one to get back to Seattle. She called Damien and you know the rest."

"All except for where she got the money. I never gave it to her."

"I'm afraid you won't like this part. She stole it out of Aunt Edie's purse."

Once again, Jenna felt ill. "Oh, no."

"We already had a talk about that. And about how worried you had to have been. She's sorry she upset you and she promises to write Aunt Edie a note and ask her forgiveness."

"Yeah, well, she'll be doing more than that. She'll be

babysitting and mowing lawns until she's paid Aunt Edie back every penny."

"A good idea," Mel approved. "Why don't you let her stay with me for a while and I'll supervise her rehabilitation."

"What, reward her for her bad behavior?"

"No, just let the dust settle."

"You know what's so sad about all this? I was planning to surprise her and you and bring her for a visit tomorrow."

"Maybe I'll lay on the guilt and mention that. We'll have another talk in the morning. And now it gets worse."

How could it?

"She told her father that she knows you'll pay Aunt Edie back since you won all that money at the casino and now you're rich."

Another wave of nausea hit. Damien knew about the money. If he knew how much Jenna won she'd be hearing from his lawyer. That revocable settlement had sounded like such a good idea at the time. "This way, if your income takes a dip you can renegotiate," her lawyer had told her. There'd be some renegotiating, all right.

But maybe… "Did she tell him how much?"

"I'm afraid she did."

"Oh, boy."

"Maybe he won't do anything."

And maybe Jenna would wake up in the morning and discover she'd turned into a mermaid. "I've got to go, Mom."

"Of course. You probably need to process all this."

"No, I need to go throw up."

# Chapter Nineteen

*To Do:*
*Give up*

In spite of the fireworks up and down the beach, the Fourth of July had been lackluster for Jenna. She'd sat on Aunt Edie's back porch along with her aunt, Pete and Seth and stared unseeing at the enormous bursts of color splashing against a black sky. Aunt Edie had made Italian sodas and baked brownies. Jenna had passed on the brownies and only taken a couple of sips of her drink.

"She'll miss you and come back," Aunt Edie had predicted.

"I don't know. She's wanted to be with her father all along." And, after the Fourth, that was where she was going. Damien's parents were making room for her in the spare bedroom. It would be shopping trips with the rich grandma by day and horror movies at night with Damien and Aurora the princess. "He's perfect, you know," Jenna had added bitterly.

"Perfect until he isn't," Seth had said. "If he's anything like you say he is, her eyes are going to get opened pretty quick."

That made Jenna sad, too. She hated the idea of her daughter having to be disappointed in her father.

"It will all work out," Aunt Edie had assured her.

Yes, one way or another. It was that "another" Jenna was worried about.

Her worries increased when she got the letter from Damien's lawyer on Friday. *As there has been a change in your circumstances*, it began, and then went downhill from there.

She called her lawyer. "Well, this could be a problem," he said, "because of the revocable settlement."

The cursed revocable settlement! That had been meant to work in her favor. Now it was screwing her over. "What do you suggest I do?"

"You could go to court and fight him. Of course, you'll spend some money doing that," the lawyer cautioned. "I suggest you pay him to make him go away. We can negotiate something with the stipulation that he can't increase the maintenance. No coming back to the well again."

"Okay, make a deal," she said, and ended the call with a frown.

"Is he going to take all your money?" Aunt Edie asked, making Jenna almost drop her phone.

She'd been sitting on the back porch, sure her aunt wouldn't hear, but there Aunt Edie stood in the doorway, her brow furrowed.

"Have you been eavesdropping?" Jenna teased. That would teach her not to go far away from the house for important calls. She'd been so caught up in her anger she'd never even heard the door open. She managed a smile. *See? Everything's fine.*

Aunt Edie didn't smile. *Who do you think you're kidding?*

By the time their friends arrived for the usual Friday night gathering neither of them was in a party mood. In fact, Aunt Edie didn't look well.

Their discouragement didn't go unnoticed. "Has something bad happened?" Nora asked.

"You could say that," Jenna replied, and shared the latest development. She tried to gloss over the dire implications, but her aunt wasn't stupid. Watching the old woman's lower lip tremble made Jenna want to cry.

"It's sick and wrong," Courtney said. "What are you going to do?"

Jenna knew what she'd like to do. Send the poor excuse for a man that was her ex a bomb in the mail. "I'm going to settle before he hauls me into court."

"Men are such bums," Courtney said in disgust.

"Not all men," Nora corrected her.

No, only the ones in Jenna's life.

"Between Damien and Uncle Sam I'm not going to end up with enough money to put the roof on the Driftwood," she confided to Tyrella when her aunt wasn't listening.

"Don't you give up. We'll go back to praying."

Jenna was too discouraged to pray and said as much.

"That's why you've got friends," Tyrella said.

"And which one of you has a big pile of money sitting around with no place to go?"

"Don't worry. We'll think of something," Tyrella said, and hugged her.

Short of robbing the bank, Jenna didn't see any way of getting that money.

After the women went home and Aunt Edie went to bed, she made her way to the beach with some newspaper, matches and kindling. With the aid of the moon she found a couple of pieces of dry wood and made herself a fire. Who knew how much longer she'd be able to stay, how many more beach fires she could enjoy?

"I thought this fire belonged to you," said the familiar deep voice. Seth sat down on the log next to her.

"I needed a beach fire." Actually, she needed a fairy godmother.

"There's something about the beach," he said. "You come here and your troubles can't find you."

"Yeah, right. Mine found me just fine."

"Only temporarily. The tide can wash them away."

"That was very poetic," she complimented him.

"Yeah, that's me. Poetic." He draped an arm around her. "What's wrong now? Your kid's safe, you're rolling in dough. How come you're not smiling?"

"Because my ex found out I was rolling in dough. There won't be enough left to roll in by the time he's done."

"That sucks," said Seth, the master of understatement.

"I needed that money. Oh, Seth, what am I going to do?"

"I wish I had a solution for you."

"Nothing's turned out the way I expected. I thought we'd all be so happy here. I thought I could help Aunt Edie. Instead, we did all this work for nothing and I can't finish the renovations. Nobody will stay at the Driftwood and we'll lose the place and that will break Aunt Edie's heart. And my daughter…" Didn't want to be with her. Jenna's throat constricted and she couldn't finish the sentence.

Seth tightened his hold on her and pulled her against him. "I'm sorry, Jenna. I'm really, really sorry. I wish I could make it all better for you. I wish life was like the movies."

Now she was sobbing, and he kissed the top of her head and continued to murmur that it would all be okay. But it wouldn't. The fire finally died and she stopped crying. He put out the embers, took her hand and led her back through the dunes to the house, neither one speaking.

Finally, at the stairs to the back porch, he turned her to him and kissed her. It melted her, not with passion but with tenderness. Yes, if only they'd met years ago, before Damien, before Seth's troubles. He'd have become an English teacher and they'd have come to the beach every summer. He'd have helped Uncle Ralph keep the place up and they'd have both been there for Aunt Edie and there'd have been no need for huge chunks of money to repair the damage done by the sands of time. If only you could go back.

But you couldn't. You couldn't even hang on to the present. That quickly moved into the past, slipping away. She clung to Seth in an effort to hold the moment, but at last he broke them apart.

He held her firmly by the arms. "You're a brave woman, Jenna. Remember that. No matter what happens, remember that."

No, she wasn't brave. She bit her lip and nodded and went into the house. She wanted to climb into bed and pull the covers over her head just like her daughter would.

Her daughter.

Jenna cried herself to sleep.

It was a troubled sleep, with her on the beach, trying to run in the sand and getting very little traction. People kept rushing past her—Damien, holding hands with Aurora and waving and laughing, her daughter chasing after them.

"Wait, Sabrina!" she called. "Don't leave me."

But Sabrina kept running, her hair, once again reddish gold, flying in the wind.

And there went Aunt Edie. She was a wraith, floating on the wind, crying. Her cries turned into howling and the wind picked up and Jenna whimpered, "I'm sorry, Aunt Edie. I'm sorry."

She was crying when she woke. The sun was streaming in her window and the dolls on the window seat were smiling at her, mocking her. She grabbed a tissue from the box on the nightstand and blew her nose, picked up her cell phone and checked the time. Nine a.m.

Nine in the morning and she didn't smell breakfast. That wasn't normal. She went downstairs and found the kitchen empty. No Aunt Edie making bacon or sitting at the table sipping coffee.

Filled with dread, Jenna ran back up the stairs to her aunt's room. She knocked on the door, then opened it and stepped inside. Aunt Edie was still in bed. Oh, dear God.

Jenna ran to the bed. "Aunt Edie!"

Her aunt opened an eye and looked at her. "What time is it?" Her voice was so weak.

"It's nine."

Aunt Edie sighed and the eye shut again. "I'm tired, Jenna."

Oh, no. Oh, no. Aunt Edie was never tired.

"Are you okay?" What were the symptoms for a heart attack again? Sweating, headache, confusion. No sweat on her aunt's forehead. "What day is it?"

"It's Saturday, dear. Let's sleep in."

Okay, no confusion. Still. "But you never sleep in."

"I know. I just don't want to get up."

Her aunt was, indeed, sick. Sick at heart.

"You stay in bed and rest," Jenna said. "I'll make you some tea and toast."

Aunt Edie said nothing, just lay there.

Jenna tried not to sob as she went downstairs to the kitchen. Her poor aunt. She'd looked to Jenna to rescue her and this was what she'd gotten.

Pete banged on the kitchen door and Jenna let him in.

"You're not dressed," he said accusingly, taking in her sleep T-shirt.

"We slept late."

"Where's Edie?"

"She's in bed."

Pete's cranky expression turned to concern. "In bed? Is she all right?" His voice was threaded with panic.

"She doesn't feel well."

"Why haven't you called the doctor?" he demanded, marching to the kitchen phone. "Edie's never in bed at this hour of the morning. You should have known something was wrong."

She'd been in bed herself, so how could she have known? She kept the retort to herself. Pete was worried. She got that.

"Lizzy," he growled into the phone. "Get ahold of Doc and tell him to come over to Edie's place. Something's wrong... I know it's his day off. So what? Tell him to get out of his damned golf cart and get over here right away." He hung up and glared at Jenna. "You should have called the doctor."

She nodded, took the toast out of the toaster and put jam on it.

"I'll take it to her," he snarled, grabbing the plate out of her hand.

For once, he actually wanted to be useful, so she didn't

argue with him. Instead, she made tea and followed him
up the stairs with her aunt's favorite mug, a large white
ceramic one with blue seagulls soaring across it. Gulls
Just Want to Have Fun, it reminded her. Yeah, they were
having fun now.

By the time she got to the bedroom, Pete had put an
extra pillow behind Aunt Edie's head. He was sitting on
the side of the bed and coaxing her to have a bite of toast.

"Come, on, Edie old girl. It will do you good."

"I'm not hungry," she said querulously, and turned
her face away.

Pete looked ready to cry. Jenna already felt the tears
welling.

She knelt at the bed. "How about a sip of tea?"

"I just want to rest," Aunt Edie said, eyes shut, tears
slipping down her wrinkled cheeks.

Jenna bit her lip and patted her aunt's arm. She and
Pete exchanged worried glances.

Silence reigned in the room as they waited for the
doctor to come. It seemed like an eternity before the
doorbell rang.

Jenna went downstairs and opened the front door to
find a man who looked to be somewhere in his fifties
with red hair, a slightly jowly chin and a deep tan. He was
wearing golf clothes and carried a medical bag.

"I'm Dr. Fielding," he said. "I understand our Edie's
not feeling well."

"She didn't come down to make breakfast," Jenna
said. That made her sound like a disappointed child.
"She's always up early and puttering in the kitchen."
Her voice caught.

"Let's check her out," he said, and Jenna led him upstairs to her aunt's room.

Aunt Edie lay still as death, her face turned away. She looked so pale.

"About time you got here," Pete snapped as they walked in.

The doctor ignored him. "Well, now, Edie, what's going on?"

"I don't need a doctor," she said, her face still turned.

"Probably not," Fielding agreed. "Let's check you out, anyway."

Jenna and Pete watched as he took her pulse and her heart rate. "Can you smile for me, Edie? Raise your eyebrows? Squeeze my hand?"

Aunt Edie complied but didn't look happy about it.

"Have you been taking your aspirin?" the doctor asked.

"Yes. I just want to rest," she said irritably. "Every once in a while a woman needs to rest."

"Very true," said the doctor. "How long have you been feeling tired?"

Since Jenna let her down.

Edie was done talking. She clamped her lips together and closed her eyes again, and her three visitors left the room.

"What's wrong with her?" Pete asked once they were in the front hall.

"Her heart and blood pressure are fine. She has no symptoms of stroke or heart attack," said Fielding.

Pete threw up his arms, losing patience. "Then what's wrong?"

"Nothing physically."

"Well, then, what?" Pete demanded.

"I think she's depressed. Have you had some bad news recently?" the doctor asked Jenna.

She nodded. Damien again. He'd been bad news for years.

"Edie's never depressed," Pete insisted.

The doctor ignored him. "Rest and relaxation will do her a lot of good. I can prescribe something," he said to Jenna.

The one thing her aunt needed most, he couldn't help with, but she nodded. He wrote out an illegible prescription, told Jenna to call him if anything changed and left her and Pete standing in the hall.

Pete held out his hand. "I'll go pick up the prescription."

She nodded and handed it over, then went back upstairs to her aunt's bedroom, pulled up a chair beside the bed and settled in to keep vigil. Aunt Edie said nothing.

Pete returned half an hour later and sat down on the other side of the bed. "The doc prescribed some pills for you," he said to Aunt Edie.

She plucked at her bedspread. "I don't want any pills. I just want to sleep. Can't you both go away and let me sleep?"

Gruff old Pete seemed to cave in on himself.

"Okay, Edie," he said, his voice breaking. "I'm here if you want anything."

He and Jenna tiptoed out of the room. "What are we going to do?" he whispered once they were on the landing.

"I don't know," Jenna whispered back. How did you help someone find hope when she'd lost it?

# Chapter Twenty

*To Do:*
*Make soup for Aunt Edie*
*Clean Roger's cage*
*Cry*

Jenna cleaned Roger's cage and made some chicken soup for her aunt. It seemed silly to be making soup in July but it was all she could think to do to help Aunt Edie feel better.

Actually, the only thing that would make her aunt feel better would be to learn that Jenna had been able to catch hold of the money that was slipping away. She was going to try and dribble out money to Damien in as small amounts as possible, but he'd demanded a chunk up front. That coupled with what she owed in taxes had crippled them, blowing away much of her windfall. Herbie didn't extend credit and her charge card was maxed out. And then there was that bank loan, lurking in the shadows.

"I've been a foolish old woman," her aunt had said after the party broke up Friday night. "Trying to hang on to the past and drag it with me into the future. Things change. Things fall apart. Things die."

And right there, before Jenna's eyes, a part of her aunt had died.

She wasn't interested in the soup when Jenna took some up to her. Pete, who was still sitting by her bed, passed up the offer of food also. He was almost in as bad a shape as Aunt Edie.

Jenna went back downstairs, did some paperwork, cried. Cleaned the downstairs bathroom. Cried. Baked cookies—they weren't as good as Aunt Edie's—and cried some more.

She checked on her aunt, who was awake but in no mood to visit and refused to take her medicine. Finally, she got in her car and drove to the pier, sat down and watched as a little fishing boat bobbed out to sea. How easy life looked out there on the water. No worries. No disappointment. Just the sun and the summer breeze.

Aunt Edie wouldn't have any worries once they sold the place, Jenna reminded herself. She'd be able to live quite comfortably.

Comfortably, but not happily. Her life's blood was the Driftwood Inn. She was fading away right along with their hopes for keeping the place going. If they lost the Driftwood Inn Jenna knew she'd lose Aunt Edie, as well. The woman would die of a broken heart. She already was.

Her mom's shift at the grocery store had ended. Jenna put in a call. "Aunt Edie's not doing well."

"Oh, no," Mel said. "What happened?"

Jenna relayed their latest misery and her mother listened, making the appropriate sounds of sympathy as she talked.

"How about you?" Mel said at last. "How are you doing?"

"Rotten. It seems so unfair. All that hard work and then that money came in, like a fairy tale. But instead of a happy ending we got hit again. And now, we're almost back to square one."

"Not quite. You have some money."

"Not enough. I don't know what else to do."

"Do you want me to come down there? I have tomorrow off."

There wasn't anything her mother could do to improve their circumstances but Jenna said an emphatic yes.

"I'll pack a few things and start down right away," Mel said.

Her mother would have to work on Monday so it would be a short visit, but even a short visit was better than nothing. A shot of moral support and maybe Jenna could find a way to keep going.

A few minutes after she finished talking to her mom Jenna's cell rang. Sabrina!

She pressed the phone icon and eagerly accepted her daughter's call.

Sabrina barely gave her time to say hello. She was crying. "I want to come home."

"Sweetie, what's wrong?"

"Daddy doesn't want me here. All he cares about is Aurora."

No, all he cared about was himself.

"Please, Mommy, let me come home."

Mommy. She hadn't been Mommy in a long time. Once more her daughter was a little girl. With a big hurt. What on earth had happened?

"Of course, you can come home. Grandma's coming down. I'll have her pick you up."

"Okay," Sabrina said, catching in a ragged breath.

"I've missed you. It'll be good to have you back."

"Oh, Mommy!" And the crying started again.

It took a few moments to calm her daughter, and several reassurances that no, Aunt Edie wasn't mad at her for what she'd done. "But you'll have to earn the money to pay her back."

"I know. I will."

"Okay. You get your things together and Grandma will be there soon."

"Okay." Sabrina sounded relieved.

She wasn't half as relieved as Jenna. She put in a call to her mother and explained what had happened.

"I'm on my way," Mel said. "See you soon."

Soon couldn't come soon enough. Sabrina wasn't the only one who wanted her mommy.

Jenna called Damien and told him Sabrina had had enough.

"That's fine with me," he said. "She's been a real handful. You've let her turn into a brat."

"She wasn't a brat before you left," Jenna snapped, and cut off the call.

He didn't deserve his daughter's love. He didn't deserve anyone's love. She wondered how long before Aurora would figure that out.

Who cared? The important thing was that Sabrina would soon be back where she belonged. Jenna drove to the house feeling as jubilant as a woman who was about to see her dreams go up in smoke and possibly lose a dear relative could feel.

Maybe seeing Sabrina would perk Aunt Edie up, give her a reason to keep going. Jenna hoped so.

Back at the house, Pete was still sitting vigil and Aunt Edie was lying in bed with her eyes closed. "Why don't you take a break?" Jenna suggested. "I'll sit with her."

He nodded. "I need a drink," he said, and left the room.

"How about you, Aunt Edie," Jenna whispered. "What do you need?" As if she couldn't guess.

She fetched herself a glass of water and tried to coax Aunt Edie into trying one of her cookies.

"I'm not hungry," Aunt Edie said, eyes still closed.

"I don't blame you for not wanting one. They're not as good as yours."

No reply.

"Really, nothing I make in the kitchen's going to be as good as what you make. You're still the best cook ever."

Still no reply.

"I have a little bit of good news," Jenna ventured. "Sabrina's coming home. I think she missed us."

Aunt Edie responded with a light snore.

A snore was better than nothing. Hopefully, seeing Sabrina would perk her up.

It was nearly eight when her mother and Sabrina rolled in. Jenna had been sitting on the front porch waiting, and at the sight of them she raced down the steps.

Sabrina dashed from the car and into her arms. "Mommy! I'm sorry. I'm really, really sorry."

"I know," Jenna said, and kissed the top of her head. "Now, come on. Let's see if your grandma needs help with her suitcase."

Her mother had packed lightly and so, other than a bag of groceries, her mom's vintage train case and Sabrina's backpack, there wasn't much to bring in. "I'll take your things up to my room," Jenna said to her mother. "You can sleep with me. Sabrina, why don't you go put that milk and orange juice in the fridge."

Sabrina nodded and disappeared into the kitchen and Jenna led her mother upstairs. Once they were in the bedroom and out of earshot, Jenna asked, "How is she?"

"Pretty unhappy. I'm afraid she's had a rude awakening." Mel shook her head. "Every girl wants to think she's her daddy's little princess. Sadly, Damien has another princess."

"So, they ignored her," Jenna guessed.

"Pretty much, and the times they did take her out I guess Aurora got bossy. I think the final nail in the coffin came when she overheard them arguing about her. Aurora wanted her gone and I'm afraid Damien didn't exactly stick up for her. He said something to the effect of them having to suck it up. At least, that's what Sabrina heard."

"Good Lord," Jenna said in horror. How it must have hurt to hear that coming from the father she adored. "What did I ever see in him?"

"A handsome, talented man. One can hardly blame you for assuming he had a heart."

"I hate for her to see what a jerk he is."

"She was going to at some point. Find some good male role models down here and she'll be okay."

Jenna thought of Seth Waters, white knight. And Brody, who'd been unwilling to take so much as a penny of the money she'd won. Yes, her daughter did have some good role models here.

"How's Edie?" Mel asked. "Any better?"

Sabrina was in the room now. "What's wrong with Aunt Edie?"

Jenna's right eye began to twitch. "She's not feeling good."

"Has she got a cold?"

"No, it's a little more serious."

Sabrina's eyes got wide. "Is she going to be all right?"

What to say to that? "I hope so."

"What's wrong with her?"

"She's wearing out, honey," Mel said softly.

Sabrina's brows knit. "No." She shook her head. "No, she can't…die." She rushed from the room.

"Sabrina!" Jenna called, and ran after her, chasing her into Aunt Edie's bedroom.

Aunt Edie was still as a corpse. Sabrina fell by the side of her bed and threw herself on the old woman's arm. "Don't die, Aunt Edie. Please don't die. I'm sorry I took your money. I'm so sorry. I'll pay you back every penny. I love you. Please don't leave us. Please." She started sobbing and, watching her, Jenna felt her own tears returning.

A moment later, an age-spotted hand with blue vein ridges lifted and rested on Sabrina's pink hair.

"We need you. Don't leave us," she begged.

Jenna took her daughter's arm. "Come on, let's let Aunt Edie rest."

Sabrina sobbed her way out of the room, ran into her own room and slammed the door.

"Let's go downstairs and have some iced tea," said Mel. In the kitchen, she found the cookies Jenna had made sitting on the counter and bit into one. "These are good."

"Not as good as Aunt Edie's." Jenna fell onto a kitchen chair. "She's dying, Mom. I let her down and I've done nothing but bring stress into her life. I got her hopes up when I won that money, and shot them down again. I don't have enough money to fix the roof and get linens and…" She shook her head. "The vinyl in the bathrooms. I had myself convinced we could actually get people to stay here with that crumbly old vinyl. I just wanted a roof, damn it."

Mel sat down next to her and laid a hand on her arm.

"Honey, this isn't about you failing. It's about you trying. Your aunt knows that. We all know that."

Jenna rubbed her face, trying to scrub away her misery. "I always loved it here. I wanted to be back. To stay back."

"You can still stay. Yes, you may have to sell the Driftwood, but that doesn't mean you can't rent a little house down here, run your massage business. Date those handsome men your sister's been telling me about," she added, a smile in her voice.

Jenna dropped her hands and frowned. "She told you?"

"Of course. You know your sister can't keep a secret. And you wouldn't be able to keep it from me much longer, either, you know that."

"I'm so done with love," Jenna said.

"But maybe love's not done with you," said Mel. She got up, poured a glass of iced tea and set it in front of Jenna along with a cookie on a napkin. "Come on, drink up. Eat. Your adventure's not over and I suspect you're going to need your strength."

She needed more than strength. She needed money.

And her daughter needed her. Sabrina surfaced from her room with red, swollen eyes. Cookies held no appeal and she didn't want to text or watch TV. It seemed all she wanted was to stick to Jenna's side. Finally, at ten, worn out by her emotions, she went to bed.

Pete came back shortly after she'd gone, wanting to know how Aunt Edie was doing. "No change," Jenna said, and introduced him to her mom.

He doffed his hat and said the required, "Nice to meet you."

"Nice to meet you, too," Mel said. "And thank you

for being such a comfort and help to my aunt these past few years."

He shot a look Jenna's direction as if wondering what she'd been saying.

Tonight she had nothing bad to say about him. She merely smiled.

"I try," he said. "I care about Edie."

"I can see that you do," Mel said. "I'm sure she'll be better in the morning."

He nodded, looked at the floor, then left.

"He's driven me nuts ever since we arrived," Jenna said, "but tonight I feel sorry for him. He really does care about Aunt Edie."

They sat up talking until almost midnight, when Mel finally yawned and said, "I think I need to go to bed. You coming?"

"In a little bit," Jenna said, and let her mother go on up without her. She looked out the kitchen window. No fire on the beach tonight. Maybe Seth was over at the Drunken Sailor, playing pool.

Or maybe he was in his room. She slipped out of the house and across the parking lot to room number two, knocked softly on the door. No answer.

Maybe it was just as well. Who knew what she'd have done in her present state of mind.

She finally went to bed. Her mother was already asleep, breathing softly. Melody Jones never snored. She was much too ladylike for that. Everything she did, she did with grace and calm, even sleeping.

"Oh, Mom, if only I could be more like you," Jenna murmured. She got ready for bed, then climbed in next to her mother and snuggled close. "Please don't leave me for a long, long time. I couldn't survive."

Mel sighed as if to say, "Don't worry, I won't."

Jenna closed her eyes and finally, finally went to sleep.

On Sunday morning she awoke to the smell of coffee. She opened her eyes. Her mother was still next to her in bed, sound asleep. Had Sabrina gotten up?

She went to her daughter's room and, finding it empty, smiled. This was a new and improved Sabrina, up early and making breakfast. Aunt Edie would be proud. She'd get some of that freshly brewed coffee and bring it up to her.

To her surprise, she entered the kitchen to find her aunt sitting at the kitchen table, sipping coffee and offering instructions as Sabrina put together a blackberry coffee cake. Her heart caught in her throat.

"Aunt Edie!" She hurried over and hugged her aunt and Aunt Edie patted her arm. "You're feeling better?"

"Yes, I am. I'm still a little tired, so our girl is making breakfast for us."

"Blackberry coffee cake, your favorite," Sabrina said over her shoulder to Jenna.

Jenna fell onto the nearest chair, relief washing over her. "I'm so glad to see you up. You gave us a real scare yesterday."

Her aunt's smile fell away. "I'm sorry. It was selfish of me."

"Selfish to not feel good? Hardly."

"No, selfish to give up."

Oh, boy. But what if they had to? "Aunt Edie…" Jenna began.

"Oh, I don't mean on the inn. If we have to sell it, then we'll sell it."

"Sell the Driftwood?" Sabrina turned away from her project and stared at them in horror. "We can't sell the

Driftwood, not when we've worked so hard on it. Anyway, you have all that money, Mom."

"It's not turning out to be as much as I thought," Jenna said, and left it at that. Much as she despised Damien she still couldn't bring herself to paint a bad picture of him for her daughter. He'd already painted a bad enough one.

"Thanks to that horrible man of yours," Aunt Edie said, and then, realizing what she'd done, looked horrified.

Jenna braced herself.

"Is it because of Daddy?" Sabrina asked, the disappointment plain on her face.

"Things don't always go as you plan," Jenna said evasively.

"I hate him," Sabrina said with all the passion of angry youth, and turned back to her mixing bowl. Hate and love, how easily you mixed them up when you were a kid.

"You do now, but someday…" What? Jenna decided not to finish the sentence. "Anyway, things will work out," she said, bringing them back to the subject at hand.

"It's time to let go," Aunt Edie said with a sigh. "We did make so many wonderful memories here, and I have to admit, the Driftwood Inn has meant a lot to me. I loved being able to meet people and, well, those guests almost became like family," she said with a smile. "But they weren't, not really. This is my family." Her smile vanished and she dropped her gaze. "I so wanted to help you."

"We wanted to help you, too," Jenna said earnestly. And they'd all failed.

"I thought the Driftwood Inn could be useful again. I thought *I* could be useful." Jenna was about to speak, but Aunt Edie held up her hand. "After Sabrina came to my bedside last night I had a lot to think about. And do you know what I concluded?"

Jenna was almost afraid to ask. "What?"

"That maybe I can still be useful. Just because we have to sell the Driftwood doesn't mean we can't stay here in Moonlight Harbor. We can keep the house and I can keep teaching Sabrina how to cook. We'll all be together, and we'll all be at the beach. And that's what counts, isn't it?"

"Oh, Aunt Edie," Jenna said, tears in her eyes.

"I know it's not much to give you."

"It's everything," Jenna said, and hugged her.

Aunt Edie smiled and then heaved a sigh. "I'm still a little tired. I think I'll go back upstairs and rest. Maybe Sabrina will bring me some of that coffee cake when it's out of the oven."

"For sure," Sabrina said. "Do you want me to help you upstairs?"

Aunt Edie waved away the offer. "I'm not dead yet."

Thank God.

Mel came down just as Sabrina was taking out the coffee cake. "I looked in on Aunt Edie. She's in bed but she says she's feeling better."

"She is."

"Good," said Mel. "Then I can go back and not worry about you."

"But you just got here," Sabrina protested.

"I know. Sadly, I have to work tomorrow. But I'll stay for lunch. How about a beach walk? Then I'll treat you girls to some popcorn shrimp at the Seafood Shack."

They gave Aunt Edie some coffee cake and then played hooky from church, something that was more than okay with Sabrina, and walked the beach, looking for agates. This time they didn't find any, but Sabrina was happy with the beach glass she discovered.

"You'll have to show her how to make wind chimes," Mom said to Jenna.

"Can we do that today?" Sabrina asked eagerly.

"Probably," Jenna said, and her daughter smiled, then raced ahead in search of more beach treasure.

"Being down here is going to be good for her," Mom predicted.

"I hope so," Jenna said.

Her mother put an arm around her. "It will be. Things will work out."

One way or another, Jenna thought wistfully.

They returned laden with beach treasures and, even though her circumstances hadn't changed, Jenna felt as if a heavy load had been lifted from her shoulders.

"You'll be okay," her mother told her, giving her one final hug before leaving.

Yes, she would. If only...

She steered her thoughts away from the Driftwood Inn.

Mel had barely left when the doorbell rang. Jenna went to answer it, figuring it was one of her aunt's friends. Instead, she opened the door to find a chunky forty-year-old man with brown curls in the process of curling their way off his forehead. He wore jeans that were sure to show a butt crack if he bent over and a faded Nirvana T-shirt. Next to him stood a short, roly-poly woman with stringy, long brown hair and glasses. She was holding a squirming three-year-old boy with hair the same color as his father's.

The man looked at Jenna in confusion but she'd have known that snub nose and those big, brown eyes anywhere. "Winston. What are you doing here?"

His brows shot up. "Jenna? I haven't seen you in years."

"It's been a while."

"I want down!" cried the little boy, straining against his mother's arms.

She set him down and he raced past Jenna into the living room. Oh, boy.

"We came to see Aunt Edie," Winston said. "Thought she'd like to meet the wife and see Winston Junior."

Oh, yes, that was just what Aunt Edie needed when she didn't feel well. "Actually, she's not feeling too good."

"Is she okay? Is she dying?"

Did he sound hopeful? "No," Jenna said, disgusted. She could hear Roger squawking and decided she was stuck letting the invaders into the house. "Come on in," she said, and stepped aside.

"Call the cops!" shrieked Roger. "Call the cops!"

Jenna got to the living room in time to see little Winston Junior shaking the base of the cage. She rushed over and pulled his hand away. "We don't do that to Roger. He gets seasick."

"Give me whiskey," Roger begged. Jenna knew just how he felt.

Sabrina had come out of the kitchen to see what the commotion was all about and stood staring at the little terror, who was now jumping up, batting the base of the cage like a piñata. "Hey, don't do that!" she snapped, and the boy pulled his mouth down at the corners with two fingers and stuck his tongue out at her. Such an adorable child.

Winston was in the room now, along with the missus, and he flopped onto the couch. "I see she's still got the bird."

"Yes, she does. So, Winston, what brings you to town?"

"Oh, we were just driving through on our way to Oregon."

Moonlight Harbor wasn't on the way to anything.

"Thought we'd stop in. I haven't seen Aunt Edie in a while."

"You caught her at a bad time," Jenna said. Meanwhile, Winston's son was using the seashell chair for a trampoline.

"Can you make him stop doing that?" Jenna asked.

"What? Oh, sorry. Win-Win, sit down."

The child plopped onto the chair, crossed his arms and scowled.

"Maybe he'd like a cookie," Jenna said. "Sabrina, can you take Win-Win into the kitchen and give him a cookie?"

Sabrina looked at her mother as if she'd just told her to get on out there in the Coliseum and fight the lions. "Do you want a cookie?" she asked the boy grudgingly. Jenna's cookies may not have been as good as Aunt Edie's but she suspected that Winston Junior, like his father, wasn't that discriminating when it came to food.

"Yessss!" And Win-Win was off and running.

"I wouldn't mind something to eat myself," said Winston. He sniffed. "Something sure smells good."

The aroma of coffee cake still hung faintly in the air. Jenna said nothing. That had been for Aunt Edie. If Winston got near it, the rest would be gone before you could say oink.

"I'll go get us a plate," offered his wife, and waddled off to the kitchen.

"Have Sabrina put some cookies in a container to take with you," Jenna called after her. "That way you'll have something to eat on the road," she said to her cousin.

"We're not in that big of a hurry," he said. "So, what are you doing here, Jenna? Visiting?"

"I'm living here now," she said, making his easy smile shrink. "I'm running the Driftwood Inn for Aunt Edie."

"Looks like you're in over your head. The place is a dump."

"I only got here last month," she said. "It's taking some time to pull it together." No way was she telling him they were going to have to pull the plug on it. He'd be all over that, happy to help her sell it and hold his hand out for a chunk of the money. Whether it was food or money, Winston didn't care. He'd always been greedy for both. She could still see him when they were kids, whining to his parents that they hadn't given him enough spending money. It had seemed to Jenna, whose piggy bank was always starving, that he had plenty to spend, even when his father wasn't working. Which was a lot of the time.

"How are Aunt Grace and Uncle Arthur?" Her mom kept in touch with her brother even though they had little in common. Mel was a hard worker. And Uncle Arthur? He'd spent more time drawing unemployment than he had working. Last Jenna had heard he was getting ready to retire from his job as a tire salesman.

"Dad's retired now. Mom's still working."

"And how about you, Winston?"

He shrugged. "I'm in between jobs."

Of course. Which would explain why he'd stopped by to see good old Aunt Edie. Jenna knew her aunt had loaned him money over the years. Judging from the letter her aunt had included in Jenna's birthday card she was about through doing that. Which was just as well, considering the fact that they didn't have any to loan.

"Thought we'd take a run down to see Kelly's folks while we've got some time," Winston said.

And suck them dry for a while. Jenna was so sick of mooches.

"Well, Winston," she said, "I hope you guys weren't planning on staying here. There's no room." No room at the inn. Ha, ha.

He frowned. "You can probably find a corner for us somewhere. Aunt Edie's got that spare bedroom."

Jenna shook her head. "It's my office now and I can't have you sleeping on my massage table."

The frown dipped lower. "You've kind of taken over, haven't you?"

"No kind of about it," she said sweetly.

He pointed a pudgy finger at her. "You know, you always were bossy."

She had to smile at that. "That's because I'm the oldest."

"Only by six months."

She sighed. "Look, if you want to go up and see Aunt Edie, I'll take you. But she really hasn't been feeling well, so you can't stay long."

"Maybe we'll let Aunt Edie be the judge of that," he snapped. He marched up the stairs, Jenna following in his wake. "You've probably been telling her all kinds of lies about me," he muttered.

"What would I tell her? I haven't seen you in years."

"Your mom's probably told you stuff."

"Oh, for heaven's sake, Winston. Don't be so paranoid."

He stopped on a stair and whirled around to glare at her. "Paranoid? You're moved in here, happy as a clam and telling me I can't stay and you're calling me paranoid?"

"I was invited to move in," she said.

"Yeah, right," he said, and started stamping the rest of the way to the landing. "I heard you and the artist were splitting. You probably came down here and gave her some sad sob story about how you couldn't make it."

Ah, yes, good old Cousin Winston. He hadn't improved with age. "I'm making it. I have a business. How about you?"

"I'm going to be doing an internet start-up. I'll be rich enough to buy this place in two years."

"Well, go, Winston," she said, reverting to her thirteen-year-old snotty voice.

"You should be glad I came down," he said as he marched along the landing. "It's obvious you need help here." He pushed open Aunt Edie's door without bothering to knock. "Aunt Edie," he greeted her in a hearty voice.

Jenna was right behind him and saw the expression on her aunt's face. Unpleasant surprise.

"I tried to tell him you hadn't been feeling well," she said.

"Winston, what are you doing here?" Aunt Edie asked wearily.

"I was passing through and wanted to stop by and see you," he said. "You haven't met my wife yet."

"No. And I sent you a wedding present four years ago and am still waiting for a thank-you."

The tips of Winston's ears went red and even though Jenna couldn't see his face she knew it matched them. "We've been busy," he said.

"I imagine. With your little boy. I sent a card and twenty-five dollars and never heard a peep."

Cousin Winston was in deep doo-doo. "Auntie, we really did appreciate that."

"Yes, I could tell," she said. "But it was nice of you to stop by. How many years has it been now? Let's see. I think the last time I saw you was about five years ago. You wanted to start a business designing websites and asked me for money. Which I gave you. And I didn't get a thank-you for that, either."

"I'm sorry, Aunt Edie. I had my hands full trying to get it off the ground."

"And did you?"

"Uh, no. That didn't work out."

"I'm sorry to hear that, Winston."

"But hey, it's good to see you. I'm sorry you haven't been feeling well."

"I'm better now," she said.

"That's good. We wouldn't want to lose you."

"I wasn't planning on getting lost," she said shortly.

He manufactured a laugh. "Well, I thought maybe we'd hang around for a couple of days, catch up, give you a chance to meet Winston Junior."

"I don't think so, Winston," Aunt Edie said. "I'm not feeling that much better. And really, we're not in a position to entertain at the moment. Jenna has her hands full renovating the inn."

"It looks like she could use some help."

"I've got it under control," Jenna said, and he scowled at her over his shoulder.

"It was nice of you to stop by," Aunt Edie said, "but I'm sure you need to get on the road to your next adventure."

"Jeez, Aunt Edie, we just got here," he protested.

"Winston, this is what happens when you drop in on people unannounced. They can't always entertain you. I suggest the next time you take it into your head to come butter me up you at least call and see if it's convenient.

And maybe, if I ever get a thank-you for everything I've done for you these past few years or hear from you when you don't want something from me, I'll be more inclined to entertain you."

Ouch. This was a side of her aunt Jenna had never seen.

Winston bristled. "If that's the way you feel I guess we won't stay."

"I'm sure you'll be happier somewhere else," Aunt Edie agreed.

Winston said no more. He left the room in a huff.

"I never liked that boy," Aunt Edie said. "He's always been selfish. Go hustle him out before he eats everything in the cupboard."

Jenna snickered and followed her cousin out of the room.

He was waiting for her at the foot of the stairs. "You've poisoned her against me," he accused.

"I don't know, Winston. I'd say you've done a pretty good job of that all on your own."

"Fine. Let this whole place fall down around your ears. And when you need someone to come help you, don't be calling me."

"I promise I won't," Jenna said.

Win-Win and the missus were coming out of the kitchen now. The child had a cookie in each hand and his mother held a paper plate piled high with them.

"We're leaving, babe," Winston said to her just as she started to sit down.

"Leaving? I thought we were going to stay for the week."

"We're not wanted here," he said, looking loftily at Jenna. "And I never stay where I'm not wanted."

And here was yet another thing for which to be thankful.

# Chapter Twenty-One

*To Do:*
*Go to chamber of commerce meeting*
*Talk to Brody about selling*
*Don't cry!*

"Who were they?" Sabrina asked when Jenna came into the kitchen in search of lemonade and a strong dose of sugar.

"Just a cousin nobody likes," Jenna said, and snagged a cookie.

"They're not staying, are they?"

"No. I think we've seen the last of Cousin Winston." For a while, anyway. Knowing her cousin, he'd soon be hard at work repairing old offenses and trying to ingratiate himself with Aunt Edie.

Pete knocked on the kitchen door. "How is she?" he asked as Jenna let him in.

"Much better. She even came downstairs for a little while."

The relief on his face was touching. He covered it up with a brisk nod. "You tell her not to worry about making dinner. I'll pick us all up something at the Seafood Shack."

Pete the mooch springing for a meal? It was all Jenna could do not to say, *Who are you?* Instead, she said, "Thanks, Pete. That's sweet of you."

"Don't want anybody saying I don't pull my weight around here," he said. Then, pointing to Sabrina's culinary creation, he added, "I'll have a piece of that coffee cake. Probably won't be as good as Edie's, though."

Ah, yes, there was the Pete they all knew and tried to love.

It looked like life in Aunt Edie's beach house was almost back to normal. Actually, better than normal because the snotty, unhappy alien Sabrina had been replaced by a girl who was happy to help and done complaining. At least temporarily.

Aunt Edie was a little subdued, but at least she was up and moving around again.

As for Jenna, she was resigned. They were going to have to sell the Driftwood. They couldn't limp along with a half-renovated motel.

"It's still killing me," she said to Seth when he came over Monday afternoon to see if she wanted him to do anything. "And it almost killed her. I thought we'd lost her on Saturday."

"Shit. Is she okay now?"

"Pretty much. She's trying to adjust and put a good spin on things, but I know she's heartbroken. This old place is her baby. How do you give up your baby?"

"I don't know," he said, leaning against the front porch. "At least your girl's back."

There it was, the rainbow in the storm that Mom always talked about. "Yes, and it's good to have her home again. I'm just sorry she had to see the ugly side of her father."

"She would have at some point," Seth reminded her.

"I know." Jenna shook her head. "I wish I could have spared her that." She sighed. "I wish a lot of things. I'd love to be able to find a way to make things work out here. You probably won't have a room much longer," she added. "It would be great if we could find a buyer who'd keep the place just as it is, but I suspect whoever buys the Driftwood will tear it down to build something bigger."

With no character. And if that happened it really would kill her aunt. She bit her lip, willing herself not to cry.

"You don't know that for sure," he said.

"No, but I strongly suspect it. Oh, well," she added with a fatalistic shrug. "It is what it is and there's nothing I can do about it. We'll sell the place, pay off the bank, and live happily-ever-after on whatever's left and Aunt Edie's social security and whatever I can make as a massage therapist. And Pete will set up a tent in the backyard."

"Or maybe he'll finally move into your aunt's bedroom," Seth teased, making Jenna scowl. "However it all shakes out, you'll be okay. You're a survivor. You'll find a way to land on your feet."

"I hope I don't break all my toes in the process," she said.

Tuesday was the Moonlight Harbor Chamber of Commerce meeting. Jenna attended, figuring that even when she didn't have the Driftwood Inn she'd still qualify for membership thanks to her massage therapy business. Networking was important.

She wasn't very excited over the kind of networking she was going to have to do on this particular day. Trying to smile and be positive when people congratulated her on her lucky win and asked her how the renovations were coming was downright painful.

"I'm afraid much of the money had to be shared with my ex," she said as she stood visiting with some of the business owners, managing to leave out all the adjectives she longed to add. "So, we're at a standstill."

"What are you going to do?" asked Rita.

"I'm going to talk to Brody."

"You're selling?" Ellis West looked both shocked and disgusted.

"I think we're going to have to. I've run out of money. We can't open up the place in its present condition."

"That's a damn shame," he said.

"It's reality." Reality sucked.

Jenna made her way to where Brody stood, talking with Tyrella. "Hey, there," he said to her. "How's it going? When does the new roof go on?"

"It doesn't," she said.

"Herbie can't fit you in? I'll talk to him."

"It's not that. I don't have the money."

"How can you not have the money?" Brody asked. "Where'd it go?"

"It's going to my ex. Well, not all of it, but a chunk. Between that and taxes, I don't have what I need for the roof, let alone bedding, bathroom floors…" An image of the fallen-down fence and the disaster pool popped into her mind. "And the pool." Not to mention paying off the bank. "You were right all along. We need to sell. Will you help us?"

"Sure," he said, looking far from happy over getting

the listing. "Jenna, I know I advised you to sell, but I'm sorry you have to. I really am."

She wanted to say a polite thank-you, but her throat squeezed over the words like a boa constrictor and all she could do was nod and try not to tear up.

"There has to be something we can do," Tyrella said as Rian LaShell came up to talk to Brody.

Jenna shook her head. She was out of ideas.

"You know, I've been thinking about this," Tyrella said.

She didn't get a chance to go any further. "Let's all take our seats," Brody called to everyone, bringing an end to the chitchat.

"Thinking what?" Jenna asked, not wanting to let go of a promising conversation.

Patricia called Tyrella over to sit with her. "I'll bring it up when we get to new business," she said to Jenna, then went to join Patricia. They instantly had their heads together and Jenna wondered what they were up to.

She finally gave up trying to imagine. There wasn't anything she could think of that could possibly help at this point.

Lunch was served and Jenna, seated between Brody and Ellis, could only pick at her fish and chips.

Halfway through lunch, Brody called the meeting to order. Jenna tried to listen to the various reports but her thoughts kept drifting. What could she have done differently? Wasn't there some way they could hang on to the Driftwood?

Of course there wasn't. As for staying in the house, would Aunt Edie really be happy remaining there and seeing someone else with what had once been hers? How would she feel if some big-name chain moved in and took over?

"Any new business?" Brody asked.

They were on to new business already? Jenna tried to pull herself away from her miserable thoughts and pay attention.

"Yes," Tyrella said. "We need another festival."

"What else is new?" Susan Banks said sourly.

"What did you have in mind?" Brody asked.

"A fundraiser. We need to save the Driftwood Inn."

That got Jenna's attention. She looked at Tyrella in shock.

"She just won a ton of money," Susan protested. "Why on earth do we need to jump in and give her more. No offense," she said to Jenna.

"Because Uncle Sam and her ex took most of it. She needs money for a new roof or she can't open. And she needs…" Tyrella turned to Jenna. "What else do you need?"

Jenna's cheeks burned under Susan's unsympathetic glare. She stumbled down her list. "But I don't expect anyone to give me money."

"None of us can spare that kind of money," Susan said. "A lot of us are struggling to keep our own doors open."

"Perhaps we need to think in terms of a yearly event where we raise funds to help struggling businesses or help new start-ups," said Patricia Whiteside. "Once in a blue moon we all need help."

"That's what we could call the festival," Nora said. "The Blue Moon Festival. I'm sure Sherwood could help us set up a nonprofit account. Right, Sherwood?"

"Well, uh."

"Of course he can," Patricia answered for him. "I

think this is an excellent idea. How many businesses have we seen come and then go because they couldn't afford to keep their doors open long enough to establish a customer base? You all know the challenges of being a tourist-driven business when that business is seasonal."

Everything she said made sense, but Jenna felt her whole face and neck on fire as Patricia spoke. Jenna Jones, the town beggar.

"We've had a lot of discussion about trying to figure out ways to bring people down here," said Nora. "Everyone loves a festival. Think how well the Sand and Surf did."

"When would you hold it?" Susan asked suspiciously.

"As soon as possible," said Tyrella.

"We've just had the Fourth of July," Susan pointed out. "And that was a mess to clean up after."

"August," said Tyrella. "We could hold it the first weekend in August. People are still in vacation mode and haven't started their back to school shopping yet."

"That only gives us a month to plan," Susan protested.

Ellis jumped in. "What's to plan? You open your shops up, call in some vendors and everybody kicks in a share of their profits. There's always musicians looking for a venue to play at and artists who want to sell their artwork. We set up a bunch of booths on the pier and charge people for the use of them. The church ladies do bake sales, we get some carny rides in. We're good to go."

"And just where do we get the money for advertising?" Susan demanded. "Our money for the year is all budgeted."

"I'll kick in five hundred," Brody said.

"So will I," Patricia said. "And I'll give a thousand to start our fund."

"I'll donate five hundred to the cause," said Tyrella.

"Me, too," Nora said.

"I'm strapped for cash, but I can design the posters," said Rian LaShell.

Jenna could hardly believe what she was hearing. Hope and guilt warred inside her. Hope won. Maybe, just maybe, the Driftwood could be saved.

Before the meeting ended a vote had been taken and the motion to establish the First Annual Blue Moon Festival had carried. A committee had been established, consisting of Tyrella, Patricia, Ellis, Rian and Brody, and Sherwood had been put in charge of setting up a 501(c)(3) for the new nonprofit, which would exist under the umbrella of the chamber.

"I don't know how to thank you all," Jenna said, looking around the room, teary-eyed.

"No need," said Patricia. "When one of us succeeds, we all succeed. We should have thought of something like this years ago."

"Looks like you might want to hold off on listing the Driftwood," Brody said to Jenna after the meeting broke up.

"It looks that way," she said with a smile. She couldn't stop smiling. "Thank you. So much."

"I told you the money would come," Tyrella said, and gave her a hug.

"Yes, you did. And now I need to get home and tell Aunt Edie the good news." This was the medicine her aunt had needed all along.

She found Aunt Edie resting on the couch, Sabrina reading to her from her dystopian mutant teen novel. If Damien could see their daughter now…he still wouldn't want to be bothered with her. His loss. If he wanted to slack off on visitation that was fine with her. And anyway, Jenna didn't want to share.

"Guys, you'll never guess what happened at the chamber meeting," she said, rushing into the living room. "We're going to save the Driftwood Inn!"

"For real?" Sabrina asked, eyes lighting up.

"I don't understand," said Aunt Edie.

Jenna recounted the events of the meeting.

"That means we don't have to move!" Sabrina exclaimed. This from the girl who, only a short while ago, was dying to leave.

Aunt Edie put a trembling hand to her heart. "I can't believe it."

"It's true. I was there. We're going to make it, Aunt Edie. We're going to save the Driftwood."

"We need to celebrate," Aunt Edie said. "Sabrina, why don't you and I make some cookies? We'll have a beach fire tonight."

"Are you sure you're up for that?" Jenna asked, concerned.

"Oh, yes. This has given me a new lease on life. We need to party. Don't we, Sabrina?"

Sabrina was all over that, and the couch and the book were abandoned and Jenna was sent to invite Seth to join them.

"No shit," he said when she told him the news.

"No shit. The town is really coming through for us."

"People helping each other, novel idea," he cracked. "Think it'll catch on?"

"We can only hope."

Once again, a bonfire blazed on the beach. Pete had two helpings of Aunt Edie's beans and gobbled half a dozen of the oatmeal cookies she and Sabrina had baked.

Seth played his guitar and they sang "Found a Peanut" and "Ninety-nine Bottles of Beer on the Wall." Pete thought up a new ghost story to tell about a girl with pink hair who drove away the ghosts from a haunted motel only to be eaten by a giant squid that left Jenna and Seth chuckling and Sabrina frowning.

Aunt Edie didn't last long, announcing that she was tired, and Pete escorted her back to the house. Sabrina went in soon after to write in her journal, and Seth and Jenna stayed behind to let the fire die down.

"I still can't believe how quickly everything's changed," she said, watching a piece of burning wood break and fall into the flames.

"Life can turn on a dime."

"I guess the trick is to be ready to turn with it. Thanks for…being there the other night." That kiss. That had been worth a million dollars.

"I didn't do anything, but I'm glad someone's come to your rescue. If I'd had any money I'd have done it."

"You gave me comfort."

"Comfort's good. Money's better. You need to find yourself a rich man."

Where had that come from?

"Get together with somebody with money and a good credit rating and you'll never have to worry about the Driftwood again."

"If I'd found someone with money, then this festival would never have happened. Maybe," she added thoughtfully, "all our struggles here have been for a reason. Maybe the people of Moonlight Harbor needed a catalyst to help them think bigger than they'd been thinking. Maybe we all needed to realize how much we need each other."

He cocked a brow at her. "No man is an island?"

"Or even a peninsula," she cracked.

He smiled and moved a little closer, put an arm around her. "Jenna Jones, you're something special."

Was she? Nah. "I don't think so."

"I do," he said, and brushed her lips with his.

*Oh, baby.*

He gave her lips another little brush.

*Keep it up.*

And then he got serious and she turned into a melting marshmallow again. Boundaries. Where were those pesky boundaries when you needed them?

He found them just as she was about to go over the edge and pulled away, straightening her top. "I'm thinkin' we shouldn't be making a habit of this. Bonfires are dangerous."

Yes, and a girl could get burned. But darn, she'd been enjoying the heat.

He stood up and held out his hand. "Come on, time to go in."

"Do I have to?"

"We both have to," he said, and together they put out the fire.


Aunt Edie was her old chipper self again when her friends came over on Friday. Everyone was excited about the upcoming festival.

"We're going to have a booth and sell sundaes, and floats," Nora announced.

"Susan's not doing anything," Courtney said in disgust.

*Why am I not surprised?* Jenna thought.

"Which is fine with me, because I'm going to have a

fashion show on the beach and sell some of my designs. I've already got a primo spot. It pays to know important people," she added, grinning at Patricia.

"I think it will be lovely," Patricia said, "and I'm going to be one of her models."

"I hope you and Sabrina will, too," Courtney said to Jenna.

"For sure," she promised.

"If I can sell enough pieces, then maybe I can quit," Courtney said. "In fact, maybe I will, anyway," she added with a snap of her gum. "I'm getting tired of being Susan's doormat."

"We'll be hiring soon," Jenna told her. "I could use someone to work the reception desk in the evenings."

"With an evening job I could sew during the day," Courtney said thoughtfully.

"Where would you sell your clothes?" Tyrella asked.

Courtney's mouth drooped. "Good question. I can't afford to rent space."

"I've been thinking of adding a little boutique shop at my place," Patricia said. "Maybe we can work something out if your fashion show goes well."

"A boutique at the Oyster Inn? Whoa," Courtney said in awe.

"Poor Susan," Tyrella said. "She'll be out of business in a month."

"Not necessarily," said Aunt Edie, who was wearing a pair of twenty-five-percent-off pink slacks from Beach Babes. "A lot of women like her clothes."

"There's room for more than one clothing store here," Patricia said easily.

Talk about the upcoming festival continued. It seemed everyone had something planned for it.

"Ellis and I are making a dunk tank," Tyrella announced. "A dollar a pop to try and sink the members of the city council. I can think of a lot of people who will pay for a chance to do that."

"I'm going to have a booth and sell my caramel corn," Annie said. "And Emma's going to help me."

"The church women are doing a bake sale and the youth group is selling Belgian waffles," Patricia reported. "The other churches are having booths, too. Oh, and Nora's Bill is making us a giant thermometer so we can show how much money we raise."

"How's that going to work in just one day?" Jenna asked Nora.

"I don't know," she said. "He's in charge of that. I'll have my hands full selling ice cream."

"We can't thank you all enough," Aunt Edie said, misty-eyed.

"Edie, we all love you," Patricia said to her. "And really, we should be thanking you for inspiring us. It's important to pull together, and everyone benefits when we do. Anyway, our town can use a facelift and we may as well start with the Driftwood Inn."

*Shiny penny pretty*, thought Jenna. Maybe the mayor had something there.

Plans continued to move forward. Once again, the Driftwood Inn made the news. How the money was lost was handled diplomatically and the focus quickly switched from the recipient of the funds to the new festival's mission statement, which was to help deserving Moonlight Harbor businesses prosper.

"Was this your idea?" Aaron asked Jenna.

"I wish," she said. "No, all the credit goes to Tyrella

Lamb for coming up with the idea and our chamber of commerce members for supporting her. Without our local businesses, this never would be happening."

Happen it did. Come the first Saturday in August the town was once more alive with a party atmosphere. Stores were offering sales, and next to each cash register sat a giant donation jar painted with a blue moon and a starfish (one of the Friday night group's craft projects) and a little card explaining the purpose of the festival and featuring an old photo of the Driftwood Inn in its prime. Visitors were happily stuffing dollars in those jars.

They were also strolling from booth to booth on the pier at the end of town, downing ice cream sundaes and floats, Belgian waffles, elephant ears, gyros, and Annie's caramel corn, purchasing seascapes and metal fish sculptures from local artists and picking up brochures from Beach Dreams Realty and other businesses such as Top Dog Roofing. Brody had shamed Herbie into donating the labor for the new roof and then rewarded him with a free information booth. Nearby, the carnival rides were doing a brisk business, squeals and loud music filling the air, while overhead the seagulls chaperoned.

Moonlight Beach was also a hub of activity with horseback riding, street acrobats and belly dancers. Courtney's fashion show was a success and Jenna and Sabrina came away with new outfits.

Celeste and Mel and Vanita came down, and so did Brittany and her family. They all took turns watching over Aunt Edie, who was seated in a special booth filled with pictures and memorabilia from the Driftwood Inn's glory days, including the highly prized Pat Boone autograph.

"I think we've got a success on our hands," Brody said to Jenna as they took a root beer float break. "Looks like you're going to have the money you need."

"If my ex doesn't hear about it."

"Not to worry. You submit the bills and we'll pay them from the fund."

"That's a great idea."

"Hey, it protects all of us. That way we can give an accurate accounting of where the money's going and our recipients don't get accused of misspending. Don't want you running off to Vegas," he said with a wink.

"I think my gambling days are through." At least until the spousal support orders have been lifted.

The party continued until midnight on the pier with the carnival rides still going. By the time Jenna and company got back to the house Aunt Edie was looking tired.

"But it's a good kind of tired," she said. "Thank you all for coming. And thank you, dear girl," she added, patting Jenna's cheek.

"It wasn't me," Jenna told her. "You can thank your friends here at Moonlight Harbor."

"I never would have dreamed…" Her aunt looked out the kitchen window to where the night was starting to chew away a moon ready to wane. "People are wonderful."

Yes, for the most part, they were.

# Welcome to the Driftwood Inn

*To Do:*
*Put ad in paper*
*Put up announcement on the Driftwood's Facebook page*
*Get punch makings and balloons*
*Be grateful and celebrate!*

Thanks to the success of the Blue Moon Festival, the Driftwood Inn reopened on Labor Day weekend. It sported a new roof, new vinyl and shower units in all the bathrooms and new mattresses and bedspreads on the beds. Ellis West and Brody and Seth had set the fence around the pool to rights and drained it, then a pool specialist had been brought in to repair the cracks. A local artist had painted a mural on the bottom—a mermaid swimming under a full moon. Best of all, the bank had finally been paid off.

Aunt Edie and Sabrina baked dozens of cookies and Sabrina and her friend Marigold, whose family was staying at the inn, worked the open house party, moving among the guests with trays of treats. When they weren't flirting with the cute boy who'd come down with his family.

Thanks to word of mouth and a Groupon special, the

Driftwood Inn was at full capacity, and Jenna's family and friends were all packed into Aunt Edie's house, with sleeping bags and army cots everywhere. Courtney, who had left Beach Babes to come work nights for Jenna, was at the reception desk, checking in a family while Jenna mingled with everyone.

"The place is adorable," Brittany told her, taking in the driftwood and tasteful netting with its giant starfish on the outside wall of the office building and one corner of the motel. "And I love the blue with white trim."

"I like the mermaid in the pool," Vanita said. "So cute! And the rooms are darling. Well, room," she corrected herself.

The only room open for viewing at the moment was Seth's, which he'd allowed Jenna to use as her display model. Pete's was locked and off-limits.

Seth was still staying, but he and Jenna had renegotiated, and he was now a paying resident. Of course, she'd cut him a deal and he hadn't protested too much.

His was one of the sandy beach rooms, with brown carpet and a beach mural on one wall. Sabrina's picture of a moonlit beach hung in the bathroom and more of her pictures graced the walls of all the other rooms. Several guests had already raved over the cute lamps and decorations in their rooms and she smiled and thanked them and kept the fact that they were consignment store finds to herself.

Aunt Edie—dressed in a long flowing skirt and a top that Courtney had designed for her, accented with a scarf trimmed with blue sea glass and tiny shells (a Courtney creation)—was mingling with the guests and beaming and looking ten years younger. Pete, who'd actually shaved for the occasion, stood next to her, wearing slacks, sandals and a Hawaiian print shirt.

One of their guests, a middle-aged woman, came up to Jenna, gushing, "Our room is so cute. I didn't know they even made orange carpet anymore."

"Neither did I," Jenna said with a smile.

"Well, it's very clever the way you made it work," said the woman. "I guess this place just got renovated?"

"It did."

"You did a great job."

Jenna looked to where Seth stood, drink in hand, talking to Ellis West. As if sensing her gaze on him he turned and smiled at her and she smiled back. Brody was relaxing on one of the office couches, keeping Patricia company. He raised his glass in salute to her.

"*We* did a great job," she said.

More guests came in to register, this time a family with two little boys and a girl who looked to be about Sabrina's age. "This is a quite a celebration you're having," observed the mom.

"It's quite a life we're having," Jenna replied happily.

"Well, dear, you did it," her mother said a few minutes later, hugging her. "You found the rainbow in the storm."

"It wasn't easy," Jenna said, "but it looks that way."

"I'm glad for you."

"Me, too," said Celeste, who had come to stand on the other side of her. "After everything you've gone through you finally got your happy ending."

"No," Jenna said with a grin. "My happy beginning."

* * * * *

## *Some Moonlight Harbor*
### *Favorite Recipes*

---

Whenever people gather, whether it's at someone's home or around the campfire, food is a big part of the fun. Here are a few favorite recipes some of your new friends in Moonlight Harbor thought you might enjoy.

## *Best Baked Beans*

*Courtesy of Wilma Spike*
*Ingredients:*
*¼ c. salad oil*
*2 c. chopped onions*
*1 lb. lean ground beef*
*1 c. ketchup*
*2 tbsp. prepared mustard*
*2 tsp. vinegar*
*Salt to taste*
*2 1-lb. cans pork and beans in tomato sauce*
*1 1-lb. can red kidney beans, drained*

Directions:
Heat oil in pan. Add onions and simmer until golden brown. Add hamburger and brown. Drain and then add remaining ingredients. Pour into bean pot or casserole dish and bake at 400°F for 30 minutes. Makes 8 servings.

# *Tyrella's Key Lime Pie*

*Courtesy of Robin Claney*
*Ingredients:*
*1 9-in. prebaked graham cracker pie crust*
*6 yolks from large eggs*
*1 14-oz. can sweetened condensed milk*
*¾ c. lime juice*
*3 tsp. grated lime peel*

Directions:
Beat yolks in medium-size bowl until they thicken and turn light yellow. (Don't overmix.) Add condensed milk and mix well. Then add half the lime juice. Once thoroughly mixed add the rest of the juice and the grated peel. Pour into the pie shell and bake at 350°F for 12 minutes. Cool, chill and serve with whipped cream.

## *Aunt Edie's Oatmeal Muffins*

*Ingredients:*
*1 c. oatmeal*
*1 c. flour*
*1 tsp. salt*
*1 ½ tsp. baking powder*
*½ tsp. baking soda*
*½ tsp. cinnamon*
*½ c. brown sugar*
*1 c. buttermilk*
*1 egg*
*½ c. oil*
*½ c. golden raisins*

Directions:
Pour milk over oatmeal in a small bowl and let stand so the oatmeal can soak up the buttermilk. Sift dry ingredients into a bowl. Beat sugar and egg with the oatmeal mixture, then add to dry ingredients and raisins and mix. Spoon into lined or greased muffin tins and bake 20 minutes at 350°F. Makes 1 dozen.

# Aunt Edie's Shrimp Soufflé

*Ingredients:*
*8 slices of multigrain bread, diced*
*2 c. shrimp*
*½ c. mayonnaise*
*1 onion, chopped*
*1 green pepper, chopped*
*1 c. celery, chopped*
*3 c. milk*
*4 eggs*
*1 can cream of mushroom soup*
*Grated cheese*
*Paprika*

Directions:
Cut up the bread and put half of it into a medium-size casserole dish. Mix shrimp, mayo, onion, green pepper and celery and spread over diced bread. Top with the remaining bread. Mix eggs and milk together and pour over mixture. Bake at 325°F for 15 minutes. Remove from oven and spoon soup over the top. Top with cheese and paprika. Bake for one hour. Serves 6-8.

# Blackberry Coffee Cake

*Ingredients:*
*For filling:*
*⅔ c. sugar*
*¼ c. cornstarch*
*¾ c. water or blackberry juice*
*2 c. fresh or frozen whole unsweetened blackberries*
*(if using frozen berries, thaw and use the thawed juice)*

*For cake:*
*3 c. flour*
*1 c. sugar*
*1 tbsp. baking powder*
*1 tsp. salt*
*1 tsp. cinnamon*
*1 tsp. vanilla*
*1 c. butter, room temperature*
*2 eggs, slightly beaten*
*1 c. milk*

*For topping:*
*¼ c. butter*
*½ c. sugar*
*½ c. flour*
*¼ c. sliced almonds or chopped walnuts*

Directions:
Make filling by combining sugar, cornstarch, water or

juice and berries. Cook over medium heat until thickened. Set aside to cool. Sift flour, baking powder, salt and cinnamon into a large bowl and add sugar. Cut in butter to form fine crumbs. Add eggs, milk and vanilla and mix until blended. Pour half of batter into a 9x13-inch lightly greased baking dish. Cover with filling and drop remaining batter by spoonfuls over that. For topping, cut butter into flour and sugar and stir in nuts, then sprinkle evenly over top of cake. Bake at 350°F for 45 minutes. Serves a dozen.

# Acknowledgments

So many people helped me as I launched into this new series. I'd like to take a moment to thank them. (And bore the rest of you to tears.) First of all, a big thanks to Rachel McGraw, LMP, who graciously filled me in on how our muscles work and explained about the life of a massage therapist. Rachel, you've worked wonders on my aching bod. Thanks to Jed Sonstroem for all your legal input. You give lawyers a good name. Thanks to Tiffany Avery, general manager of the Ocean Shores Inn and Suites, for giving me a glimpse into what's involved in running an inn at the beach. A big thanks to Greg Fritz at the Quinault Beach Resort and Casino for answering my many questions about gambling and slot machines. Speaking of, I had lots of help in that department. My buddy Alexa Darin shared many of her tips for winning. Jane Lines let me look over her shoulder as she played the slots. (Ah, Gerhardt, if you hadn't talked me out of it I could have won three hundred bucks on her machine!) Thank you, too, to Missy and Crystal, security guards at the Quinault Beach Resort and Casino, who filled me in on what they do to keep everyone (and their money) safe. Thanks to Karen Schanberger for proofing my casino scene. Obviously, anything I got wrong about playing the slots is nobody's fault but my own. And a big thank-you to Roger Spiese (aka Roger 2.0) for letting me turn you into a parrot. Roger, you're a sport. Finally, thank you to my wonderful agent and pal, Paige Wheeler, and to my adorable and clever editor, Michelle Meade, and all the staff at Harlequin MIRA who work so hard to turn my books into something I can be proud of!

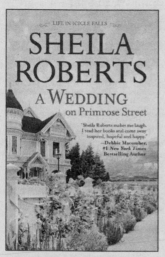

# HARLEQUIN®

# SPECIAL EDITION

### Life, Love & Family

*The Nanny's Double Trouble*

NEW YORK TIMES BESTSELLING AUTHOR
*Christine Rimmer*

Save **$1.00**

on the purchase of ANY
Harlequin® Special Edition book.

Available wherever books are sold, including
most bookstores, supermarkets, drugstores
and discount stores.

---

# Save **$1.00**

## on the purchase of any Harlequin® Special Edition book.

Coupon valid until August 31, 2018.
Redeemable at participating outlets in the U.S. and Canada only.
Not redeemable at Barnes & Noble stores. Limit one coupon per customer.

**52615665**

**Canadian Retailers:** Harlequin Enterprises Limited will pay the face value of this coupon plus 10.25¢ if submitted by customer for this product only. Any other use constitutes fraud. Coupon is nonassignable. Void if taxed, prohibited or restricted by law. Consumer must pay any government taxes. Void if copied. Inmar Promotional Services ("IPS") customers submit coupons and proof of sales to Harlequin Enterprises Limited, PO Box 31000, Scarborough, ON M1R 0E7, Canada. Non-IPS retailer—for reimbursement submit coupons and proof of sales directly to Harlequin Enterprises Limited, Retail Marketing Department, 225 Duncan Mill Rd., Don Mills, ON M3B 3K9, Canada.

5 65373 00076 2 (8100)0 12356

**U.S. Retailers:** Harlequin Enterprises Limited will pay the face value of this coupon plus 8¢ if submitted by customer for this product only. Any other use constitutes fraud. Coupon is nonassignable. Void if taxed, prohibited or restricted by law. Consumer must pay any government taxes. Void if copied. For reimbursement submit coupons and proof of sales directly to Harlequin Enterprises, Ltd 482, NCH Marketing Services, P.O. Box 880001, El Paso, TX 88588-0001, U.S.A. Cash value 1/100 cents.

® and ™ are trademarks owned and used by the trademark owner and/or its licensee.

© 2018 Harlequin Enterprises Limited

HSECRCOUPBPA0518

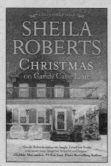 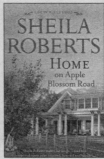 

# SHEILA ROBERTS

| | | | |
|---|---|---|---|
| 33003 | STARTING OVER ON BLACKBERRY LANE | ___$7.99 U.S. | ___$9.99 CAN. |
| 31879 | HOME ON APPLE BLOSSOM ROAD | ___$7.99 U.S. | ___$9.99 CAN. |
| 31815 | A WEDDING ON PRIMROSE STREET | ___$7.99 U.S. | ___$8.99 CAN. |
| 31661 | THE LODGE ON HOLLY ROAD | ___$7.99 U.S. | ___$8.99 CAN. |
| 30790 | CHRISTMAS IN ICICLE FALLS | ___$7.99 U.S. | ___$9.99 CAN. |

*(limited quantities available)*

| | |
|---|---|
| TOTAL AMOUNT | $ _____ |
| POSTAGE & HANDLING | $ _____ |
| ($1.00 for 1 book, 50¢ for each additional) | |
| APPLICABLE TAXES* | $ _____ |
| TOTAL PAYABLE | $ _____ |

*(check or money order—please do not send cash)*

---

To order, complete this form and send it, along with a check or money order for the total amount, payable to MIRA Books, to: **In the U.S.:** 3010 Walden Avenue, P.O. Box 9077, Buffalo, NY 14269-9077; **In Canada:** P.O. Box 636, Fort Erie, Ontario, L2A 5X3.

Name: _____

Address: _____ City: _____

State/Prov.: _____ Zip/Postal Code: _____

Account Number (if applicable): _____

075 CSAS

mira

Harlequin.com

MSR0518BL